THE COUNTERFEIT GUEST

Rose Melikan

sphere

SPHERE

First published in Great Britain in 2009 by Sphere

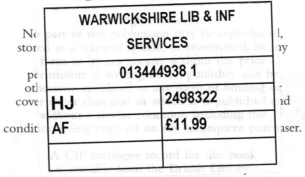

ISBN 978-1-84744-135-5

Typeset in Bembo by Palimpsest Book Production Limited,
Grangemouth, Stirlingshire

Printed and bound in Great Britain by Clays Ltd, St Ives plc

Papers used by Sphere are natural, renewable and recyclable
products made from wood grown in sustainable forests and certified
in accordance with the rules of the Forest Stewardship Council.

Mixed Sources
Product group from well-managed
forests and other controlled sources
www.fsc.org Cert no. SGS-COC-004081
© 1996 Forest Stewardship Council

Sphere
An imprint of
Little, Brown Book Group
100 Victoria Embankment
London EC4Y 0DY

An Hachette Livre UK Company
www.hachettelivre.co.uk

www.littlebrown.co.uk

For Tim; a great friend to have in your corner.

Acknowledgements

I am very grateful to friends and family, whose support and encouragement aided the production of this book, and I would particularly like to thank Clare Alexander, Jeff Dalley, Miranda Griffin, Antonia Hodgson, Sriya Iyer, Quentin Stafford-Fraser and Jane Stevens for their advice, criticism, and technical assistance.

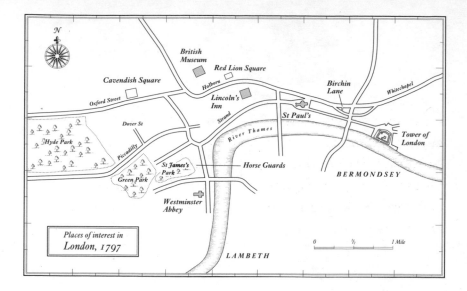

Places of interest in
London, 1797

British Museum

Red Lion Square

Cavendish Square

Holborn

Lincoln's Inn

Birchin Lane

Whitechapel

Oxford Street

Strand

St Paul's

Dover St

River Thames

Tower of London

Hyde Park

Piccadilly

Horse Guards

BERMONDSEY

St James's Park

Green Park

Westminster Abbey

0   ½   1 Mile

LAMBETH

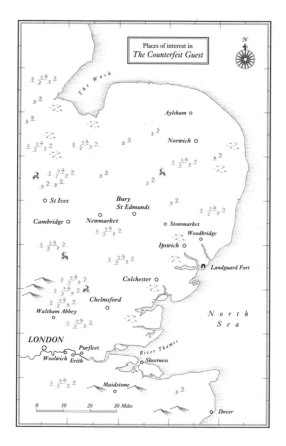

Places of interest in
The Counterfeit Guest

The Wash

Aylsham

Norwich

St Ives

Bury St Edmunds

Cambridge

Newmarket

Stowmarket

Woodbridge

Ipswich

Landguard Fort

Colchester

Chelmsford

North Sea

Waltham Abbey

LONDON

Purfleet

Woolwich Erith

Sheerness

River Thames

Maidstone

0   10   20   30 Miles

Dover

1

On the Suffolk coast some eight miles east of Woodbridge stood what had once been a priory for women adhering to the Cistercian order. Its appearance had changed over the centuries, and the nuns had long since departed. Yet it was called White Ladies in their memory and, in the spring of 1796, it was to be restored to female rule. A young woman named Mary Finch had inherited both the estate and a considerable fortune, and she had resolved to make her home there.

This resolution could not be enforced immediately. Miss Finch had come to Suffolk under somewhat unusual circumstances, and the lawyers had only recently determined that she was indeed the rightful owner of White Ladies. Various practical matters would also have to be settled before she could take up residence. So, for the time being, she remained at nearby Lindham Hall, as the guest and protégée of its owner, Mrs Tipton.

Lindham Hall was another sphere of feminine influence, a fact to which Cuff, the only masculine member of the household, could testify. Cuff held the offices of coachman and porter, and between Mrs Tipton, Peggy the maid, and Pollock the cook ('them old cats', as he was wont to call them, when he thought no one was listening), he rarely had a moment's peace. Mary Finch also made occasional demands of him, but he did not mind these, somehow. Indeed, sometimes he went so far as volunteering his services, and he joined her in the flower garden on a sunny May afternoon without the least prompting. Observing the slim, straight figure poised on the edge of the lawn, a figure that managed to exude energy even when motion-less, he reflected that Miss Mary surely had a way about her.

Mary was deeply engaged in horticultural matters and did not hear him approach. Fashionable ladies, she was convinced, spent a great deal of their time arranging flowers, and she knew little of the art. As a first step in her education she must learn the names of all the likely blooms, and now she repeated, 'Wallflower, wind-flower, cowslip, narcissus, rockfoil,' in the direction of the items in her basket.

'Just so,' agreed Cuff, nodding and touching his hat. 'And that one there?' He pointed at the colourful bed with the toe of his boot.

'Lungwort – what an unpleasant name! Like something witches might use for their spells.' A breeze lifted the curls that had escaped confinement while Mary's attention had been else-where, and her smile was similarly mischievous.

Cuff bent and plucked a pale blue flower to add to her collection, and Mary said, 'Forget-me-not. I did not pick any, as they are so small.'

'No, best left where they are, perhaps.' After a moment Cuff added, 'Nothing for him, then, miss?' removing his pipe from between his teeth and frowning, as if its failure to draw had something to do with his question.

Mary shook her head, and her voice lost a little of its enthusi-asm. 'Not yet.'

The rather complicated logic of Cuff's remark had not confused her. 'Him' referred to a Royal Artillery officer of their acquaintance named Robert Holland. He was part of the unusual circumstances that had first brought Mary to Suffolk and had set in motion what she still privately called her 'Adventure'. Few people were privy to everything that had happened during those strange weeks in October when she had helped to defeat a French spy, and those few had been sworn to secrecy. For his part Cuff knew only that there was a sort of understanding between miss and the captain, and that he, old Cuff, meant to help it along.

The help he provided was of a particular nature. The two young people wished to maintain a correspondence, but they could not do so openly. Holland's letters to Mary, therefore, arrived under cover to Mr Josiah Cuff, and Mary's to Holland were posted by the same J.C. (Mary had also coached him in a likely story should a letter be queried, for she had no confidence in his innate powers of deception.)

'It has been less than a fortnight,' she explained, fretting with her scissors. 'I mean . . . not quite yet.'

'You know best, miss.'

Mary nodded, but she was far from certain that she *did* know best. It was all very difficult. She had not actually seen Holland for more than six months, and their communications in the meantime had been very sparse. In part this was because words did not flow easily from the captain's pen. Indeed, he seemed to hesitate over every line. His efforts had also been restricted, however, by circumstances beyond his control. He held a staff appointment at the regimental headquarters at Woolwich – a place known as the Warren – but in November he had been sent to Gibraltar, ostensibly to oversee an extension to the great siege tunnels. This had not been the only, or even the primary, reason for his employment there, but the epistolary effect had been the same – the mail did not travel very quickly between Gibraltar and Suffolk, and there was always the chance that shipwreck or enemy action might disrupt it altogether.

The character and frequency of Holland's correspondence had naturally affected Mary's. She could hardly answer his cautious reports, in which details of fortress routine featured prominently, with wild displays of emotion. Her letters must mirror his, with accounts of her days at Lindham Hall, or the progress of her legal affairs, or references to the weather. Nor could she reply too promptly. If *he* waited a month between letters then so must she. None of this was the result of indifference or coquetry on her part, but rather a half-understood notion that she must not commit herself any further than she had done. What did she really know of Captain Holland, after all? A correspondence like theirs was not strictly proper – not proper at all, in fact – and people who did improper things often suffered for them, or at least were found out. And being found out, especially whilst she was under Mrs Tipton's authority, was not a pleasant prospect.

Squaring her shoulders and lifting her chin, the latter a particular gesture of decision, Mary told herself not to think about Captain Holland and informed Cuff that she must go inside. He agreed, saying it was just like Peggy to come out for a squint, and then they'd catch it. They parted on those wise words, Mary to the Hall, where she intended to arrange her flowers, and Cuff to the stables to give the harnesses a thorough clean, by which he meant that he was going to have a nap.

Mary pushed the heavy front door closed behind her, kicked off her old boots, and retrieved the neat leather slippers she had left in the passage. She had promised Mrs Tipton to give up ineligible footwear, but with a private exception for gardening, long walks, and any activity that might prove particularly wet or muddy. Others of Mary's station might not have taken such a frugal view, but she could not easily forget a girlhood of genteel poverty and, until very recently, the prospect of a straitened adulthood. Perfectly good shoe leather – or boot leather – oughtn't to be wasted.

Having made the necessary change, she dropped her boots into the large urn that held a collection of walking-sticks, a sword that had allegedly seen action at the Battle of Sedgemoor, and Mrs Tipton's umbrella, and proceeded with her flowers to the kitchen. From there she was ordered to the pantry by Pollock, who suspected that worms and other undesirables were concealed among the blooms, and she wouldn't tolerate none of them crawlies in *her* kitchen. It was from the pantry, therefore, that Mary emerged some time later, clutching two jugs of tastefully arranged spring flowers. One she placed on the sideboard in the entrance hall, and the other she carried into the parlour. This was strictly the second parlour, for the first parlour was grim and uncomfortable, as befits a room preserved for 'best' and, consequently, almost never used.

As Mary crossed the room Mrs Tipton awakened. She had

been 'resting her eyes', but now she sought to ward off any suggestion that she had been asleep and might have missed something. She was a small, sharp, imperious old lady, and she blinked at Mary from behind steel-rimmed spectacles. 'Ah, there you are at last,' she cried. 'What have you been doing?'

'Gathering these flowers, ma'am, as you asked. I hope you are pleased with them? The garden is looking lovely in the sunshine.'

'Yes, yes – very pretty. And where is Mr Cuff? He ought to have been helping Peggy to lift the stair carpet, but I expect he has made himself scarce, as he generally does on such occasions.'

'No, ma'am, indeed, he was helping me,' said Mary, loyally, although she had heard something about the carpet project and suspected that it had stimulated his interest in the garden.

Mrs Tipton made a scoffing sound and then declaimed point-edly on Cuff's several shortcomings, all of which threatened to undermine the smooth operation of the household. 'Something will have to be done about it,' she decreed. 'That is how all the trouble started in France, you know.'

'In France, ma'am?' asked Mary, trying not to smile.

'Certainly. Servants getting above themselves, and people unwilling to take a firm hand. And what has been the result? Revolutions, and guillotines, and now this fellow Bonaparte. Well, I shall soon put an end to it. We shall have no *Rights of Man* at Lindham Hall, nor any other nonsense.'

Mary had to bite her lip to maintain her countenance. 'Oh dear.'

'It is a serious matter, and one must regard it as such. Heaven help us if we go the way of the French – the whole country in an uproar and men taking off their breeches.'

Mary knew rather more about the political situation in France, and she attempted to explain. 'I think, ma'am, that you mean—'

'I *mean* men with no breeches,' Mrs Tipton repeated, her eyes flashing. She disliked being interrupted. '*Sans culottes*, they call themselves.'

'Yes, but they—'

'A perfectly ridiculous practice when it comes to governing

a country, but history provides us with many instances of men behaving foolishly, and this is but the latest. In fact . . .' She hesitated as it suddenly occurred to her that this was not the best topic of conversation to pursue. Young persons were impressionable, after all. '. . . your letters have arrived,' she finished.

'My letters?'

'Yes, certainly – on the table.' Mrs Tipton gestured irritably. She also disliked being misheard or misunderstood.

Mary likewise decided to abandon the *sansculottes*, albeit for different reasons. Instead, she gathered the small pile of neatly folded and sealed papers and sat down on the sofa. She was used to her friend's crochets, and she quite enjoyed receiving letters, particularly those that did not engender anxiety. Before she had come to Suffolk a letter had been a rare event. Her circle had consisted of other penurious females, and no one else had had occasion to write to her. Her circle was still small but lately she had begun receiving invitations to dinner parties, and dances, and musical evenings, often from people whom she did not know, but always expressing an earnest desire for her presence. This was what came of being well off, and it was really very charming.

Mary smiled as she glanced at the first message, and Mrs Tipton's own gaze softened into complacency. Almost since Mary's arrival at Lindham Hall Mrs Tipton had entertained an ambition for her – that she should succeed in County society. This ambition might have had something to do with Mrs Tipton's lack of a daughter to mould and influence. On the other hand, she liked to mould and influence most of the people with whom she came into contact. However it had come about, Mary Finch was her particular project, and Mrs Tipton was not displeased with the changes she had wrought during the past seven months. Mary had always been a pretty girl, but pretty in spite of her dowdy, unadorned gowns and ingenuous manner. No one could have mistaken her for anything but a schoolmistress or governess. Yet now her celery-coloured muslin might have been described in the pages of the *Lady's Magazine*, and the colour set off her auburn curls admirably.

That is what a pretty girl needs, mused Mrs Tipton, *a proper setting. And now that those rascally lawyers have consented to turn over her inheritance, who can say what might happen?* It was fortunate that Mary had neither the freckles nor the pale complexion that often accompanied red hair – *no, auburn,* she corrected. And as for the sharp temper . . . 'Well?' she demanded, nodding at the letters in Mary's lap. 'What is the tally?'

'Dinner at Woolthorpe Manor in a fortnight.'

'Yes, very well.'

'A card party at Miss Carmichael's.'

'Negligible, and she will undoubtedly attempt to throw that nephew of hers in your path, which is tiresome. When is it to take place?'

'Saturday.'

Mrs Tipton pursed her lips. 'Do not reply straightaway. Something better may arise.'

'And there is to be a concert at Ickworth Lodge. The countess of Bristol begs we will attend.'

'Hmm. The Herveys are curiosities and not in the best of taste, but a plain refusal might do you harm in other quarters. We must consider how best to respond. What sort of concert?'

Even when she remembered to control her smiles or frowns, Mary's eyes often testified to her state of mind, and now a sense of fun shone through the green depths. '"In the Italian style".'

'Good Lord,' complained Mrs Tipton with a shudder. 'A decent collection of letters, however. What is that thick one?'

'It looks,' said Mary, turning over the wrapper, 'to be from Storey's Court, but I do not think it is Sir William Armitage's hand.'

Mrs Tipton urged her to open it. 'If they are planning a ball you must certainly attend. With Susannah Armitage as good as married there may be some excellent opportunities. There is the carriage to consider, for I do not know that Mr Cuff can drive such a distance . . . his rheumatism, you know, but I daresay something can be contrived.'

'I beg your pardon? Oh, yes,' agreed Mary, absently, as she continued to examine the packet. Was it really a ball? She had received a letter from Sir William quite recently, and he had said nothing about any sort of entertainment. Of course, he might have forgotten. She could almost hear him gaping at Lady Armitage and murmuring, 'A ball, my dear? Here? Ah, certainly, but remind me when it is to occur?'

She smiled. Sir William had proven himself an exceedingly good friend. He had been ever so helpful about her Adventure; it was because of him that Mrs Tipton had never been alarmed or distressed by it. He had managed to charm her, which was no mean feat, and he had not minded her outrageous hints about helping Mary to find her place in society. On the contrary, he had immediately invited Mary to spend Christmas at Storey's Court! Were it not for Sir William she would never have met Susannah and Charlotte, and of course he was Captain Holland's cousin—

Captain Holland.

All at once Mary experienced that prickly, shuddery feeling that Peggy said was caused by someone walking across your grave. That was nonsense, but might something have happened to Captain Holland . . . and Sir William had learned of it? Gibraltar was probably a very dangerous place – there were tunnels, after all – and if he *had* received bad news, dear Sir William would certainly write to her straightaway . . .

Her fingers were shaking. Something *had* happened, and she had been bothering about card parties and Italian singers!

'They might send a carriage and servant for you,' mused Mrs Tipton. 'It would be a thoughtful gesture on Sir William's part, and I am sure that if he were reminded . . .'

Mary tore open the seal; the paper inside had a black border. 'He is dead!'

'. . . of our situation. *What* did you say?'

Mary was reading quickly, and now she frowned in confusion. The colour had drained from her face, and she felt stricken and relieved at the same time. 'It is . . . dreadful news . . . Lady Armitage writes, and there is a message from Susannah as well. It was an apoplexy, they believe, and . . . the doctor says he did not suffer.'

'But what *is* it?' demanded Mrs Tipton.

'It is poor Sir William . . . He is dead.'

2

The death of Sir William Armitage dealt a stunning blow to Storey's Court, his Norfolk estate. The house itself, an eminently comfortable, if somewhat eccentric mansion, went into deep mourning, with black baize hangings at the windows and wreaths of willow and rosemary at the doors. The servants were also transformed into silent, ghostly figures, who performed their duties without a smile. The butler, Jeffries, tearfully obscured his master's portrait with a black veil and adorned those of other deceased Armitages with black bands, as if thereby they might meet their kinsman in properly sober attire. Few lights were lit in the public rooms other than the twelve, large, silver candlesticks that burned each evening in the drawing-room. This was where the body had been laid out, and where tenants came to pay their respects in a solemn procession. The death of a landlord inevitably provoked uncertainty among those who lived under his regime, but Sir William had been both respected and liked, and the men and women who sought admittance at the kitchen door in their Sunday clothes expressed genuine sadness at the loss of the 'good gentleman'.

Many who knew the Armitages in happier times would have said that Sir William was ruled by the female members of his family, and therefore his passing would but dimly affect the actual conduct of his affairs. To a certain extent this was true. He had retired from public life, and in his retirement he had liked to avoid 'unpleasantness' whenever possible. His wife, by contrast, was a woman of definite opinions and not easily swayed from her purpose, while the liveliness of one daughter and the beauty of the other also made them remarkable. However, the three ladies felt their loss most keenly, although they behaved differently in consequence. Charlotte, the younger daughter, was inconsolable and initially refused even to acknowledge what had happened, while her mother and elder sister masked their grief with action. Lady Armitage grappled with her late husband's legal and business affairs, and issued detailed instructions to the funeral-arranger she had summoned from Norwich, while Miss Susannah Armitage eased the distress of the servants and tenants, and tried to make comfortable the family members and friends who were descending upon Storey's Court.

Mary was immediately immersed in an atmosphere of gloom and anxious activity when she and Mrs Tipton arrived. Indeed, their arrival contributed to the latter. Mary's presence had been particularly requested by Susannah, but Mrs Tipton had, unfortunately, not been included in anyone's calculations. As it was quite impossible that a girl of twenty-one – an *heiress* of twenty-one – should make the journey alone, however, Mrs Tipton, a fragile septuagenarian, had necessarily accompanied her. (Mary had not been convinced that a solitary journey was impossible, but she had been overruled.) The appearance of an unexpected guest momentarily disturbed Lady Armitage's arrangements but, like Marlborough before Blenheim, she speedily rearranged her forces. The result saw Mrs Tipton settled in the Jasmine Room, a school friend of Sir William whom Lady Armitage had never liked removed to a large closet renamed the Blue Room for the occasion, and an unusual, octagonal-shaped apartment at the top of the house given to Mary.

'Of all the rooms in Storey's Court I like this one the best,' Susannah affirmed when she appeared with a cup of tea and an offer to help Mary unpack. 'I do hope that you will be comfortable.'

'I think I should be very hard to please if I were not,' said Mary. The room was certainly charming, with its vaulted ceiling and lime-washed walls of stone. The furnishings were all in blue and green. 'It is like being in a tower,' she murmured, opening one of the windows and gazing out.

Susannah stood against the adjacent wall and kept her gaze directed into the room. 'It used to be the nursery, you know, and we had the most marvellous games . . . sometimes we pretended that I was a captive princess, and our cousin Bobs would rescue me.' She smiled gently. Grief had, if anything, rendered Susannah more beautiful than ever. Her hair fell in a golden shower about her shoulders, and her long-sleeved mourning gown was of a severe, almost medieval style. It was not difficult to imagine her a princess in fact, as well as imagination. 'Charlotte ought to have taken a turn, but as the princess generally stood at the window and waved her handkerchief, or listened for the rescuers at the keyhole, Charlotte always insisted on being the wicked gaoler or one of Bobs' loyal henchmen.'

'Y-es, I expect she would,' said Mary, flinching at the mention of Captain Holland and then telling herself that she had done no such thing. 'How did they manage to rescue you?'

'Sometimes the wicked gaoler was slain on the stairs,' Susannah admitted, 'but sometimes, well . . . we oughtn't to have done it, but if you are careful you may get right out onto the roof from here, and sometimes the rescuers came that way.' She joined Mary at the window and explained the process. 'You hold onto the sill and let yourself down until you reach that ledge, and then you walk along it – it is wider than it looks – to that lumpy bit, which you climb.'

Mary leaned out to measure the distance to the ground, and Susannah added, hurriedly, 'I oughtn't to have let Charlotte do such a thing, but I thought that if I could do it—'

'*You* climbed onto the roof?' demanded Mary. It was the last sort of admission she would have expected from the demure Susannah.

'Only once, and it was dreadful, but I knew that, once she had seen Bobs do it, there would be no stopping Charlotte. She might even have tried it on her own, which would have been very dangerous.'

Mary nodded. She did not mention that such a hazardous and potentially fatal activity could have been avoided by the simple expedient of informing a responsible adult, being well aware that this would have been impermissible under the laws of childhood.

'We oughtn't to have done it,' Susannah repeated, 'but . . . I do not suppose that we shall ever have such fun again.'

Susannah's hand was beside hers on the sill, and Mary squeezed it companionably. 'I am so sorry for you. It has been a terrible blow.'

'We never knew that Papa was ill, beforehand, so we did not have the chance to accustom ourselves to it . . . or even think that it might happen. Really think about it, I mean, for of course people die . . . all of the time.'

Susannah's sentence ended in a quavering swallow, and Mary drew her away from the window. They sat, arm in arm, on the low bench at the foot of the bed. 'It is very hard when someone dies unexpectedly,' she agreed, 'but it must have been worse if he had endured a long illness.'

'Yes, of course you are right, and I must not . . . but poor Lottie. These last few days have been worse for her. She has been dreadfully upset . . . and I fear that Mama is beginning to lose patience with her. Mama has had so much to do, you know.'

'I am certain that you both have,' said Mary. 'Would it help at all if I were to have a talk with Charlotte? Do you think she would like it? It is a family matter, I know, but—'

'Oh, *would* you?' cried Susannah. She had been wiping her eyes with a handkerchief, and now she clutched it to her breast. 'I did not like to bother you. If our cousin were here he would do it, but— And she admires you so much.'

Mary completed a discreet search of Charlotte's bedchamber, her maid Elsie's room, and the kitchens before she sought expert assistance in locating her quarry. Jeffries, conducting a lonely vigil in the drawing-room, suggested that she try the stables. Apparently he had been arranging for food to be sent there,

12

secretly. 'I'm grateful the nights have been so mild,' he sighed. 'You won't give her away, I'm sure, miss?'

'No, indeed,' said Mary. They were standing beside the coffin, now enclosed in lead and a wooden casket, richly upholstered in black velvet with gilt and brass fittings. She had never seen death so magnificently arranged. Despite the engraved inscription plate and the heraldic figures, it was difficult to associate the massive box with Sir William, and yet, somehow, she felt that she was speaking as much to him as to the butler when she explained that she would not reveal Charlotte's hiding place if she did not wish to be found. 'I hope that she will agree to come into the house, however.'

'That's right, miss,' replied Jeffries. 'I daresay you'll know how to put it to her.'

On venturing into the stables Mary wondered whether Jeffries had been mistaken or Charlotte had moved to another location. The stalls were either empty or had four-footed occupants, and none looked to have been recently vacated. In the end it was Clemmie, Charlotte's chestnut gelding, who gave the game away. There was an open loft above the stalls on one side of the building and, after Mary had stroked him and given him a piece of sugar, he stood staring upward in a marked manner.

'Good afternoon, Charlotte.'

Silence.

Mary raised her voice. 'I know that you are up there in the loft – Clemmie has pointed you out.'

There was a rustling from somewhere above, and then a girlish voice complained, 'You tricked him into giving me away.'

'No, he simply appreciated that stables are for horses and houses are for people.'

A tousled, fair head appeared at the edge of the loft, and several wisps of straw floated down to the ground. Clemmie nodded and made a sound between a huff and a snort. 'I suppose I ought to come down, now that I have been discovered,' said Charlotte, grudgingly.

'Unless you are the princess held captive by the wicked gaoler,' Mary agreed. 'I expect that she generally combed her

13

hair, however, or her rescuers might not have been so keen to free her.'

'*I* was *never* the princess.'

Presently Charlotte descended from the loft and joined Mary in front of Clemmie's stall; a slight, rather dishevelled figure. Her costume of unrelieved black made her look younger than her fifteen years, and her usual rosy, cheerful countenance was sallow and wan. She presented a truculent front, hunching her shoulders and scuffing her shoe against a wooden post, but this crumbled when Mary turned to her with a sympathetic smile. All at once she was in her friend's arms, clutching fiercely and whispering, 'I did not mean to stay away so long, only it was so terrible, you know, and when they brought the . . . coffin downstairs, and we were obliged to look at poor, dear Papa in his nightcap— Mama said that I ought to kiss him, but I simply couldn't.'

Mary agreed that she would have found it difficult, had it been her father, but after the tears subsided she suggested that Charlotte might not find the current arrangements quite so off-putting. 'The . . . structure is much less *coffinish*, now – more like a large treasure chest, and very magnificent.'

'Oh. That is not so bad.' Charlotte drew back but continued to hold Mary's hands. 'Do you think that Papa will forgive me for *not* kissing him?'

'Of course he will,' said Mary. 'And he is in heaven now.'

'Yes, but I suppose I have made everyone else cross as well, and *they* are not in heaven.'

'Well, they have been worried, so you mustn't mind if they are a bit sharp, just at first.'

'Mama, you mean. Susannah is never sharp, however naughty you have been.' A faint smile had crept, reluctantly, to Charlotte's lips with these words, but now it disappeared. 'I suppose a great many queer people have arrived by now . . . our relations.'

Mary acknowledged that she had encountered several persons named Armitage since arriving at Storey's Court, although she could not attest to their characters. 'And I expect that they are not so very odd.'

14

'Oh yes they are,' Charlotte retorted. 'The Gorgons, for instance – only they are not so much odd as bad. Very likely there are some of them prowling about.'

'*Gorgons?* What on earth do you mean?'

'They are really our cousins – Armitages, although the particularly grand ones have turned themselves into Hyde-Armitages. But we always call them "Gorgons", because they are so awful. I read about them in a book; they turned you to stone if you looked at them, and our Gorgons could certainly do that.' Charlotte paused, conscious of Mary's enquiring look, and acknowledged, 'It is hard to explain Gorgon-ness unless you have actually seen it; they are terribly proud, and nasty . . . and of course they treated Cousin Sophia *very badly*. My cousin Robert's mother,' she added.

'Captain Holland, do you mean?' Again Mary's heart seemed to skip a beat, but she sternly ignored it.

Charlotte nodded. 'Yes, of course. I had forgotten that you know him. I daresay you will want to hear all about it.'

Mary did want to hear, but she did not feel quite comfortable asking. And yet, not to ask seemed false – very much like the falseness of her unacknowledged correspondence. Even as she debated with herself whether she could justify remaining silent, however, Charlotte began her account, and Mary's conscience was salved. It was impossible *not* to listen, after all, and Charlotte ought to be distracted from her own sorrows.

Thus, through no fault of her own, Mary learned that Sophia Armitage had fallen in love with a handsome but penniless gentleman named Mr Holland. Sophia's father, as might have been expected from his title 'the Old Gorgon', had forbidden the match on pain of disinheritance and other terrible and unfair penalties. The marriage had taken place nevertheless, and the young couple had settled down to what would have been a happy, if impecunious, wedded life. Unfortunately, however, tragedy had struck with the untimely death of Mr Holland – probably while performing a noble act. The grieving Sophia, abandoned by all the family apart from Sir William and Lady Armitage, had been obliged to come and live at Storey's Court.

15

Even accounting for a certain degree of poetic licence on Charlotte's part, it was a sad story, and Mary knew from her own experience how family members could fall out with the bitterest consequences. A quarrel between her own father and uncle had lasted for more than twenty years, and there too a marriage had been the root of the trouble. 'Poor Sophia,' she agreed. 'What was she like?'

'Oh, I never knew her,' Charlotte confided. 'She died when Bobs was a little boy, and he is miles older than Susannah and me. I know that she was very beautiful because I have seen her picture, and Mama says she was quite shy and delicate. I expect it was because of the tragedies. Then Bobs went away to the military academy, but he always came home to Storey's Court during the holidays – that was before he went to India. But the Gorgons simply ignored him – they still do.'

'How very spiteful of them,' cried Mary, 'for I suppose there is no question of . . . money any longer.'

'Oh, no. Although Bobs is quite poor, really.'

'But he must feel it – their unkindness, I mean. I know I should.'

Charlotte considered this. 'Perhaps he does. He never talks about things like that. But we mind for him, Suz and I. I wish he were here now. It is too bad, having to make do with the Gorgons, when we would so much rather have Bobs.'

'Is he coming, do you know?' Mary could feel a blush rising as she asked the question. 'I suppose you have written to him?'

'Yes, of course – Susannah wrote straightaway, and he ought to have arrived by now.' Charlotte brooded. 'How far is it to Woolwich?'

'Oh, a good long way,' said Mary, sounding very much like someone who had not calculated the exact distance. 'And . . . is that where he is?'

'Yes, I think so. Why do you ask?'

Mary started to answer, but had proceeded no further than a flailing, embarrassed gesture when Charlotte continued, 'He *was* at Gibraltar – that is in Spain, you know – but he came back to England in April.'

So casually spoken, those words provoked a wave of confused emotion. Relief that he had returned safely and dismay that he had not written to tell her so. Mary struggled to reply naturally, focusing her gaze on the hay-rack in Clemmie's stall. 'Ah, did he? I mean, how interesting. Yes, very likely he is in Woolwich, then, as you say, and very likely to be here . . . in a day or so.'

Fortunately, Charlotte was too absorbed by her own anxieties to notice those of her friend. 'I hope so. We want him dreadfully, you know. I am afraid that the funeral will be . . . I may not be able to bear it, if Bobs is not here.'

'Well, you needn't attend if you do not wish to,' Mary reminded her. 'Some ladies feel—'

'Oh no, that would be cowardly,' scoffed Charlotte. 'Of course I *must*— And you are coming, aren't you?' Her voice quavered again with the second question.

Mary reassured her, 'Yes, certainly – and I am sure that Captain Holland will be here as well. The funeral is not until Tuesday, so there is still plenty of time.'

'Ye-es.'

'And no doubt *he* will be quite cross if he hears that you have been fretting about him.'

Charlotte's worried frown relaxed. 'Yes, and he will tell me not to be a silly shrimp, and did I expect him to *fly* to Norfolk?'

'Precisely,' Mary agreed. 'And now, shall we . . . return to the house? I daresay we can creep in without anyone seeing – especially the Gorgons.'

'No, we shall keep a particular lookout for them. And Mary, you will be a dear, won't you, and not say a word about this to Mama? About the Gorgons, I mean. She has never quite approved of our calling them that.'

'Oh, no, certainly not.'

3

Captain Holland did not arrive in a day or so. In fact, on the morning of the funeral the mourners assembled without him. Ill-defined groups formed on the gravel drive at the front of the house, waiting for the signal to proceed to the estate chapel, but no signal was forthcoming. As the minutes passed, carriages from Aylsham arrived, bearing those who could not be accommodated at Storey's Court, and this provoked a further delay. The air was warm and sultry, and the sun, beating down upon a company dressed in black cloaks, scarves, and gloves, did not improve anyone's temper.

Moving among them was a youngish man of middling height, properly if modestly dressed in a black suit. It was hard to describe him more distinctly, as he had the kind of bland, uninteresting face that did not impress itself on the viewer. No one actually recognised him, but the number gathered for the funeral was sufficiently large and varied that no one thought it odd. The Norfolk Armitages assumed he had married into the Hertfordshire branch of the family, while those from Hertfordshire believed him to be related to Lady Armitage, and the Hyde-Armitages thought he had probably come up from Town. The last guess was the most accurate, but the man was not attached to the Treasury or to any part of the government, as might have been expected given Sir William's long public career. He strolled anonymously between the various groups, watching and listening. His glance fell upon Mary and lingered there until his sense of duty obliged him to move on to more likely objects.

Quite unconsciously, Mary was engaged in a similar exercise. Chairs had been provided for Mrs Tipton and another elderly lady, and Mary was standing beside them, making desultory conversation. At first this absorbed all her attention, but gradually she became aware of male voices behind her.

'Eleven o'clock ought to *mean* eleven o'clock. I hate this hanging about.'

'You are too used to having your own way, that is your trouble. You should try hanging about in court all day, waiting for his lordship to grace us with his presence.'

'But I was expressly informed— And besides, that is an entirely different matter. *We* are being made to wait because of this infernal crowd, and most of them have only turned up because they got wind of a legacy. Like pigs to the trough.'

'Well, if you had ever been in a courtroom you might perceive some similarities. And to be fair, how often have *you* visited Sir William since we were children?'

Mary turned slightly and perceived two gentlemen whose sombre attire did not diminish their air of fashion. There was a sufficiently close resemblance between them to suggest that they might be brothers, although the elder had a rather heavy, dull expression. Mary thought that he was probably the one who did not like hanging about; he had a watch in his hand and was staring at it fixedly.

Her guess was swiftly confirmed as he continued, irritably, 'Oh, hardly ever. One only sees people – family members – on these occasions. Weddings and funerals – uncomfortable clothes and a devilish amount of money spent.' Frowning, he pondered this sentiment and added, 'I suppose that fellow Holland is somewhere about?'

'I expect so,' said the younger man, mildly, 'but I do not suppose I would recognise him.'

The elder prodded him familiarly. 'Well, I daresay you shall do, before all of this is over. He is sure to turn up, pockets to let and begging bowl to the fore.'

The younger man caught Mary's unfriendly gaze. 'Mind your manners,' he breathed.

'Eh? What was that?'

'Nothing,' sighed the other, as Mrs Tipton rose and tottered away on Mary's arm, 'only you might try to keep your voice down. As you said, there is quite a crowd, and it does no good to dig up family skeletons.'

The elder glanced around him. 'Ah, perhaps you are right.'

'Of course I am right. Now be a good fellow and tell me, who is that very pretty girl over there, walking beside the old hen?'

The other gentleman did not know, and the object of their scrutiny rapidly passed out of sight. Too rapidly for Mrs Tipton, who could not walk so quickly with a single cane, and protested that she was being dragged – positively dragged. Indeed, Mary was moving at a decided pace as she struggled to regain her temper. *Insufferable Gorgons!* she fumed.

Presently Mrs Tipton's protests had their effect, and the two of them halted on the opposite edge of the crowd, where a servant was handing out sprigs of rosemary. Mary lowered her chin and managed a contrite smile. 'I beg your pardon, ma'am, only . . .' Scanning the gathering, she noticed a plump, earnest-looking young man, apparently adrift. He was Mr Grantley Molton, whom Susannah was engaged to marry, and when Mary waved discreetly he joined them with a relieved smile.

'Good day to you, Miss Finch,' he remarked, 'and to you, ma'am – although it is a melancholy one, to be sure. One does not know quite where to put oneself on such an occasion. I much prefer the hunting field to this sort of show – I suppose we all do.'

'I should have thought you would be with Susannah,' replied Mary. 'You are practically one of the family.'

'Well, not quite,' said Mr Molton, 'and I do not like to presume. One oughtn't to be too forward, you know. I feel for poor Susannah, however. This has been a very sad trial for her. And for Charlotte and Lady Armitage, of course. But Susannah . . .' He sighed in sympathy.

Mrs Tipton observed him critically. 'A tearful girl, is she? Well, you must cure her of that.'

'She is tender-hearted,' Mr Molton corrected.

'Then you had better be prepared to stand by at the end of the service in case of a collapse. And mind you have your handkerchief ready.'

'Yes, I shall, ma'am, to be sure.'

He would have said more, but at that moment the door of the house opened and the casket appeared, now shrouded by a white pall and borne by six burly servants. The funeral-arranger slipped past them and began manoeuvring everyone into the procession that would accompany Sir William on his final journey. Mary and Mrs Tipton were placed among a miscellaneous group near the back, which suited Mrs Tipton's speed of walking, if not her sense of precedence. Everything seemed to take a great deal of time, for some people either did not listen to the instructions or forgot them and had to be recalled to their places. At last they were ready to set off.

Despite the late-morning sun, the chapel was pleasantly cool. Although it had not been used for general worship for at least forty years, members of the family were still christened, married, and buried there, especially when, as on this occasion, the congregation could not be accommodated in the tiny village church. Among the crowd of black backs, shoulders, hats, and veils, Mary could only just see Lady Armitage, Susannah, and Charlotte in the front pew on the other side of the aisle, together with Lady Armitage's brother. Behind them sat Mr Molton and a gentleman whom Mary did not recognise. Then Mr Fortescue, the curate from the village, gave a modest cough and the service began.

The familiar words, '*I am the resurrection and the life, saith the Lord: he that believeth in me, though he were dead, yet shall he live,*' transported Mary from the chapel to other churches she had known, other funerals. She remembered the day, four years previously, when her own parents had been buried. It had been a cold, grey morning in February, so cold that by the end of the service her hands and feet had become numb, and she had stumbled to the graveside as if walking on blocks of ice. Ice had entered her heart, too, for a while, for she had lost everything – home, happiness, security – and had been left alone in the world. At least the Armitage ladies were spared that fate.

They rose to sing the twenty-fifth psalm, and Mrs Tipton uttered a humph of satisfaction. She objected to the modern displacement of metrical psalms by hymns in some parishes (her own especially), which she considered the first, dangerous step towards Enthusiasm, Free-thinking, and Dissent. Mary, who did not agree with her, nodded absently, and found her gaze drawn to the gentleman beside Mr Molton, first because he was not singing and then because his person was so arresting. She would not call him handsome for, judging by his grey hair and the creases around his eyes, he was beyond the age at which a young lady (even secretly) might venture such a compliment. Nevertheless, his angular features, bold eyes, and firm, upright carriage were very striking, and he was dressed in the most immaculate, well-cut suit of black and pearl grey that Mary had ever seen. He made Mr Molton look rather shabby and unkempt in contrast, and even faintly ridiculous, when he turned over two pages in the psalter and lost his place. Was the unknown gentleman sneering at Mr Molton? He seemed to incline his head quizzically towards his neighbour, and Mary bristled. *He is not elegant but sleek, and anyone who displays such . . . superiority cannot have been a real friend of Sir William.*

At the conclusion of the service Mr Fortescue and Lady Armitage's brother accompanied the coffin into the chancel and thence through a door and down into the crypt. When they had disappeared, the widow and her daughters stepped out of their pew. Mary turned to observe their progress down the aisle, and her eyes met those of Captain Holland, who was standing among the servants at the rear of the chapel. She flinched and instantly dropped her gaze. Then she looked again and saw him turning towards the door with Charlotte on his arm. The slow, somewhat haphazard flow of departing mourners increased the distance between them, and when Mary finally emerged into the sunshine again, she could not immediately pick him out.

'Well, well,' said Mrs Tipton, 'I would not give a great deal for another of that man's sermons, but I am glad that a proper solemnity was observed throughout. I daresay that is why no one fainted. There is nothing like Tate and Brady for stiffening the sinews. I once attended a funeral where members of the congregation were dropping like ninepins. It was a particularly hot day, of course, and several of the family were Methodists. Rather effusive, if you know what I mean, and much given to hymn-singing.'

Another lady joined them, dabbing her eyes with a lace handkerchief. 'What a lovely service,' she sighed, speaking with the freedom that some people experience on public occasions. 'But what a sad, sad day this is, and *poor* Miss Armitage . . . like a wilting rose.'

'It comes to us all in the end,' said Mrs Tipton, briskly, 'and some of us were pretty poor flowers to begin with.'

'Mm,' agreed Mary, scanning the crowd covertly. 'Shall we step into the shade?'

'Lady Armitage seems to be bearing up,' continued the moist lady, nodding towards a small group standing apart. 'She has always had such a *presence*.'

Mary concurred in what she hoped was a casual tone of voice. 'And there is Captain Holland. The dark-haired gentleman in the blue coat,' she added, as the lady craned her neck to see.

'Ah, yes,' she affirmed. 'The very tall person who has neglected to wear a mourning scarf. I wonder that no one thought to . . . He is a relation of Sir William's, is he not? That is to say, a *connection* of some sort?'

'Of some sort,' agreed Mrs Tipton. 'So, he has arrived at last. One is frequently told that military men are punctual, but one lives and learns. How do you find him, Mary?'

'I think he looks very tired, and indeed *I* think . . .' A pert defence of the captain hovered, but remained unspoken. Instead, Mary contented herself with a condemnatory frown

23

at the two ladies and asked, 'Hadn't we better start making our way back to the house? It is rather a long walk, if we keep to the path.'

With the service over, the thoughts of many turned to luncheon. It was the sort of thing that no one liked to mention, but everyone expected. Like a burial or interment, a hearty meal was a natural consequence of a funeral, and even those guests who were leaving that afternoon had no intention of doing so on an empty stomach. Storey's Court did not possess a large hall, and it would have been difficult to accommodate everyone indoors. Fortunately, however, the threat of rain had passed, and luncheon was served on the lawn. Long tables groaned under enormous quantities of food and drink, and the sight reassured those persons for whom breakfast seemed a long time ago. Some of the more discriminating guests did complain about the informality of an outdoor meal, and remarks were made about the insufficiency of chairs and the very real danger of sunstroke. Mrs Tipton was among those with something to say on that matter. Mary was used to this, however, and, having settled her friend in a comfortable spot beneath a cluster of lilacs, she undertook to ferry across cold meats, bread rolls, pickled eggs, cheese of various sorts, and salamangundy from the luncheon tables.

One of the least considerate conventions of the after-funeral luncheon was that those most severely affected by the death should circulate among their guests and offer *them* consolation and thanks. Captain Holland was so unmoved by convention, however, that he convinced Lady Armitage and her daughters to remain indoors and not bother with anyone. The news of Sir William's death had reached Holland only the day before, and he had posted to Norfolk overnight from Woolwich. As a consequence he was unshaven, travel-worn and, as Mary observed, very tired. He was damned, however, if the ladies were going to be obliged to appear 'on parade' without a chance to recover from the strain of the funeral. Unfortunately, if they were to be let off, he must take their place, and he disliked assuming the role of host at Storey's Court. There were certain

24

to be Gorgons present who would say that he was putting himself forward and taking advantage of Sir William's generosity. Well, that couldn't be helped.

He stood on the edge of the paved terrace and scanned the lawn, taking in those faces that he recognised and those he did not. His glance settled for a moment on the bland, non-descript young man, and a vague question began to form itself. Before the task was completed, however, he located Mary sitting comfortably under the trees. How beautiful she looked, and elegant: a finer, more polished version of the girl he knew.

Money, of course, generally had that effect. He now knew that Mary Finch had a fortune of seven thousand pounds a year, or so Sir William had said. Seven thousand pounds a year. How often had that golden figure appeared in Holland's imagination during the past month. In a stroke it had transformed her life and established an immense gulf between the two of them. Holland had realised it straightaway, and if he had not, Sir William's words on the subject would have removed all doubt. 'Old Finch has left her a fortune indeed,' he had written, 'and with it the chance to become a great lady. Which means that you must give her up, I am afraid. For as things stand, you cannot make her an offer that would bring advantage to her or credit to yourself. I am sorry, Bobs, but that is the truth of it.'

Yes, that was the truth of it, and it was hard. Seeing her now, however, aroused a combination of emotions that Holland found even more disturbing. How could he wish her well and resent her fortune at the same time? Would it be selfish to speak to her or cowardly to avoid her? She was sitting with Mrs Tipton – *by God, is that old . . . lady fated always to be at Mary's side?* He frowned, reflecting on the likelihood that any conversation he initiated in *her* presence might be successful. 'Everything all right, Jeffries?' he asked, as the butler approached.

'Yes, sir, I am just going to replenish the stock of pale ale. Such a warm day, you know.'

'Mm.' Holland knew that he ought to turn away, but instead

he waited for Mary to notice him. She had seen him in the chapel, surely she intended to speak with him – she would wish to do so. Holland was not sure what he wished, but that made no difference to what he expected of her. She need only turn her head slightly, but now she was nodding in the direction indicated by Mrs Tipton's elevated cane, and she did not turn.

Eventually he became aware of someone standing on his other side. 'Sorry— Ah, Mr Quincy, sir.' He extended his hand. 'Thank you very much for coming. I hope you're well?'

'Oh, tolerably, tolerably,' returned the short, bewigged gentleman who had been Sir William's solicitor. 'Although an affair such as this,' he shook his head glumly, 'makes one aware of the ticking clock. *Tempus fugit*, you know, Captain Holland.'

Holland did not know, but he nodded politely.

'I came up from Town last week, to be of such service to Lady Armitage as lay within my power and, of course, there was a great deal to be discussed. Sir William had an admirable grasp of legal affairs, and he had made his wishes known to me some time ago. Still, it is surprising how many details are left unresolved until, ahem, until the melancholy event actually takes place. In his heart of hearts each man deems himself immortal, whatever religion and experience teach us.'

As Mr Quincy expanded on the essential human vanity of considering oneself the centre of the universe, Holland was wondering whether it would be possible to end the conversation without causing offence. Then he heard '. . . a brief word with you?' and turned in surprise towards the speaker.

'*In private*,' Mr Quincy added, in a low, confidential tone that Holland found even more surprising.

'Yes, all right,' said Holland, and when Quincy added that there was no time like the present, he motioned to the lawyer to precede him into the house. They passed through the drawing-room, nodding at acquaintances, and turned into the passage beyond. At the end of this was a small room with a view down to the lake: Sir William's study. Being quiet and out of the way, it had been given over to Mr Quincy as an office during his stay. The two men entered and closed the door.

'I regret that I was not able to explain the position to you earlier,' said Quincy, adjusting his spectacles on his nose and setting a leather wallet and several small boxes on the desk in front of him. Apart from the presence of the lawyer's portmanteau and the various items it had disgorged, the room had not been altered since its late owner's death. There was an empty sherry glass on the mantelpiece, and a newspaper lay open across the most comfortable armchair, which had been drawn up close to one of the windows. On the floor beside it a moderate tower of books had collapsed into an untidy heap. 'I always find it best to make the position clear when there is anything unusual. It helps to prevent bad feelings.'

'The *position*?' asked Holland, distractedly. Although usually he was quite unaffected by intuition or inexplicable sensations, upon entering the study he had been strangely conscious of his cousin's presence. He had almost seen Sir William rising slowly from his chair and crying, 'There you are, Bobs,' his habitual greeting whether Holland had been away for a month or a year.

'Yes, sir, of the will.'

'Sir William's will?'

'*Yes*, sir.' Quincy smiled, wondering who else's might possibly have been meant. Still, he found it refreshing that Captain Holland could be so unmindful of the situation – and quite unusual. Quincy had seen far more instances of bereaved relations springing lightly from the throes of affliction when the reading of the will was proposed.

In fact, Holland was mindful, although he did not reveal his thoughts so openly. As the lawyer consulted some papers, Holland seemed again to hear Sir William's voice: 'As things stand, you cannot make her an offer that would bring advantage to her or credit to you.' But now the words sounded wholly different: not condemning but qualifying. 'As things stand your offer would be dishonourable . . . but not if your circumstances changed.'

And they *would* change if Holland were to receive a fortune of his own. *No, not a fortune*, he quickly reminded himself, *that wouldn't be fair to the girls – but something.* He had never given the matter much thought before, but it was not a groundless notion, surely. Sir William had always been fond of him and had helped him in the past. Why shouldn't he have done so again, in his will?

Holland could feel his heart begin to pound. *As things stand.*

'Ah, yes, here we are,' announced Quincy, producing a page of notes. 'This is not the will itself, you understand, for that shall be read later in the presence of all the beneficiaries, when Lady Armitage is ready.'

'*Not* the will,' repeated Holland, frowning. 'But you said—'

'That there were unusual circumstances, yes, indeed. I break no confidences if I tell you that, although he was land rich, Sir William was, relatively speaking, cash poor. Most of the real property, such as Storey's Court, is subject to an entail and passes to Miss Armitage quite irrespective of the will.'

Holland nodded. 'Yes, I knew that.'

'And the remainder of his estate, apart from a few small legacies, will go to provide for his widow and younger daughter, as must be adjudged right and proper.' Quincy gazed over his spectacles at Holland, slightly curious as to the effect his words might have. If he expected a display of emotion he was disappointed, for Holland merely nodded a second time. What he was feeling at that moment was another matter, but the lawyer knew nothing of that.

Quincy coughed and then lowered his eyes to the paper. Perhaps he found Holland's reserve disquieting, or, perhaps he was not looking forward to what remained of his task. 'You will be wondering in what way you are concerned in this.'

Holland smiled faintly. 'You wanted to prevent . . . bad feelings.'

'Yes, in part, but also Sir William had in his keeping some items that belonged to your mother, the late Mrs David Holland. The will is silent on this point, but I know it to have been Sir William's wish that these items be delivered to you at his death, if he had not done so during his lifetime. Various . . . documents, and these boxes contain the pieces of jewellery described in this list. I have taken the liberty of examining them, and they are all correct.'

Holland glanced at the list: his mother's wedding ring; a pair of ebony hair combs; a gold-coloured bangle; a diamond bracelet. 'Where did the bracelet come from?'

'I believe it was a present from Sir William,' said Quincy. 'Jewels are outside my province, but a reputable London jeweller could tell you its value.'

Holland sat for a moment, considering. Then he leaned forward and untied the strings that fastened the leather wallet. What was revealed made him sit back in surprise. It might have been his own face staring up at him. She had drawn it, a pencil sketch whose caption read, *David, on our wedding day, 1765*. Underneath was a curious collection: a packet of letters to Mrs D Holland; a handkerchief embroidered with her initials; what looked like the dried remains of a nosegay tied up with a piece of ribbon; the stub of a charcoal pencil; a diary.

The items meant nothing to Holland: odd mementoes of a person whom he had never known. 'Why did Sir William keep these?' he asked. 'Did he think I'd want them?'

Quincy nodded slowly. 'Perhaps. Sir William also laid it upon me to explain certain matters to you if he had not already done so. These . . . items, or some of them, are related to what I have to say.'

The study door opened, and Lady Armitage stepped into the room. 'Good gracious, Robert, how you startled me. What *are* you doing?'

'Oh, nothing,' he replied, rising quickly from the hearth and replacing the poker. Black, feathery remnants of paper lay smouldering in the grate, and the atmosphere was vaguely smoky. 'I've been looking at some things Quincy was keeping for me – nothing important.'

'Apparently not.'

29

'There didn't seem much point . . . but I'm afraid I made a bit of a mess.'

She shook her head. 'Not at all. I cannot quite face this room yet – cannot face making a decision about it, but in the meantime it needs a good clean.' She slowly crossed the room and took up a position in front of the window. She was a slim woman, finely boned, and above her black gown her face looked bloodless, like delicate porcelain. 'Do you know, we had the most difficult time – Mrs Ramsay and I – arranging for this room *ever* to be tidied. Sir William was fond of having it just so.' She smiled tremulously. 'I believe he preferred the dust and cobwebs to remain rather than have anything moved from where he had placed it.'

'I think he was fond of everything about this house,' said Holland. 'Will you . . . stay on here, you and the girls? I mean, with Susannah getting married—'

Lady Armitage sighed and glanced towards him. 'We have not discussed it. And you oughtn't to speak of her marriage as a certainty . . . at least, not to Mr Molton. There is no formal engagement, you know, merely an understanding, and a wedding is quite impossible until Susannah is out of mourning.'

'Oh, yes, I forgot. How long does the mourning last?'

'For the girls, six months. For myself . . . a year and six weeks, I suppose.' She smiled ruefully. 'Here is a puzzle for you, Robert. These are the periods that were prescribed by the French court. Ought we to adhere to them because they were set down by a king, or abandon them because he was a Frenchman? What is done in France, nowadays, I cannot imagine.'

Holland shrugged; such matters were beyond him. Lady Armitage removed the newspaper and sank gracefully onto Sir William's favourite armchair. 'I think I shall need at least a year and six weeks to recover. How tired I am.' She considered Holland as he stood behind the desk, toying with a letter opener. Their relationship had not always been a smooth one; certainly the two of them had seemed to rub each other up the wrong way more frequently than any of the other members of the Storey's Court household had done.

I do not dislike Robert, she said to herself, *that would be too bad, an unjust condemnation. It is true I have never loved him, but then he is not my son. I am . . . fond of him, and I have always been just. Surely that is sufficient.* Having reached this reassuring conclusion she unbent slightly. 'Whatever happens with Storey's Court – and I do not expect anything to happen straightaway, or perhaps at all – I hope we shall continue to see you, Robert, as often as your duties permit. Indeed, we shall *expect* to see you.'

'Thank you, ma'am. That's very good of you.'

'It is nothing of the kind. I pray you will not be so . . . absurd as to imagine that Sir William's passing will have any effect on . . . we four.'

'No, but . . . thank you for telling me.'

As soon as the servants began to clear away the luncheon things, Mrs Tipton announced that it was time to go inside. She did not like to be present while crockery was removed and tables disassembled. It gave one the feeling of being a sort of debris, she complained. While agreeing that the sight of a plundered sideboard was a gloomy one, Mary chose not to retire for a refreshing sleep, but to take advantage of the afternoon sunshine. Mrs Tipton considered this most irregular, but acquiesced because she was very tired and suspected that Mary would do as she liked as soon as Mrs Tipton's eyes were closed. She did, however, extract a firm promise from Mary not to remove her hat under any circumstances.

The Storey's Court gardens – English, French, and oriental – were all in bloom, and strolling through them Mary's thoughts wandered along similarly divergent paths. The sight of the carefully tended beds and sculptured arbours made her think of Sir William. He had been keenly interested in garden design, and had even corresponded with Mr Humphry Repton on the subject. It was pleasant to see the colourful, harmonious results of his labours, yet sobering to think that his death had made no difference to them. *Of course, God is the true author of these beauties,* she reminded herself, but somehow that acknowledgement did not lift her spirits. Nor were they much improved when she turned to a second object of reflection, Captain Holland. Ought she to seek him out? Certainly she would like to see him and speak with him, but doing so was not such a simple matter. Even under normal circumstances it might involve a certain amount of . . . scheming, if only to avoid Mrs Tipton, and the circumstances were hardly normal. An assignation seemed heartless on the afternoon of a funeral – even thinking about it made her feel uneasy. And yet . . . not speaking with him, or doing so only in company, upon indifferent topics, would be terribly hard.

Mary's perambulations took her, almost unheeded, to the raised pool in the French garden, and she stood close to the edge, oblivious to the statues of porpoises and tritons rising imperi-ously from the water. She was still considering whether an attempt to discover why Captain Holland had not informed her of his return to England *would* qualify as an assignation, when a move-ment to her left distracted her. She turned and was surprised to see the elegant gentleman from the funeral. He bowed and, after a brief hesitation, apologised for disturbing her.

The suddenness of his appearance, coupled with Mary's earlier, unfriendly thoughts about him, confused her momentarily, but she managed a suitable reply. His grave, well-modulated voice and perfect politeness, moreover, asserted themselves in his favour. After they had introduced themselves he explained that his carriage was being prepared and, in recognition of the journey, he was taking the opportunity to stretch his legs.

'You do not stay for dinner this evening, sir?'

He shook his head. 'No, I believe that ought to be reserved for close friends and family members, in courtesy to Sir William's widow, who will not relish the prospect of further entertainments.'

'Indeed, no,' said Mary, thinking that his view was very con-siderate. Curiosity made her want to ask what had prompted him to attend the funeral, if he could claim neither kinship nor friendship with Sir William, but she refrained. Notwithstanding, he explained that he had come to support an acquaintance who *was* a close relation. 'My conduct might be considered eccentric, but I have been away from England for many years, you see, and have now few intimates in this country. So I am perhaps more willing to expend my energy in the service of friendship than men who are more amply endowed.'

Mary assured him that such eccentricity as he described was wholly admirable, in her opinion. Was not friendship – real friendship – among the highest qualities and most important bonds?

'Certainly it is a bond that extracts a high price on occasion,' he agreed.

They spoke for a few minutes longer. The gentleman praised the gardens, which endeared him to Mary, but their conversation ended on a sour note when he admitted that, were he the owner of Storey's Court, he would very likely sell it – always assuming that he could obtain a good price. It was a fair enough pile (she disliked that word), but rather small for a country house and inconvenient for Town. Privately Mary recognised these limitations, but she wondered that anyone could dismiss a property – a home – so casually on the very day of its owner's funeral. *You forget that he never knew of Sir William's fondness for Storey's Court*, she told herself, *surely he did not mean to be impolite*, but when they parted she regretted that so refined a gentleman should need to have excuses made for him.

It was nearly five o'clock when Mary finally returned to the house. The afternoon had passed without her noticing, and she felt slightly uncomfortable as she mounted the steps to the front door. The door opened before she could touch the knocker, and a relieved Jeffries greeted her with a hurried bow. 'Ah, Miss Finch, there you are.'

'Yes, I am sorry,' said Mary, guiltily. 'Have you been looking for me?'

'No, miss— I mean . . .' He frowned and started again. 'I beg your pardon, but Mrs Tipton has been asking for you. She and the other ladies are in her ladyship's book room, you see.'

'Ah, and I had better join them. But perhaps . . . Will I have

33

time to change before dinner? I ought to have done so earlier, I know.'

Jeffries was already motioning her along the passage. 'Right this way, miss – very fetching, I'm sure. And I expect that dinner may be delayed somewhat tonight,' he added.

'Oh? Is . . . is anything the matter, Jeffries?'

His face immediately resumed its habitual grave, anonymous expression, but he did not offer a smooth denial as he would ordinarily have done. He liked Miss Finch; she was rather like his own young ladies. 'Well, miss, since you ask, on top of everything else, we've had a spot of bother – her ladyship and I – as regards the seating. There were to be fourteen tonight, and we had but six gentlemen to eight ladies. That was bad enough, but now that Master Robert – I mean, the captain – has had to leave we must begin again.'

Mary started. 'Captain Holland? He has gone?'

'Yes, miss, about half an hour ago. "Urgent business at Woolwich", I believe he said. And now we shall be thirteen, unless something can be contrived, and thirteen, you know, is a very unlucky number.'

They stopped outside the door of the book room; Mary could hear muted voices from within. 'Yes, very unlucky,' she agreed.

'Well, we mustn't grumble, with there being a war and all, but you would think that an exception might have been made just this once, on account of it being poor Sir William's funeral, but then Master Robert – the captain, I mean – has always been a bit of a jack-in-the-box and— Oh, yes, that reminds me . . .' He began searching in his pockets. 'He asked me to give you a message. Here it is, miss.'

She did not answer, and he slipped the paper into her hand. Then, nodding politely, he continued down the passage, muttering to himself about nobody liking jelly apart from Miss Charlotte, and if *she* had the headache that would bring them down to twelve.

Mary stared at the paper, folded into fourths and bearing her initials, and slowly opened it.

Storey's Court
24th May 1796

To Miss Mary Finch,
I write in haste, but entirely sensible of the situation, regretfully to inform you that I can see no possibility of continuing the friendship with which you have honoured me. I apologise for any actions on my part that may have caused you distress, and I ask that you will also forgive my communicating with you now in this way. Although shabby, it does have the virtue of brevity. With all my best wishes for your health and happiness, I remain your respectful servant,
Robert Holland

4

On the tenth of October, a year to the day from when she had first set eyes on White Ladies, Mary finally came into residence. The process of renovation had taken longer and been more complicated than anyone had expected, for it had included restoring the house's medieval features, bringing the cooking facilities into the modern era, and doing battle with the damp and draughts of several centuries. Some of the furnishings had also been changed, for what had contented an elderly, reclusive bachelor did not satisfy an energetic young woman with artistic sensibilities and a willingness to spend money (ineligible boots notwithstanding). So she had pored over catalogues, samples, and swatches, and in the place of threadbare carpets and gloomy portraits she had purchased new fabrics and papers in the style of Robert Adam, and had ordered furniture from Thomas Sheraton's warehouse.

The result would have shocked the late Mr Finch and his pious predecessors, but when Mary took possession she felt not a little pride. Perhaps the house *was* rather remote, and her own associations with it were not *entirely* pleasant, but these were trifles when compared with the thrill of ownership. Not so very long ago the thought of owning a property of any kind would have been ridiculous – an aspiration far beyond her means. If White Ladies had been a tiny cottage it would still have been hers and treasured for that reason. But it was *not* a cottage nor anything like, and this thought, as she passed from one elegant room to another, was also pleasing.

Mary did not enter into her kingdom alone. With her own fortune secured, she had acted straightaway to share it with the two people who had befriended her at the unremarkable girls' school where she had taught Drawing and History after the death of her parents. Mary's offer was fortuitous from several points of view. Miss Marchmont and Miss Trent were spinsters of a certain age, and they joyfully accepted liberation from the toils of the schoolroom. Furthermore, a young lady conscious of her reputation could not easily live alone, even if she wished to, and Mary would have been obliged to find suitable companions in any case. It was to her credit that she thought of her friends first, and her reputation not at all.

Her generosity quickly bore fruit, for no sooner had the three of them crossed the threshold of White Ladies then they began what seemed to be a charmed existence, from which everything that was dreary or difficult had been banished. They found good servants, nothing leaked, and the rents were paid on time. The weather stayed fine well into November, and even when a gale came roaring in from the sea, all of their chimneys were spared. Mary bought a pair of mild-mannered geldings and took up riding, and when not engaged in that interesting pastime, her world revolved around parties, outings, concerts, and assemblies.

Her friends supported her in these endeavours, not only as faithful chaperones, but also in what might be deemed their professional capacities. In her past life, Miss Marchmont had taught Deportment as well as Mathematics, and under her tutelage Mary learned popular country-dances like the Maid of the Oak and the Prussian Rose, along with cotillions and allemandes for more grand occasions. Miss Trent's needlework had always been admired, and now she produced a steady stream of lace-trimmed collars and embroidered handkerchiefs to enhance Mary's wardrobe. Both ladies delighted in Mary's success and seemed to be experiencing through her the delights that their own girlhoods had lacked. Privately, Mary called them her fairy godmothers.

Nor was the title misplaced, for like those benevolent spirits, the Misses Trent and Marchmont were bent upon securing Mary's happiness. Of course, they worried about her expenses at White Ladies; for them the lessons of poverty were even more ingrained, and everything in Suffolk seemed very expensive. But more than that, they longed to see her suitably married. Supporting one's old friends was all well and good, they felt, but Mary ought to aspire to marriage and children, for therein lay true contentment, security, and womanly virtue. Having little experience themselves of courtship and none of marriage, they turned for advice on these matters to Mrs Tipton. She was very well-suited to giving advice, as there were few subjects in which she did not consider herself an expert, and this one was particularly dear to her. Some of what she said was nonsense and some was worse, but she was a keen observer of her class – the rural gentry – and generally knew to a nice detail what could and could not be done.

When Mrs Tipton paid them a visit, therefore, Miss Marchmont and Miss Trent were keen to seek her guidance. A conference on Mary's Future took place one afternoon in the smallest of the White Ladies sitting-rooms, not long after the house had been re-opened. The ostensible reason for the visit was to render judgment on the new library curtains, but the conversation soon shifted to the subject that was uppermost in everyone's thoughts.

Mrs Tipton sipped her tea meditatively and eyed her colleagues. 'Love, of course, is the principal difficulty to be overcome.'

'Oh, yes,' agreed Miss Trent. She was a thin, grey-haired woman, earnest and timid in equal measure. 'But Mary is such a *dear* girl – I am sure a great many gentlemen must fall in love with her. Very likely *all* of them.'

'No, no,' scoffed Mrs Tipton, privately dismissing Miss Trent as a well-intentioned simpleton, 'I mean that something must be done before she fancies herself *in love*. As comprehended by a young person, love causes no end of trouble. Even the most gentle, accommodating girl may indulge in high drama for the sake of it, and if she already has a strong character – as Mary has – she generally becomes mulish in the extreme. If we can get her safely married before there is any nonsense, it will be better for everyone. I hope you have not noticed any symptoms?'

'Of love?' queried Miss Marchmont. 'I do not think so. There have been no sighs or complaints that no one understands her, and no mysterious letters read in secret or clasped to the bosom.' In character as well as person Miss Marchmont was rather a substantial lady, and might have stood up to Mrs Tipton were she not, like everyone else, slightly afraid of her. 'And Mary has been very busy with the estate, of course, and putting this house to rights.'

Mrs Tipton nodded, but she was not wholly convinced. She also thought that 'bosom' was a low expression, except when used in church as the attribute of a patriarch. 'Well, mark my words. Love is the danger, especially with a girl like Mary.'

This discussion of love naturally developed into a lecture about the wrong sorts of husband. Mrs Tipton ran briefly through the more significant masculine flaws – drunkenness, brutality, arrogance, lack of common sense – and advised that Miss Marchmont and Miss Trent be particularly on their guard for any suitors exhibiting them. She wondered whether Miss Trent would recognise foolishness in anyone else, but that lady's query on the best sort of profession for a husband restored a measure of confidence. Mrs Tipton frowned thoughtfully; professional men of any description were somewhat suspect. Who would burden himself with a profession if he could avoid it? Nevertheless, a lawyer might become a judge, and a parson might become a bishop. If one could not marry a title, one could look out for a likely prospect. Not that Mrs Tipton was the least snobbish about such things as titles and nobility, but it was well to be aware of the opportunities, and a crest did smarten one's carriage amazingly.

'What about the services in that respect?' asked Miss Marchmont. 'Generals and admirals, you know. Admiral Hood was made a lord last year.'

'Hmm, yes, possibly,' Mrs Tipton allowed, 'but military men are very awkward husbands. If, as at present, there is a war, they are apt to be killed, which may be unpleasant and is sure to be difficult. If there is no war, then they are a nuisance, disconsolate because they have nothing to command and given to imposing martial discipline on the household.' There were also, she explained, certain worrying tendencies to consider. The Army was full of younger sons and men of dubious character – their families happy to be rid of them for the price of a commission. 'Having no money of their own, they are generally on the lookout for a rich wife.' She looked meaningfully at her audience.

'Oh, dear,' murmured Miss Trent. She had always thought soldiers rather dashing, and this brusque account of their failings made her feel ashamed. In her anxiety she added an extra inch to the muffler she was knitting for the poor, her needles clacking feverishly. It was with considerable relief that she heard her friends acknowledge the decided glamour of the military profession, which made officers so dangerously appealing to unsuspecting females.

'If only they dressed like parsons and spoke like bankers we should all be spared a great deal of trouble,' complained Mrs Tipton.

'Few women are proof against a red coat,' agreed Miss Marchmont with a hint of a smile. '*Scarlet fever*,' she added, and Miss Trent nodded worriedly.

'Precisely. And that is why—'

'What were you saying about scarlet fever?' asked Mary, slipping into the room. 'Is someone ill?'

'Good gracious, Mary,' cried Miss Trent. 'How you made me jump.'

Mary stooped to recover the ball of wool that had been flung from Miss Trent's lap and run along the floor. 'I beg your pardon. I thought you would have heard me coming along the passage . . . but you were doubtless deep in your confabulations.'

'Confabulations indeed,' sniffed Mrs Tipton, but she

acknowledged Mary's curtsy and studied her closely as she sat down at the empty place on the sofa.

Mary was conscious that she was under scrutiny, but felt that she was as near to being mistress of the situation as was possible with Mrs Tipton. 'How are you keeping, ma'am?' she asked.

'At my age, if one does not actually collapse, one must be considered to be doing well,' that lady replied. Mary handed her a plate of small, individually iced cakes, and she glanced at them suspiciously before taking one. 'These are very rich for everyday.'

'But you do not visit us every day,' Mary replied with a smile, 'and as we were intending to show you our new things, I daresay Cook wanted to make something especially nice as well. She is very particular about her cakes, you know.'

'Indeed. Well, everything is very lovely – lovely and expensive. You have spent a good deal of money, and I expect you have enjoyed it. Nor is there any harm in that. If one can afford it, one ought to be extravagant once in one's life. But what are you going to do now?'

This was not the question that Mary expected. '*Do?*' she asked.

'You mustn't simply idle away your time. No woman can afford to do that. You *ought* to be thinking about marriage.'

Miss Marchmont and Miss Trent glanced at each other. Neither would have had the temerity to speak so boldly.

Mary managed to avoid frowning, but she wished that Mrs Tipton had said something else. Not sure how best to respond, she nodded. 'Mm.'

'Good. A wise woman makes use of such advantages she has, while she has them. An ample fortune, of course, is always an excellent recommendation, but one mustn't discount the importance of a pleasing appearance. Men never do.'

Mary nodded again.

'I suggest that you look to marry one of our Suffolk gentlemen – someone of substance and a good family, whom everyone knows. I am aware of several eligible young men – youngish – and I daresay one of them would suit.'

That a third nod would be tolerated was too much to hope, and Mary cautiously added, 'Yes, perhaps.'

Even this, however, was insufficient, and Mrs Tipton glanced at her sharply. 'What do you mean by that?'

'Nothing, only I do not wish to marry someone merely because he is suitable.' After a moment she added, with a touch of piquancy, 'Perhaps I shall never marry at all.'

Miss Trent gasped, and the word 'mulish' formed itself on Mrs Tipton's lips. 'Well, well,' she observed instead. 'I trust that your heart is in no way engaged at present?'

'No, ma'am, it is not.'

'I see. There was a time when you entertained a fondness for that fellow Holland, Sir William Armitage's cousin. Something to do with the militia, I believe.'

'He is an *artillery* officer, and . . . it was he who rescued me from the smugglers, when I first came to White Ladies,' she added to Miss Marchmont and Miss Trent in a gentler tone, although her glance had not lost its keenness.

'Ah, yes,' noted the former, while the latter breathed, 'How perfectly marvellous.' Neither dared to look at Mrs Tipton.

Mary, however, continued resolutely. 'But that is all over now, and really, I cannot tell you anything more about him or what he is doing.'

She was telling the strict truth, for she knew nothing of Holland's movements since the day of the funeral, or even whether he was still in England. She had received letters from both Charlotte and Susannah, but none had mentioned Holland. As for the note that he had left at Storey's Court, she had taken its request at face value, although the pain of doing so had been considerable. It was now one of her particular objects to forget him.

Holland was still in England, and on this particular afternoon he was at Fort Cumberland, near Portsmouth. To be strictly accurate, he was sitting in a creaking, uncomfortable, straight-backed chair outside the office of the fort's commanding engineer, Colonel Frederick Mulcaster. A desk separated Holland from the colonel's adjutant, a fresh-faced lieutenant in the uniform of the East Middlesex regiment. The scratching of the lieutenant's pen was the only sound in the room, apart from the occasional creak when Holland shifted in his chair. From outside came the clarion voice of a sergeant unhappy with the progress of the men under his command, and the myriad noises of a fort undergoing repairs and rebuilding.

The outer door opened, and a large, florid, harassed-looking officer strode into the room, his coat covered with a fine layer of brick dust. He brushed his sleeves ineffectually and glared first at Holland and then at his adjutant, both of whom had risen at his entrance. 'Well, what is it?'

'Excuse me, sir. This is Captain Holland, come down from Woolwich. And I have those calculations for the stone-cutting that you asked about.'

'Good. Give them to me later. Sorry to have kept you, Captain Holland. My name is Mulcaster, and I have charge of this damned show.' He motioned for Holland to precede him into his office and asked his adjutant to get them something to drink.

Colonel Mulcaster sat down at his desk with the sigh of a man who had been on his feet all day and studied Holland from over the rim of his sherry glass. 'Your health, sir.' He drank, and continued, 'Well, and what do you think of this place?'

'The work seems to be progressing, sir.'

'Progressing, but at the devil of a pace. Do you know we have been at it for almost thirteen years, and we are not a quarter of the way finished? What if the French come tomorrow? Or next year? How shall we fight them off? We lack guns, ramparts, and men.'

'You think an attack likely?'

'God knows. The French seem to be making all the running in this war.' Mulcaster drained his glass and set it down on a detailed drawing of a section of the north wall. 'Well, there it is. There you have Fort Cumberland. Behind schedule and over the estimate, thanks to a crowd of rascally contractors, ill–considered plans, and a commanding engineer who may be past his prime.'

He paused to give Holland an opportunity to intervene, and when it was not taken up he continued. 'It is not my way to beat about the bush, sir. Doubtless you have your orders, and I do not intend to make trouble, but I must tell you that unless you have come to do something about my guns I do not take it kindly that the Board should be poking its nose in my affairs without so much as a "by your leave".'

Despite the increasing vehemence with which these remarks were delivered, Holland relaxed slightly. 'Excuse me, colonel, but I'm from the regiment, not the Ordnance Board.'

His words produced a distinct thawing in Mulcaster. 'What? Oh, yes. The youngster did tell me, but . . .' He shook his head and then frowned thoughtfully. 'Say, are you to do with the, er, *laboratory*?' He uttered the last word quietly and with a hint of respect. In addition to being the headquarters and store-house of the Royal Artillery, the Woolwich Warren was where the creative, secret work of the regiment took place.

'That's right, sir. Just at the moment I'm a sort of jack of all trades.'

'What the devil does that mean?'

What it meant was that Holland was in a state of professional limbo. For almost two years he had worked closely with Colonel Congreve, the chief of the laboratory, acquiring a wealth of confidential information along the way. This information had proven so tempting to the French government that a plot had been hatched to kidnap Holland and pry it out of him. Although the plot had failed, it had disturbed the Board of Ordnance, which governed the artillery. Fearful of the risks that Holland's expert knowledge created, the Board had immediately whisked him off to Gibraltar for safekeeping. He had been recalled after several months, at which point it had been decided neither to remove him completely from experimental work nor to lock him up more securely at Woolwich, but instead to keep him on the regimental staff and employ him on lesser, largely routine tasks.

Rather than say any of this, Holland merely explained, 'I'm doing the rounds of the Portsmouth district: Southsea Castle, Fort Blockhouse, the Portsmouth gun wharf, Priddy's Hard, and Fort Cumberland. There's Priddy's gunpowder, of course, but I'd also like to see the shot furnace they're building at Fort Blockhouse. And several of our invalid companies are scattered about — I'm here to show that the regiment hasn't forgotten them.'

'Quite an agenda,' said Mulcaster. 'And what about my guns?'

'Well, sir . . . what's your current ordnance?'

'Ten 32-pounders and fourteen 18-pounders, and some other rubbish from the old fort — the master gunner could tell you the calibres, but I doubt we have shot for them. What we need is ten more 32-pounders.'

Holland considered. 'I can't promise it will do any good, sir, but I'll try to get you the guns, and I'll report that you're short of men — of gunners. There seem to be plenty of redcoats about.'

'Come, that is decent of you,' acknowledged the colonel, 'very decent. I— My apologies for thinking you were a damned Ordnance spy. It has been preying on my mind all day.' Mulcaster sighed thoughtfully. 'You had better mind how you go from now on. There are master gunners at all the forts hereabouts and local Ordnance personnel, and all of them jealous buggers. You mustn't expect any more of a welcome from them than . . . well, than you got from me.'

'That's all right, sir,' said Holland. 'I'm used to it.'

'Well, you know your business best. Have another glass?'

'Thank you, sir.' Holland sat back in his chair for the first time since entering the room. Nodding towards a pair of curved swords mounted on the wall behind the colonel, he observed, 'Those are a fine pair of talwars, sir.'

'Ah, yes, do you think so? They are amazingly balanced, and Damascus steel, of course. I got them at Pondicherry, in '61.' Mulcaster took one of the swords down and fingered the blade before handing the weapon across.

'Very fine work, sir. And they keep their edge better than any of ours.'

45

'You were in India yourself, Captain Holland?'

'Yes, sir. I had a Company commission before my regimental one came through.'

'Did you see much action?'

'A bit, sir. I was with Lord Cornwallis in '91 and '92.'

Mulcaster nodded. 'Hot work.'

They continued to talk about India, the likelihood of a French raid on Portsmouth, and the fort's shortcomings in a friendly, desultory way, until the decanter – the very large decanter – was empty. Then Holland suggested that he ought to have a word with the fort's master gunner.

'Of course, by all means,' replied the colonel, walking him somewhat unsteadily to the door. 'And when you go to Priddy's Hard – I had better mention this now, before I forget it – you will have to do with the storekeeper, and he is called Sicklemore. Fellow stands on his rank – a damned civilian, of course, but you must give him his Army rank as a member of the local Ordnance Board – takes offence otherwise.'

'Yes, sir. I'll remember.'

'And that is not all,' Mulcaster continued, lowering his voice to a confidential rumble. 'He cannot resist a wager. You will never get away without a wager. How many ships come in for powder every month? What is the distance across Forton Lake? How many barrels of powder are there in the depot's magazine? That sort of thing. Do you know how many barrels the magazine at Priddy's Hard holds when it is full?'

'No, sir.'

'Four thousand, two hundred and thirty-eight. Remember that, now. Four thousand, two hundred . . . and thirty-eight. Enough to give us a bit of a fright if it went up, eh?'

'Yes, sir. I trust they're careful with their cigars.'

Holland was spending the night at Fort Cumberland, and that evening he dined in the mess. Communal dining of this sort was not usual for him, for the Warren had no such arrangement, but he knew the routine well enough. The early stages tended to be the same everywhere – the juniors on their best behaviour in the presence of the commanding officer, the seniors under an obligation to keep the conversation flowing, and the guests respectful and attentive, not wishing to be caught out by any local customs. Later, of course, things could change, but that was why it was important to keep one's eyes open.

To begin with, Holland followed this laudable practice, and also did his duty towards both the wine and the conversation. As the evening advanced, however, his concentration slackened. Mulcaster had escaped after the loyal toast, and of the locals only the younger officers remained, determined to see out the last bottle. Most were subalterns, decent enough fellows, but bored by fort routine. The others were guests: a Navy captain, a half-pay colonel in the Light Dragoons, a major of the 38th Foot, and Holland himself. Now the differences in rank, service rivalries, and the amount of drink could easily lead to trouble.

Holland was tired, and without intending to he began daydreaming about Mary Finch. He did not think about her very often, really; he did not *want* to think about her at all. But sometimes a chance word could bring things back, and tonight there was a cold wind blowing, and the rain was falling in fitful bursts, just as it had on the night it all began. It was strange how things happened, or didn't . . .

The insistent voice of the dragoon colonel forced its way into Holland's recollections. 'Men of rank, I tell you, that is the answer. Do you agree, sir?'

Holland raised his eyes to find everyone looking at him. He had no idea what they were talking about. 'Rank?' he asked.

'Good breeding,' explained Balfour, the Navy captain. His deep-set brown eyes and prominent brow gave him a thoughtful expression, and his accent clearly identified him as a Scot.

It emerged that one of the subalterns had purchased a captaincy in another regiment and would shortly be leaving Fort Cumberland. This, in turn, had sparked a wider discussion of service promotion and its objects.

'Never ask a gunner about promotion,' bawled the major, a glowering, bull-necked man, whose face had become an unpleasant red. 'They've got to sit on their arses and wait for the fellow next on the list to peg out.'

'I see. So there is no promotion by purchase in the Royal Artillery, sir?' asked Captain Balfour.

Holland shook his head.

'Then we have something in common, for we too have our officers' list, according to the date on which a man is commissioned captain. Once he reaches post rank in our service, the holy list determines the pace of his advancement.'

The cavalry officer tried to make a point about the hierarchy of men, but the major's louder voice easily defeated him. The wine was also having its effect generally around the table, and a variety of opinions, some of them coherent, were expressed. A salacious account of the exploits of someone called 'the grand madam' caused the subalterns at the end of the table to collapse with laughter, and it was with difficulty that they were recalled to the gravity of their seniors' conversation.

Holland, likewise, had no desire to make a contribution, but for some reason his opinion was repeatedly sought. At last he shrugged and answered in a low voice, 'If an officer's good at his job, he ought to advance. I don't give a damn about anything else.'

'You have very democratical ideas, sir,' observed Balfour. '"*A man's a man for a' that*," eh?'

'Democratical?' roared the major. 'Ruination of the country, you mean. I've heard of these . . . societies, with their goddamned oaths and petitions. They're nothing but a pack of traitors.' He stared implacably at Holland across the table.

'I'm no Democrat,' Holland warned, 'or any other sort of politician, thank God,' and several of the others murmured their agreement.

'No, no, of course not,' Balfour agreed. 'Nor are any of us here, I will take my oath upon it. Not Democrats, I mean. But as for being politicians, that is another matter entirely.' He gazed at his associates. 'Consider, gentlemen – we must keep order among the men under our command, not only in battle, but generally. How we do it, whether by fair words or foul blows,

48

is a political matter, and it makes us politicians. Don't some of us know as much about tyranny and liberality as any who have sat upon a throne or called a council chamber to order? Of course we do, and our decisions are every bit as important for our lads – and perhaps for the nation.'

A sense of uneasiness crept around the table, inspired partly by Balfour's words and partly by the befuddled senses of those who heard them. No one spoke, and then Holland asked, 'Is that what you meant when you said "A man's a man . . . for all that"?'

Balfour shrugged. 'Yes, perhaps, but it wasna my own expression. It is poetry written by a man of my country that has become very popular on the streets of Glasgow. It sounds best as a bit of music, if you do not mind the dialect.' Swallowing a sip of port he tapped the table and began to sing in a clear baritone:

> 'Is there for honest poverty
> That hings his head, an' a' that;
> The coward slave – we pass him by,
> We dare be poor for a' that!
> For a' that, an' a' that.
> Our toils obscure an' a' that,
> The rank is but the guinea's stamp,
> The man's the gowd for a' that.
>
> What though on hamely fare we dine,
> Wear hoddin grey, an' a' that;
> Gie fools their silks, and knaves their wine;
> A man's a man for a' that:
> For a' that, and a' that,
> Their tinsel show, an' a' that—'

He broke off and smiled again at the company. 'Perhaps I had better stop there. The fellow who wrote the words *was* a sad, democratical fellow, I am afraid, and I mustn't speak out of turn here, of all places.' He inclined his head slightly, as if in apology to some military deity who might have been offended by the lyrics.

'Huh,' grunted the major, heavily, as he stared into his empty glass. 'Democratical . . . traitors the lot of 'em.'

One song usually had the effect of triggering another, but not on this occasion. In fact, the conversation faded to weary, jaded murmurings, and the company broke up shortly afterwards. As he crossed the courtyard on the way to his quarters Holland found himself walking beside Balfour, who alone seemed still to be in a good humour.

'Promotion was ever a sore topic among officers,' he observed with a shake of his head. 'We perhaps ought to have stuck to safer topics, like the ladies.'

Holland smiled briefly. 'They're worse, in my experience.'

'Yes, perhaps,' agreed the Scot, chuckling. 'And the politics. I hope I did not touch you there, sir?'

'No. I don't think I'd have sung that song, though, not in the mess.'

'Och, it *was* late in the day to be starting that hare.'

'Is that what you were doing?'

'Well, perhaps I was. It wasna good manners, but I am afraid that political questions will need answering soon enough. And if laddies with guns start arguing politics, well, you know what happened in France. It is a wise man who looks to his own house when he sees his neighbour's is ablaze.'

They parted, for Captain Balfour was returning to his ship. As he walked away he began to whistle the tune of his song, and it seemed to Holland that he could still hear it long after the darkness had swallowed up all other sounds.

Balfour's poem was not generally recognised in England at that time, although the message it contained would have been considered noteworthy in a variety of circles, both high and low. On that very night there was a man lounging in a tavern called the Three Mariners who would have found those words, and the fact that they were known by a serving Naval officer, very interesting indeed.

No one could have truthfully described the Three Mariners as a genteel establishment, or even a strictly honest one. If it had been either of those things, its regular patrons would have shunned it. Located in the village of Lambeth on the south side of the Thames, the Three Mariners had much less in common with its neighbour, the archbishop of Canterbury, than it did with the transient population of watermen, sailors, pilots, and fisher folk who plied up and down the river, or with the crimps, thieves, beggars, and whores who waited for them on shore. To such people, taverns like the Three Mariners were familiar haunts – comprehensible, if not strictly comfortable.

The etiquette of the place was certainly understood by the man in the corner of the snug that night. His position exposed him to the worst of the tobacco smoke and the stale, greasy kitchen odours, but he was more interested in keeping a tactful watch and a secure position in case of trouble, than in the salubriousness of his environment. For trouble, in some form or other, was certainly a possibility. If it came, he knew that his fellow patrons would remain passive out of sheer bloody-mindedness, while if his identity were to become known he could expect far worse. This was because he belonged neither to the river nor to the shore, although his work obliged him to partake of both worlds. He was, in fact, an agent of one of the several intelligence services working, more or less covertly, in London at that time. His activities, however, were not guided by Horse Guards or the Admiralty, nor by the Home Office, Foreign Office, or the City police, but by an individual whose contact with government was so ephemeral as to be almost non-existent. This was a secretive, eccentric, even strange person named Cuthbert Shy, and his agents were known as Shy's Men.

There were some people, quite highly placed, who insisted that there was no such person as Cuthbert Shy, and that his ring of agents was a myth put about to confuse the French intelligence services and frighten any disaffected Englishmen or radical Irishmen who might otherwise cause trouble for the authorities. Gossip and rumour were a natural consequence of war. It was hardly surprising, therefore, that a figure like Cuthbert Shy should have emerged. But as for there actually being such a man, surely, that was a very different matter. Who had ever

51

seen the fellow? Did anyone admit to having met him? Where was his office? He certainly did not seem to receive payment for his activities – which was a telling argument in some quarters – or at least if he did, it was extremely well camouflaged in the Secret Service Fund accounts.

Shy's agent in the Three Mariners did not trouble himself about such details; his own concerns were far more practical. He was responsible for Matters of Interest south of the river. In order to collect information on this subject he drew upon a motley collection of spies, informers, and more or less trustworthy vagabonds. They frequently heard things, and sometimes they reported them at pre-arranged locations like the Three Mariners. The agent called it 'collecting the mail'. But the mail was late tonight, and that was troubling. Not only was he expecting a meeting with one of his most reliable contacts, but also he had heard that the contact would bring important information – news of an alliance between the French and an English traitor. It was exactly the sort of thing that Mr Shy would want to know, but the night was passing. If it grew much later the agent would have to leave the Three Mariners and try his luck at another 'letter box'.

A slight, obviously drunken man reeled dazedly into the pub. The fellow's clothes were filthy – he had clearly fallen in something unpleasant at least once – and he had shaved none too recently. Neither of these qualities had any particular effect on the company, although his haphazard attempts to solicit the price of a drink bore little fruit. He was advised to 'Mind my glass, you clumsy sod', while a sailor told him to 'Bugger off, mate', but without any real hostility.

'Any chink, gov?' the fellow whined, steadying himself against the agent's table and staring down at him with bloodshot eyes. 'Price of a cuppa? Chap's got to eat,' he added, none too logically. 'You can spare a pig, can't you? 'Alf an 'og?'

'I've no change,' the agent replied, 'but you can finish this if you like.'

The drunkard took the proffered glass, sniffed it dubiously, and drained it in one gulping swallow. He belched noisily and wiped his mouth on his sleeve. 'Don't think I like your draught, mister,' he complained, returning the glass with a shaky hand.

'Suit yourself.' The agent shrugged.

'Aw, don't be like that, gov. I'll 'ave another, see if I don't. A man's got to 'ave a drink, ain't he?'

'Have as many as you like,' replied the agent, dryly, 'but not from my purse.' He stood up and eased past the drunkard, brushing aside the ineffectual hand on his arm and ignoring the fellow's renewed pleas.

The frustrated petitioner staggered forward, then back, then sat down on the floor rather more heavily than he had expected. 'Any change, gents?' he called, gazing up hopefully at those around him. ''Alf an 'og for a poor cove wot's dry as dust?'

Having shouldered his way onto the street, the agent took a deep breath and turned into the alley that ran parallel to the river. He did not stop to look at the scrap of paper that his contact had passed to him, along with the empty glass, but hunched his shoulders and kicked a loose cobblestone out of his way. It was a clear night; the rain had stopped, but there was no breeze to dispel the dank smells of the river. The whole process had taken longer than he would have preferred, but he had what he wanted — at least he hoped he had. There was still the report to write, however. He began to walk faster.

He was debating whether to hail a waterman or cross the river at Westminster Bridge, and he did not hear the men behind him until it was too late. A sharp struggle, a blow to the stomach, and his knees buckled beneath him. *Now that was stupid of you*, was the only observation that occurred to him as he felt the warm blood spill through his fingers.

His assailants pulled him quickly into the shadow of a timber shed and skilfully rifled his coat and waistcoat pockets. They found a battered watch lacking its chain, a purse containing a few shillings, a cotton handkerchief, and a folded piece of paper bearing three words in a scrawled hand: *RABELAIS PHOEBUS RAT-CATCHER*. In short, nothing of obvious value.

Having stripped him of his coat and shoes, they dumped his body in the river.

5

Autumn faded into winter, and as the weather closed in it was impossible to maintain the heady programme that had so delighted Mary. Nevertheless, she and her friends entertained very creditably at White Ladies. Tea parties and literary discussions were excellent opportunities for showing off Mary's intellectual accomplishments, (Mrs Tipton warned against too liberal an exposition in this area), and the improvements she had made to the estate, (Mrs Tipton considered White Ladies one of Mary's particular assets, especially for the more artistic gentlemen). In early December such a gentleman paid a visit, and he and Mary spent an agreeable afternoon discussing the tie-beams and purlins in the refectory ceiling. But when he called a second time and she was out, she did not regret having missed him. This seemed to be her attitude towards all of the gentlemen of the neighbourhood, even the most eligible. It was, to those who looked upon marriage as the crowning glory of Mary's career, the only cause for concern. She was pleasantly polite in masculine company, but she gave no indication of deeper feelings, or even, as Mrs Tipton complained, of preferring any one of them to a block of wood.

Mary did not, in fact, find any of the Suffolk gentlemen particularly appealing, but that had more to do with their blockheadedness than with any bruises her heart had sustained during the previous spring. Or so she told herself. Nevertheless, it took very little to turn her thoughts in Captain Holland's direction. A reference to Storey's Court or the Armitage family was sufficient, and so she experienced a little thrill of excitement when a letter from Charlotte Armitage appeared on the breakfast table one morning shortly after Christmas. The letter justified her reaction, although not in the way that she had imagined.

'Listen to this,' she cried, breaking in upon a rambling conversation between Miss Trent and Miss Marchmont about the failure of the recent peace negotiations, which poor Lord Malmesbury had conducted so bravely. 'Susannah Armitage is to be married at last, but *not* to Mr Grantley Molton. To a Colonel Crosby-Nash.' She lowered the paper. 'I believe I met him, briefly, at Sir William's funeral. An elegant gentleman . . . rather *mature.*'

'But what of the engagement?' demanded Miss Marchmont. 'Do you mean to say that it has been broken off? How astonishing.' Neither she nor Miss Trent had actually met Miss Armitage or Mr Molton, but they had heard all about them from Mary, and therefore commented freely on their doings as if they were all old friends.

Miss Trent was in the act of pouring tea, and the pot hung, suspended, in her frail grasp. '*Poor* Mr Molton,' she cried. 'Such a nice, polite young man, and so devoted to Miss Armitage. What can have happened?'

Mary shook her head. 'Charlotte's explanation . . . and her handwriting . . . are not very clear. They were obliged to put off the wedding, you know, and perhaps—'

'It seems to have happened very quickly,' complained Miss Marchmont, aggressively buttering a slice of toast. 'Those two girls are scarcely out of mourning, and Miss Armitage engaged already? It is quite unseemly. What can Lady Armitage have been about to allow such a thing?'

'Dear, dear,' murmured Miss Trent, 'it *does* seem distinctly . . . I do hope . . . but you know there is *love*, Sarah. One must make allowances for that. And dear Miss Armitage is such a *lovable* girl.'

Miss Marchmont pursed her lips. 'That was what we all thought first time round. Then it was Mr Molton she loved, and now I suppose it is this fellow— What is his name, Mary?'

'*Colonel Crosby-Nash.*'

'You need not speak so loudly – I am not hard of hearing. In fact, my hearing is as acute—'

'I beg your pardon,' said Mary, 'I think that I remember Susannah mentioning . . .' She set down the letter and hurried from the room, explaining, 'She wants fatherly advice,' over her shoulder.

Miss Marchmont and Miss Trent stared at each other, but before either had time to voice a question, Mary had returned, brandishing a second letter that she had retrieved from her study. 'Here it is,' she urged, 'a letter that Susannah wrote a little while ago. I did not take any notice at the time – or rather I did not imagine that it had anything to do with romance, but perhaps it explains what has happened.

We are all very quiet here, as you would expect, but we have been much heartened by visits from my uncle. My mother relies upon him a great deal, for he has been much in the world, and knows far more of its workings than we do. We used not to see so much of him, but since the melancholy events of the spring he has been a tower of strength. The loss of my dear father has demonstrated to me the necessity of relying upon a gentleman, not only of character and situation, but of worldly experience. You, dear Mary, are clever enough – ahem – but in my own case, I feel the need for guidance most keenly. You will know that, as my dear father's heiress I now have considerable responsibilities, and I am persuaded that I shall best discharge these with an experienced, one might say fatherly, guide.'

'How lovely,' beamed Miss Trent, before adding, perplexedly, 'but what does it mean?'

'Well, Charlotte describes the colonel as a friend of her uncle's. Perhaps *he* is the fatherly guide – the colonel, I mean. He is not a young man and . . . I expect he knows more of the world than Mr Molton.' Mary tried to remember her own conversation with Colonel Crosby-Nash. 'He has been abroad for a number of years, I believe.'

'And if both her mother and her uncle regard the colonel as the more suitable,' added Miss Marchmont, 'I do not doubt that Miss Armitage has also been convinced. It stands to reason that she should be. *Some* young people have the proper respect for their elders' advice.'

'Oh, yes, certainly,' Miss Trent agreed, 'but I *do* feel very sorry for Mr Molton.'

'Yes, it is all up with him, I am afraid.' Miss Marchmont shrugged. 'I daresay he will go into a decline.'

'My dear Sarah, you really mustn't joke about it.'

'It is not in the least a joke – declines are all the rage,' Miss Marchmont protested. 'First love, and then a decline. Well, well, what a piece of news. And Miss Charlotte Armitage will undoubtedly keep us informed. I look forward to the next instalment.'

Charlotte did more than keep them informed. In early March she visited White Ladies, brimming with news about the wedding itself, which had recently taken place. The first opportunity to broach the subject came on the afternoon of her arrival, when she and Mary went riding. Mary was not a very experienced horsewoman, and the two animals set off down the lane at a pace that Charlotte privately dismissed as 'plodding'. When she concluded that their speed was unlikely to be improved upon, and a run across country not to be hoped for, she fell back on conversation.

'Well, what do you think of this business of Susannah's?'

Mary frowned and glanced quickly over her shoulder in the direction of her groom, who was accompanying them at a polite distance. Polite, but within earshot. Within earshot of Charlotte, certainly.

Charlotte, however, had no such qualms. She told Mary not to mind and everyone would know about it soon enough. 'My maid Elsie is probably in the kitchens at this minute, telling all she knows, and why should the servants not have a good gossip? There is no other news worth hearing.'

Rather than attempt to answer this question Mary returned to the previous one. 'What do you think about it?'

Charlotte shrugged her shoulders. 'The deed is done, so we must reconcile ourselves to it. And him. I do not think I shall ever call him "Arthur", however.'

'No? Why not?'

'He is very old, to begin with. He must be past *fifty*!'

'That does not make him Methuselah, you know,' laughed Mary. 'I exchanged only a few words with him last spring, but he struck me as . . . very distinguished.'

Charlotte acknowledged this point, grudgingly, but maintained that Colonel Crosby-Nash was not the sort of old person whom one could easily like. He was not *jolly* old, but *frosty* old, and not the least bit fun or interesting. He had been a soldier, but despite having spent years and years in India, he had not had a single adventure, or brush with death, or anything.

'But that was not his fault, surely.'

'They were always fighting when my cousin Bobs was in India, and any officer with the least enterprise . . . But I believe the colonel had something to do with supplies or wagons, or something dreary like that, so perhaps he had to stay behind when anything exciting happened.'

'Yes, he might have been desperate to have a go at whomever they were fighting, and been obliged—'

'To annotate a list of soldiers' bootlaces,' finished Charlotte, laughing. 'Or discover whether the horses' blankets had been handed out.'

'No, *I* meant,' urged Mary, 'armies need supplies, you know. I am sure you are being most unfair.'

Charlotte was not convinced. '*You* have met him – did you like him?'

'Well . . .' Mary hesitated, trying to be just. 'I thought he was very impressive. There was a kind of certainty about him, and confidence . . . I cannot quite explain it.'

'He is very rich, of course,' said Charlotte. 'Mr Molton has a comfortable fortune, and he is the heir to Fordham, which is quite near to Storey's Court, but the colonel made an enormous amount of money when he was in India. I daresay it was while everyone else was fighting, and now he has a great, vast, splendid house in London, *and* an estate in Kent, and a shooting box somewhere in the North!'

'So he is Croesus, rather than Methuselah,' said Mary, pleased to shift the conversation away from her own assessment of Colonel Crosby-Nash. 'Did Susannah care about the vast splendidness?'

'Well, she likes nice things, of course, but *no,* I do not think that she did care so very much . . . but Mama was terribly impressed. It is the only thing anyone seems to talk about: money and the three per cents.' Charlotte gazed longingly at a stretch of open ground visible through a gap in the hedgerow, which was simply begging to be galloped across.

'People are very anxious, you know, on account of the war.' Mary guided her horse past the gap, apparently without noticing it.

Charlotte sighed. 'Yes, and I suppose they are being *responsible*, but I think it is very dreary. Do you know, when he came to call, he and Mama and Susannah would go into the drawing-room and talk about economics. I could hear them through the door sometimes.' She grimaced. 'And that was how he courted her! Can you imagine? But when I asked Susannah how she stood it, she said that the colonel was a very knowledgeable gentleman who was helping her to understand her responsibilities. Mama thinks he might be made a baronet.'

'Are baronets particularly noted for being responsible?' asked Mary with a smile.

'No,' giggled Charlotte, 'but I think she prefers the idea of Susannah possibly becoming *Lady* Crosby-Nash to her being plain *Mrs* something else for ever and ever.'

'Mrs Molton, for instance.'

'Yes, it is hard luck for him,' Charlotte allowed, 'but I never really thought that he and Susannah were terribly in love. They could not be married straightaway, because of the mourning, but if they had been consumed by a burning passion they might have run away to Scotland, where you can be married whenever you like by a blacksmith. It is what I should have done. But instead, she stayed at Storey's Court, and he stayed at Fordham, and between the colonel, and economics, and Susannah being responsible, by the time the mourning was finished,' she shrugged, 'that was that.'

'Everything has certainly happened very quickly,' said Mary, remembering Miss Marchmont's complaint.

'I suppose that Colonel Crosby-Nash did not want to hang about. Not at—'

'"Not at his time of life", you were about to say,' chided Mary. 'You are terrible, you know. I pity the poor man.' She turned away slightly to disguise her smile.

'I only meant that he had made up his mind,' Charlotte protested, 'but the other is true as well. And now they have gone to London, and they are to stay there for the rest of the Season.' She sighed, and then, flashing a glance across at Mary, asked, 'Does it not sound wonderful, "the London Season"?'

Mary had been once to the capital, but under very unusual circumstances. Fashionable London, the London of 'the Season' was a mystery to her, but the words conjured up a series of delightful prospects. Music, dancing, visits to the theatre, picture galleries, and dinner parties where the conversation ran to topics other than the shooting. The country entertainments she had experienced must pale in comparison to those of the great city. 'It *would* be—'

'It would be perfectly splendid,' finished Charlotte. 'And shouldn't you like to go to London yourself? *I* am going,' she added, airily.

Mary halted her horse. 'You cannot mean— Lady Armitage is never giving you a Season at your age.'

'Well, no,' Charlotte admitted. 'I am only to go for a fortnight, and I am only allowed to attend the ball given by Susannah – but it sounds the most complete thing. Mama said it was better to visit London in small doses, and that I might go this year as a sort of treat after the horribleness of losing dear Papa. Next year she and I may go for an entire month.'

She urged her horse forward again, and Mary was obliged to follow. 'But . . . you cannot go on your own *this* year, surely?'

'No. There is my uncle, of course, and Susannah – although Mama says I mustn't vex her, now that she is married, which I suppose means that she thinks I vexed Susannah *before* she was married. But that is beside the point. I am going, and I think you should too!'

'Thank you very much,' said Mary, 'but your uncle is hardly likely to invite me, and I cannot simply add myself your party!'

'Oh, that makes no difference,' scoffed Charlotte, 'we have been obliged to accept visits from any number of tiresome people at Storey's Court whom we had not invited, and you would not be tiresome at all! However, I am *not* staying with my uncle, at least not if you come too. We would stay at my house. Ten Cavendish Square came to me by Papa's will, you know, which was terribly kind of him. And it just so happens that Admiral Verney, who generally lives there, has gone to Bath to restore his health. Is it not perfect?'

'Not for Admiral Verney. You are not responsible for his gout, I suppose?'

'No,' laughed Charlotte, and then, sobering slightly, she asked, 'you would be allowed to come, would you not? I mean, no one tells you what to do . . . no one whom you must obey? We were not allowed to do anything, hardly, during the mourning – not that we wished to be particularly merry.'

Mary shook her head, smiling gently. 'No, of course you did not, but you oughtn't to be in mourning forever. Your father would not have wished it. And as for myself, there is no one whom I must obey.' As she spoke the image of Mrs Tipton appeared in her mind's eye. Mrs Tipton objected to London (she had never been there), as a place where dangerous, loose-living men conspired to ruin inexperienced young ladies, both morally and financially. Fortunately, however, her views did not hold universal sway at White Ladies; it was one of the many charming features of its regime. 'You know,' she admitted, her

61

smile broadening, 'I meant to go to London last spring, but I never managed it.'

'Then there is no excuse for not managing it now. And think of the fun we shall have! We can drive in the park, and go shopping, and visit St Paul's cathedral and the Tower of London, and Susannah will be close by. Perhaps there will even be *illuminations* and a royal salute, such as they are having now for Sir John Jervis. I *do* think the Navy is splendid.'

'Very splendid, but wait a moment. I cannot abandon Miss Trent and Miss Marchmont, even for royal salutes.'

'They can come too,' said Charlotte, largely. 'In fact, it would be a good thing if they *did* come. For while you are quite responsible enough, you are not very old, and it would be very useful to have elderly ladies who could accompany us on outings. I believe Mama would prefer it.'

'Miss Marchmont and Miss Trent are not elderly,' laughed Mary, 'and never let them hear you say such a thing.'

'Well, that is even better,' said Charlotte, with scarcely a pause, 'because then they will not tire quickly and always want to go home for cups of tea and to put their feet up. There – have you any other objections?'

'Hmm,' said Mary, gravely, 'let me reflect. Other objections . . . No, not that I can think of.'

Charlotte laughed delightedly. 'You *are* droll. So you will come?'

'Yes, I think I shall.'

'Hooray!' cried Charlotte. 'Let us go and write to my mama and Mrs Arbuthnot – she is the housekeeper at Cavendish Square – right away. Do you think that these old armchairs of yours might manage a canter? I am certain a gallop is quite beyond them.'

'Of course they may canter,' replied Mary, patting her horse's neck. 'And do not call them "armchairs". You will hurt their feelings.'

The flow of letters back and forth between White Ladies, Storey's Court, and 10 Cavendish Square removed any lingering doubts from Mary's mind. Lady Armitage gave her benevolent approval of the scheme, and Mrs Arbuthnot confirmed that everything at Cavendish Square would be ready for the young ladies by the time of their arrival on the twentieth of April. In consequence, apart from The Trip to London, very little was discussed, planned, or even considered for the remainder of Charlotte's visit.

Miss Trent had to be talked into joining the party.

'You two go ahead, and I hope you have a marvellous time, but I do not think—' 'Oh, come, Miss Trent, we cannot take a holiday without you! We would not enjoy ourselves in the least.' 'But hadn't one of us better stay here and look after things?' 'No, Charlotte assures me that we are superfluous to White Ladies – everything will carry on very well without us.' 'Besides, Hetty, there is the matter of your umbrella. I know very well that you have set your heart on an umbrella of green silk, like the one that Mrs Tipton has. Where do you think such things are made? London, of course.' 'But mightn't you—' 'Certainly not. You must pick it out yourself. We could not possibly take the responsibility.' 'Well, then, if you are sure.'

There was not the slightest necessity that they travel by their own carriage; the regular service would suit them perfectly.

'The regular service? Won't it be very cramped and incon-venient?' 'It would be cramped for you, Charlotte, with your great, vast wardrobe.' 'My wardrobe is not vast. I think you are most unfair.' 'You forget, I saw the number of trunks you brought with you to White Ladies. Poor Wallis was staggering under the load.' 'Yes, well, but imagine what odd people you might encounter travelling post!' 'Nothing of the kind. And . . . unusual companions make the journey more interesting.'

What about servants?

'I presumed that there was a regular staff at 10 Cavendish Square.' 'Oh, yes, of course, but I shall certainly bring Elsie.' 'I haven't got a lady's maid.' 'I know, and I do not understand how you manage without – but then you are very clever. But in London . . . why, with all the outings, and entertainments, and the ball, it will be quite different.' 'Oh, dear. I suppose we shall be obliged to be elegant all of the time. Shall we manage it, do you think, Miss Marchmont?' 'You two may go in for elegance – Hetty and I shall strive for the sensible, qualified by the comfortable.' 'Are you not forgetting Miss Trent's umbrella? She will be the most fashionable of us all!'

And shopping.

'Think of all the wonderful shops! My mama says that one may find every sort of pretty thing in London.' 'Hmm, yes, I might try to find a new boot-scraper.' 'A *boot-scraper*? You cannot— Oh, you are teasing me, Mary, aren't you?' 'I might be.' 'And do *you* love shopping, Miss Marchmont?' 'I like it well enough, Miss Armitage, although I appreciate that my responsibility lies primarily in curtailing the shopman's more extravagant flights of fancy and keeping an eye on the purchases you *do* make.' 'And we must all be on our guard for sharp practices. Some of these London people may believe they can take advantage of such country mice as ourselves.' 'You *are* a dear, Miss Trent. I think we shall all have such fun!'

Despite her assurances about the regular service to London, Mary decided to reserve three places on the mail coach. '"If a thing is worth doing it is worth doing well",' she explained, when Miss Marchmont baulked at the extra expense. 'And we shall be doing well when we reach Cavendish Square two hours earlier than if we had gone post.'

The journey itself was largely uneventful. At Ipswich, where they dined prior to boarding the mail, the landlady of the Great White Horse required only a moment or two of concentrated effort before she remembered Mary 'quite perfectly' from the occasion of her previous visit to the inn, when she first came to Suffolk. 'There was that terrible crash on the Stowmarket road,' she continued, 'and the poor gentleman dying in our best room but one. Not that there is aught to worry about on *your* journey, ladies,' beamed the landlady, 'the mail is that safe and ever so convenient, I always say.'

This advice proved well founded, for after Ipswich they

bowled along through the vernal darkness, with smooth changes at Stratford and Colchester. The coachman and guard were extremely polite, not only moderating their speech for the sake of their female passengers, but also stopping twice to fetch down Miss Trent's trunk – first when she could not find her handkerchiefs, and then when she forgot to put them away again.

At Witham they acquired another passenger, a tall, angular clerk named Wilcocks, who was taking some important documents to counsel's chambers. He was very politically inclined, and for the next stage of the journey he enlightened them upon the state of the nation and how the government could benefit from his advice. In particular, he would take a firm hand with regard to the criminal activities of the Channel fleet.

'The Channel fleet?' asked Mary, when he eventually paused for breath. 'I beg your pardon, but has something happened?'

'Indeed it has, miss,' cried Mr Wilcocks. 'The sailors have mutinied. The ships were ordered to sea on Sunday, but the crews refused to sail.'

This charge was greeted with creased brows and pursed lips; it sounded highly suspect. 'Surely no captain would ask his men to sail on Easter Sunday,' urged Miss Trent.

'Such are the requirements of war, ma'am. And to refuse an order on that sacred day surely compounds the men's wickedness.'

'The requirements of the men's souls—'

Mary cut her off. Miss Trent had certain Non-Conformist tendencies that, if indulged, might lead the discussion into deep theological waters. 'But why have they mutinied?'

Mr Wilcocks uttered a critical humph. 'They want higher pay – well, and who would not? But I know what my employer would say if I declined to execute his orders because I did not care for the size of my pay packet – and better provisions, and *better* officers. I can see you scarcely credit it, my dear ladies, but I assure you it is so. These . . . rascals have the audacity to criticise their lawfully authorised superiors.'

'Where are they now?'

'In Portsmouth — unless they have escaped to France and surrendered themselves and their ships to the enemy.'

'Would they really do such a terrible thing?' asked Miss Marchmont.

'They have raised the red flag of rebellion at the masthead and supplanted their officers — there may be no limits to their treachery.'

Mary frowned at Mr Wilcocks' highly coloured language. 'But what is being done about it? I mean, to end the mutiny?'

Lord Spencer, the first lord of the Admiralty, had gone to Portsmouth to speak with the sailors and attempt to negotiate a settlement, but Mr Wilcocks considered this an act of supreme folly. The mutineers were like badly behaved children, who neither understood nor deserved reasoned argument. They must be compelled to return to their duty, and the sooner the government grasped the nettle, the better.

As Mr Wilcocks spoke, Mary's opinion of his intellect became more apparent in her expression. 'Yet, if they are in possession of the ships,' she argued, 'I do not understand how they can be compelled. Surely Lord Spencer must reason with them, or it is he who shall be stung.'

'And if they have organised this . . . mutiny and set down their demands,' continued Miss Marchmont, more temperately and with a warning glance at Mary, 'they strike me as being quite capable of understanding the first lord's arguments.'

'I am sure that *English* sailors would be reasonable,' said Miss Trent, 'and good-hearted. Our guard, you know, was once a sailor. That is how he learned to tie down our luggage so efficiently.'

Mr Wilcocks favoured them with a knowing smile. 'I do not believe that you ladies quite understand the situation.'

Mary attempted to disabuse him of this view, but Miss Marchmont's voice was louder. She agreed that very likely they did *not* understand it, and might they seek further illumination from the report in his newspaper? Mr Wilcocks was more than willing to explain the salient facts, but she dissuaded him. They would be sorry to bother him with silly questions that could be answered by reference to the printed account. If they were then still *at sea*, perhaps they might apply to him for clarification?

'Of course. It would be my pleasure.'

The handing over of the newspaper brought the conversation to a close. Not only did the ladies take a very long time to read the article on the mutiny, they seemed to find the entire contents of the newspaper of absorbing interest. Mr Wilcocks watched them for a time, their heads bowed earnestly over the printed pages; Miss Marchmont was wearing her reading spectacles. Presently he began to grow bored. He had dined very well, and the motion of the carriage was making him drowsy. When he began to snore gently the three bowed heads rose, and their owners exchanged complacent smiles. Mary carefully folded the paper and replaced it on the seat beside him, and Miss Trent got out her knitting.

'What a tiresome fellow,' whispered Miss Marchmont, 'braying at us in that odious way. But you mustn't try to argue with that sort of man. You will never shift him, and the effort will give you the headache.'

'Yes, you are right,' Mary agreed, for the interval behind the newspaper had soothed her temper. 'But the mutiny sounds very bad. If the men are adamant, how will it ever be resolved?'

Miss Trent reminded her that wiser heads than theirs were at work on the situation, but her repeated mention of 'the first lord' made Mary wonder whether her friend had unintentionally endowed the chief political officer of the Navy with divine authority.

Miss Marchmont nodded, yawning. 'And perhaps it has been exaggerated — someone like Mr Wilcocks may have written that account.' She yawned again and removed her spectacles. 'He has at least set us one good example, and I propose to follow it. Let us hope for a quiet night.'

Mary was unable to sleep, but the darkness, the steady rocking, and Mr Wilcocks' snores caused her to drift into a comfortable languor. In this condition her thoughts moved easily between the past and the present. *London very dangerous . . . the mails safe and convenient . . . crash on the Stowmarket road . . . the Great*

White Horse . . . dangerous . . . sailors must be taught a lesson . . .
sailors and soldiers . . . White Horse . . . White Ladies . . . the first
time I saw White Ladies was with Captain Holland.

Captain Holland. Mrs Bamford, the landlady at the Great
White Horse, had not forgotten him either. 'What of that other
gentleman? *Captain* Something, wasn't he? He's passed through
our place once or twice since then, and ever so gallant in his
blue coat – almost better than a red one.'

It was coming on for evening when Holland made his way
from the main laboratory building to his quarters in the Warren.
It had been a long day, and Holland's mind was still full of
experimental data and how the quantity of smoke must be
balanced against the longevity of the burning item. His orderly,
Gunner Drake, met him at the bottom of the stairs.

Drake was a spare, wiry individual with greying hair and an
expression at once knowing and suspicious. 'Visitor up top for
you, sir,' he explained with an eloquent jerk of his head. 'It's
that there Dick— Er, *Major* Whittington.'

Holland frowned his surprise and quickly asked, 'Supplies?'

'No brandy and the sherry's precious low,' replied Drake. 'I
was just on me way to cadge some off of Lieutenant Evans.'
And it'll be poor, mean stuff, he continued to himself, *but beggars*
can't be choosers, and them wot can't afford to buy nothing decent . . .

'Yes, and he owes me,' said Holland, completing the thought
that passed between them. 'All right. Carry on then.'

Holland ran up the bare wooden stairs, his pleasure at seeing
his friend slightly dimmed by his anxieties as a host. He tried
to remember when he had last seen Major the Honourable
Francis – generally known as Dick – Whittington. *Six months?*
Probably closer to eight. Given the proximity of Woolwich to
London, it ought to have been more recent. Then again, there
was a gulf between the Foot Guards, one of the most exclusive
regiments in the Army, and the Royal Artillery. Their officers
existed in different worlds, both within the service and without.
The Guards tended towards the more glamorous side of warfare
while the training of the gunners inclined to the scientific, and

sometimes there was little sympathy between them. Holland and Whittington had known each other for a good many years, however, and their relationship was generally a harmonious, if not quite an equal one.

'Evening, Dick,' said Holland, motioning his friend not to stir from his seat on one of the dilapidated armchairs. 'What brings you south of the river? Heard anything new about this mess the Navy's got itself into?'

'And to you, old fellow,' replied Whittington in a leisurely tone. Both men were in uniform, but there the similarity ended. Whittington was the sort of person who always looked and sounded comfortable. He was well-groomed, his uniform fitted perfectly, and his long, booted legs rested easily on the dented fender. An expensive pair of leather gloves had been tossed onto the floor, and the pale hand he raised in greeting displayed a heavy gold signet ring. 'In answer to your second question, the first lord has not yet returned from Portsmouth, but everyone is hopeful that the compromise he has offered – in particular the pay increase – will be accepted. In answer to your first question, I am here to look at a horse, of all things – and to see you. An odd idea, I know, coming to Woolwich for a horse, but—' He frowned as Holland sat down opposite. 'By God, what is that appalling odour?'

Holland smelt the sleeve of his coat. 'Ah, that'll be me, I'm afraid.'

'Hang it out of the window,' Whittington called, as Holland retreated to his bedroom. 'Or better yet, burn the thing.'

The article in question was Holland's oldest uniform coat, which was not only much worn, but also stained by oil, charcoal, and the various chemicals used in the regiment's laboratory. He returned in his shirtsleeves.

'Rather too much of the infernal region about you for my liking,' Whittington continued. 'You know, brimstone.'

'Yes, sorry. I've been mixing the stuff all day,' Holland explained, 'and I'm used to it.'

'Oh, and what are you working on, if it is not too much of a secret?'

69

Holland shook his head and resumed his seat. 'They don't trust me on anything really secret anymore. It's a kind of bomb. The idea is to make a great deal of smoke, quickly, without a flame. Quite an interesting problem, actually.'

'This is deemed a valuable addition to the art of warfare by your masters, I take it?'

'Well, think of it as a kind of covering fire, to protect an advance or a retreat.'

Whittington nodded. 'Yes, I see. Rather ignominious, however, creeping about in a cloud of smoke.'

'Better than being dead,' said Holland. 'But about the mutiny, you think a rise in pay will do it?'

'Probably, if something is also done about bad officers.'

'Well, so long as the Channel fleet puts to sea again . . . though I suppose the North Sea fleet can watch the Texel and stop the Dutchmen coming out.'

For some time there had been rumours that the French were keen to attempt a landing on British soil, this time with Dutch aid. Sceptics pointed to the two recent failures in Ireland and Wales. Even the French would not be so foolish as to try a third time. The more pessimistically inclined, however, argued that the Irish invasion had only failed because of bad weather. If the Navy were to be convulsed by mutiny, both the Irish and the English coasts could be in danger.

Holland and Whittington analysed both positions until Whittington grew bored with the exercise. He shrugged his shoulders and complained that it was all a nuisance. What was the good of strategy when the most carefully laid plans could be undone by a gust of wind or a shift in the tide? 'And you know, this matter of my horse is even more depressing.'

Holland smiled tolerantly. 'All right – what happened?'

'A very sad story, I am afraid. He sounded absolutely perfect: an eight-year-old liver chestnut stallion of seventeen hands. Good bloodline, excellent manners, used to military exercise, and a friend who claimed to have seen him said he was the genuine article. I really had my heart set on him, even to the extent of coming all the way down here to settle the bargain, but when I saw him, it was not to be. Having been promised Pegasus I was presented with Rocinante.'

Holland disliked learned references, which he assumed these were. *Dick and his flourishes.* 'What's happened to . . . Pompey, wasn't it?' he asked, filling Whittington's glass with the last of the sherry.

'Nothing, apart from the fact that he is getting on in years, and he had colic pretty badly this past winter. Still game as ever, but he really deserves a spot of retirement. I would never take him abroad.'

The allusion to foreign, and therefore active, service touched a nerve with Holland, and he felt an ungenerous relief when Whittington admitted that he knew of no actual plan. Nevertheless, if English troops *did* return to the Continent the Foot Guards would probably be among them, while Holland would be stuck in Woolwich, unless the war really got going, and new artillery battalions were raised.

'It is your own silly fault for joining the branch of the service with the worst queue of officers and no means of jumping it,' said Whittington. 'And you are lucky to have this staff job. Why you are in such a hurry to get yourself shot to pieces is beyond me. Ah, there you are, Drake – and with a second bottle, stout fellow! You have saved us. How are you keeping, by the way? Are you longing for some honest soldiering instead of all this experimental sorcery?'

'Can't complain, sir, thank you very much.' Drake did not approve of Major Whittington, and he privately muttered, *Honest soldiering my arse,* as he filled their glasses.

'That's right, leave the bottle,' said Holland, fixing Drake with a look, 'and now that you're here, why don't you stay to supper, Dick?'

'Indeed. A capital suggestion.'

'Reckon we can fix up somethin', sir,' Drake observed in a long-suffering tone.

'Oh, no, let us go out, by all means,' urged Whittington. 'We might try our luck at the Clarendon Hotel in Blackheath.'

Holland rapidly calculated the likely cost of a meal at that elegant establishment. 'All right, if you like. See to the horses, will you, Drake?'

Drake was tidying up the room – not that anything was out of place – and he almost dropped the gleaming inkwell he was 'dusting'. *The Clarendon 'Otel! And who'll be payin fer that little treat? Captain Haitch can't afford it, and since when 'as 'is bloody lordship got so generous as to throw money about on anybody but 'imself?* 'I ain't so sure about Ranger's near foreleg,' he warned. 'It's been a mite swollen lately.'

'It was fine this morning.'

Drake shook his head slightly, but answered in the affirmative. *A fool and 'is money – if any – is soon parted for good and all.*

When the door had closed behind his reluctant subordinate, Holland resumed. 'To be fair, of course, I couldn't jump the queue even if it were allowed. No tin.'

Whittington nodded, although he had not needed to be told. The state of Holland's uniforms, the mean accommodation, and the lack of anything decent to drink all told the same story. He felt a twinge of conscience. Was his friend very hard up? Ought he to offer him a loan? Would it be possible to mention the subject in such a way that avoided embarrassment to them both? Probably not, but he had better pay for dinner. 'What you need,' he advised, 'is to find yourself a rich wife.'

Holland flinched as if he had been cut. '*What?*'

'I do not say that you must be wholly mercenary, only that you should fall in love with a rich girl and not a poor one. I am sure it is quite easily done.'

Whittington's tone was sufficiently impersonal, and Holland relaxed again. 'Mm, I see.'

'It is what I should do,' Whittington continued, thoughtfully, 'what I *mean* to do, in fact. If a girl is of a good family, with passable looks and twenty thousand pounds, she can have me. If she is very pretty she need only have ten thousand, and if she has thirty thousand, I shall keep my eyes closed. Not a bad bargain, I think. She would become Vicountess Bamfield, after all, in the fullness of time. What more could she want?'

'Nothing, I suppose. What are you going to do about your horse?'

Whittington burst out laughing. 'By God, the noble art of conversation is not lost in you, Bob.'

'No, I only meant—'

'I know precisely what you meant, but I am serious! The young ladies of the stage are all very well when one is amusing oneself, but there are such things as the family honour . . . and the family purse. Both must be kept in good nick. However, as it is unlikely that the Honourable Mrs Whittington will turn up in the next day or so, and I want to break in a new mount gradually, I thought I would have a look at Tattersalls. They ought to have something suitable, although I shall probably have to pay above the odds. Why don't you come along? There is a sale on the day after tomorrow.' Whittington took another swallow of the execrable sherry and shuddered faintly. 'You really ought to come up to Town more often. Get away from this ghastly place.'

'What's wrong with it?' asked Holland, the wariness returning.

'You have been shut up in the Warren for far too long if you need to ask. That is the worst of you gunners, you have no interest in anything that does not explode.'

Holland nodded, smiling slightly. Whittington also felt the release of tension and, chiding himself, he made another effort to lighten the atmosphere. 'My friend, I hope they never send you abroad, however much you complain. Woolwich is certainly your Lagado.'

'Lagado?'

'You know, the Grand Academy of Projectors? Gulliver's visit to Balnibarbi? Dean Swift's masterpiece?' prompted Whittington, as his hints failed to provoke a response. '*Swift*,' he repeated.

'No.'

'Good God, man, what do you read?' Whittington rose to his feet, masking this further embarrassment with exasperation. Everything he said seemed to be coming out wrong tonight.

He crossed the room to peer at a small bookcase. 'Ha! Just as I thought. This proves my point exactly: Gray's *Treatise on*

Gunnery; Le Blond, *The Arms and Machines Used in War*; Muller, *The Attack and Defence of Fortified Places*; *The Doctrine of Projectiles*— Good God! I was not aware that projectiles *had* a doctrine. Robbins, of course, and Vauban . . .' His finger traced to the end of the shelf. 'But what is this? *The Poems of Alexander Pope*.' He leafed through the volume and gazed back at Holland, who seemed suddenly nervous. 'You surprise me. Have you *read* these poems?'

Holland shrugged. 'Yes . . . some of them. Swift's a poet, is he?'

'Er, yes, but he also wrote prose. He is most famous for a very humorous piece, a comic novel called *Gulliver's Travels*, in which the hero visits a number of very odd, imaginary countries. In one of them, a place called Lagado, is the Grand Academy of Projectors.' As his explanation proceeded, Whittington perceived it was going to fail, but he carried on gamely. 'The Projectors are scientists, of a sort, and philosophers, and they spend their time attempting strange, impossible things, like . . . drawing sunbeams out of cucumbers or turning ice into gunpowder. It is highly diverting.'

'Mm.'

'And, naturally, it always makes me think of your laboratory.'

The clock outside struck the hour, and Holland said they ought to go. Whittington agreed with a feeling of relief. He was happy to leave the dingy room and the awkward conversations it seemed to inspire. As they strode across the courtyard his usual suavity returned. 'The best thing about London,' he observed, 'is the number of pretty girls that one sees.'

'You'll be able to find the Honourable Mrs Whittington.'

'In fact,' Whittington continued, 'I am acquainted with several splendid young persons who would do for you, and if you were to drag yourself away from this place, I might even introduce you.'

A disapproving Drake was waiting for them in front of the main gate, together with Ranger and Pompey. 'It'll be short commons for us, after tonight,' he muttered, and Ranger tossed his head in sympathy.

'I have only one request,' warned Whittington, as he swung himself onto his horse's back.

'What's that?'

'You must promise not to talk about smoke bombs. Even the most obliging girls tend not to appreciate them. They are funny that way.'

'All right, damn you,' laughed Holland, and they clattered down the empty street together.

6

London in springtime was delightful, especially for those residing at a fashionable address like 10 Cavendish Square. The house was conveniently situated in a pleasant neighbourhood, and while Admiral Verney's furnishings were rather austere, the ladies were thrilled to learn that no less a person than Lord Howe had dined at the massive oak table. Miss Trent professed to admire the portrait of Admiral Verney that hung above the drawing-room fireplace. Even when he was directing cannon fire from his quarterdeck, she felt, he maintained a fatherly air.

The capital, however, boasted far more notable attractions. Charlotte wanted to see them all, and Miss Marchmont and Miss Trent wanted to see all those that were suitable. Upon arriving, Miss Marchmont had straightaway purchased a reliable guidebook. Armed with her copy of the *Ambulator,* she conducted her charges, for so she considered them, on tours incorporating '*whatever is most remarkable for antiquity, grandeur, elegance or rural beauty*'. These sometimes seemed to Charlotte to come perilously close to *lessons*, as both Miss Marchmont and Miss Trent slipped easily into a pedagogical style, and Mary enthused upon anything of a remotely historical nature. Thus, rather too much time was taken up with how the Tower of London had been constructed and its significance for medieval government, whereas Charlotte wanted to see the lions, or at least to hear more about beheadings. Fortunately, however, these were minor inconveniences, and scholarly pursuits were leavened by concerts, visits to the theatre, and shopping expeditions. Miss Trent's green silk umbrella was an early purchase.

More serious matters were being debated in other quarters during those fresh April mornings and showery afternoons. Businessmen in the City feared that the bullion shortage must affect the stability of the Bank of England, while in Whitehall government ministers wondered when the policy of blockade would exhaust either British resources or the patience of neutral states. The men who dwelt in the slums and rookeries, for whom financial insecurity meant starvation and war meant enforced military service, were also considering whether their lot was a fair one. Few of these problems were meant to cloud the days of well-to-do young ladies, however, and when Mary enquired about the Spithead Mutiny, her questions were greeted with indulgent smiles. That she should add an interest in politics to her other accomplishments was considered charming, but not one that ought to be encouraged. It was the work of wiser heads, she was reminded, to wrestle with such things.

Perhaps she agreed. Certainly as she sat with Susannah in the upstairs parlour of 10 Cavendish Square her thoughts were not employed upon matters of state. Since arriving in London and seeing Susannah installed at Scarborough House, the vast, splendid residence in Dover Street, Mary had experienced a growing concern. Susannah had a gentle nature, but this tempered, rather than did away with, her playfulness and spirit of fun. She might lack her sister's dynamism and oppose some of the latter's more outrageous schemes, but more because she foresaw their ultimate, unpleasant consequences than because she was unmoved by their immediate charm. What could account, therefore, for her present dull withdrawal? Her beauty was undiminished and might even be said to have improved, but somehow its effect was not altogether pleasing. She was like a painting whose creator had failed to capture his beautiful sitter's vital spark.

The most likely causes of the trouble had swiftly occurred

to Mary, but thus far neither had convinced her as being correct. Yes, Susannah had been shaken by the death of her father, but she was no longer weighed down by grief. Sir William seemed to belong to her past life, and she regarded herself as a wife first, rather than a daughter. *As she ought*, thought Mary. Susannah's marriage too seemed happy enough, in so far as Mary could judge such things. They had dined with the colonel and his bride only once since coming to London, but the setting had been exquisite, and the colonel had been both fond and attentive. Charlotte might still judge him 'frosty old', but Susannah had appeared more than content, and had hung upon his every word.

And yet, something *was* wrong; Mary was convinced of it. Now, however, she answered brightly when Susannah asked whether she was enjoying her visit. 'Oh, yes, very much. You know, Dr Johnson said that when one was tired of London, one was tired of life.'

'Did he? Yes, I suppose he did,' replied Susannah with a bland smile. 'He was very clever, I expect.'

Mary observed her from behind lowered lashes. Was it better to ignore this lethargy, or ought she to confront it? She did not wish to intrude, but it seemed cold-hearted to pretend that all was well when it so plainly was not. 'Of course, it is only natural that you should miss Norfolk,' she ventured, placing a comforting hand upon Susannah's clasped ones. 'Your mother, and Storey's Court.'

'Well, I— It is all so different from what I am used to, from what . . . I am a very lucky girl, I know that,' said Susannah, seeming to struggle with her conscience. Then she brightened and raised her drooping head. 'And we may be going into the country ourselves shortly. To the colonel's— To *our* house in Kent.'

'That sounds lovely,' Mary agreed, and she allowed herself to be reassured. Perhaps it was merely London life that did not agree with Susannah. Certainly she would see more of her husband in the country, and if she was looking forward to that, Mary's worst fears were either misplaced or exaggerated.

She replenished Susannah's teacup with an elegant flourish, and continued, 'London *does* take some getting used to — so big and noisy, and everyone rushing about. Charlotte, you will not be surprised to learn, is extremely taken with Town life — as she imagines it after less than a week.'

Susannah nodded. 'Dear Lottie can be rather . . . *decided*. What did you tell me of her latest mission? Something for the ball?'

'New gloves,' Mary reminded her.

'*Gloves*?' repeated Susannah, blankly. 'But surely—'

'Yes, I know,' Mary laughed, 'but Charlotte is convinced that her gown will be ruined if worn with her wholly irreproachable, I should even say *highly elegant*, gloves. No gentleman will consent to stand up with her, her first ball will be an utter failure, and she will return to Storey's Court in disgrace. The glovers of London are her only hope of avoiding this terrible fate, and she has enlisted Miss Marchmont's assistance in her quest for the perfect article. I do not expect them to return until they have visited every shop.'

'Poor Miss Marchmont! I hope she will not be too exhausted to enjoy tomorrow evening.'

'Oh, no, and she has devised a plan, she and Miss Trent, to keep a check on Charlotte at the ball. It would not do to give her a free hand, however it has been gloved. She is not yet sixteen, after all.'

'No.' Susannah frowned thoughtfully. 'I think she might dance with our uncle, or one or two of the other gentlemen — I could point them out — but that must be my task, in Mama's absence. I would not interfere with your friends' enjoyment for the world.'

'They will not mind it in the least,' cried Mary, shaking her head. 'In fact, I doubt you could stop them. They like managing things, and you will have quite enough to do. Though, I must say that you seem very calm about everything. I would be on fire with anxiety, worrying about all the last details . . .'

Susannah seemed to wilt again; she stared down at her cup of tea and fiddled with the handle. 'Well, I *would* have been dreadfully worried,' she acknowledged, 'only I have had very little to do. You see, Mrs Crawford has been managing Scarborough House since the colonel returned from India, and she is very experienced. She knows what is suitable for an event of this kind, in London – and so does the colonel. They are both far cleverer than I am.'

A disturbing thought occurred to Mary but was immediately dismissed. Mrs Crawford might have a great knowledge of London society, but she was also a hard-faced, humourless woman of sixty-five. 'Well, I do not think—'

'It is true,' Susannah assured her. 'I know how to do things in the country well enough, but in Town people have very different standards – even the servants are different. I am sure I would make the most dreadful mistakes, whereas this way everything will be done in the first style.'

To be found deficient in such an important wifely skill as organising a ball was clearly distressing to Susannah, but Mary decided not to disagree with her. Things *were* different in London, after all. 'At least you will be able to enjoy yourself tomorrow,' she urged. 'You . . . you are looking forward to the ball, are you not?'

Susannah produced her bland smile a second time and said she was sure it would be lovely.

The conversation turned to more mundane matters. The ladies of 10 Cavendish Square had been invited to come early to Scarborough House, and then to spend what was left of the night there, after the ball's conclusion. This invitation, gratefully accepted, necessitated a consideration of logistics and a possible re-consideration of attire. One could not make a last minute change of gown, shoes, or gloves if one had not brought one's entire wardrobe along to Scarborough House, and that would not be possible.

'I hope that none of us becomes over-wrought,' said Mary, with mock seriousness. 'Perhaps I ought to consult Miss Trent. I am certain she will know of a remedy or tonic that is just the thing for excitability. A sort of *slow-you-down* rather than a *pick-you-up*.'

Susannah neither laughed nor offered a comment, and Mary

was grateful when the appearance of the parlour maid provided a distraction. 'Beg pardon, miss. Colonel Crosby-Nash is downstairs.'

'Oh, why, ask him to step up,' Mary replied, directing a surprised glance at Susannah. 'Were you expecting him?' she added, when the door had closed behind the servant.

Susannah was already on her feet, clasping and unclasping her hands. 'Ye-es, I thought he might . . . if he finished his business at his club. Did I not say?'

'Perhaps you did, but it does not signify either way. I only wish that Charlotte were at home.'

'Do not mind that,' murmured Susannah. 'He . . . does not quite approve of Lottie, you know . . . not all of the time. *He thinks she is unruly,*' she finished in a hurried whisper.

Then the parlour door opened, and Colonel Crosby-Nash was announced. The first thought that occurred to Mary was that he did not look as if he cared a great deal about organising balls. Not incapable, but unlikely to be interested in deciding between lilies and gardenias, or what sorts of iced drinks should be served to ladies who had been dancing all evening. He was handsomely dressed in a dark green frock coat over a pale silk waistcoat, fitted nankeen pantaloons, and hussar buskins, and through a combination of gravitas and vigour avoided appearing either too young or too old. His piercing glance, moreover, seemed to take in every detail of his surroundings and instantly determine its significance. He strode confidently into the room and favoured Mary with a curt bow. Susannah's hand he raised swiftly to his lips, and then he conducted her back to her chair.

'Good afternoon, Miss Finch. I am happy to see you again,' he announced. 'Have you been gossiping about tomorrow's doings?' He stood behind Susannah's chair, and presently he began to toy with a curl of her hair that lay upon the back of her neck. A flush of colour slowly spread across her face.

In a way that she could not explain, Mary found his action brutal. The incongruousness of that sentiment, however, disturbed her. How could such a fond gesture – a caress – betoken anything but affection? Surely she was letting her imagination run away with her . . . but what was she imagining? With a conscious effort she replied normally. 'Yes, sir, I am afraid that we have. This will be my first Town ball, so of course I am looking forward to it. It certainly sounds very impressive.'

He raised his eyes slowly, and when they met Mary's she wanted to look away. 'Well, when one has acquired a beautiful jewel, one must do something *impressive* to show her off,' he observed.

'The colonel is so very generous,' breathed Susannah.

'Not at all, my dear. If I set out to do a thing, I like to do it well.'

Susannah fidgeted, and he smiled. 'As modest as she is beautiful. My *"pearl without a spot"*, as the poet says. I hope, Miss Finch, that you and Charlotte are making the most of the other opportunities London has to offer, during your visit?'

'Indeed, yes, I believe we are.'

'Excellent.' His expression softened, and after a moment he walked to the fireplace and stood with his hand upon the mantelshelf. 'Perhaps you will manage to tempt my dear wife into joining some of your expeditions . . . shopping or sight-seeing.'

Mary was surprised by the request, and it showed in her voice. 'Certainly, of course,' she replied and then turned to Susannah. 'I daresay you have already visited most of the places on our list, but I hope you know that you are welcome to join us whenever you like, if you can stand Charlotte's pace.'

'Oh, yes,' Susannah agreed, with an earnestness that Mary could not quite decipher.

'My business affairs have taken a great deal of my time during these last weeks,' Crosby-Nash explained, 'and in consequence I have not been free to entertain my bride as much as I should like. I am afraid that she has been pining, shut up in Dover Street and not daring to venture out alone. At least, that is my fear. Is it justified, my dear?'

Susannah glanced up at him. 'I have been perfectly content, Arthur, but . . . I shall go along, on the very next outing,' she promised.

He smiled tolerantly. 'It is just as you like, only I would not want you to feel that you must be always at home.'

'No.'

'And if you *do* accompany your friends, how shall you manage things?'

'I shall order the carriage.'

'And?'

'Direct George or Matthew to attend us.'

'Just so.' He nodded, adding to Mary, 'I have had to explain to Susannah that the use of one's carriage and the attendance of a footman are essential for a lady of quality in London, if she is not to be mistaken for . . . a person of a questionable character or situation.'

The colonel's position meant that Mary could not look at husband and wife together, but must choose which to observe. Politeness required that she acknowledge his remarks, but she wished that she could tell how Susannah was receiving them. Did she feel chastened by this little lecture on etiquette, or did she consider it part of his 'fatherly guidance'? *I know how I should regard it,* thought Mary. She smiled pleasantly, however, before replying. After all, he was not *her* husband, and there was little point in arguing. 'I expect that Susannah is used to the greater informality of the country, sir – as I am. The precautions that you mention would certainly not have occurred to me in Suffolk. However,' she added, trying to be fair, 'I understand that London ways are different.'

'Indeed they are,' he agreed.

The day of the ball dawned bright and fair, but in Woolwich Robert Holland awoke with a pounding headache. He opened his eyes – or rather, one eye; the other was swollen shut. Having slowly assumed an upright position, he raised a tentative hand to assess the damage: a black eye, without a doubt, and a split lip.

Footsteps in the passage were followed by a deferential knock. He would soon know the worst of it. 'Come in, Drake.'

Drake stepped briskly into the room, whistling under his

breath as he always did first thing in the morning. The tune died on his lips when he surveyed the battered figure in the tumbled bed. He merely placed a mug of tea on the bedside table, however, and observed, 'I 'ope the other chap come off it worst, sir?'

Holland grinned at him. 'He did.'

'Dead, is 'e?'

'Do I look that bad?'

'Well, you ain't likely to win no beauty prizes, sir, I don't think. 'Ow'd it 'appen?' Drake's tone descended from the familiar to the conspiratorial. 'Low pads been up to their tricks again?'

Holland shook his head, wincing abruptly. '*Bugger*. No, it was nothing.'

'Don't look like nothing.' Drake stared at him. He knew that Holland had gone into Woolwich town with another officer, and if there hadn't been trouble with civilians . . . 'Say, it weren't one of the lads, was it? The bloody fool!'

'Pipe down, will you?' Holland complained. 'You're not doing my head any good.'

'But strikin' an officer – that's an 'anging offence.'

'Of course it is, so you'd better forget about it.'

'But . . .' Drake's dismay faded to indignation. 'You won't be forgettin' that there shiner in an 'urry,' he grumbled. Folding his arms, he studied Holland dispassionately and asked whether he was going to be sick. On being informed that a basin was not necessary he turned to the matter of rehabilitation. 'Right. Then I reckon you'd better 'ave a poultice fer that eye. I'll fetch up the 'ot water.'

'I don't need a poultice,' Holland argued. 'How bad can it be?'

Drake replied by taking down the small mirror from the wall and handing it over. Holland glanced at himself. The dried blood made it look worse, of course. 'The swelling will go down if you leave it alone.'

'Not soon enough, it won't,' Drake pronounced, shaking his head. 'Ain't you forgettin' tonight, sir?'

'Tonight?'

84

'Miss Susannah's – that's to say, Mrs Crosby-Nash's – ball. An 'ighly elegant affair, I don't doubt.'

'Oh, Christ,' groaned Holland, in a tone that indicated he certainly had forgotten.

'Can't 'ave you turnin' up in company, lookin' like you've gone ten rounds with Mendoza, now can we, sir?'

The possibility of avoiding the ball altogether occurred to Holland, followed closely by the conflicting thoughts of disappointing his cousins, of his dislike of balls and large parties, and of breaking his promise to attend the damned thing. And Mary Finch; she was in London, and she would doubtless be there tonight. *Damn it all.* 'No, I suppose we can't.'

'Right you are, sir,' said Drake, all brisk efficiency. 'I'd best be off for that 'ot water, then.'

In accordance with the strictures of London society, the ladies of 10 Cavendish Square made the journey to Dover Street that evening in the Armitage carriage. As a result their characters were preserved but their ensembles were not, and they arrived in a somewhat creased and fractious state. Fortunately, Susannah was on hand to offer practical aid in the person of her maid, who knew a great deal about smoothing ladies' gowns and repairing tousled coiffures, and to reassure everyone that they looked perfectly lovely regardless.

In the case of Mary and Charlotte, this was quite true. Mary had chosen an open robe of gold tabby over an ivory satin round gown. The former was cut in a plain, Classical style, and the latter was delicately embroidered at the neck and sleeves. She also wore her hair simply, in gentle curls and ringlets, and this provided an effective foil to her jewellery – an unusual necklace of small gold loops, threaded together to form a rope, and matching earrings. As befitting someone who was not yet sixteen, Charlotte wore a round gown of pale blue lutestring, and her hair was swept back from her face and tied with blue ribbons. The effect was both artless and charming, particularly because she had been forced to give way to Miss Marchmont on the subject of rouge and white paint, both of which had been strictly forbidden. When informed of this tyranny, Susannah expressed sympathy to Charlotte and pressed Miss Marchmont's hand in gratitude, before completing her sister's dress with the gift of a single strand of pearls.

Not surprisingly, the two elder members of the Cavendish Square party paid less attention to the demands of fashion as regards their own attire. Nevertheless, they were tremendously, if secretly, excited to be attending so grand an affair, and they each managed to achieve a certain éclat, in their different ways. Miss Marchmont had refused to countenance the fad for high waists and the absence of stays, as the combination would, she claimed, make her look like a pouter pigeon. Instead she had opted for a more 'traditional' gown and half-robe, both of grey satin, but topped by a stylish turban of Indian muslin and black velvet bandeau. Miss Trent, by contrast, had insisted that she did not require a new gown of any description, and indeed her beautiful lace curricle and cap – both the product of her own hands – had quite transformed her steel-blue chemise gown into an elegant, if restrained, ensemble.

Invitations to the ball were inscribed for eight o'clock, and such was the prestige of Scarborough House that almost all the guests had arrived by half past. There was a constant procession of carriages stopping outside the mansion and disgorging their elegant passengers. Depending on their beauty or political persuasion, arrivals might be greeted by cries of admiration or scorn from the crowd of onlookers, but a cordon of footmen and lamplighters preserved them from any actual jostling. Once inside they were shown first into the upstairs library, where little rounds of toasted cheese and several varieties of punch were served, and where they were greeted by their host and hostess.

Then it was time to go down, as the sound of music promised further delights. Despite being situated in the centre of the house, the high ceiling and pale walls contrived to give the ballroom a light, airy feeling, while the two large chandeliers provided a brilliant display. There was a balcony at one end of the room, which housed the orchestra, and their pleasing strains would dictate the progress of the evening. Lavish arrangements of fresh flowers completed the simple decorations, and the heady scent of lilies, roses, and carnations filled the air.

At precisely nine o'clock Susannah and Colonel Crosby-Nash opened the ball. Despite the difference in their ages, they made a handsome couple. Susannah was surely the most beautiful woman in the room in a gown and petticoat of pale pink sarsenet, trimmed in Italian lace, and with a blaze of diamonds around her neck, while the colonel was severely elegant in black and white. They performed an accomplished minuet, and probably no better situation could have been devised for showing off Susannah's natural grace. If some of the ladies were waiting for her to miss a step they were disappointed, and certainly none of the gentlemen entertained such uncharitable thoughts. Then the music changed, and the assembled company seemed to breathe and look about them. Gentlemen remembered their partners and led them to the floor for an allemande. Now the atmosphere became heady, vibrant, and the more general movement created a beauty of its own. As the patterns of the dance shifted, there was a kaleidoscope of lilac, ivory, primrose, and aquamarine, with occasional bursts of amber and jade. Sombre, masculine hues provided a counterpoint to the ladies' finery, but here and there the more striking colours of military uniforms might be picked out.

Mary watched from among the chaperones who were seated under the balcony at the far end of the room, and it seemed to her that Susannah had been right – the elegance of a Town ball was altogether different from what she had experienced in Suffolk. It was not that the ladies' gowns were more stylish or the gentlemen more handsome, although this was generally the case. Rather, everyone moved more serenely and spoke with a greater confidence, so that individual imperfections of appearance did not seem to matter. They were the leaders of society, or at least of that segment of society that mattered, and they knew it.

Whether she aspired to join that world of wealth and privilege Mary was not certain. It seemed to her that with serenity came coldness, and confidence was not easily distinguished from disdain. Succeeding among these great people might prove as costly to one's character as to one's purse. At least for that evening, however, she could not long remain a passive observer. She attracted the attention of several gentlemen, each of whom would have outshone a country assembly, and they encouraged her to think herself exceedingly handsome, charming, and a most delightful creature. When she was not dancing she was certain to have at least one attendant eager to provide her with a glass of punch, or to sit with her or walk with her, and if six different suppers were to be provided, she could have had a different partner for each.

Mary's success was not generally repeated among her friends. Despite their early triumph, Susannah and her husband did not dance together again, and after mingling briefly among some gentlemen of his acquaintance, the colonel departed the ball-room. During the next few hours he returned occasionally but always remained a spectator. For her part, Susannah danced several times with different partners, gracefully, but with no apparent enthusiasm. Charlotte, by contrast, was all too willing to dance. Unfortunately, due to the high standards set by Miss Marchmont and Miss Trent, her partners were few and un-inspiring. She danced twice with her uncle and once with a bespectacled gentleman who had something to do with the Board of Trade. At one point a young cavalry officer attempted to storm the citadel, but a baleful look from Miss Marchmont obliged him to retire from the field.

It was while encamped between her two minders that Charlotte at last perceived the arrival of a champion. 'Look, there is Bobs, at last,' she cried, as she perceived her cousin at the entrance to the ballroom.

'Yes, dear,' agreed Miss Trent. 'You mustn't point,' she added, placing a restraining hand on Charlotte's arm. 'And you mustn't stand up.'

'But he is to dance with me,' Charlotte protested, 'and he does not know it yet.'

'A lady waits for her partner,' affirmed Miss Marchmont from Charlotte's other side. 'She does not bellow at him from across the room.'

Charlotte sat back in her chair with an unladylike huff. 'Do not fret,' whispered Miss Trent, who could never maintain a stern front for long. 'I daresay he will be here directly.'

Her prediction was mistaken, however, for Holland made his way first to Susannah. They stood for a while together, Holland with his arms folded, and Susannah wielding a languid fan. A servant produced glasses of champagne, and Holland downed his in a swallow.

'Oh, look,' cried Charlotte, 'he has been in a fight.' Thanks to Drake's poultice, the swelling had been reduced, and Holland could open both eyes. In compensation, however, the area around his injured eye had come out in a vivid purple, and when he turned in response to something Susannah said, it was on prominent display.

'Not *quite* what we want,' remarked Miss Marchmont, cocking a critical eyebrow. 'Not *precisely* the latest fashion, I think, even in London town.'

'What a colour,' said Charlotte, admiringly. 'Perhaps that is why he is so late. The Woolwich coach was attacked by robbers, and Bobs had to fight them off.'

'Shh, dear,' Miss Trent murmured, and Miss Marchmont urged, 'You must pretend that you have not noticed it.'

'What?' demanded Charlotte. 'Bobs!' she cried, motioning furiously, and he moved at last in their direction.

Mary observed all of this from a discreet distance. She had known that Holland would be attending the ball – at least that he had been invited – and she had told herself more than once that she could meet him with the utmost tranquillity. Unfortunately, this did not now seem to be the case. Seeing him and wondering what he was thinking made her feel awkward; neither angry nor wounded nor fearful, but an unsettling combination of all three. Yet she could not look away nor direct her own thoughts more pleasingly.

Then a timely interruption occurred. A bashful admirer, who thought Mary's heightened colour and the set of her shoulders particularly charming, summoned up the courage to speak to her. This broke the spell, or whatever influence Holland exerted over her and, as the gentleman at her side announced that their common acquaintances in Stowmarket would be glad to hear that she was enjoying herself in London and looking so well, she watched Holland and her friends with apparent contentment. Holland, she thought, looked quite grim – but then he often did – and now he was engaged in a conversation of sorts with Miss Marchmont and Miss Trent. Introductions, judging by the former's imperious nod and the latter's nervous, flapping gestures. Might he be enquiring about Mary at all? Had he seen her? Would he look in her direction? Did she want him to?

Before Mary could frame an answer to any of these questions, Charlotte sprang to her feet and drew her cousin in the direction of the dance floor. As she studied his retreat, Mary felt strangely let down, although there was no good reason for this. Why had she imagined that his presence at the ball would have anything to do with her? It quite clearly did not. *And so be it. I do not care in the least.*

She exhaled decidedly and surveyed the scene. Holland's departure meant that it was safe to return to her seat – not that she had moved to avoid him. Disengaging herself from the Stowmarket man, she collected two glasses of punch and presented them to her friends.

Miss Trent smiled at her fondly. 'Ah, thank you, my dear. Are you tired? It is *such* an exciting evening. I hope you have been enjoying yourself?'

'Yes, I . . . The music is very good.'

'And your gown is lovely,' agreed Miss Marchmont. 'I had my doubts about the colour, you know, but it is just the thing for you.'

Mary smiled complacently. She had chosen her gown quite carefully and felt that the combination suited her. She was not a schoolgirl, after all, and could carry off a certain degree of sophistication. On the other hand, she had no desire to stun the assembled company with what might be considered a showy display. She had never worn such an expensive gown, and as for her jewellery, well, if a thing was worth doing . . . Yes, everything was as she could have wished.

She felt rather less comfortable a few minutes later when the music ended and Charlotte returned to them, with Holland reluctantly in tow and no chance of escape. *Oh dear.* Was it possible to assume a pose that conveyed a polite interest in what was going on around her and also suggested that she had not noticed Captain Holland? The best she could manage was a somewhat awkward tilt of the head that actually made her appear to be eavesdropping on the ladies seated on her other side.

'What fun!' cried Charlotte, her eyes shining. 'Miss Trent says that dancing makes her dizzy, but you really ought to have a go, Miss Marchmont. Bobs will take you, won't you? He does not know so many steps,' she confided, 'but I daresay *you* know them all and can show him if he goes wrong.'

Miss Marchmont resisted that tempting proposal, and Charlotte carried straight on. 'Well, and Mary – *you* are quite a hit. Everyone is asking about you, calling you "the Suffolk Heiress" and saying that *copper* is worth its weight in *gold* nowadays. What do you think of that?'

Miss Marchmont answered for her. 'I think it is ridiculous,' she sniffed, 'and in very poor taste.'

'They mean her hair,' Charlotte confided to Miss Trent, 'which is not *really* coppery, but I suppose it was the best they could do, and I think it is very nice when people pay you compliments! Bobs, did you not say that Mary was looking very pretty tonight?'

'Er, yes.' Holland had managed to draw back, as if he hoped to be excluded from the conversation. When Mary uttered an equally hesitant reply, however, and flickered a glance in his direction, he edged forward as if he were going to speak to her. Instead, Miss Marchmont affirmed that there was 'no copper for sale hereabouts', in a tone worthy of Mrs Tipton, and he retreated again, looking uncomfortable. Then someone called his name, and he turned to acknowledge the newcomer. 'Evening, Dick.'

Dick Whittington shook his head affably. He was even more handsome than usual in his dress uniform. Drake had done his best to bring Holland 'up to the mark', but the contrast was decided. 'I thought I saw you across the room,' Whittington reported, 'but did not credit— Good God, man, been walking into doors again? That was clumsy of you.'

'It was a *fight*,' piped Charlotte, taking immediate offence. 'And Bobs knocked the other man down, only—'

'Shh, Lottie,' murmured Holland, frowning at her.

'I beg your pardon, ma'am,' replied Whittington, bowing gravely. 'If the other fellow was knocked down, that changes everything. Captain Holland, may I be introduced to your fair protector . . . and her friends?'

'Yes, sorry. Major Whittington – my cousin, Miss Armitage, and Miss Finch, Miss Marchmont, and Miss Trent.'

'Ladies,' said Whittington, taking all of them in with a smile, 'I am honoured to make your acquaintance.' Leaning towards Charlotte he added, conspiratorially, 'I have known your cousin for a great many years and so presume to bait him on occasion. Am I forgiven?'

'Well, I suppose so,' replied Charlotte, smiling in spite of herself. She gave him her hand, and when he kissed it in token of her graciousness, he won her over completely.

The relationship between Charlotte, Susannah, and Holland was soon explained. 'Ah, so *that* is what has dragged our gallant gunner up to Town,' said Whittington. 'Family feeling. How awfully cosy. You must know, ladies – and I hope you will not come down on me for this, Miss Armitage – that generally speaking nothing short of a direct order from the master general of the Ordnance would bring Captain Holland to an affair such as this one. Am I right, Bob?'

'I suppose so, more or less.'

'But now you are here and I daresay enjoying yourself. Perhaps there is hope for you after all. Ah, the music is starting again. If you are not already engaged, Miss Armitage, might I have the privilege?'

'Yes, of course,' laughed Charlotte, and Whittington led her away on his arm.

Holland stood for a moment, irresolute, and then extended

his hand to Mary. He did not speak until she had taken it, and then asked, 'Will you dance with me?'

His hand felt hard as it closed around hers, and she rose to her feet without looking at him. 'Very well,' she murmured and then nodded her assent, for she was aware that her voice had been scarcely audible. The thought of refusing had flashed momentarily, but it had somehow failed to spark the appropriate conduct.

'Oh, wait!' cried Miss Marchmont. 'Mary! I do not think—'

Holland stepped aside so that Mary could precede him. 'Don't worry,' he said, looking back. 'She won't come to any harm with me.'

'I sincerely hope not, sir. Be so good as to bring her straight back as soon as this dance is finished.'

They danced. At least, there was no better name for the exercise, although dancing is generally adjudged to be enjoyable, and neither of them took any pleasure from what they were doing. Holland was lost in bleak recrimination. Why had he not left her alone? He knew very well what she must think of him, but it couldn't be helped. She could not possibly understand his decision, and he could not possibly explain it. Mary felt as if she were dancing with a stranger – or worse than a stranger, a dear friend who had consciously chosen disregard and indifference. He did not shrink from touching her, or even helping her when she missed a step, but that was because his hand was anonymous.

The pain of that anonymity grew steadily, and when they reached the end of the line of couples Mary perceived that she was crying. They were not fierce, burning tears, but she could not control them, and anyone looking at her would surely notice. Even he . . . *That* humiliation had to be avoided, whatever else happened. She turned away from Holland and the other dancers, and towards the knots of people gathered on the edge of the dance floor. Once she thought she heard someone speak her name, but she shook her head and carried on, hardly noticing where she was going. Holland stepped out of the dance and watched her disappear into the crowd, but he did not follow.

As she walked, her face averted, Mary upbraided herself. What was the matter with her? She had never felt so weak and spiritless, and over such a little thing. To cry because someone did not care for her. *Coward!* Well, if that were so she could at least do her best to conceal her weakness until she could master it. In the four corners of the room stood pairs of large porcelain vases, each filled with sprays of flowers and greenery. She slipped behind the nearest, intending to remain out of sight until she could compose herself. *If I may only be quiet for a little while,* she thought, *I shall be able to return to the others, and no one the wiser.*

She stood for a few minutes in the secluded nook, breathing deeply and forcing herself to think about bland, pleasant things, such as sheep, and the new flagstones that were to be laid in the courtyard at White Ladies. It was also important, she knew, not to rub her eyes; rather she must allow her tears to dry and blink back any new ones that threatened to fall. Red, puffy features would certainly give her away to such keen observers as Miss Marchmont and Miss Trent.

Presently, she was able to look about her. It was surprising how much shelter the vases and greenery actually provided, together with the shadows, which were notable in this particular corner because the candles in the wall sconce had burned out. She could observe the bustle and movement of the ballroom quite candidly and yet remain unobserved. There was Charlotte, dancing at last with the young cavalry officer, while across the way a lady in turquoise silk looked to have spilled something down the side of her gown and was trying to conceal it with a beaded shawl. Captain Holland was not in plain view, fortunately, and now her breathing was almost completely steady.

Mary was wishing she might moisten her handkerchief and wash her face, when she suffered a new shock. The wall beside her appeared to be *moving* – or could it be some trick of the shadows? She retreated into the very corner and observed a part of the wall very definitely swing towards her. Then she relaxed. It was, of course, a door to the servants' passage, painted

94

to look as if it were part of the wall, and in the gloom she had not noticed it. She kept still, however, for her presence would seem distinctly odd to the servant who emerged from the passage and equally difficult to explain.

A man emerged, and then a second, who pushed the door closed. Now, if either turned round they would see her, for only the deep shadows remained for protection. She pressed back against the wall, but they were more interested in the room before them.

Mary let her breath out slowly. The first man was a servant – she recognised the Crosby-Nash livery, and he was carrying a tray. The second, however, cut a very strange figure, for his carefully starched cravat, powdered wig, and silk stockings marked him as a guest at the ball. Why was such a person creeping about in the servants' passage?

She asked herself that question as she studied the two men, and now they were conversing, the taller man – the servant – bending deferentially to the shorter. They both spoke in low voices; if she had not been so close behind them she would never have caught their exchange.

'If you are ready, Cit— I mean—'

'I know precisely what is meant, but you must use greater care! Always!'

'Yes, of course,' murmured the servant. 'Your pardon.'

'Very well,' replied the other man. 'Now, if you have composed yourself, let us make our way to the front of the house.'

'Your pardon again, but are you sure this is wise? You could easily remain another night, you know. It would be safer.'

The shorter man shook his head. 'No, there are other matters requiring my attention that I must be at liberty to pursue. That was the last set of dancing, was it not? If I make my departure now, with the crowd, the risk will not be very great.'

The servant's answer was inaudible, but a chuckle passed between the two men, and then they stepped forward into the room. Mary followed them.

She was immediately swept into a milling throng. The music had ended, and now couples stood together, congratulating each

95

other on their prowess during the evening, while singletons darted in and out, attempting to locate those whom they must collect before departing. Liveried footmen were circling, bearing wraps and capes, and announcing that his lordship's carriage was at the door.

Holland was in the entrance hall, waiting for his hat to be produced, and suffering himself to be pushed slowly backwards as more imperious guests thrust towards the door. He seemed to observe them phlegmatically, but that was because he neither saw nor felt the press of the crowd. Instead, he was occupied with the memory of Mary Finch gliding towards him, the candlelight casting a golden glow upon her hair and shoulders, and the touch of her gloved hand when their palms met in the dance. How he had wanted to entwine his fingers with hers, to draw her closer and to see her smile at him, but none of these things had happened. No, instead he had been cold and heartless; he had made her cry.

Well, you made her cry. For one night you were a bastard, but wasn't that better than being one for the rest of your life? And this will surely be the end of it; you won't see her again. He forced himself to repeat that conclusion and to acknowledge that it was for the best. While not an arrogant man, it had not previously been Holland's practice to doubt himself, but he did so now. Tonight had proven how strong was the temptation to go back on his decision, and to let the future take care of itself. But that would be weak, selfish, and he was damned if he would do it.

A sudden movement brought him out of his reverie. He was standing at the foot of the great circular staircase, and an older gentleman attempting to make his way tripped against the edge of the bottom stair. Holland hauled him upright, and they exchanged pleasantries appropriate to the occasion. 'Sir, I am obliged to you,' said the one, adjusting his wig. 'Hell of a crush,' the other agreed.

A footman appeared with Holland's hat, and the older gentleman called for a linkboy to light him to Arlington Street and the White Horse Cellar. He was somewhat undersized, but he moved and spoke with the confidence of a man used to being obeyed. His embroidered waistcoat, diamond cravat pin, and lace cuffs might have conveyed the dandy if coupled with a foppish demeanour. As he wore them, however, they indicated a refined sense of taste.

'May I offer you the benefit of my light, sir?' he asked, glancing up at Holland. He had pale blue eyes, which were remarkable in an otherwise sallow visage, and his thin face bore the scars of childhood smallpox. 'I am concerned that the streets are dangerous at this time of the night, even for a gentleman of your pro . . .' His voice trailed off as he noticed the other's black eye, and his expression became sceptical.

Holland smiled wryly in acknowledgement of the joke. He certainly did not look as if he could take proper care of himself. 'No, sir, they aren't safe, and I thank you for the offer, but I'm heading in the opposite direction.' Drake's impudent query came back to him, and he resisted the temptation to explain that the other chap 'ad come off it worst.

Mary stood on tiptoes, craning her neck. She had lost track of the short gentleman, but the servant was ahead of her and to the left. She followed him into the supper room. There was a blockage of some sort – a few of the guests had consumed too much wine – but if she circled round to the right, she thought she would intercept the servant *and* his charge before they reached the entrance hall. Why she wished to do so she could not say, other than that their conversation had fired her curiosity. As she made her way through the crowd she found herself face to face with Dick Whittington.

'Ah, Miss— *Miss Finch*, are you all right?'

She attempted a smile, while at the same time striving to keep the servant in view. Was that his wig, bobbing like a seagull on the crest of a wave? 'Yes, of course. I am quite well. Such a lovely evening.'

Under the glare of the chandelier, however, her tearstains were visible, and Whittington was not deceived. 'Has something happened? Can I help at all?'

'No, no, really.' Someone jostled her, and she was conscious that this made her appear to be in need of assistance, of a strong manly arm upon which to lean. Whittington provided one. *Oh, you are a nuisance,* she sighed, for now she had lost sight of the servant and must continue to smile winningly at Whittington. If only he would forego his gallant ministrations!

He was oblivious to her irritation. 'Might I ask, have you been long acquainted with Captain Holland?'

Here was an even less appealing topic, and she answered cautiously as he steered her past an obstacle. 'N–no, not very long. Why?'

'No reason, only I saw you dancing with him a while ago, and later he walked past me without a word. Do you happen to . . .' His thoughtful frown faded into a smile. 'The sly dog! I beg your pardon, Miss Finch, but are you by any chance an admirer of the poetry of Mr Pope?'

This query was so unexpected that she stared at him, her chagrin momentarily forgotten. 'Why, yes, I am,' she admitted, mystified. 'Why do you ask?'

'Oh, no reason,' he laughed. 'Come along. Let us see if we can find him.'

This suggestion provoked an entirely different, and more powerful reaction. 'No, please!' she cried, 'I would really rather . . .' But Whittington had plunged back the way she had come, and as he had hold of her arm she was obliged to follow.

7

For all its bright beginnings, the evening ended badly for Mary. She and Major Whittington did not find Holland (a failure for which Mary was profoundly grateful), but the process of searching for him was unnerving, and she returned to her friends more jostled and buffeted than she would otherwise have been. Miss Marchmont was not pleased by the escapade and said so, while Whittington's arch glances, before he took himself off, were irritating in the extreme. Finally, and surprisingly, Miss Trent made a contribution to Mary's low spirits. Mary had retired wearily to bed when her friend appeared, still wearing her ball gown and in a buoyant, even ebullient, condition.

'My word,' she simpered, 'I hardly know whether I dare speak to you!' and when asked to explain this extraordinary remark, replied, 'You are "the Suffolk Heiress", now, and no longer our own dear Miss Finch. You are quite beyond the common touch.'

Mary responded in confusion and dismay. 'Miss Trent!' she cried, sitting up in bed. 'What can you mean? *You* have never felt this way, surely? Nor Miss Marchmont?'

Miss Trent hastened to reassure. Of course, *they* could never be deceived by appearances, or what people said; such a thing would be *quite impossible*. She then flitted lightly on to a consideration of the different varieties of punch served at the ball (all delightful) and whether any might have contained alcohol. This, and an observation on the invigorating effects of mint cordial, caused Mary to bite her lip, but afterwards, when she was alone, the question of her own situation returned.

It had never occurred to Mary that the receipt of a fortune might have changed her. Yes, certain outward trappings had been added – and very pleasant ones, too – but none that had affected her essential character. She was the same as she had ever been, and no one who knew her could possibly think otherwise. Miss Trent's remarks, however, called that view into question. If she *looked* to have changed, perhaps those who had not also passed through the crucible of Mrs Bunbury's school for young ladies, or who did not view the world through a prism of sunny simplicity, might take appearance for reality.

Captain Holland, for example. Might his behaviour towards her be the result, not of indifference, but of an unwillingness to express his affections, now that she was wealthy? It seemed unlikely; had he not specifically said that money did not matter? True, he had spoken on the assumption that she might *not* inherit her uncle's fortune, but surely a principle that worked in one direction was equally applicable in the other? And later, when he *had* known that she would inherit, he had expressed his feelings in no uncertain terms (she blushed at the recollection). It was fair to say that he had not known the extent of her wealth when he had behaved so warmly. Could that have made the difference? He had imagined her receiving a modest competence and an unsuitable, draughty house, and instead she had become . . . the Suffolk Heiress?

Perhaps. Mary knew very well that Captain Holland possessed an . . . unbending personality; it was impossible to convince him of anything about which he entertained the least suspicion. And as she recalled the events of the previous year, it seemed highly significant that his letter breaking off their friendship had come in the spring, soon after the full extent of her inheritance had been determined.

Well, if that explained the captain's conduct, what ought now to be done about it?

★   ★   ★

It had been expected that all the ladies of Scarborough House would breakfast in bed on the morning after the ball. When the maid bearing a tray cautiously opened the door to Mary's chamber, therefore, she was surprised to find its occupant not only awake but up and dressed. 'Why, good morning, miss,' she cried. 'You're an early bird, you are. I do hope none of us has gone and woke you.'

Mary was seated at her dressing table, apparently observing her reflection in the mirror, but seeing instead the events of the previous night. The greeting disturbed her meditations, and she began to brush her hair. 'Oh, no,' she said with a smile. 'I could not sleep, that is all. I expect I am not yet used to the sounds of London. They are . . . very different from those of the country.'

The girl arranged the contents of her tray upon a small table beside the window. 'Aye, it's a terrible racket, if you're not used to it, what with the dustmen, and tinkers, and sandmen, and I don't know what bawling up and down the street. But this here is nothing compared to Billingsgate of a morning. Cook sends me there when we know the master wants a bit of fish for breakfast. You wouldn't credit some of the things they say, and loud enough to wake the dead.'

She brooded, frowning, and then brightened. 'And you ladies deserve your sleep after all that lovely music and dancing last night. Wasn't it a grand evening?'

'It certainly was,' said Mary, poking at an unruly curl. 'You are Sarah, are you not?'

'That's right, miss. Shall I pour out for you?'

Mary shook her head. 'No, thank you.' She was not very hungry, but she allowed herself to be helped into the chair that Sarah obligingly held for her.

Sarah's mind was still upon the ball. 'Emm and me – we were helping with the supper – we never saw such a sight as all those ladies and gentlemen, dressed as fine as could be, and the tables fit for a king. You were ever so pretty, miss, if you don't mind me saying so. We saw you dancing with a gentleman – and he was ever so handsome. Emm says you can't beat a

101

gentleman in regimentals, which is true most of the time, but for a ball, I say proper evening dress takes the prize.'

This comment did nothing to strengthen Mary's appetite for breakfast, and when she was alone again she returned to her dressing table. There, concealed under a hand mirror, was a letter on a distressingly similar subject. She had written and re-written it in the early morning hours, when her own thoughts, more than the tramp of London traffic, had disturbed her slumber.

She lifted the mirror and read the address: *Captain R. Holland, Royal Regiment of Artillery, The Woolwich Warren, Kent.* The simple, apparently confident pen strokes conveyed nothing of her present anxiety. *Ought I to send this? A lady does not chase after a gentleman, but waits for him to act . . . And if he does not? If he has made it exceedingly clear that he will not?* She pondered this. Captain Holland could be very stubborn, and some might say that she was demeaning herself by pursuing him. Ought she to be put off by such concerns? *You have written the letter*, she told herself, *and you must send it. To falter now would be the worst sort of cowardice . . . scarcely worthy of the term.* With that warning she snatched up the letter and swept out of the room.

She continued to encourage herself as she made her way towards the main staircase at the front of the house. There was a general air of stillness, but surely the other servants would be up and about. One of them would take her letter. Indeed, it should be put into the post now, before anyone else saw it or the worse-than-cowardly feeling recurred.

As she approached the stairs, Colonel Crosby-Nash's voice became audible from the entrance hall below; he at least, was another early riser. Mary peered over the banister and then retreated a few steps, intending to wait until he had gone. Her position prevented her from seeing the person to whom he was speaking. From their exchanges, however, it was clear that they were friends. Mary paid little attention to their conversation, but she could not help watching as they made their way to the door. They shook hands, and she saw the other man's face. Then she looked again.

The front door opened, and Mary darted to the window opposite the head of the stairs. This afforded a good view of Dover Street, and she could observe the man quite clearly as he descended the front steps and walked smartly away. The sight kept her at the window long after he had disappeared, and the letter to Captain Holland remained, unheeded, in her pocket.

'Should you like to be considered a busybody, Miss Finch?'

The voice pierced the low buzz of conversation. It was the second evening after the Crosby-Nash ball, and Mary and Susannah were wedged into a corner of the duchess of Gordon's crowded drawing-room in Pall Mall.

'I beg your pardon, sir?'

'A busybody – I asked whether you should like to be considered one.' The speaker, a young, expensively dressed man, gazed down expectantly at Mary through a quizzing-glass. It had the unfortunate effect of magnifying his eye to an alarming extent, and now it blinked at her. 'Of course you should not like it, as I have been explaining to my friend Browne, but that is merely because society does not care for the expression. If I asked, "Do you like to be considered one who is interested in his fellow man?", your answer would be quite different.'

'Different from what, Mr Waterbury?' asked Mary with an attentive, if slightly fixed, expression of enquiry. 'I was not aware that I had made any answer.'

'Ha, she hasn't answered,' crowed Mr Browne, a plump gentleman on Mary's other side. He rocked onto his tiptoes whenever he spoke, and as he did so now he bumped into her. 'What do you say to that, Waterbury?'

'Ah, but you acknowledge my point. You acknowledge that we are all of us prisoners of words. Be one's conduct what it may, the words we choose to describe it determine whether it shall be judged well or ill.' Waterbury executed a dramatic pause. 'The name is all.'

'Rubbish,' scoffed Browne, and then in quite another voice, 'My word, I wish someone would open a window. It is dashed hot in here.'

It was indeed very warm, and Mary was finding the attentions of both gentlemen rather tedious. She glanced across at Susannah, who was listening to Waterbury's observations with a look of dismay. Susannah was not at ease among what she described as 'very clever gentlemen', and it was because she had expected them to feature largely at the duchess's rout that she had begged Mary to accompany her. Colonel Crosby-Nash had been unable to attend, and Susannah had not felt able to face the ordeal alone. Nor had she been willing to decline the invitation. The duchess had attended *their* ball, and so, to Pall Mall they had come.

'I say, there is a man who will aid my cause,' cried Waterbury, peering and waving. 'The attorney general, don't you know. He will affirm the importance of words – terms of art and so forth. *Jargon*. Sir John!' he called.

'The attorney general, good God,' murmured Browne, and this time he sank slightly. 'I do not care to bandy words with him! Mrs Crosby-Nash, what do you say to a glass of something? It is grown so devilish hot all of a sudden. Ha! *Devilish . . . hot*? Do you see? May I escort you?'

'Oh, yes, please,' nodded Susannah, 'if you think it would not be *very* rude.'

'Nothing like it,' affirmed Browne, and with a helpless glance in Mary's direction Susannah allowed herself to be drawn away.

Mary awaited the newcomer with an interest that only partly reflected her wish to end the conversation with Mr Waterbury. Sir John Scott was one of several gentlemen of the government who had interviewed her at the conclusion of her Adventure. On that occasion she had found him pleasant, if given to over-qualification, and she wondered whether he might be in a position to help her now.

'Miss Finch,' he said, 'how happy I am to see you once more. I trust you are well – although my eyes tell me that you must be.'

'Ah, I see that the two of you are already acquainted,' said Waterbury, his quizzing-glass flashing as he looked first at one and then the other.

Sir John bowed. 'Indeed, sir, you are correct. The profession certainly lost a great interrogator and searcher-out of truth when you decided against the bar . . . but I mustn't forget my errand. I am charged by our hostess to beg you will be so good as to give your opinion in a matter of precedence – of etiquette. It is a question of the nicest distinction, I believe.'

Waterbury's expression lit up; he was always happy to be of service to her grace.

'There, sir,' said Sir John, indicating two elderly gentlemen conversing on the other side of the room, one of them with the assistance of an ear trumpet. 'I believe they will be able to explain the matter to you.'

'Certainly,' agreed Waterbury, waving in their direction. 'They look sadly perplexed. Miss Finch, will you excuse me? Sir John?'

'Do not let us detain you,' said Sir John, and Mary nodded. They exchanged amused glances as Waterbury hurried away.

'Did the duchess *really* want Mr Waterbury to mediate between those gentlemen?' asked Mary.

'I may possibly have overstated the matter ever so slightly,' admitted Sir John, 'but I daresay he shall discover some topic upon which he may provide assistance – some outlet for his particular, ahem, genius. But this is rather a sad crush, and he may return. Shall we seek out a more comfortable spot?'

'Yes, please,' said Mary, and she took his arm.

The parlours on either side of the drawing-room had been set up for card playing, but as yet none of the duchess's guests had made use of them. Mary and Sir John, therefore, were able to find seats well away from the heat and noise of the drawing-room, where their conversation could not easily be overheard.

'Ah, that is better,' he remarked, taking his ease. 'I do not much care for affairs of this sort – too much like a riot for my tastes. A sociable riot. But sometimes needs must. You would perhaps be surprised how often a favourable vote is the result of drawing-room conversations and not of speeches made on the floor of the House. Of course, I am neglecting my duty in that respect, just at the moment, but I think I might be excused. Tell me, how are you enjoying London?'

'Oh, very much so,' said Mary, 'but I wonder whether I might . . . consult you on a matter? I believe it may be of some importance, although what Mr Waterbury said—'

'My dear young lady, do not say that you have been disturbed by that silly fellow!'

'No, but . . . well, you shall make up your own mind, of course.'

Sir John sat back in his chair. He had anticipated a light-hearted flirtation with Miss Finch – wholly innocent, of course, and quite a pleasant way of passing the evening. Now he perceived that another role was required of him, and he was enough of a philosopher to accept it with a good grace. He thought he had a good idea of what might be troubling such a pretty young woman, and his expression assumed the gravity of the old married man, well used to offering advice in matters of the heart.

In this case, however, he had misunderstood, for Mary was concerned, not with her own situation, but Susannah's. The marital woes of a woman whom he had never met were not particularly intriguing, but Sir John listened politely. Politeness ripened into interest, however, as Mary described the Scarborough House ball. He nodded as she queried the colonel's frequent absences during that evening, and frowned at her mention of the two men emerging from the servants' passage.

'There are several reasons why a gentleman might wish to move privately from one part of a house to another,' he warned.

'Yes, sir,' Mary agreed, 'but one reason might be that he wished to keep his presence a secret.'

'Why, then, do you imagine that he was dressed like a guest attending the ball?'

'In case he was discovered, or had to make just such a departure as I witnessed.'

'Perhaps,' acknowledged Sir John, slowly. 'And yet, you cannot affirm categorically that he did not actually attend, can you? I imagine that it was a very crowded affair . . .'

'I only saw him the one time, creeping about in the shadows,' urged Mary, but candour demanded that she acknowledge the

106

lawyer's second point. 'I suppose that he *might* have been present at some other stage, but—'

'But you do not think it likely. Now, now,' he cautioned, as Mary started to protest, 'I do not mean to disparage your view. Indeed, I would go so far as to suggest that the gentleman's conduct might be described as somewhat curious.'

'But that is not all,' Mary continued, ignoring Sir John's tepid endorsement. She had dropped her voice with the mention of the men and the passage, but now her whispers assumed a distinct urgency. 'On the morning after the ball I saw the servant a second time, *not* dressed in livery but instead conversing with Colonel Crosby-Nash in a most familiar manner. No one, seeing them in the entrance hall of Scarborough House, would have imagined them to be master and servant, and yet the man I saw had most certainly been *in service* only the night before!'

'Hmm, this begins to sound . . . I believe you said that, on the night of the ball, the er, gentleman from the passage implied that he had already spent a night at Scarborough House. Might it be possible to—'

'Yes, I wondered about that,' said Mary, nodding, 'and it seemed to me another highly suspicious detail. Susannah – Mrs Crosby-Nash – had said nothing about a visitor, and although the housekeeper seems to make a good many of the decisions at Scarborough House, surely Susannah would have *seen* him or known something of him.'

'One might certainly expect it in the ordinary course of events.'

'And *mentioned* him in regular conversation,' added Mary. 'It stands to reason. So, this morning,' and now she hesitated, 'I made an examination of that passage, the one that leads to the ballroom.'

Sir John gaped at her. 'Indeed. And what did you find?'

'Well, the passage leads to the kitchen, but partway along it there is a staircase, and at the top there is a *secret room*, completely contained *within* the house!' She returned his gaze, not without an expression of triumph.

'Did you venture within?'

'No. The door was locked.'

'So you cannot precisely affirm that there *is* a secret room.'

'Well, no,' Mary acknowledged, 'but what else could it be? A secret . . . *cupboard* at the top of a private stair? It must be a room, and I daresay that if someone wished to spend a night in Scarborough House, without his presence being generally known, that is where he would stay. And if an associate − dressed as a servant − were also close by, he could look after him, provide him with food and drink, and even help him to depart at a convenient moment.' The look of triumph returned.

'Perhaps.' Sir John sat silently for a while, and then gazed at Mary from beneath bushy eyebrows. 'I presume that you have not mentioned your . . . explorations to anyone? Nor your suspicions? Good. I would strongly advise you not to do so.'

'But what is to be done?' asked Mary, and when he pursed his lips and offered a half shrug, she continued, urgently, 'Come, sir, something is wrong − you know that very well − or at least you suspect it, and something must be done about it. I would like to do *something*.'

'Would you, indeed? Something that would be helpful? I make no promises, mind.'

'Yes, of course. Mrs Crosby-Nash is my friend, remember, and I fear . . . I am uneasy about her. If there is some trouble, or some . . . mystery—'

Sir John motioned for silence and adopted the same condition himself, his fingers pressed together and the tips tapping against his lips. After a time he cast an appraising look at Mary. Then he sighed and shook his head. He slipped his watch out of his waistcoat pocket and considered the time before resuming his cogitative posture. 'The hour is late for a poor, hard-working servant of the Crown,' he remarked at last, 'and I shall have a busy day tomorrow. Dear, dear. Could I prevail upon you, Miss Finch, to come and see me in my chambers?'

'Your chambers? Why, yes,' agreed Mary, baffled by this abrupt change of tack.

He patted her hand reassuringly. 'I do not mean to amaze you, my dear, it is only that I think it advisable that you tell your story to someone who understands these things more completely than I, and if the arrangements can be made for you to do so tomorrow then so much the better.'

Mary found it difficult to gauge her own feelings the following morning as she entered the cab that was to take her to Lincoln's Inn. The air was cool and fresh and, to her willing mind, it felt like the sort of day when something might happen – but whether that something would be good or bad she could not tell. That Sir John Scott should have asked for this meeting, despite his cautious scepticism, must mean that the information she had uncovered was important, but how? She supposed that it had something to do with the law, since it concerned Sir John, but what were the arrangements that he had spoken of? And what sort of legal matter could be beyond the cognisance of the attorney general of England?

The arrangements had been made by the time Mary arrived at Sir John's chambers in Lincoln's Inn, and he explained them in a dry, measured tone, with none of his usual twinkle but all of his professional hesitation. Firstly, if she were so minded, she would meet another gentleman for whom her information might be of some interest. While not strictly part of the government, this gentleman was one in whom the government had the greatest faith, and who had performed a number of essential services in matters of a highly confidential nature. Secondly, because of the nature of this gentleman's work, it was important that he be neither well known nor linked too closely with anyone in government, and particularly with the attorney general. For that reason Sir John could not entertain the gentleman in Lincoln's Inn; rather, Mary must go to him. Sir John's clerk, Peters, would see that she reached her destination safely and would return her to Cavendish Square when her business was completed.

'And I would like to make one additional point,' said the attorney. 'As I have suggested, *officially* I know nothing about the gentleman or his affairs. Nor do I wish to know about either. However, after your interview is concluded, I would be grateful to know whether you are content with your situation as you understand it. Not what that situation involves, mind you, merely whether you are content with it. If the answer is "yes", then the matter may very well pass completely out of my hands. In fact, I am quite certain that it will. Do you understand?'

Mary nodded. She had remained silent throughout the attorney's explanation, despite the sense of rising apprehension. Sir John's warnings, duly given, only sharpened her curiosity, but she was aware that she must not demand many answers at this stage. 'Might I ask one question? What is the gentleman's name?'

Sir John smiled, and the curtain of his reserve parted slightly. 'It is Shy. Cuthbert Shy. Rather an odd sort of name, but I believe – so I have been told – that he is rather an odd sort of person. Shall I ring for Peters?'

It took the best part of an hour to reach their destination. The journey was roundabout, involving three hackney cabs, a stroll among the print shops in St Paul's churchyard, and a visit to a Bond Street confectioner's. At one point they descended from their vehicle and walked for some distance, conduct that seemed to serve no purpose other than to enable them to hail another cab and resume their journey in the opposite direction. Throughout this strange performance Mary was grateful for the presence of Sir John's clerk, the silent but efficient Peters. Not only did he negotiate the awkward route with apparent ease, but also his modest, unassuming, wholly ordinary appearance was reassuring. Mary even began to enter into the spirit of the thing, as she imagined it. They were engaged in an elaborate game of hide and seek, rendered oddly amusing by the fact that they did not secure a hiding place, and no one was seeking them.

When they parted at the front door of a modest residence in a neighbourhood Mary did not know, therefore, she felt a momentary trepidation. The game had ended, and what would happen now? Peters explained that he would not wait to see

110

her inside, but promised to collect her in due course. How he intended to inform himself that her interview had concluded was not revealed. Mary watched him depart and took a deep breath. There was nothing to do but carry on, and she lifted the iron knocker and rapped in what she hoped was a confident manner.

A servant who did not ask her name conducted her to a simply furnished study and then departed without a word. Almost immediately another door opened and a tubby, middle-aged man with bright blue eyes and a florid, cheerful expression stepped into the room. He greeted her briskly, shaking her hand and motioning her to a chair by the window. 'Good morning, Miss Finch. I am Cuthbert Shy. Thank you for consenting to my little stratagems.'

'Not at all, sir,' replied Mary, falling cautiously back upon convention. It would have been difficult to say what she had expected of the mysterious Mr Shy, but the individual before her was certainly a surprise. In his old-fashioned tie wig and long, moleskin waistcoat he reminded her of a grocer or chandler, and his surroundings reinforced this image of modest rectitude. The single bookcase was empty apart from a Bible, a collection of Addison's essays, and what looked to be a trio of ledgers bound in red leather. There were no paintings on the walls, only prints, and the carpet looked to have been selected purely for utility by someone who knew the value of a shilling. Outside she could see a tiny walled garden, with neat rows of vegetables standing on either side of a gravel path.

Mary watched in silence as Shy retreated to the desk in the centre of the room and began ransacking its drawers for a pen, penknife, ink, blotter, and paper. When he had collected all to his satisfaction, he placed them on the small table beside Mary's chair and then sat down in the chair opposite. There was something faintly amusing about his performance, and she was wondering whether Sir John might have made some mistake when she suffered an even greater surprise.

'Oh, but I am afraid that it would never do,' Shy complained, leaning forward in his chair and blinking at her earnestly. 'It is all very well for *public* men to cut a figure – I daresay some of them like it – but when one aims to do one's work in private, anything remarkable is out of the question. Of course, doing the other thing may put people off, or call into question one's authority, but those are minor difficulties which one hopes may be overcome by other means.'

'I . . . yes, I expect so,' Mary agreed, and as she conceived a slight change in his expression, a hint of keenness behind the round, placid visage, she felt as if she had been caught in some childish act.

He nodded. 'Precisely. I am glad that we understand each other. Mistakes, particularly those made at the outset, can often be corrected, but a taint in character is another matter. Now, do you know why I agreed to see you, Miss Finch? There were two reasons, and I shall tell you both. Firstly, you have the attorney general's recommendation. He is not the sort of man to jump without being doubly sure of his landing, so if he says that something might possibly interest me I can be certain that it shall. Secondly, I know of your involvement some time ago in the matter of the French agent, Paul Déprez. You conducted yourself with courage and intelligence on that occasion, which leads me to believe that you are not generally unreliable.'

Although her heightened colour remained, the mention of her Adventure caused Mary's back to straighten and her chin to rise. She *had* behaved creditably on that occasion, even if she could not immediately see beyond a moleskin waistcoat. 'I hope I am not, sir.'

'So do I – very much so. Now, before we continue, I am afraid that I must make a request. You have guessed it, I am certain, but let us be clear. It is essential to me that you remain absolutely silent about this meeting and anything that we may discuss. Do you agree?'

The difference between the tone of his speech and its subject matter was so marked as to be slightly bewildering. The keen, knowing look remained, however, or Mary thought it did, and she nodded in reliance upon it.

'Very good, then let us come straight to the point. I should

112

like to hear what you can tell me about your friend Mrs Crosby-Nash and her husband.'

Mary let out her breath, not having realised that she was holding it. 'Well, sir, it is all rather . . . complicated. Where shall I begin?'

'Wherever you like,' said Shy. 'Ladies, in my experience, tend to regard questions like a dinner party with several removes before the roast, whereas gentlemen regard them like fences to be jumped straightaway, whether their horse is ready or not. One method fills the listener too full of soup to enjoy his meat, and the other obliges him to climb out of the ditch and start again. Of course, I prefer the golden mean, but let us follow your inclinations and see where they lead us.'

With that encouragement, Mary set to her task, and Shy, sitting back in his chair and rubbing his eyes behind his spectacles, contributed nothing beyond the occasional nod. When she began to describe the events of the Scarborough House ball, however, he became more demanding. 'A trifle more of the soup, if you please,' he urged, still with his eyes closed, 'and do not forget the fish.' Everything about the evening interested him, and he asked her to compile a list – with descriptions – of every person she could remember.

'I am afraid,' said Mary, as she appended the names of the servants, 'that this menu will prove exhausting.'

'Not at all, Miss Finch. I think you will find that I have a prodigious appetite. Tell me again – with the most careful attention – *precisely* what passed between the two men who emerged through the gyp door.'

She complied, and then he pressed her for details about the second sighting of the supposed footman and her attempted survey of the secret room. Mary was conscious that the latter was not very helpful and explained that she had not explored farther for fear that she might be discovered and her presence in that part of the house questioned. 'But I am certain that a room lies behind that door.'

'Oh, yes, quite,' Shy agreed, 'and there is such a thing as chancing one's luck beyond reason – which seems a contradiction, but isn't.

113

Not to be recommended, however.' He fell silent then, drumming his fingers on the arm of his chair and surveying the tidy row of young carrot plants in his garden. Without shifting his glance he asked, 'How would you describe Colonel Crosby-Nash?'

Mary was becoming used to Mr Shy's sudden changes of direction, which were rather like the journey he had prescribed for her, but now she frowned before answering, conjuring the colonel's image in her mind. She did not know where this particular question was tending, but she was certain that a straightforward portrayal was not what was required. 'I would call him elegant, calculating, and strong-minded.'

'Very good,' Shy affirmed. 'And to those attributes I might add that he is a very dangerous man.'

'*Dangerous?*' A vague, if terrible fear sprang suddenly from the confusion of Mary's thoughts. She could feel her heart beginning to beat in thick, heavy strokes.

'Very much so. You have performed creditably in my little examination, and this is your reward: I am going to confide in you.' He paused. 'You know that Colonel Crosby-Nash has a considerable fortune. Now, wealthy gentlemen – and ladies – are entitled to use their wealth in whatever way they like, although most are drearily predictable. They fit up great houses and amuse themselves with entertainments of various sorts. The colonel does these things, of course, but I believe he has also turned his attention to other, more singular activities: treason, rebellion, and the more important forms of espionage.'

Mary stared at him. 'Espionage? Good Heavens, sir! And yet—'

'And yet, he is a member of the most fashionable clubs in the capital. He attends royal levees, and when he hosts a ball . . . you have seen how eagerly his invitations are taken up.'

'But how can these things be? As you say, he is accepted everywhere. But if he is a *criminal* . . . why has this been kept secret? It is . . . and my friend has *married* him!'

'She has been cruelly deceived,' Shy acknowledged, shaking his head, 'and I am sorry for it. But you see, what I have just told you is absolutely confidential. Colonel Crosby-Nash stands unconvicted of any crime, nor is he even suspected, in any official way.'

'But *unofficially*, is it true? You are certain?'

'Yes, I am certain, but I can produce little actual evidence to support my view.'

'What does Sir John say?'

Shy smiled gently. 'Sir John has a great capacity for doubting, you know, and he tends to concentrate on what can be proven, rather than what one believes . . . or even *knows*. Of course, such is his professional character, and one oughtn't to rail against it.'

Mary considered this. Sir John might be a doubter, but for all that he had sent her to Shy. 'I believe he has the utmost confidence in you, sir,' she said, slowly. She offered the compliment partly for her own sake. Shy's claims, indeed everything about him, seemed fantastic, and the recollection of Sir John's faith established a connection of sorts to the ordinary world.

'Does he?' queried Shy, raising an eyebrow. 'Well, that is good of him.' He rose from his chair and began to pace the room, slowly moving between his desk and the window. 'You may be aware that the situation of this country is very precarious. Abroad, our military allies are either unwilling or unable to act, while French forces sweep across the continent. At home our finances are strained almost to the breaking point, while Anarchists and Republicans do their best to promote disorder and rebellion. Believe me, I do not overstate the case. And now there is mutiny among the Channel fleet. Perhaps the grounds of complaint are genuine, but the timing strikes me as extremely convenient for our enemies.'

'Do you believe that Colonel Crosby-Nash—'

'He may be involved,' said Shy, shrugging, 'and he may have other . . . irons in the fire. Also, while I have no evidence that he is a traitor, I expect that there is a connection with the chief French intelligence agent working in this country. You know, of course, that the French have their spies, just as we have ours.'

The back of her throat went dry, and she swallowed before speaking. 'Like Mr Déprez.'

'Yes, although the fellow that I am looking for is far more dangerous. Déprez was an adventurer, who played his own game for the thrill of the thing; my man is a patriot. He behaves too ruthlessly to be anything else, you see. He organises the affairs of others, and for him it is not an amusement. My hope is, that by fixing my gaze on the colonel, I may not only frustrate *him* but, perhaps, gain a clearer view of the man behind him.'

Mary remained silent, absorbing what she had heard. If anything, Mr Shy's story was becoming more extreme, but it was also drawing her in. Her own Adventure was proof enough that spies and renegades were real, and Mr Shy doubtless had a greater experience than she. Perhaps adventures happened more frequently than one might think. Perhaps they were all around. *I suspected that something was wrong at Scarborough House,* she silently urged, *I knew it.* Aloud she asked, 'Are you hopeful of discovering evidence against Colonel Crosby-Nash?'

Shy said that he was hopeful, up to a point. The colonel had been under observation for some time, but with few tangible results. 'You will say, perhaps this is because there are no results to be found – the colonel is a wholly virtuous individual who knows nothing of villainous Frenchmen. I say, in answer, that my men face a difficult task. Crosby-Nash spends a great deal of his time in what one might call a charmed circle, consisting of the members of his clubs, his associates from India – all of whom know each other – and the persons to whom he extends a particular invitation. It is no simple thing to introduce a stranger into that circle, yet I wager that is where our friend does a great deal of the business that he wishes to keep secret.'

'The ball would have been a perfect occasion for a secret meeting,' Mary suggested. '*I* noticed his comings and goings, but I doubt others did.'

'No, nor how one particular visitor was spirited out of the house, in full view, yet without attracting the slightest attention to himself.'

116

'I am sorry that I was not able to see his face clearly.'

'That *would* have been a most valuable coup,' Shy agreed, 'or if you could have communicated your information in a more timely manner – not that the delay was your fault. Still, what you have told me is exceedingly interesting and, no doubt, will prove valuable in due course.'

He smiled at her placidly, and she wondered whether this marked the end of their discussion. It certainly sounded as if it did. Presently he would thank her, and whatever mechanism existed for summoning Mr Peters would be put in train. Then a cab – or perhaps a series of vehicles – would return her to the safety and security of 10 Cavendish Square, and that would be that. The adventure, if there were to be one, would continue without her, and she experienced a feeling of distress at the prospect. It was somehow unfair to make this amazing revelation, to admit her to a secret world, and then to exclude her again with a tidy, dismissive thanks. *I could almost wish—*

'I always think that one oughtn't to make rash decisions,' mused Shy. 'Do you agree?'

The question startled her. 'What? I mean, I beg your pardon – I mean, *yes*.'

'And yet it occurs to me that the best way of obtaining valuable information is not to attempt to insert a stranger into the colonel's circle, as I mentioned, but to recruit the services of someone who is already in that privileged position and has already proven herself well-qualified for the task.' He glanced at her. 'What is your own opinion?'

Mary found herself laughing, despite the seriousness of the situation. 'I am surprised that you ask me,' she said, 'for you seem to know my thoughts before I have finished thinking them. But do you also know that my visit to London is nearly over? I return to Suffolk in a few days' time, while the colonel will shortly go into Kent.'

Shy considered this. 'Must you return to Suffolk? Might you not prolong your stay? And might you not thereafter go to Champian Hall – that is the name of his estate in Kent – as a companion to Mrs Crosby-Nash?'

It would be possible, at least as a practical matter. Mary could please herself, after all, and Susannah had mentioned that she would welcome company – she was rather lonely, although she would not admit it. 'I . . . *perhaps* I might,' she temporised, but even as she spoke her heart began to beat more strongly, and she was asking herself whether she should undertake this task, or whether she was mad to consider it.

'"Perhaps" is such an agreeable word – so brimming with possibilities,' purred Shy. He shrugged his shoulders. 'But you must decide whether you would actually care to undertake this proposition, not in a fleeting moment of whimsy to please a funny little man, but seriously. What I am asking is highly important, but it is not simple. There is the task itself – gathering information about a man who does not wish his secrets to be disclosed – and then there is the nature of the work. Spying, even on an enemy, is not a decent job, particularly for a young lady such as yourself.'

A young lady who fits up a great house and amuses herself with entertainments, added Mary, with private irritation. Had she in truth become such a person, concerned only with satisfying her own vanity? She frowned. 'But this work is important, and there is my friend to consider – Mrs Crosby-Nash. If her husband *is* a renegade, he cannot be trusted. He might decide that she is a burden, or she might even discover something that would put her in danger!'

'Either is certainly possible.'

'Then she must not be left alone with him,' cried Mary.

'It is probably not the situation that her friends would prefer,' Shy acknowledged.

'I do not suppose you could . . . get her away from him, somehow?' She gazed at Shy hopefully.

'I do not think so,' he admitted. 'At least, not without considerable time and effort. My resources are not limitless, you know, and it would be extremely unwise to do anything that would arouse his suspicions.'

'Yes, yes, of course,' Mary agreed, hurriedly, 'it was foolish of me to suggest such a thing.'

118

'Not at all – it was a most worthy sentiment. However, if you—'

'If I went with them to Kent, I would *not* arouse his suspicions, for he knows that Susannah and I are friends, and . . . I could observe him and keep watch over her at the same time.'

'Indeed, Miss Finch,' said Shy, smiling, 'I believe you are also able to read *my* thoughts. More importantly, I believe that we are in agreement about how to proceed.'

8

Mary stepped into the cab that was to return her, circuitously, to 10 Cavendish Square. On the seat beside her was a parcel of books; a morning's innocent purchases, should anyone question her absence. That Mr Shy should have thought of such a thing and made provision for it gave her a slight chill. *Good or bad*, she mused, *you wondered which it would be and now you know that it is very bad indeed. So bad that stratagems and precautions are necessary straightaway.* She did not regret her decision, however, and now that she knew the worst she felt strangely calm about what she must do. That such a dangerous man as Colonel Crosby-Nash should be abroad – abroad and working his mischief unchecked – was simply not to be tolerated. Whatever she could learn about him, and however she could protect Susannah, these must be her objects.

The faithful Peters also resumed his place and signalled for the driver to set off. They drove for a few minutes in silence, and he watched Mary unobtrusively. He was an observant man, but he knew how to keep silent – he would not have retained his place with Sir John if he had not had that skill – and he could sense the change in Mary. During the earlier journey she had been wondering; now she was planning. Before she had been uncertain; now she was determined. He knew the answer to his question without asking it, but he was a good servant and asked it nevertheless.

The cab turned a corner, and Mary lifted the books onto her lap. 'Yes,' she replied, steadily, 'you may inform Sir John that I am quite content with my situation.'

Shy had given Mary only a general insight as to how the adventure might proceed, but it did not require any deep reflection to know that her first task must be to attach herself to the Crosby-Nash household. In the days that followed, therefore, she made a point of visiting Susannah and falling in with her modest suggestions for how they might amuse themselves. These, unfortunately, did not tend to involve her husband, but the resulting familiarity between the two women produced the desired result: an invitation to Champian Hall.

As Mary was congratulating herself on her first success, however, her confidence suffered a knock. A consequence of the extra attention paid to Susannah was that Mary had spent less time with her other friends, and it was with a sense of guilty surprise that she realised that their own departures were fast approaching. She was obliged to bar them from the Kentish invitation – or rather to discourage Susannah from including them – as their presence would undoubtedly complicate her work. In Charlotte's case this was easy enough, for she had no desire to take a holiday with the colonel. Excluding Miss Marchmont and Miss Trent was more difficult. It never occurred to them to feel slighted, but that very humility, and the selfless pleasure they took in this latest opportunity for their dear friend, made Mary uncomfortable. *Knowing that one has done what was necessary*, she brooded, *does not prevent one from feeling mean.*

Perhaps for that reason she agreed to accompany her friends on their final outing to purchase a present for Lady Armitage. After much discussion, a bottle of scent from Golding's, the queen's perfumer, had been resolved upon. Such an establishment would provide an eminently suitable product, and by focussing their search in this way, they would avoid a repetition of the Great Glove Search. In truth, the outing would not be quite so restricted, for Miss Marchmont wished to visit a

121

shop in Vine Street that sold lead pencils, and Miss Trent, inspired by the prospect of royal perfume, had hit upon the notion of surprising Mrs Tipton with an offering of tea from Antrobus, Seaman & Antrobus, who were teamen to His Majesty. After consulting Kent's *Directory* their plan of campaign was agreed: pencils in Piccadilly, tea on the Strand, and thence to Golding's on Cornhill.

Everyone was rather tired by the time they reached the last of these, but Golding's revived their spirits. Mary and Charlotte particularly enthused over the variety of perfumes, all in dainty crystal bottles or porcelain flasks painted to look like vases of flowers, or water jugs, or figurines. Nor were they obliged merely to look, for the proprietor's wife encouraged them to try this one behind their ears, another on their wrists, and a third on the inside of their elbows. One potion made Charlotte sneeze, but she nevertheless thought they were all wonderful, while the array of silver pomanders, engraved bergamot boxes, lotions, powders, and perfume burners caused Mary to forget about any other investigations.

They emerged some time later with a bottle – a very small bottle, for Charlotte had already managed to spend a great deal of her pocket money, somehow. Miss Marchmont met them on the pavement, confessing that the various odours, however pleasing individually, had been too much for her in combination. She was waving a handkerchief to dispel any lingering traces.

'And I daresay it shows a want of patriotism in me,' she acknowledged, 'but *really*, the one supposed to be the queen's favourite reminded me of nothing so much as a pair of wet boots, drying by the fire. I do hope you have not purchased any of that one?'

'Oh, no, something far more elegant. *L'eau* means water, you know,' Charlotte confided to Miss Marchmont, who nodded gravely. 'You mustn't think that the *fleurs* – the flowers – are in any way low or common.'

'No, indeed.'

'Exceedingly *un*common, I am sure,' said Mary, smiling, and then her expression changed to a quizzical frown. 'We seem to have lost Miss Trent.'

'No, she had an errand at a jeweller's in this neighbourhood,' replied Miss Marchmont. 'She is coming just now, I believe.'

Miss Trent rejoined them, slightly breathless, and, after having been assured that she had not kept anyone waiting, explained that she had popped round to Hardy & Son's in Birchin Lane to execute a commission for Susannah. The clasp on her bracelet – the very beautiful one she had worn at the ball – had come loose and required mending.

Miss Trent has taken Susannah's bracelet to be repaired? Mary thought this rather odd, and particularly when she learned that the commission had not actually come from Susannah, but from her husband. Why would Colonel Crosby-Nash have asked Miss Trent to perform such a service? They were hardly on familiar terms, and – kind-hearted as she was – dear Miss Trent was not the sort of person in whom the colonel would naturally confide.

Mary considered this as they climbed into the carriage for the journey back to Cavendish Square, and she scarcely contributed to the discussion of confectioners' shops and whether they really ought to buy something to recover their strength. She could not remember the bracelet that Susannah had worn at the ball, and she could not see her way to enquiring about it now. It would sound very strange, coming in the midst of Miss Marchmont's testimonial on behalf of Banbury cakes. *But surely Birchin Lane is rather an odd address for a fashionable jeweller? Would a gentleman like Colonel Crosby-Nash not prefer Bond Street or St James's?*

'Oh! Wait!'

Mary was startled out of her contemplations by Charlotte's sudden cry, which she repeated, more forcefully, to the coachman by thumping the roof of the vehicle and calling up to him through the lowered window.

'My word, what is the matter?' demanded Miss Marchmont. 'Have we run someone down?' They were in the middle of a busy High Holborn.

123

The carriage rolled to a stop and Charlotte descended. 'No, no,' she laughed, 'it is only . . . I have ordered something, and I remembered it just now as we passed. I shan't be a moment.'

Miss Trent peered out of the window. 'Good gracious, a saddler's,' she gasped, apparently only slightly less shocked than if Charlotte had swept into a gin shop. 'What can be happening?'

Mary frowned ruefully and made to follow. 'Please do not fuss,' she urged, cutting off any further exclamations. 'I will see to it.'

Cradock & Renorden's, the establishment that had claimed Charlotte, advertised a range of saddles, whips, and similar items. As Mary entered she reflected that her presence in this masculine enclave might not actually lend much propriety to the situation. She was relieved, therefore, to discover that the front of the shop was not populated by rough-looking men in leather aprons, or men of any sort, apart from the clerk, who was dutifully attending to Charlotte from behind a counter. Mary listened gravely while Charlotte explained that, as she would shortly be leaving London, her order must be sent on to Norfolk, as soon as it was completed. The name was Armitage, she affirmed, and he doubtless had it recorded somewhere.

When the clerk disappeared behind a curtain, perhaps to consult with the leather-clad men in the distant reaches of the shop, Mary's demeanour changed. She drummed her fingers on the counter and cast a frosty glance at Charlotte from the corner of her eye. 'Is *this* what accounts for the void in your pocket money?' she asked.

Charlotte nodded, not at all abashed. 'Yes, I am afraid it is – but *really*, I do need a new saddle very badly. It is false economics not to invest in the best tack that one can afford, you know, besides being cruel to one's horse. Just imagine if I were to injure poor Clemmie by riding him with an uncomfortable, *worn* old saddle.'

Mary maintained a critical air, but only with difficulty. 'How do you know that the saddle you have purchased for a vast sum will suit Clemmie any better?'

'Oh, I am certain it will,' Charlotte assured her. 'Cradock &

Renorden were particularly recommended to me by Major Whittington. You remember, we met him at the ball? He said that for a good, everyday saddle, one must come to Cradock & Renorden, and that is precisely what I want. So you see, I am not being extravagant in the least!'

The clerk returned before Mary could express an opinion on the subject, and he affirmed that the item would be with the young lady in a fortnight. Charlotte's smile of triumph, and the fact that he had not overheard the discussion of finances, emboldened him, and he wondered whether he might be of further service to the young lady in respect of a bridle or head collar. Charlotte wavered, but Mary assured him that their requirements had been amply provided for and steered Charlotte to the door.

'You really oughtn't to have gone into a shop like that, you know,' said Mary, once they were outside again. It was nearly four o'clock, and the street was busy with traffic of all kinds. They walked arm in arm to avoid being separated or jostled as they made their way back to the carriage.

'Why ever not?' demanded Charlotte. 'I do not think that Major Whittington would play me a trick. He and Bobs are the best of friends, and if he *were* to give me bad advice, I daresay Bobs would thump him.'

Mary stopped short, perhaps to allow a lawyer in wig and gown to push past, and then answered steadily enough, 'Yes, I daresay. What I meant, however, was—'

'Dear Bobs,' sighed Charlotte. 'I hoped he would come and see us again, before we returned home.'

'I . . . I expect he is very busy.'

'Yes, that is what he said. I do think it is unfair, however.'

Mary remained silent. She did not want to ask about Captain Holland, and actually refrained from doing so until they had reached the side of their vehicle. 'You have heard from him, then?' she murmured.

'Oh, yes,' said Charlotte, as she opened the door. 'Bobs is a very good letter-writer.'

★   ★   ★

125

That accolade was more remarkable for its fondness than its strict accuracy. As Mary could have testified, Holland was not merely a poor, but an unreliable correspondent. Almost a week had passed, for example, since he had received her letter, and yet he had made no reply. The press of work might have accounted for the lapse, but somehow she did not think this was the case.

In fact, Holland not only meant to ignore her letter, which had spoken so shyly about character, disposition, fondness, and the negligible effect of fortune upon any of them, he had meant to destroy it. Yet neither had happened. The letter itself had found its way into the pocket of his second best uniform coat, and there it had remained. He felt the familiar rustle when he rose from his desk that afternoon, and as he walked towards the river, intending to stretch his legs, he rehearsed its familiar, painful contents, like a wound he could not leave alone. When he reached the dock, however, a sight rarely seen in the Warren drove all other thoughts from his mind. Two small children, a boy and a girl, were climbing on the crane used to load and unload river-borne cargoes.

'Oy, you two!' he shouted, quickening his step. 'What do you think you're doing there?'

They turned to face him, their guilty expressions changing quickly to pleased smiles. 'Captain Holland!' they called, the little boy even hanging on one-handed in order to wave.

Holland muttered an expression unsuitable for youthful ears, and in a louder voice ordered, 'Jack, climb down now – both hands. Chloe, stay where you are.' Reaching up, he lifted the little girl to safety. When both children were on the ground he considered the pair of them: Captain-Lieutenant Jack Dalton's son and daughter. Holland could not remember their ages, but they were certainly too young to be climbing about on a crane over the Thames – and what the devil were those slackers in the guardhouse doing, not to have stopped them?

He glanced at the building in question, apparently closed and any inhabitants uninterested in what might be occurring around them. Then a guard emerged, and Holland hailed him in no very friendly tone. 'You there! Woken up at last, have you? Pass the word for Gunner Drake. Tell him he's wanted here, on the double. And now,' he continued, folding his arms and fixing his charges with a stern look, 'what's going on? Who is in charge of you?'

'No one,' piped Chloe, with evident pride. She was a pretty child, although at present her long yellow curls were wind-blown, and the front of her pinafore was distinctly grubby. 'We've been in the coal yard.'

'I can see that. You shouldn't go in there.'

'Why?'

Holland frowned, but before he could answer she continued, 'We saw men sifting muck and digging a ditch. One of them called to me, and I waved to him. He hadn't any teeth in front.' She showed him hers in a fierce grimace to illustrate the contrast.

'Of all the . . . have you been on the convicts' wharf?' Holland demanded. 'How did you get down there?'

'We climbed over the wall,' Chloe explained. 'Jack boosted me, and I—'

'All right, never mind. Just don't do it again.' He turned to Jack, whose clothes were in a comparable state to those of his sister, although his bore grass stains in addition to coal dust. 'But what are you doing here? Here in the Warren, I mean.'

'Mama brought us, but then she had to go away again, and she said we were to wait.'

'She never told you to wait for her on the docks.'

'No, sir,' Jack admitted, 'she said to play in the storekeeper's gardens.'

'Then why didn't you?'

There seemed to be no answer to this question, or at least Jack could not explain the chain of events that had begun with an energetic game of animal tag and ended with the abortive attempt to climb the crane, by way of visits to the stables, the engraving shop, the saltpetre storehouse, and the coal yard. He remained mute, therefore, and only stared at his inquisitor.

Chloe stepped into the breach. 'Jack threw coal in the river.'

'Tattle-tale!'

127

'And a man saw him. Jack said that I was to say that I had done it, but—'

At this point the situation deteriorated rapidly. Jack cried, 'Traitor!' and struggled to inflict an appropriate punishment on his sister, while Chloe, in attempting to escape, stumbled on the cobbles and sat down hard. Tears immediately welled up, and her lip quivered. 'Oh, oh!' she cried.

Holland attempted to prevent further hostilities and offer consolation to the wounded, but his efforts had little effect on either party. 'He kicked me!' Chloe wailed. 'No I never,' stormed Jack, while looking as if he fully intended to make good the accusation retrospectively.

'All right, all right, nobody's dying,' complained Holland. 'Steady on, both of you.' Then he straightened at the sound of a more welcome voice.

'Wot's all this then, sir?' asked Drake. 'Bit of a lark? Why, good afternoon, Master Jack, Miss Chloe. Now wot 'ave you gone and done?' He knelt beside her, smiling and shaking his head ruefully.

'Oh,' moaned Chloe. 'Jack hit me, and my petticoat's torn!' She raised her arms to Drake, and he picked her up.

'Liar!' Jack struggled for an appropriate term of abuse. 'Frenchman!'

'Pipe down,' Holland commanded, tightening his hold on Jack's hand. Then he added in a lower voice, 'Mrs Dalton is meant to be coming for them . . . God knows when.'

'Well, well, you're all right now, Miss Chloe, I'm sure, and I don't see no tear, neither,' Drake assured her. 'That's often the way of it, sir, with ladies. They 'as their whims and distractions, you see, which makes 'em unaccountable. I ain't seen Mr Dalton at all today.'

'I'm not surprised.' Holland turned to Jack. 'Does your father know you're here?'

The boy gaped. 'Maybe.'

'Where'll we put 'em for safekeeping, sir?' asked Drake. 'Guard 'ouse?' He winked at Jack.

Holland endeavoured to control his irritation. 'I suppose . . .

they had better wait in my rooms until someone can come and collect them.'

The children cheered, and Drake added, 'Just as you say, sir,' while avoiding Holland's eye. Chloe had wound her grimy hands around his neck, and now Drake also had the appearance of one who had been playing in the coal yard.

The rather unusual party made its way towards the officers' quarters, and Holland's back stiffened as he intercepted the amused glances of his colleagues. When they passed a company of men an anonymous voice enquired with apparent innocence, 'Is that what they get up to on the staff, lads? Playin' nursemaid while we does all the work?'

'Silence in the ranks!' bellowed the sergeant.

Another voice, seemingly wishing to be helpful, observed, 'You left yer bonnet at home, mate.'

'Oy,' thundered Drake. 'Just you watch yourself, there. I 'eard that.'

'Quack, quack.'

'Leave it,' Holland muttered, as Drake halted and glared ominously into the ranks of scrupulously blank faces. 'What's your company, sergeant?'

'Captain Fanshawe's, sir.'

Fanshawe. I might have known. 'What are you up to, standard drill?'

'That's right, sir.'

Holland thought for a moment. 'Tell Captain Fanshawe, with my compliments, that these men might benefit from parbuckling the 42-pounder. You know the one I mean?'

'Indeed I do, sir, but Captain Fanshawe . . . I believe he's gone into the town, sir.'

'Well, then carry on and inform him afterwards.'

'Yes, sir. Teams of four on the rise, sir?'

Holland nodded, smiling faintly. The weapon in question, an enormous old siege gun, was used principally to teach the men how to roll, or parbuckle, a gun barrel. As a light exercise it could be moved across level ground; rolling it uphill was a rather more arduous task.

129

'They got no discipline, that lot,' Drake complained, as the men marched away.

'No, I know it. Let's go.'

Drake continued to give vent to his irritation in muttered observations. 'Nothin' but gallows bait – that's wot they are. I'll give 'im "quack, quack". See if I don't.'

'Captain Holland?' asked Jack, anxiously, as he hurried to keep up with the other's longer strides. 'Shall you have to tell about the coal, sir? Father says that when a fellow commits a crime in the regiment he is thrown into the cells and not given any dinner.'

Holland sighed. 'I suppose I might overlook it, as it's a first offence.'

'I . . . it was only a few pieces.'

'Well, don't do it again,' ordered Holland, in what he hoped was a suitably admonitory tone. 'And . . . and you shouldn't offer to hit a girl.'

'I know, sir,' admitted Jack humbly.

They stopped at the bottom of Holland's staircase. 'I'll 'ave a go at finding Mr Dalton, shall I, sir?' asked Drake, making as if to pass Chloe into his officer's arms.

'Oh no you don't,' Holland replied. 'You take them upstairs – give them something to eat, or . . . I don't know. I'll find Dalton.' Freeing his hand from Jack's clammy hold, he added, 'and you might try . . . cleaning them up a bit.'

Although he profoundly disliked what he called 'pushing about bits of paper', Captain-Lieutenant Jack Dalton had spent the last several days performing precisely that exercise. Holland found him in the company commander's office, wading through a pile of ordnance dockets, muster rolls, medical reports, stabling accounts, and an on-going correspondence relating to the loss of a quantity of slow-match four years previously. Dalton's company had finally received orders for service abroad, and as well as equipping the men and arranging for transport, the Ordnance Board required that any outstanding queries – however ancient or irrelevant – be resolved before they sailed.

'Look sharp there, Mr Dalton!' commanded Holland, leaning

in at the door. Dalton was Holland's closest friend in the regiment. They usually saw things in the same way, although Dalton was livelier, more enthusiastic, and typically used five words for every one of Holland's. His enthusiasm had landed him a wife that he could ill afford, and two children had swiftly followed. 'Did you know your two little ones were in the Warren today?'

The stocky, sandy-haired officer looked up, his mind still on travelling blocks and forage carts. His distracted air was not unlike that of his young namesake. 'What? Yes, Kitty said something about it. Isn't she back yet?' He passed a weary hand over his eyes. 'Damn, you've made me lose my place. You should always warn a fellow when you mean to interrupt him. They're . . . One of the storekeeper's clerks has them in hand.'

'Not when I saw them five minutes ago,' Holland replied. 'They were hanging off one of the cranes, about to fall into the river.'

'What?!' Dalton stood up quickly, scattering documents and upsetting a nearly empty bottle of ink. 'Damn it!'

'They're not there *now*. They're in my rooms, confound them, probably turning the place upside down.'

'Ah, well, that's all right then.' Dalton sat down again, grinning, and picked up his pen. 'A bit of domesticity is just what you need — I've always said so.'

'No, it bloody well isn't all right. Come and collect them! And what's your wife about, leaving them at the storekeeper's? Haven't we enough awkward sods of our own without Jack and Chloe adding to them?'

'I don't know. She said something or other . . . You know Kitty — she's a law unto herself, and quite beyond the ken of a mere husband. Keep an eye on the next generation of Daltons for half an hour, will you? I'm nearly through with this lot, and then I can take a break.'

Holland folded his arms uncompromisingly. 'Half an hour,' he affirmed.

'Thanks, Bob. I'll be as quick as I can.'

'Good,' grumbled Holland, and then, 'got your orders for Canada at last?'

131

Dalton nodded, already back to his papers. His pen commenced its scratchy progress across the page.

'And Captain Adair has left everything to you, of course?'

'It is as you see it. I am but the hands and eyes of the Great Man. His is the controlling genius.'

'Some genius. When are you off?'

'We leave for Halifax in a fortnight's time, or so it has been revealed to me.'

Holland watched as his friend added up a column of figures and recorded the result in a careful hand. 'Which means you will be sailing next week for the Cape?'

Dalton smiled a second time and sat back in his chair. 'Very likely.'

Mary did not forget Miss Trent's errand in Birchin Lane, but as her friends made their final preparations for departure she wondered whether she had been wrong to regard the incident as suspicious. Observing Miss Trent re-packing a trunk because dear Charlotte did not appreciate how difficult it was to refresh silk that had become badly wrinkled, Mary could well imagine her offering her services to Colonel Crosby-Nash. And why should he not have appointed her his courier, knowing that it would give her pleasure to be of assistance?

Mr Shy had explained that Mary should purchase brightly coloured flowers from the vender who frequented Cavendish Square if she had anything to report. If she discovered nothing she should purchase white flowers, and he had urged her to do so regularly so that he would know that all was well. What, precisely, would follow a purchase of vibrant snapdragons or columbines was not clear, for thus far Mary had confined herself to more pallid blooms. She did so again on the following after-noon, when she also bade farewell to Cavendish Square. There was no point in raising Mr Shy's hopes with an unlikely piece of speculation. If she began bothering him with such things, he might question the wisdom of recruiting her in the first place, and even undervalue any important information that she discovered.

That was always supposing, of course, that she *did* discover anything. Even after Mary took up residence at Scarborough House, finding out the colonel's secrets was not easily done. He did not regularly submit himself for examination, and when they did meet she was too self-conscious to be an effective interrogator. Whereas she might have raised the progress of the Naval mutiny as a topic of general interest, for example, now she hesitated to do so, fearing that he would suspect her motive. Nor was it a simple matter of observing his activities away from Scarborough House. He spent a great deal of his time 'on business', and she could hardly intrude upon such matters.

When she added up what she had achieved since agreeing to help Mr Shy, therefore, Mary found the result underwhelming. She had asked the colonel roundabout questions to do with his past, and she had managed to join two innocuous outings. For the first of these she had been one of a foursome (the others being Susannah, Crosby-Nash, and his little mongrel dog, Slipper), on an afternoon drive and a stroll in Green Park. On the second she and Susannah had gone with the colonel to an artist's studio. Through none of these did Mary feel that she learned anything worthwhile. Undoubtedly Mr Shy was aware that the Crosby-Nashes were a moderately well-to-do family in Leicestershire. Nor did it seem likely that the painter of society portraits, who boasted repeatedly of his early friendship with Sir Joshua Reynolds, was a secret conspirator. The outing to Green Park, too, had been a disappointing affair, with Slipper the most vocal member of the party. His habit of barking and crying whenever the carriage slowed had made conversation almost impossible until they had reached the park. Once there he had tugged and scrabbled, deaf to all commands that he behave himself, and had finally pulled the lead out of Susannah's hand and escaped. A man had brought him back, but the fact that he spoke only to Susannah, and that Slipper appeared to have bitten him, had convinced Mary that there had been no criminal assignation.

She told herself that things would be different once they were in Kent, but this was scant consolation for her present failure. Having set her mind upon a particular goal, she was not altogether patient about its achievement. It was with particular irritation, therefore, that she learned of Colonel Crosby-Nash's decision not to accompany the ladies to what would be their final London entertainment at the King's Theatre. Over breakfast he explained that he was obliged to dine with some gentlemen at the Rainbow Coffee House. Fortunately Susannah's uncle had agreed to attend the performance in his stead, so they would not be denied their outing.

'What, by the way, is the programme,' he asked, with the air of one trying to advance the conversation over an uncomfortable passage.

'It is an opera called *Nina* by Giovanni . . . Paisiello,' replied Mary, thinking to herself that the Rainbow Coffee House was where someone called Mr De Costa, an Indian agent, conducted his business. (The colonel had mentioned the name before, and she had looked it up in the *Directory*.) 'The heroine is driven mad by the supposed death of her beloved.' She was studying a description of the opera together with a list of the performers, and she reported, 'It is described here as "a comedy of great beauty and sentiment", so perhaps it will end well.'

'Oh, yes,' said Susannah, meekly.

Why do you not ask him to cancel this dinner with his Indian friends and honour a promise to you that was made weeks ago? thought Mary, raising her eyes to observe Susannah's profile, but aloud she asked, 'What do you suppose is a "zampogna"?'

Crosby-Nash was spooning honey onto a slice of bread. (He generally ate sweet things at breakfast, Mary had discovered.) 'I beg your pardon?'

'A zampogna,' Mary repeated. 'This account states that "*a shepherd attracts Nina's attention with a zampogna, and she follows him to the village*".'

'It certainly sounds mysterious, and I shall look forward to knowing for certain after this evening.' The colonel nodded pleasantly at his wife. 'Mind you do not leave the performance early, my dear – at least not until the zampogna makes its appearance.'

★   ★   ★

They enjoyed the opera very well, particularly the first act, when the shepherd played such a beguiling tune on his zampogna that he seemed more pied piper than Italian rustic. During the interval, however, they endured several conversations with people who knew one or other of them, or wished to do so. The opera was a popular one and had drawn a large audience, but Susannah was too beautiful not to attract attention. Mary too, did not lack admirers. To the world she was still the Suffolk Heiress, after all, whatever role she had chosen for herself.

Mary replied at random when asked her opinion on the timbre of the heroine's voice and the fluency of her recitative, however, for Susannah's bracelet had been commented upon, and Mary realised that here was the object of Miss Trent's mission – the very bracelet she had taken to be repaired. *How odd to see it at last,* she mused, as Susannah held out her arm to display the shimmering band. It was a slim, elegant example of the jeweller's art, a circle of small gold leaves set with diamonds, and it sparkled brilliantly on Susannah's gloved forearm.

'It was a wedding present,' she explained, 'from my cousin, Robert.'

Mary started; it was impossible not to, and a confusion of emotions assailed her. Surprise, dismay, and even jealousy. Captain Holland had bought this beautiful thing, but not for her! Never for her . . . Susannah was given diamonds – diamonds! while she was simply cast off, her letter ignored . . . She could feel her face becoming hot and looked away. *Stop this nonsense,* she scolded herself. *He may surely buy a present for whomever he wishes, and how can you possibly be jealous of Susannah – your own friend . . . and a married woman?*

Then the curtain rose for the second act. As the audience's attention was focussed on the hero – who had not been killed in a duel and still loved the heroine, despite her madness – Mary's own thoughts gradually turned from Captain Holland to his gift. Seeing that bracelet caused her to formulate a plan. She spent the remainder of the evening thinking it over, and by the time the hero had been presented to the heroine, pretending to be an emissary from himself so as not to startle her, Mary had determined to put it into execution. It was a simple enough matter; in fact it was so simple that had she not been frustrated by her inability to communicate *something* of importance to Mr Shy, she probably would not have considered it. But now that she had done so, well, why not? Nothing might come of the scheme – very likely nothing would. This did not daunt her, however, and as the hero and heroine, now recovered, embraced upon stage together with her father, who had been the cause of all the trouble, Mary thought that anything was possible.

Rarely had Mary suffered such vexation as when she awoke the following morning and remembered that it was Sunday, and her plan must be put off. She set off with even greater excitement, therefore, on Monday. Carefully clad in the least expensive of her morning gowns and a plain straw hat, she carried a brooch whose fastening she had bent apart. Her heart was beating more rapidly than usual, for while she congratulated herself on slipping out of Scarborough House without anyone noticing, the task she had set herself was rather unnerving. It was only the second time that she had undertaken a journey alone in London. The first had been when she visited Sir John at Lincoln's Inn, and she told herself that what she was doing now might be just as important. She walked purposefully, nevertheless, even hurriedly, along Dover Street – head down and clasping the walking-stick she had taken up at the last minute as a possible defence against ruffians or importunate persons. When she reached Piccadilly unscathed, she hailed a cab and asked the driver to take her to Hardy & Son's – watchmakers and goldsmiths – in Birchin Lane.

The street itself looked distinctly ordinary. Directly opposite Hardy & Son's was a grocer's, and the shops on either side were a stationer's and a notary public. Farther along were larger buildings, and Mary stood for a few moments watching the clerks trooping into their offices. This was certainly not a

136

fashionable part of town, but neither was it derelict. The men who passed her appeared serious and businesslike, as if they had important matters to consider, probably with other serious and businesslike men nearby. A few of them looked at her curiously as they passed, and once she was asked if she had lost her way, but generally Birchin Lane was too busy to concern itself with her.

Hardy & Son's was smaller than the jewellers' shops that Mary had visited in Bond Street and rather meanly lit. When she stepped through the door, she felt as if she were entering a gloomy parlour, unfashionably decorated and bearing little evidence that customers were either frequent or particularly welcome. A bell had sounded when she opened the door, and after a moment a woman appeared. She was tall and thin, with a stern, if dignified expression. Her eyes were dark, and her grey hair was pulled severely away from her face in a tidy arrangement of looped braids. The girls who worked in jewellers' shops often wore their employers' handiwork, at least if they were pretty; there was no better way to show off a necklace or a pair of earrings. This woman, however, was plainly dressed in grey satin, with no adornment apart from a small cameo at her throat.

She unfolded her hands and bade Mary sit down. 'Good morning, madam. How may I help you?'

Something about the woman's manner, and the fact that she was obviously neither of the proprietors, put Mary off. She felt as if she had been caught whispering in church by the parson's wife – his very formidable wife. The woman opposite did not quite seem at home in the little shop, but neither did she look like a criminal conspirator. Her manner was too *upright*, and not in the least furtive or calculating. Nothing was happening quite as Mary had expected, but she smiled politely and launched into the story she had prepared. It was received steadily, with neither frown nor smile but only a brief nod, which might have signified agreement with Mary's assertion that a friend had recommended the excellent repairs made by Hardy & Son's, or merely an unwillingness to disagree with what was being

137

said. When Mary produced the brooch and explained how it had been damaged, she attempted a modest joke. It produced no response. Mary was not a flirt, but she could not help thinking that a man would have shown more interest, and she regretted the absence of Hardy, or preferably, Son.

The woman turned the brooch over; she had fine hands, with long, elegant fingers. Then she raised her steady gaze to Mary and seemed to study her. 'One moment, if you please,' she said, and walked serenely out of the room.

Alone in the shop, Mary was tempted to speak or clear her throat, if only to break the suspense, for there *was* something suspenseful in the atmosphere. The street outside had grown quiet, and inside there was only the ticking of an ornate gold clock on the sideboard. Ought she to stand up and perhaps examine the glass-topped counter of watch fobs and card cases? In another shop she might have done so, but here she felt too awkward to move. The faded rug had a dog-eared corner. She tried to flatten it, but the crease was too strong, and it turned over as soon as she raised her foot.

'There you are, madam,' said the woman, and she pressed something into Mary's hand. It was the brooch.

'Why— You have fixed it!' cried Mary, in genuine surprise. 'How clever of you.'

'The fastening was bent,' replied the woman. 'It was a simple matter.'

She stood over Mary, arms folded again, while Mary returned the brooch to its small velvet pouch, and thence to her reticule. Would it be possible to prolong the interview? Only for so long as it took her to convince the woman to accept a fee for the work done. A shilling was handed over, and that was that.

Mary pulled the door closed behind her, the bell ringing again to signal her departure. She gazed back through the glass, but the woman was already gone, back into whatever workshop or private rooms lay beyond the dismal parlour. Rather than retracing her steps Mary walked down Birchin Lane towards Lombard Street. The larger buildings were offices, and they all seemed to be the premises of particularly dull businesses such as insurance agents, stockbrokers, and notaries. Each one had a neatly swept front step with railings, and a gold nameplate beside the door. It was difficult to imagine anything more solid and dependable.

In Lombard Street Mary hailed a cab that would take her back to Scarborough House. It would certainly be another day of white flowers for Mr Shy.

9

The carriage door closed with a satisfying thud, and the vehicle swayed into motion. It was a splendid machine, large, imposing, and exuding wealth. Outside it was painted a gleaming chocolate brown below and primrose yellow above, with a thin stripe of red in between. The last colour was repeated inside, in the red leather upholstery. Throughout there was a great deal of brass trim, all of it highly polished, and when the team of six matched bay horses tossed their well-bred heads, they revealed more brass work upon their bridles and harnesses. On the box sat the coachman and groom, both resplendent in the green and gold Crosby-Nash livery.

Mary was lost in her own thoughts as the carriage drew slowly into Pall Mall. She had assumed that Mr Shy would send instructions before she departed for Kent, but this had not happened. Then, on that very morning, she had received a letter from Coutts, her London bankers. It was written on the firm's stationery and was even signed by Mr Herbert, with whom she had previously dealt. Its contents, however, referred to a conversation between them on banking and investment matters that had never taken place.

Thos Coutts & Co.,
59 Strand

9th May 1797

Miss Mary Finch,
Scarborough House
Dover Street

Dear Miss Finch,

 I am happy to be in a position to provide further information on the subjects we discussed when you honoured us with a visit on the 28th of last month.

 Firstly, as regards the government funds, one would like to say that, having rebounded modestly to the level of fifty-three, the three per cents shall not fall beneath a value of fifty, but a prudent banker must not engage in such wishful thinking! While I believe that − failing a new and unexpected crisis − we may cautiously hope for a slight strengthening in the months ahead, perhaps to a level of fifty-three and a half, I must advise you that no loss in value is impossible.

 Next, as regards India, suffice it to say that our balance of trade with that region is not in an altogether healthy state. Last year the official value of imports was in the area of five millions, while the value of goods exported was less than two millions − and five for two is hardly a fair exchange! Of course, this is not necessarily such a sad state of affairs for someone with investments in India, and the situation may be improved further if the Company is able to expand its trading contacts with China.

 Both of the above, of course, will be profoundly affected by the answer to that most important question: shall we have peace? There have been some hints upon the subject in the French newspapers, but I do not like to speculate further until our government, or other reputable source, provides more detailed information. Needless to say, peace in Europe would have the most favourable effect upon our financial interests at home as well as in other quarters of the globe, but I remain doubtful as to its occurring in the immediate future.

 Finally, your information about the Spanish silver dollars was correct

141

in all but one particular. They have been issued, at least in small numbers, and have a nominal value of four shillings and nine pence. They are only bank tokens, however; they are not statutory currency and cannot be used as such. I have taken the liberty of enclosing one of these interesting trinkets for your further study and amusement. On this specimen both our king's effigy as well as that of the Spanish monarch may be distinguished. Such is not always the case, I am sorry to say, due to the careless way that some of them have been stamped.

I trust that the above information is of use to you, and I remain, Miss Finch, your most obliged and respectful servant,

William Herbert, Esq.

Somewhere among those tepid remarks, Mary believed, lay the key to her future conduct – but where? Perhaps the bank token itself? It might be a badge of identity – a way of communicating with the agent to whom she must report – but she was warned against using it. The letter also mentioned Indian affairs, and Colonel Crosby-Nash had been to India. Or perhaps the reference to France was significant? She sighed. It was simply not possible to understand the letter yet. She must be patient and wait upon events.

In a conscious effort to avoid discouraging thoughts, Mary turned her attention to the passing scene, which Crosby-Nash was rather pompously describing. 'And there you see Horse Guards, where the Duke of York and his friends decide how and when we shall confound the French.'

'The Duke of York?' asked Susannah, tentatively.

'He is the commander-in-chief, my dear. And just here – on this side of the street – is the Banqueting House. A very splendid building.'

'Why is it called "the Banqueting House"?'

'I have not the slightest idea, apart from what is apparent from its name. It is the place where the king – King Charles – was executed.'

'How perfectly dreadful. *I* should not like to attend a banquet in such a place.'

'No indeed,' agreed Crosby-Nash with a tolerant smile. 'Most disloyal.' Susannah's hand had slipped beneath his, and he gave it a slight squeeze. 'And yet, some would say that a tyrant forfeits the right to his subjects' loyalty, so that the moral as well as the natural consequence of tyranny is revolution.'

Something, perhaps frustration or a desire to show herself clever, prompted Mary to remark that the remedy for tyranny might be worse than the disease. The words were no sooner out of her mouth than she regretted them, however, for Crosby-Nash smoothly asked whether she was thinking of the situation in France. 'No, although I suppose— But I was thinking of Charles I, of course, and your historical allusion. Surely the men who brought about his ruin were no better than he was.' She finished brightly. 'Cromwell and his friends.'

'Ah yes. Quite.'

'And Charles II was crowned king in the end,' she added, 'while several of the regicides were executed – even Cromwell, who had already died. His body was dug up, beheaded, and hanged in chains.'

'Indeed,' observed Crosby-Nash, 'you are a fount of grisly information, Miss Finch.'

'Isn't she clever?' Susannah beamed and, turning to her husband, added, 'Mary told us ever so much about Westminster Abbey . . . which king followed which, and who was the wisest. I wish that I knew more about history.'

'Well, my dear, surely that wish is easily gratified. A course of reading would improve your knowledge, and books are readily at hand.'

'Yes, of course,' agreed Susannah. 'I only meant—'

'I fear that you did not mean anything by such a casual statement,' complained Crosby-Nash, his tone gently mocking. 'Wishes, which of their nature, cannot be gratified other than by magic, ought to be reserved for things that are otherwise out of one's reach, such as wisdom. But I should have thought that getting the names of the kings of England by rote ought to be within anyone's grasp with a little application.'

Susannah admitted that this was so, and Mary had to recite

Miss Trent's adage about a hasty tongue to herself three times to give her temper time to cool. If the colonel had wished to strengthen his guest's resolve against him, he could not have chosen better. *Odious man!* Her next remarks, however, were temperate. Accompanying the family carriage were four vehicles carrying the servants, baggage, and supplies necessary for a visit to the country, and she observed casually that their cavalcade must make an impressive sight.

Her words seemed to amuse Crosby-Nash. 'Do you think so, Miss Finch?'

'Yes. It is like . . .'

'Juggernaut?' he suggested. 'You know the word?'

'No, I am afraid that I do not.'

'Ah, I beg your pardon. A consequence of my years in India – one becomes familiar with the local expressions. "Juggernaut" refers to the cart bearing the Hindu god Jagannath. Such is their reverence that the faithful are said to throw themselves beneath the wheels of his cart in ceremonial processions.'

'Oh, my,' breathed Susannah, 'the poor people!'

'And while I do not give myself such airs, I should explain that, just as the god's cart stops for no one – not even the faithful – so a juggernaut is taken to mean a massive, irresistible force or conveyance . . . like our not inconsiderable train.'

The proprietors of Hardy & Son's usually dimmed the lights, fastened the shutters, and locked the door to their establishment promptly at six o'clock. The regular routine was followed on that evening, but the premises did not become altogether quiet. As the shadows lengthened and the other denizens of Birchin Lane departed, four men made their way to the shop and were granted admittance. They did not arrive together, but one by one, the earliest at the front entrance and the others at the small, private door to the rear. The tall, severe woman in the grey satin dress let them in; she was alert to the faint tap at the window, the cough, the whistle, even the way one man's shoe sounded when he knocked it against his walking-stick.

Each man entered the darkened building silently and proceeded to the candlelit room behind the shop front. In an ordinary jeweller's this would have been the workshop, and it served that purpose even at Hardy & Son's. Business was business, after all, and it was said that the patron had been apprenticed to a watch-maker in his youth, which explained his fondness for tinkering with bits of delicate machinery or designing settings for precious stones when he was at leisure. A workbench occupied one wall, therefore, and on it stood a lathe, an anvil, and two sets of scales. A glass cabinet on the opposite wall contained an assortment of tools and supplies necessary for the practitioner: a set of winding keys; hammers, callipers, and pliers of various sizes; oils, grease, and rouge powder, each in the appropriate container; cloths and abrasives; a magnifying glass.

In the centre of the room, however, was a rectangular wooden table covered with a white cloth. Here the four men sat, each in his appointed place and leaving vacant the chair at the head. They formed a strange tableau, in part because of their silence, but also because they seemed to have little in common. One looked to have come straight from the docks, while his nearest neighbour wore the black velvet frock coat and tie-wig of the physician. His was the stick – gold-headed – which had made the familiar tap-a-tap. The man opposite them was clearly a tradesman of the middling sort, a brewer; and the last, who sat at the foot of the table, was an office clerk. Indeed, he had come from one of the nearby buildings, where he managed the ledgers of a respectable firm.

The woman returned with an oil lamp whose light dwarfed that of the flickering candle and inspired something like an air of hospitality in the room. The men nodded at each other in greeting, and acknowledged the woman when she served coffee in small, porcelain cups. The man from the docks sat back in his chair and swallowed his coffee in an open-mouthed gulp, rattling the cup when it was returned to the saucer.

The brewer frowned disapprovingly. For him the meeting was a serious occasion; he had put on a clean blue necktie and been particularly careful to preserve his striped stockings from harm, and there was Chabot – grubby as usual and smelling

145

of fish. Why, he had not even the sense to remove that disgraceful knitted cap. 'Chabot, you are a pig.'

'Eh? *Le poseur?*' demanded the other, glowering.

'No, no, Chabot,' explained the clerk, patiently, '*le cochon,* not *le poseur.*' He was the youngest of those present and the only one ever addressed by his first name, André. An unfortunate cowlick made his hair part awkwardly, and the front of his coat was shiny from frequent pressing, but his expression was both ardent and intelligent.

The big man smiled rather foolishly. 'Ah, *le cochon,* yes, ha ha! That is well, but a happy prig – a Citizen Prig.' He had large, powerful hands with dirty fingernails, and his smile revealed a missing front tooth.

'*Pig,* not *prig,*' muttered the doctor. He was starting to dislike these meetings – the enforced camaraderie with men like Chabot and that conceited fool, Huber; the anxiety that one's life was about to be turned upside down by some ill-judged affair; the feeling of always being under observation, of being tested.

'Yes, pig,' Chabot agreed, but before he could explain further André rapped his knuckles on the table. 'Please, my friends, citizens. Let us call the meeting to order.'

'Where is the patron?' asked Huber, petulantly. 'Does he not join us?' Huber harboured a secret jealousy of the clerk, or rather he imagined it to be secret. That such a young fellow – clever, admittedly, but exercising no authority in his place of work – should presume to do so here was irritating. That he should have the confidence of their chief was even more so.

'Yes, I expect him in a short while,' replied André, with just the degree of certainty that irked the brewer. 'And, in the meantime, we may safely proceed in his absence. I am authorised to receive your reports.' He produced a leather satchel, from which he extracted several sheets of paper and a bottle of ink. Having set these on the table, he drew the lamp closer to himself and selected the longer of the quill pens he carried in his buttonhole.

The men presented their reports in turn, starting with Huber and finishing with Chabot. For the most part these were received silently; the men who had already spoken looked relieved, and those yet to do so seemed more concerned with rehearsing their own accounts than with criticising their fellows'. Occasionally André interrupted his note-taking to pose a question or to glance thoughtfully at the speaker, and when each report was concluded he read aloud what he had written for confirmation or amendment.

When the task was completed the woman returned a second time. Still exercising an unusual prescience, she rolled back the carpet that was spread across the floor behind the table. There appeared to be nothing unusual in the expanse of polished wood thus revealed, but after a short while a section was lifted from below – a hidden door – and a diminutive figure emerged through it, seemingly out of the earth.

Like Mephistopheles when Faustus summoned him to make a bargain for his soul, thought the doctor, and would have said so, had he dared. Instead, he rose with his fellows and intoned, 'Welcome, *Citoyen Patron*.'

'English, please,' urged the new arrival, motioning them to be seated. He sometimes used another name, but here, among his colleagues, he preferred the title of 'Citizen'. The woman removed his cloak, complaining that it was wet through; as were, no doubt, his shoes and stockings, and he rolled his eyes. 'Nonsense – there has been only a brief shower of rain, and I avoided the worst of it.' To the men he continued, 'You must use English at all times, and properly! You could perhaps manage a bit more practice, eh Chabot?'

'Yes, Citizen Patron, I expect so,' said the other with a grin. He had pulled off his hat, revealing a bullet head with close-cropped hair that failed entirely where a wide, pinkish scar curved over one ear. 'But on the docks we save our breaths for working.'

'Of course, of course, but do not forget to practise, eh? Each one of us can better himself, looking out for ways to serve our cause more effectively.'

Everyone agreed that this was true, and the man addressed as Citizen Patron took his place at the table. His cloak had certainly protected him from the rain, for beneath it his dark-blue cutaway

147

coat was spotless, and the starched, intricately arranged neck cloth was undisturbed. Although he was not a young man, he wore the wide, red sash about his waist that had been affected by those with revolutionary sympathies some years hence, and his physique was still sufficiently trim that the style did not look ridiculous. But was he indeed a revolutionary? The very neatness of his dress spoke against it, together with the powdered wig and the bunch of flowers in his buttonhole. On the other hand, the Jacobin Robespierre was said to have dressed in just such a style.

He read through the reports prepared by the clerk, donning a pair of spectacles to do so. His questions were few, but always clear and to the point. Afterwards, there was a wider discussion among the group, and the woman produced more coffee and a cake iced with marzipan.

'A boat is easy,' Chabot claimed, swallowing hastily. 'I can get just such a boat, whenever he is needed, but André must provide the papers . . . the plans.'

'That can also be done,' murmured the clerk. 'I know how the orders and deliveries are conducted, and I can produce the necessary tickets – even those that require a signature. The other documents, those of a scientific nature, can be obtained from a gentleman of my acquaintance who is an astronomer.'

Huber looked sceptical. 'An Englishman?'

'Yes, but he knows nothing of political matters, and we are friends. He would have no suspicions even were I to ask him questions that were far more unusual.'

'He is a fool,' muttered the physician.

'He is trusting,' corrected Citizen Patron, 'and he is loyal to that trust, that friendship with Citizen André. We must all of us keep that in mind,' he continued, removing his spectacles and placing them in a silver case. 'Work can always be found for a fool, if he is loyal – which is comforting for some of you, eh? But if a man is disloyal . . . if he cannot be trusted, then he is worthless to me and to our cause, whatever his cleverness or his courage. Indeed, he is worse than that, for he is dangerous. He threatens us. Do you understand?'

148

They nodded, some smiling, and answered, 'Yes, Citizen Patron.' Huber considered mentioning a scientific gentleman of his own acquaintance – a completely reliable customer and also highly intelligent – but thought better of it. He did not wish to undermine the youngster, after all, but would speak about the matter privately with Citizen Patron on another occasion.

The meeting broke up shortly thereafter, its participants departing as they had come until only André and Citizen Patron remained. Of the other three, the last to leave had been the physician, who had taken his chief aside for a professional consultation regarding the latter's spectacles. Were they performing satisfactorily? Soon, perhaps, a stronger prescription would be necessary for very delicate work. After he had gone and the woman indicated that all was quiet, the remaining two men had a further conversation.

'Maurice knows a great deal about the eyes,' acknowledged Citizen Patron, 'particularly mine. It is a pity, therefore . . . You know that his daughter has become engaged to a man who was formerly the secretary to *Philippe-Ègalité*?'

André was gathering up his writing materials and did not meet his chief's gaze. 'I had heard of it, but ought we to condemn a man because of an employment before the Revolution? And the *duc d'Orléans* broke with the king, after all.'

'Yes, and then aspired to his crown. The Orléanists are traitors, and Maurice should not have permitted his daughter to become entangled with them to any degree. It was a violation of his duty as a father and of his duty to his comrades. This secretary is probably one of the duke's natural children. A serpent in Maurice's bosom.'

'You think that this man . . . I think his name is Christophe, will entangle Maurice in some treacherous actions? He has never behaved disloyally.'

'Nor do I accuse him of such, but I am fearful of what may occur in the future. Maurice does not take sufficient care – I fear that he will compromise himself to our enemies. He will give something away or allow them to exercise a hold upon

149

him, and either could prove fatal to us. He has become too comfortable in his new life, I fear, and has forgotten true virtue. His London practice and his wealthy patients absorb his energies.'

'His most recent dossier was not very complete,' acknowledged the clerk, 'as I am sure you noticed.'

'Indeed, it was both sparse and guarded – the sort of report presented by a man who is either neglecting his work or who does not wish to reveal too much.'

'Perhaps at our next meeting—'

'Unfortunately, we cannot wait so long,' said Citizen Patron, shaking his head. 'If our plans are betrayed now we face the most serious consequences.' He observed André gravely. 'Will you arrange it?'

The other man nodded. 'Of course. I will send word to Chabot tonight. "*If it were done when 'tis done, then 'twere well if it were done quickly.*"'

'It certainly would be, but I would not give Chabot the benefit of your learning. His English is atrocious, but fortunately his most important work does not require communication.'

They parted on those words, for the clerk had his commission to execute. The journey took him south of the river to Bermondsey. Chabot was employed as a labourer at St Saviour's Docks, and he had rooms above a glue-maker's shop in Trotter's Alley. André did not expect him to be at home, so he merely left a card under the mat. On the card was written an address in a much more fashionable part of town, the letter R, and three black crosses.

A handkerchief was a poor shield against the odours that seeped from the workshops and warehouses, even at night: glue, turpentine, brine, and smoke all contributed to the noxious air. André was thankful that he need not linger to deliver the message personally or explain its meaning. Chabot would understand his instructions and carry them out faithfully. Promptly too, so long as he had not gone out drinking. Only when his wits were confused by drink or anger did he become less than a perfect instrument of his chief's will.

In fact, Chabot had decided not to spend the night carousing, or at least not heavily. He returned to his lodgings at ten o'clock, and by eleven he was at the appointed address in Holborn. A light was burning in one of the downstairs rooms and another in the front passage, so he rapped a particular tattoo with the heavy brass knocker. He had been to this house once before, and he knew the routine. The servants retired early, so if the master was at home he would answer the knock; if not, no one would. Chabot did not care either way; if his business could not be completed now, he would wait.

The door was answered by the master of the house; he was in his dressing gown and had removed his wig. 'What is it?' he demanded in an urgent whisper.

'Important news.'

'You had better come inside.'

The door closed behind Chabot. Presently, the light in the downstairs room was extinguished – it was the study, where the master of the house generally received his patients. Some time later, the door opened again and Chabot slipped out. No one saw him, for he had also darkened the front passage, and the street was quiet. He had waited for almost half an hour in the study, with no animate company but the ticking clock, but he had not minded. On his way back to his small, miserable rooms in Bermondsey he experienced a passing regret for what had occurred, but this did not trouble him for long. He was sleepy, and Citizen Patron knew best.

Later that week the following account appeared in the *Times*.

Maurice Lacour-Perrey, the eminent oculist and émigré, was found dead on Wednesday morning at his home in Red Lion Square, Holborn, under the most terrible circumstances. On attempting to serve Monsieur Lacour-Perrey breakfast, his unfortunate daughter discovered his body in the study, where he had been most foully murdered. It is believed that he surprised a robber, who compounded his crime by strangling his victim so severely as to break his neck.

151

10

It was barely forty miles from London to Champian Hall, but the journey took a day and a half because Colonel Crosby-Nash preferred a sedate speed. They were going into the country for peace and solitude, and he questioned whether those were best achieved at a breakneck pace. His preference also afforded them ample opportunity for observing the Kentish country-side, in which they took great pleasure. The blossom had finished, but the neat orchards of apple and cherry trees were still very pleasing, and there were the young hop vines to admire, and the well-kept vegetable gardens, while patches of bluebells, cowslips, and daisies brightened the verge when their way took them into meadows or woodlands.

Eventually they left the Maidstone road and turned south onto a narrow track. As the trees grew more closely upon either side, their course became more secret and more inviting. The hamlets they passed, scarcely more than a few silent dwellings, did little to break the spell. Then they emerged into a valley, and the carriage negotiated a slow turn onto what appeared to be a private drive. They were almost there.

'What is that curious piece of stonework, colonel?' asked Mary, pointing towards what she had first taken to be a milestone.

'Merely one of my Indian trinkets, and not a particularly fine specimen. You will see some more interesting pieces shortly.'

The ladies uttered a collective 'Oh' as the carriage rumbled across a stone causeway, and Mary peered out of the window to observe their passage over a low ditch. Crosby-Nash, for whom the sound had not been a surprise, explained that a stream had once flowed there, doubtless to feed the moat.

'*Is* there a moat?' cried Susannah, 'such as a *castle* would have? Oh, my dear Arthur—'

'Patience.' He raised a reproving finger. 'The trees are shaping up nicely, but they obscure the house. You will get a better view in a moment, Susannah – when we have passed through the gatehouse.'

'*The gatehouse?*'

'Rather a grandiloquent term, but most of the structure remains. There has been a certain amount of wear and tear, I am afraid, and I should not advise— Ah, here we are.'

The carriage turned and rolled to a stop. Without further explanation the colonel disembarked, and Mary and Susannah followed in silent wonder. Before them stood an ancient square tower – the gatehouse – built mostly of stone but with an upper storey of brick. The ranges on either side comprised buildings or walls – it was difficult to tell which, for here and there a narrow window appeared, or the evidence of one. Access to the gatehouse was by way of a low, double-arched stone bridge, and beneath this was, as promised, a moat.

'I am afraid the gatehouse was not made for vehicles such as ours,' Crosby-Nash explained. 'The carriages will go round, but I much prefer this way, even if I must rely upon my own powers of locomotion to use it.'

Mary and Susannah echoed this sentiment. Neither had seen a castle before, other than the Tower of London, which belonged to the king and was therefore wholly different from one's own castle. They crossed over the bridge and through the arched passage with a sense of delighted trepidation, as if a knight in chain-mail might be about to challenge them, or a wizard might be lurking behind the nail-studded oak door. No such persons appeared, however, and the gloom of the gatehouse gave way to an open space, a lawn with neat gravel paths, and at once they received their first surprise. This was not a castle courtyard – there was no castle, for one thing, and the 'court' was open on one side. To their left stood a wall, somewhat ruined, but with recognisable battlements. To their right, however, was only a ruined tower, beyond which all traces of wall disappeared, the gap being filled instead by a stand of young lime trees. And before them stood Champian Hall. Mary gazed up at the long stretch of mellow brickwork, whose elegant lines were hidden here by a spread of ivy and interrupted there by small, mullioned windows; at the imposing front door, and at the vast dormered roof, with several elegant spiral chimneys rising over all.

Smiling, Colonel Crosby-Nash resolved the mystery. There had been a considerable dwelling on the site since the tenth century, although nothing remained of the medieval structure beyond a section of the foundations, the east and south walls, and the gatehouse. Even the moat was not quite what it seemed, for it had survived on only two sides. The rest had been filled in many years previously, for the convenience of the house and grounds. The present Hall had been built during the reign of Elizabeth and extended in the last century.

Susannah said that it was still very lovely, and she reckoned it was much more convenient than a castle. Mary agreed and asked whether the estate had been long in the colonel's family.

'Oh, no, not two years. I won it in a game of cards shortly after returning to England.'

'You *won* Champian Hall?'

'Yes. The former owner had a prolonged run of bad luck, and rather than giving up the game, insisted on playing a final, ill-advised hand. He had lost all of his ready money at an earlier stage in the proceedings, so he was obliged to surrender this estate. Good afternoon, Mrs Saunders,' he continued, nodding at a small, soberly dressed woman who stood on the lowest of the front steps. 'We have arrived in good time, as you see. This is Mrs Crosby-Nash – my dear, Mrs Saunders is our housekeeper.'

'Good afternoon, sir. Good afternoon, ma'am. I hope you have had a pleasant journey.'

154

'Yes, very pleasant,' said Crosby-Nash. He issued instructions to Mrs Saunders and then directed Mary and Susannah away from 'the anarchy' and towards the formal gardens that fronted part of the west and south sides of the house. The two ladies walked arm in arm, their progress repeatedly interrupted as one or other stopped to praise the yew hedges, the borders of lavender, the marble sundial, and the intricate design of flagstones that surrounded it. They were filled with enthusiasm for the remains of the massive walls that had once protected the house and grounds from attack. While no longer suited to such a role, they formed a backdrop to the gardens and linked the three surviving towers that stood guard over the property.

Susannah was particularly taken with the several espaliered apricot trees. 'We have never been able to grow apricots at Storey's Court,' she confided. 'How impressed Mama would be to see these doing so well.'

The colonel did not immediately join their conversation, but followed along behind at a leisurely pace. At last he reintroduced the matter of Champian Hall itself; were the ladies shocked by the manner of its acquisition? Mary said no, because the colonel had risked his money fairly against the other man's, but Susannah was more tender-hearted; she felt sorry for anyone who had lost his home, whatever the circumstances.

'Well, my dear, you must try to comfort yourself with the knowledge that he was rather a rascally fellow, who failed to disclose the sad state of the roof or the existence of a sizeable mortgage upon the property, when I agreed to accept it in payment of his debts. I have been obliged to spend a considerable sum of money on the place.'

'It looks to have been money well spent,' said Mary.

Crosby-Nash nodded graciously. 'It is not, perhaps, the property I would have chosen, but I have become rather fond of its quirks and oddities, in the process of trying to change them.'

'You do not feel that you have an obligation to previous generations to maintain it on their behalf?'

'No, indeed,' laughed Crosby-Nash, 'for if they were anything

155

like the generation with whom I have had to deal, they did exactly as they wished with the place, and sons liked nothing better than to rip out what their fathers had installed. I have uncovered the plans for some of the building work carried out by one of my predecessors in King William's day. It makes an intriguing study – for those who are interested.'

'Mary loves very old things,' confirmed Susannah. 'Old books and papers.'

That remark caused Mary a slight pang of anxiety, as she did not want to be considered curious, or the sort of person who made enquiries. Thinking that an interest in her own property must be uncontroversial, she turned the conversation to White Ladies. She even extended an invitation to Crosby-Nash to visit, so long as he did not expect to win it from her in a wager.

'Certainly not, Miss Finch,' replied Crosby-Nash, smiling. 'But are you in truth a gambler? Some ladies are very partial to the exercise, I know, and play for high stakes.'

'Well, sir, I have never tried it,' Mary acknowledged, 'but I fear I would dislike losing too much to gamble on winning.'

'You are very prudent. But let us go inside. We could all do with some refreshment, I believe, and Champian Hall has much yet to show you.'

The colonel's arch tone had put Mary on her guard, but it failed to prepare her for what came next. At some point in the house's history the dimensions of the great hall had been adjusted to provide a separate entrance chamber. It was rather stark, with plain, whitewashed walls and a floor of polished stone. A moderate fireplace, lacking much in the way of orna-mentation, was set into the rear wall, with only a single, uncomfortable-looking oak chair to keep it company. As one entered the room, however, little of this was noticed, for the eye was immediately drawn to a large painting, or fresco, on the wall above the fireplace. It depicted a strange creature, possessing the legs and body of a man, an extra pair of arms, and the head of an animal. The creature appeared to be dancing and his expression, in so far as this was revealed by his small, twinkling eyes and the jaunty angle of his ponderous snout, was good-natured.

'*Oh, my,*' gasped Susannah, retreating a step.

'This is Ganesha, or Gonesh, as we call him in Bengal,' Crosby-Nash informed them, 'the elephant god of the Hindus. He is considered the destroyer of obstacles, and in token of the many and varied obstacles that I have overcome in respect of this house, I decided to have his image painted. Very striking, don't you think?'

The great hall was even more startling. Its panelled walls had been painted a vivid yellow with the trim picked out in red, white, and black, while mounted heads of tigers, leopards, buffalos, and a rhinoceros replaced the more familiar trophies of elk and deer. The skin of one of the tigers lay in front of the fireplace at the far end of the room; elsewhere the floor was covered by large, brightly coloured rugs. The furniture was sparse, but similarly exotic: a few chairs, either ornately carved or fashioned from delicately braided osiers, and three or four low tables. One of these bore a chess set, in which white and black were represented by the military forces of the East India Company and those of a native prince, respectively, while others displayed a miscellany of painted bowls, ivory boxes, and bronze or stone statues. Adjacent to the fireplace stood an ironbound chest, flanked by a pair of enormous, curved tusks. Only the long oak dining table in the centre of the hall was undeniably English, and it had been rendered unusual by the addition of a runner of green and gold silk, and three silver lanterns.

The transformation of a Tudor country house into what Mary supposed must be an Indian palace was certainly unexpected, and she could not decide whether she liked it. It was clear that Susannah did not, but equally clear that she would offer no criticism.

'Are those elephant tusks, sir?'

'They are indeed, Miss Finch.'

'And did you . . . hunt all of these animals yourself?'

Crosby-Nash nodded. 'India is a great country for sport.'

If Mary had liked the colonel she would have pressed him

for details of his exploits, but as matters stood she did not mean to. They were not friends, after all. 'You must have many happy memories of your time there,' she observed instead.

'Yes, I daresay I must. I spent a good many years there, you know, and they say that once Mother India has entered your soul, she can never wholly be displaced.'

'A very beautiful country, then.'

'Yes, beautiful but also terrible, and sometimes both together. Remarkable, certainly.' A silence followed this observation, which grew larger and slightly uncomfortable.

'Yes, it must be . . . very remarkable,' agreed Susannah at last, in the voice of one who felt obliged to make a contribution. 'How did you . . . Was it very difficult to bring all of these things home?'

'There are ways and means, my dear, ways and means. The Company manages to look after its loyal servants tolerably well, most of the time.'

Mary was observing the housekeeper as she issued directions for the disposition of boxes and trunks, and aloud followed the train of her own thoughts. 'I wonder what the servants make of your changes to— Oh! I beg your pardon, colonel.'

'Not at all, Miss Finch – your suspicions are well-founded. I did encounter certain prejudices among the indoor servants who had known the place under my predecessor. I was obliged to let them go and, unfortunately, the denizens of Saxonhurst – that is the name of our nearest metropolis – have not seen fit to provide replacements. In consequence, I generally keep the house closed, apart from Mrs Saunders, and bring down my staff from Scarborough House when I mean to make a visit. London servants are generally less parochial, I find, and several have been with me since my time in India. Now, let us not stand about any longer. Perhaps we might take some refreshment in the upstairs parlour, and you will wish to see your rooms.'

The influence of Mother India was not quite so pronounced in the upper rooms, although Mary's bedchamber featured a heavy oak dresser surprisingly partnered with a bedstead of

158

rosewood and silver, and they consumed tea and cakes in a room painted a shade of green not usually seen in England. Afterwards an attitude of serenity, which had been growing upon him since their arrival, inspired the colonel to produce some of his 'particular treasures' for the ladies' enjoyment: a bowl shaped out of a kind of cream-coloured jade, inset with rubies and gold flowers; a gold statue of an enthroned goddess, adorned with snakes whose eyes gleamed of silver; a silk tapestry more than three hundred years old; a series of delicate miniature paintings depicting Indian gods and heroes. They were all of unusual beauty and interest, and Crosby-Nash's explanations of the paintings evoked a mythological world that was both exotic and familiar to his listeners – Vishnu's incarnation as a great, grey fish to save mankind from a tremendous flood, and Gazi Pir, who could charm tigers as effectively as St Francis and carried a cobra as his staff.

'Now let me tell you about the woman whose husband was killed by a snake sent by Manasa, the golden goddess. The loyal wife not only protected his body from wild animals, but also performed other heroic deeds, which so impressed the gods that they granted her a wish. Naturally, she asked that her husband be returned to her.'

Other plausible wishes occurred to Mary, but she asked whether the wife's had been granted.

'There was a certain awkwardness about it, as I recall,' acknowledged Crosby-Nash, 'but it had nothing to do with the gods. The poor fellow's leg had been eaten during an earlier part of the story and had to be recovered. It *was* recovered, however, and I believe the principals all lived . . . happily ever after.'

Despite its initial surprises, life at Champian Hall quickly fell into a recognisable pattern. Crosby-Nash reacquainted himself with the business of the estate; Susannah worked away at her needlepoint, hoping that an embroidered pillow or a fire screen might render the place more homely even as she loyally praised her husband's Indian furnishings; and Mary tentatively resumed

159

her enquiries. She gained access to the library, which proved to be the colonel's private sanctuary. Here he wrote his letters, read the newspapers he had sent down from London, and occasionally discussed country business with local worthies like the doctor and the magistrate.

Having perceived the importance of this room, Mary was initially at a loss to know how best to proceed. Crosby-Nash did not tend to announce his daily programme, and Mary could not risk being discovered poring over her host's papers. Yet only by a careful perusal of his desk was she likely to uncover important information. Help appeared from an unlikely quarter: the colonel's dog, Slipper. Slipper was not a very appealing animal. He was not handsome, and he had bitten one of the footmen during the journey to Champian Hall, but he had a redeeming attribute; he could discern his master's approach. As soon as she became aware of this ability, Mary cultivated Slipper's friendship. In fact, they became inseparable.

Slipper did not particularly care for Mary's habit of spending so much time indoors, nor did he understand her interest in the library. He was content, however, to doze on a comfortable chair until something exciting happened. Mary's own attitude towards her activities was more complicated. She told herself that discovering dangerous, criminal conduct was a worthwhile – even noble – act, and she certainly believed it, at least when considered in that way. The secret, stealthy manner in which she was obliged to behave, however, was beginning to make her uneasy. Then there was the actual discovering. She had examined the colonel's private papers and found nothing that was actually criminal. The suggestion that her host might not be an evil man ought to have pleased her, but instead it fed her discomfort. For she must continue to spy and interfere, hoping to uncover something that would justify her otherwise reprehensible acts. Mr Shy had been convinced that the colonel was a villain . . . but Mr Shy was not there.

Mary was thinking about this as she made her way along a passage towards the rear of the house, with Slipper trotting along beside her. A recent edition of the *Times* contained a reference to the Cabinet Council, and Crosby-Nash had circled it. How often did this body meet, she wondered, and what sort of matters did they generally discuss? Would the king attend?

The preserved carcass of a crocodile, looking incongruous on a Jacobean sideboard, elicited a low growl from Slipper, and royal practices were forgotten. Mary scolded Slipper for his incivility. 'You challenge this crocodile every day, and not once has he offered even the slightest hint of a reply.'

'I reckon the old feller's scared o' Mister Slipper, miss,' suggested a voice from behind them. 'He don't dare to come down off his perch, not with Mister Slipper about.'

Mary turned to see one of the young under-gardeners, and she smiled a greeting. 'Good morning, Tom. How is your father today?'

'He's terrible bad with his foot, which he hurt last night steppin' on a nail,' Tom explained, shaking his head. 'I'm off to see that tinker feller now for a swallow of somethin' for the pain.'

'Oh, dear,' said Mary, 'I hope it is not a serious injury. And you say that a *tinker* may help him?'

'That's right, miss. He's got all sorts o' cures and simples, he has, along of the usual run of— Hey, no more you don't!' he cried, as Slipper transferred his attention from the crocodile to Tom's boot.

'Slipper, behave yourself!' Mary ordered and, braving the growls of protest, obliged him to endure the ignominy of being held, infant like, in her arms. 'I am afraid he is in rather a bad humour this morning.'

'There's no bounds to him,' Tom agreed. 'Best if I puts him out. We can put him in kitchen garden if you like, and you can see him – and tinker – directly.'

'Oh, the tinker has come to the Hall, has he?'

'Aye, miss, in the kitchens. And he's askin' for the ladies o' the house, like they does. Them sort always likes to show the ladies a bit o' this and that.' Tom smiled knowingly.

The tinker's name was Romney. 'Jack Romney, that's me, ladies and gents.' He was a spare, rather elderly man, with a thin, piping voice and bright black eyes that darted back and forth, assessing his potential customers. His glance fell upon Mary, and he bowed. 'I reckon I've something here as would interest a pretty young lady like yourself, miss. What'll it be, now, bit o' lace? Bottle o' scent? These buttons is finest ivory.'

Mary would have preferred to remain at the back, but the assembled footmen, under cooks, and maidservants parted, and she was obliged to advance towards the tinker and his tray of finery. 'I am really here only to look,' she admitted.

As she watched the little man ply his trade Mary began to think it highly unlikely that she would avoid making a purchase of some kind. He seemed to know just what to say to encourage his audience to part with their money. 'You wants to make old bones, don't you, missus? That tonic'll set you up for certain. Why, I drinks it meself every day, and look at me!' 'Oh, no, my girl, you want the violet ribbon, next but one. Only violet ribbons with eyes like yours.' 'You fancy that knife, lad? I ain't surprised. That's Sheffield steel, that is.' Tom bore away a small brown bottle, whose contents were promised to make his father's injured foot 'right as rain by the morning – see if it ain't so.' Only Slipper seemed unimpressed by Romney's patter; his critical voice could be heard from outside, and occasionally he scratched importantly at the door.

Romney did not long allow Mary to remain a mere observer. On the contrary, he repeatedly caught her eye, gesturing towards something on his tray or from his pack, and shaking his head regretfully when she declined. 'Packet o' tea, miss? Come all the way from China it has. I don't say as it ain't had the custom paid on it, as that would be tellin'. But why should the old Company have it all its own way, that's what I says. Or how about this bit o' Spanish lace? Just four shillings and nine pence. You heard what they say about ladies o' Spain, ain't ye? Well, they wears lace like this here. A bargain at four and nine.'

'No, thank you.'

'Just as you like, miss. That's right, my good fellow, them laces'll suit you grand at sixpence. 'Fraid I can't let that pack of cards go for under a crown, my lad. Don't you know that cards is the devil's playthings? Got to make a bit o' tin if I'm goin' to risk me soul for sellin' 'em, ain't I? Now, how 'bout this here comb, miss? Real tortoise-shell and no mistake. Ain't it lovely? Wait a mo, I've another, have it out o' me bag directly minute. Here you are, miss, got the pair off a chap in London, just back from India. Best Indian stock.'

Mary had no real interest in the combs, which she thought rather ugly, but out of politeness she asked the price.

He eyed her, considering. 'Well, miss, for you we'll say five shillings. That's five shillings for the pair of 'em. Five for two.' He raised both hands, the right palm outward, and the left with thumb and forefinger displayed.

The sight revived an almost forgotten memory, and Mary suddenly found herself answering, 'Five for two? That is hardly a fair exchange.' She glanced at him, trying to keep her expression calm. Was she right? The reference in Mr Herbert's letter to Indian imports — was that the clue? Was *this* Mr Shy's agent?

Romney gave nothing away. 'Can't see you getting a fairer one,' he complained, shaking his head. 'Them is genuine Indian treasures, from Bombay itself. Can't get no more Indian than that, I reckon. Five shillings for the pair. Why, I'd never stay in business if I let all me stuff go so cheap.' He sighed ruefully. 'But we can't resist the ladies, can we?'

'Very well.' She shrugged with a fair show of indifference. 'I shall take them, please.'

'That's right, miss, I knew as you'd see the rarity of 'em. Worth every penny.'

Mary passed him the required sum, wondering what would happen next. She was disconcerted when Romney simply handed over the combs and seemed to lose interest in her. He answered someone's question about balls of string, and she stepped back, uncertain. Then a crash from outside indicated that Slipper had moved on to the flowerpots, and she thought she had better intervene.

She had almost reached the garden door when a voice behind her arrested her flight. 'Wait a moment, miss. You've gone and forgot your change, you have. There you are.' He pressed the coins into her hand, adding in an urgent whisper, 'St Stephen's churchyard – this afternoon at three. And don't bring that bloody dog.' Then he turned away from her. 'Don't want anyone sayin' as I ain't honest. Honest as the day is long, that's me.'

'No, I mean, of course. Thank you.'

Mary's enthusiasm was sufficient to propel her out of the kitchen, through the garden, and away from Champian Hall. Crossing the bleaching ground she passed through the orchard and into the meadow that led down to the river. All about her wildflowers blossomed in profusion among the swaying grasses; in the distance the sun glinted off the slowly turning mill wheel. The atmosphere of suspense and uncertainty that had over-shadowed her since she had accepted Mr Shy's commission was gone, replaced by a sudden, confident energy. Once again she felt part of something vital, important, and most of all, immi-nent. Slipper, momentarily cowed by her sudden appearance amid the wreckage of the pottery, now perceived that mischief was the surest means of obtaining a really thrilling walk, and he raced around her, barking and encouraging her to venture closer to the river, where he understood water voles were sometimes found.

The kneeling figure trimming the rough grass around the head-stone ignored the sound of a banging gate and hurrying feet. Only when he had completed his task did he sit back on his heels and toss his shears onto the ground. 'You're late.'

'Yes, I am sorry,' Mary acknowledged, trying to catch her breath.

'And I see you've brought the dog.'

'I was obliged to – I mean, I take him about with me so often. I thought it best that I not do anything out of the ordinary.'

'There's something in that, to be sure. Only see that you keep a good hold of him. He looks a bit too forward with his teeth for my liking. Well now, good afternoon to you, Miss Finch. I'm pleased to make your acquaintance at last.'

'And I yours.'

Romney gathered his tools, rose slowly to his feet, and shuffled to the next marker. 'This is my employment for the afternoon. Parson's paying me sixpence.' He indicated the headstone, an impressive piece of white marble whose effect had been marred by a pronounced lean, and explained, 'This one here'll take some time. Perhaps you'd like to keep me company?'

'Yes, of course,' agreed Mary and, dragging Slipper away from a particularly interesting smell, she sat down on the bench beside the grave.

Romney set to work, in that he turned away from Mary and made as if he had resumed his trimming. In fact, however, only a few blades of grass fell with each snip of his shears. 'I doubt anyone passes by,' he warned, still not looking at her, 'but just you keep watch.'

'I shall,' she replied, glancing about her cautiously. 'And Slipper will no doubt warn us if anyone draws near.'

'Aye, well, he's good for sommut, then. Now, let's get ourselves clear on the generalities, so to speak, before we move on to particulars. This is what we call an exceptional situation, talking direct like this. It won't be usual, and it mayn't happen again. Too risky for the both of us. For regular communications we'll use the System.'

The System, Romney explained, involved two stages and was not difficult for a body who paid attention. If Mary had any information to convey, she must first notify him by placing her Spanish dollar in the crack at the base of this particular headstone. Then she must leave her actual message, clearly written, behind a loose brick in the church wall that he would show her. She should try to leave her message promptly, but only if she had a safe opportunity for doing so. If he wished to communicate with her, he would use the same routine.

Romney continued tidying the area in front of the headstone, raking away twigs and leaves with his thin, gnarled fingers.

165

'Right. Are we finished, then, or have you aught for me straight off?'

Mary cleared her throat. 'Well, I have noticed a few things. I cannot tell whether they are important, of course.'

Romney shrugged; or rather he wriggled his shoulders impatiently. 'Just you go ahead and tell me, miss, and let me be the judge of whether they're important. Routine of the house seem regular?'

'Yes, very. Apart from the . . . *Indian*-ness, everything seems perfectly normal. I have been able to look through most of the colonel's desk. There is only one drawer he . . . keeps locked.' Mary found herself growing warm; it sounded so nasty when one spoke openly of it.

Romney did not share her qualms. 'And?' he prompted.

'He has a London newspaper sent down, and he seems to keep a very close watch on events. Although I suppose—'

'Anything in particular catch his eye?'

'Yes – political meetings. Meetings of the government – of ministers, I mean, or of the Privy Council, but also public lectures, especially those having to do with foreign trade. He often marks the reports of these meetings or underlines particular passages. I believe he made a great deal of money in India, and he may have property there, or investments. He certainly has a great many Indian *things*.' She paused, frowning. 'He has also been following the reports of the Spithead Mutiny.'

'We're all of us keen on the Navy, nowadays. Safeguard of the nation, you know, them wooden walls.'

'Yes, I see your point. And I do not understand how his being in Kent could affect a mutiny in Portsmouth. Besides, the newspapers say that it is almost over. Lord Howe was to go down on Wednesday to tell the sailors that their demands have been accepted, and they will be pardoned if they return to their duty. And if that is so—'

'The trouble at Spithead *is* almost over,' Romney agreed, 'but yesterday morning mutiny broke out among the North Sea fleet at the Nore. That's the big Naval anchorage at Sheerness – on the Kentish coast.'

'Ah, I see.'

Romney shrugged. 'Well, your eyes is better 'n mine, perhaps. But perhaps not. This *may* be what our friend is aiming at, in some way or t'other.'

'Does—' Mary consciously lowered her voice, 'does *Mr Shy* have agents in Sheerness?'

Romney looked at her for the first time during their interview. 'Best not to mention that name, miss, ever. And don't you mind too much about Sheerness neither. Our job's Crosby-Nash. Mutiny means naught to us, unless it means aught to him. That's what you must find out – whether it does.' He waited until Mary nodded and then continued. 'Now, it seems to me that we must try to open that other drawer – the one he keeps locked. Tell me about his desk. Anything unusual about it? Not one of his foreign pieces, is it?'

Mary did not believe it was. As far as she could remember, it was a perfectly ordinary gentleman's desk – rather large, with drawers on either side, and a shallow one in the centre. She thought it was made of mahogany with an inlaid top.

This description pleased Romney; he would not have liked to suggest the best method for tackling a foreign piece of furniture, which might have any number of clever safety features. Opening the drawer of an English desk, however, ought not to be beyond his – or Mary's – powers. He produced two keys, one of which he said would probably do the business. Each had a long cylindrical shank and a single, not very prominent, tooth. 'Try this one,' he advised, as he handed over the first, which was slightly larger and had a plain bow. 'You may have to wiggle it a bit in the lock, mind, so be patient, but if it doesn't work, try t'other.'

He also advised removing the central drawer and feeling along the inside of the desk for a catch or spring that might control the locked drawer. 'Whatever you do, don't go trying to force the lock,' he warned. 'Likely as not you'll mark the wood, and our friend will notice. We don't want him to begin looking over his shoulder, you know.'

'No, indeed not,' Mary agreed. 'Thank you for the keys, and I will do my best with them.'

'And there's another thing,' said Romney. 'Let's suppose that some particular friend of the colonel's was to turn up at the Hall. Don't run away with the idea, but we ought to know what they talk about.'

'Yes, I thought about that when Dr Chalmers came to tea – not that I imagined that *he* was likely to be involved in anything underhand, but I wondered how might I find out if he were? The colonel would keep any important conversations private, and he would hardly invite me to join them in the library.'

'Library, is it? Well, maybe I can get you an invitation. Won't be comfortable, mind, but it ought to serve our purpose well enough . . . if you're keen.' He glanced at Mary a second time. 'Ever heard of a priest's hole, Miss Finch?'

She nodded, and her spirits sank as she guessed what was coming. 'A secret room where a Roman Catholic priest could hide – built in the days when it was illegal for them to be in England, or when they were suspected of treachery.'

'That's right. Well, I know sommut of Champian Hall, and I can tell you that there's a priest's hole in the room above the library. A little place, with papered walls, last time I seen it.'

'I know the room you mean, It contains a great many Indian things that have no proper place – a sort of lumber-room. It is not much used.'

'All the better. Now, this priest's hole isn't very comfortable – it's a *hole* – but it's hard up against the chimney, so anybody inside ought to hear a deal of what's said in the library, what with the echoes.'

'Yes, I see.'

Romney caught the anxiety in her voice. 'You wouldn't mind creeping into a small, dark place in the floor?' he asked. 'Might make a body a bit fearful, all on her own in a place like that.'

'I think it probably would,' Mary admitted, 'but . . . if you can explain exactly where it is, and how I may find the way in, I could . . . try it.'

Romney watched her, his speculative expression gradually giving way to one of approval. 'It's only if someone *does* come, of course, any likely sort of visitor.'

168

'And you mustn't forget to explain how to let myself out afterwards,' she added, smiling wanly. 'I would not like to be locked in.'

'No, indeed. Don't want you turning into the ghost of Champian Hall, now do we?'

11

Mary was able to put her burglaring skills to work two days later, thanks to the colonel's decision to pay a visit to Tunbridge Wells. No sooner had she waved good-bye to her host and hostess than she was hurrying to the library, armed with Romney's special keys.

She softly closed the door and proceeded to the colonel's desk. Having moved the chair carefully to one side, she knelt down and surveyed the several drawers. First, she removed the central drawer and felt along the inside of the frame, fingering the runners on which that drawer moved, and even peering up at the underside of the desktop. It occurred to her, fleetingly, that this would be the most terrible moment to be disturbed, as there could be no possible explanation for her behaviour. Fortunately she was *not* disturbed, and Slipper, her accomplice and look-out, wheezed drowsily on the carpet. So she moved on to the next stage of her investigation, opening the locked drawer itself.

The slightly larger key, which Romney had suggested she try first, proved too large, but the smaller one slid easily into the lock. *Now what?* thought Mary, *twiddle it, I suppose, for it is not the proper key and must be made to work . . . secretly.* Not quite knowing what she was doing, she eased the key slowly, this way and that, all the while careful not to damage the lock in any way. The muscles across her shoulders tensed as she imagined the colonel returning and discovering that the lock was broken, or had been tampered with.

If this does not work, you must simply explain to Mr Romney that you could not manage it, she reminded herself. *Better that than make a mistake.* She leaned down, close to the floor, so that she could observe the keyhole closely as she manipulated the key. Suddenly, the lock gave a faint click and the key turned smoothly. Success! And with a smile of triumph she removed the key and pulled open the drawer.

Inside was an oddly shaped box whose decorations reminded her of the Indian containers she had already seen at Champian Hall. The lid was stiff, but when she eased it open she found a fabric wrapper, and inside that what looked like a brick. It was dark brown, with a firm, slightly sticky consistency, and a strong, sweet smell. Was it sugar? Or perhaps an Indian spice? Slipper had come over to investigate, and when Mary offered him her finger to lick, he declined. 'You are right,' she agreed, replacing the fabric and sealing the box. 'It certainly does not look very nice.'

Beneath the box was a stack of papers, and Mary examined these with more interest. Unfortunately, apart from a few marginal notations, they all appeared to be written in a foreign language . . . *whatever language they use in India*, she suspected, for certainly the swooping, curling script looked like nothing she had ever seen before. Seeing it now was extremely vexing. Mary had experience in decoding documents, but she doubted whether she would have much success attempting to translate an actual language! She might, conceivably, *copy* the documents and pass them on to Mr Romney, but that would be a lengthy, dangerous task. Perhaps—

Her thoughts proceeded no further, for suddenly Slipper thrust his head into the drawer and emerged with a piece of leather in his mouth. 'Oh! What are you doing?' she cried, lunging at him. 'Give me that!'

Amazingly, he did so, dropping the item just in reach of her hand, but then he compounded his crime by barking furiously and dancing about in passionate excitement. 'Stop! Quiet!' she

171

hissed, paralysed by a sudden fear that the uproar must bring the servants.

She scowled at him, listening keenly for any approaching footsteps, and then glanced at the leather strip. It appeared to be . . . yes, it was one of Slipper's collars, which explained his excitement upon seeing it. In the country he was generally allowed to run about off the lead, whereas in London he was subject to a more strict control. *But how strange that a collar should be kept under lock and key*, thought Mary, and she turned it over in her hands.

It was then that she noticed the collar's particular feature. It was somewhat wider than would have been expected for a dog of Slipper's size, and was made of two pieces of leather sewn together, one on top of the other. The outside piece, however, had an opening that extended to almost the full width of the collar – an opening large enough to . . . She fastened the strap to form a loop and considered it again. *Could anyone really hide something in this collar?*

Slipper lay with his head on her knee and gazed up at her hopefully. Smiling faintly, she slipped the collar over his head and watched him as he scrabbled to his feet and began to cavort and shake himself. In her mind's eye she was seeing his similarly energetic performance in Green Park, how he had run away . . . and been recaptured. *Of course! The man who brought him back. Oh, what a blind fool I have been! I thought nothing amiss because he spoke only to Susannah, but of course his message had been conveyed in the collar. And that man – I wish I had noticed his features more particularly! Slipper probably knew him and came when he called. The biting seems rather . . . but Slipper tries to bite everyone.*

The latter point was proven almost immediately, as Mary's efforts to remove the collar provoked a growl. At that moment, however, Slipper's teeth were a mere trifle. The evidence of the collar reminded her of other things that had happened in London – including the visit to the jewellery shop in Birchin Lane. Perhaps Miss Trent had also communicated a message for the colonel in ignorance. Very likely she had done that very thing. It would have been a simple matter to provide her with

172

a jewellery box with a false bottom. *I knew there was something odd about that business!* 'Hush,' she commanded, and dampened Slipper's ferocity with a swat on the nose.

Even as she was restoring the contents of the drawer and fumbling with the key, Mary was mentally drafting her report to Romney. She would mention everything – the man in Green Park, Hardy & Son's, the coffee houses that Colonel Crosby-Nash frequented, even Mr Doyle, the painter. *He will probably turn out to be the biggest villain of the lot!* she complained, ruefully, as she dragged the desk chair back into place.

Her excitement at discovering something, at last, was tempered by dismay and embarrassment at having proved such a careless observer thus far. Who could tell how much she had missed? *Well, I have learned my lesson – in future I shall report everything, and leave nothing to chance.*

After her discovery in the library, Mary found the next two days singularly dull. She did not see or speak to Romney, so she could not tell whether he was impressed with her dexterity in opening the locked drawer, or annoyed at her failure to understand the Green Park incident straightaway. And while she had not imagined that Colonel Crosby-Nash would actually *look* at all different, now that she had discovered another of his secrets, she wished he would not continue to behave so unexceptionally. To the world he was the perfect host, landlord, and gentleman. Mary suspected, but could not yet prove, that the image in each instance was counterfeit.

When she came down to breakfast on the third morning she was disappointed not to meet the colonel, whom she wanted to study, surreptitiously, before he became engrossed by the rent rolls. A question from Susannah, however, breached the gloom. It was a lovely morning, she said, and she meant to pay a visit to the parson directly she finished her boiled egg. Would Mary like to accompany her?

If she were being perfectly honest, Mary might have declined, but three contrary thoughts in quick succession prompted an affirmative answer. Firstly, one oughtn't to spend such a lovely morning wholly indoors; it was bad for the digestion, as Miss Marchmont said. Secondly, Mr Garbett, the incumbent of St Stephen's, had the reputation of an active gentleman and so was unlikely to have moist hands or a lisping, tremulous manner with visitors. He might even have a sense of humour, which was always an asset when discussing Worthy Things. And finally, Mary's interest in Colonel Crosby-Nash had caused her to neglect Susannah, and it would be too bad if a friend's innocent happiness had always to take second place to secrets and stratagems.

Such was Susannah's delight at the prospect of her company that Mary experienced a pang of guilt at the ordering of her three thoughts, and she resolved not to think about the colonel for at least the next hour. At first this proved difficult, for Susannah's manner as they made their way to the parsonage obliged Mary to acknowledge a dismal contrast. Susannah was light-hearted and cheerful; her very person seemed lifted by the spring sunshine . . . and freedom from the colonel's dampening influence? Then too, as they neared their destination, Mary could not help but recall her most recent visit to St Stephen's, and as they passed through the churchyard she looked surreptitiously for Romney or some evidence of his presence.

Once ensconced inside the parsonage, however, Mary was able to make good her pledge. Mr Garbett not only confirmed his reputation for activity, his kindliness also impressed his visitors. While not an accomplished orator, he spoke earnestly about his plans to assist the poor children of the parish. There was a village school of sorts, where his daughter endeavoured to teach the younger ones their letters, but so much more might be done. A proper schoolmaster, perhaps, to provide instruction in mathematics; a supply of books, slates, pens and paper; even a dedicated school building. At present, the scholars of Saxonhurst were obliged to meet in his own poor parlour, which could barely provide sufficient chairs, and was woefully deficient in desks and other pedagogical equipment. Did the ladies recognise his plight?

They certainly did. Mary was cast back to her previous life

as a schoolteacher, and she found herself regretting that her stay in the neighbourhood must be a brief one and dedicated to other matters. Perhaps she *ought* to have encouraged Miss Trent and Miss Marchmont to accompany her, for those two stalwarts could have done such a lot of good with whatever tools were to hand. At least more appropriate tools might be provided, however, and she and Susannah were keen to contribute financially to Mr Garbett's endeavour. If anything, Susannah was more adamant than Mary that something substantial must be achieved for the children, and she stressed her husband's interest, as well as her own.

'Indeed, ma'am, I am glad to hear you say so,' replied Mr Garbett, 'for I had conceived the opposite from my discussion with Colonel Crosby-Nash on the subject. Undoubtedly, I misunderstood him.'

'I think you must have done,' Susannah agreed, 'for the colonel has often spoken of the importance of education, and it is surely our duty, as Christians, to help those less fortunate than ourselves.'

Mr Garbett was reassured by these words, but Susannah seemed to grow vaguely uncomfortable as the discussion turned to practical matters: what ought to be purchased first, how much it would cost, and whether other notable members of the community might also contribute. Her promise of support never wavered, but gradually it became clear that her husband's involvement might be of a somewhat ephemeral nature. He was so busy and came down to the country to rest; perhaps they ought not to bother him. In fact, Susannah had money of her own, and that might be the simplest way to proceed. Mr Garbett need not mention the precise figure to the colonel.

Mary's heart sank as she listened, both out of sympathy and a fear that she could provide little else for her friend. In principle she resented any notion of bullying, and were she in Susannah's place, she would feel compelled to take a stand against the colonel's apparent tyranny. But she was *not* in Susannah's place, and drawing attention to the situation might serve no other purpose than to increase Susannah's distress. In the back of her mind, too, Mary feared that any disruption of the Crosby-Nash household might jeopardise her own work. The thought that she was indeed sacrificing Susannah's happiness for the sake of a criminality that she had not proven, added to her own despondency. It did not, however, provoke her into speech.

If the discussions with Mr Garbett ended on a restrained note, Susannah at least brightened again on their homeward journey. She was keen to be doing something useful, and she spoke of giving Champian Hall a proper airing. 'I do not mean to criticise Mrs Saunders, but some of the rooms have a peculiar . . . foreign sort of smell.'

Mary knew perfectly well what Susannah meant by a 'foreign smell'. She had noticed it herself; a thin, pungent aroma, particularly in the library, but she certainly did not want to acknowledge any special knowledge of that room. She replied, therefore, with the gloomy thought that even in this trivial matter she could not be honest with her friend. 'I suppose that foreign things smell different, just as they look different. If we were to send an English sideboard to India, the people there would doubtless think that it was very odd.'

'Yes, but why should not *English* things remain in England, and *Indian* things remain in India?' asked Susannah. 'Then we should all have exactly what we like. One is ever so much more comfortable, having familiar things about.'

'Oh, but I enjoy looking at foreign things,' Mary admitted, relieved to find herself on firmer ground, 'though I agree that it would be better to see them in their proper setting. Perhaps Kent is not . . . I have never travelled, you know, and I should dearly like to visit India – and other foreign places.'

'Really?' asked Susannah, the surprise and disbelief evident in her voice, 'but it all sounds so strange and dangerous! People there are always being eaten or carried off by demons—'

'But those are only fairy tales!'

'Well, yes . . . but I am certain that the snakes are real.'

'As are the elephants; I think it would be worth a great many snakes to see an elephant. And there are so many other interesting things . . . I daresay the food is different in India — I should certainly like to try that — and do not forget the beautiful silks that the colonel showed us.'

Susannah had her doubts about the cuisine of Calcutta, but she gave way before Mary's enthusiasm. 'There is also the colonel's special tea, which makes one intelligent,' she added. 'That comes from India.'

'Tea that makes one intelligent?' echoed Mary, surprised in her turn. 'I have never heard of such a thing.'

'Oh yes,' said Susannah, laughingly, 'but it does not seem to work on me. I daresay you are right about the other Indian things, however, and the silks *are* lovely. In any case, I mustn't be parochial, particularly in front of the colonel's friend.'

Mary's expression looked her question, but she asked it nevertheless. 'The colonel's friend?'

'Why, yes. Did I not mention him? We are expecting him today.'

With those words Mary's heart began to beat faster. She struggled to speak temperately. 'I did not . . . Do you . . . know who it is?'

'I have never met him,' Susannah acknowledged, 'but he is a friend from Town. His name is Phoebus — or that is how the colonel referred to him. I suppose it must be a sort of nickname, for no one could really be called *Phoebus*, could he?'

'I would not have thought so; I expect he has a . . . sunlit personality. But you know, perhaps we ought to hurry. It would be very impolite if we were not at home when he arrived. He is your first official visitor at Champian Hall, you know.' Mary had to resist the temptation to seize Susannah by the hand and tow her forward. *A friend from Town called Phoebus. What could be more intriguing?*

'Well, I suppose so,' said Susannah, frowning. 'But *Phoebus*. I do hope that he is not a poet, or something difficult like that.'

His name was actually William Legg, but Crosby-Nash introduced him as 'Phoebus', and Susannah privately decided that 'Mr Legg' would not have sounded much better. He did not look particularly radiant; tall, thin, and somewhat round-shouldered,

177

as if he were conscious of his height and wished to lessen it. Long black hair scraped into a queue rendered the contrast with his pale face more pronounced.

Mary greeted him politely, saying that she was very pleased to meet him, as indeed she was. 'You . . . have business in Town, sir?'

'Of a sort, Miss Finch.' He had a mellow, soothing voice and pale, soft hands.

'Phoebus is a barrister,' Crosby-Nash explained, 'and a very good one. But as he is determined to confine his practice to the criminal bar, he is unlikely to make his fortune by it.'

'Surely bringing justice to one's fellow man is preferable to facilitating the transfer of estates between idle, profligate families, whose wealth alone distinguishes them from other malefactors,' Phoebus replied.

'Oh,' murmured Susannah, duly cowed.

'I think I would also want to bring the character of one's fellow man and the size of the estate into the reckoning,' remarked Crosby-Nash, 'but I shall not engage you upon philosophical topics, for I know from long experience that we are bound to disagree.'

'I have never been able to understand the law,' Susannah admitted. 'There is the difference between right and wrong, of course, but the law makes everything very complicated.'

'Indeed it may do, ma'am, when employed by the misguided or the dishonest.'

Although uncertain whether Phoebus was agreeing with her, Susannah nodded and sought to bring her friend into the conversation. Mary, she asserted, found the law very interesting. Having no wish to become the focus of attention, Mary swiftly demurred, but Susannah was determined to be helpful. 'She has met the attorney general.'

'A very formidable gentleman,' Phoebus allowed, 'but I cannot say that we see eye to eye on a great many subjects. The complexity that you mentioned just now, ma'am, which obscures the plain distinction between right and wrong – Sir John Scott is its foremost proponent. Do you know him well, Miss Finch?'

As he turned his gaze upon her, a gaze that was much keener than before, it occurred to Mary that she must be careful. This interest in the attorney general might be wholly professional, but there was no need to emphasise her connection with Sir John. 'Oh no,' she assured Phoebus. 'We met at the duchess of Gordon's rout. Do you remember how hot it was, Susannah? He is . . . from somewhere in the North, is he not?'

'Newcastle.'

'Ah, that would explain it. He told some amusing anecdotes – at least, I believe they were amusing, for I could not always understand the dialect.' She shrugged modestly.

Phoebus nodded. 'He can be rather droll.'

'Humour; excellent,' pronounced Crosby-Nash, clapping his friend upon the shoulder. 'There is good even in an attorney general.'

That remark signalled a shift in the conversation to less contentious topics, a move that both Mary and Susannah, for different reasons, were happy to support. When remarks upon the weather and the beauty of the Kent countryside reached their natural conclusion, the gentlemen took their leave. The colonel explained that he and Phoebus had business to which they must attend at some stage, and they might as well do so straightaway.

Left to themselves, Susannah said something about fresh linens while Mary wondered how quickly she might follow the two men. She felt a pleasant shiver of excitement at the prospect. *Perhaps this is what it is like to gamble for high stakes!* It was hard to wait patiently until Susannah had finished whatever she was talking about and left the room, but Mary managed it. No sooner was she alone than she climbed the stairs and hurried along the passage in the other direction.

She stopped when she reached the upper storeroom and drew a deep, steadying breath. Then, opening the door, she stepped inside. It was a strange, silent room; a haphazard arrangement of furniture, ornaments, and packing crates, with half-drawn draperies that obscured the light. *Oh, who is—* Then she breathed again. It was only Durga, one of the colonel's

Indian goddesses. She was rather imposing, nearly four feet in height and riding on a lion. There were weapons in five of her six hands – the other held a severed head – but she was still only a statue and could tell no tales.

Mary had located the priest's hole after her meeting with Romney and even peered inside, but that was all. Now it occurred to her that she did not like small, dark places, and she particularly did not like the idea of climbing down into this one. But she *must* discover what Phoebus and Crosby-Nash were saying. Her very mission was to uncover that sort of information. How did she expect to do it if she hung about, too fearful to take up her post?

Steeling herself, she crept down the steep, narrow steps, her feet feeling the way. Now her waist was level with the floor, now her shoulders. Now she must close the door over her head – that was much harder. She felt again for the latch that would enable her to open the door from the inside. Would she find it again in the dark?

Closing the door cut off the last rays of light, and now she descended, slowly, by touch alone. The air was dusty and had a stale, dry odour, and presently she began to experience a strange, unreasonable sensation, as if the passage were somehow shrinking around her. Despite telling herself sternly that this was nonsense, the unreasoning, fearful part of her brain would not permit her to venture farther until she had held out her hand to prove that the rough wall had not moved in the darkness. *There,* she concluded, *nothing whatsoever to be frightened of, and really quite easy, when you remember the poor Fathers who were obliged to hide here for hours or days at a time!* She hoped they *had* been poor Fathers, wishing only to practise their vocation, and not papal assassins or revolutionaries hoping to blow up Parliament.

The sound of muffled voices, and perhaps Mary's unspoken admonitions, helped to restore her composure. *You are here to listen, remember, and not to ponder priestly inspiration.* Close on her left side was the coarse stonework of the chimneybreast, and at her feet she could see the faint hint of reflected light.

She was inside the wall of the library, beside the fireplace. Now the voices were quite audible; she could even place them in the room. Crosby-Nash was on her right-hand side, probably sitting at his desk; Phoebus was in front of her, in one of the comfortable chairs. There was a moderate thud; that would be Slipper, jumping down from the sofa.

From the tone of the men's voices it was clear that their conversation was not altogether friendly, as brusque, apparently awkward questions from Crosby-Nash prompted sulky, defensive replies from his visitor. It took a few exchanges, however, before Mary could understand the substance of their remarks and realise that she was indeed on the brink of something important.

'And yet all of this failed to move them.'

'No, no,' Phoebus complained, 'it was not like that. I would have succeeded – my fellows *did* make some headway, but the timing of the thing was wrong. I had so little warning that a mutiny was imminent; there was not time to plant the necessary seeds. We were constantly reacting to events . . . and once Lord Howe arrived we were lost. He is a kind of hero to the sailors, and I simply could not compete. It was "Good old Black Dick, he'll see us right. He won't let us down." Of course, Howe is merely the tool of ministers, but the sailors could not see it. In the end, they threw away their chances.'

'And may do so again at Sheerness.'

'Possibly, but the situation there is wholly different. The leadership is of another stamp, for a start, and I have had time to plan things more carefully. You are a great one for finding fault with what has already occurred. It is easy to be wise after the event.'

'Yes, and wisdom at some stage is better than none at any time. The mutiny at the Nore looks to provide us with a second chance, and it oughtn't to be squandered. If you had discussed it with—'

'With the rat-catcher? I do not like him.'

'I know you do not, but that does not make him worthless. His situation gives him access to information and to individuals in authority. It is always well to know what is taking place in the enemy's camp.'

Phoebus made a scoffing sound, and Mary could imagine him waving his arm in a dismissive gesture. 'I have a more valuable weapon than the rat-catcher.'

'Indeed?'

'Yes, *indeed* – the Irish.'

Now it was Crosby-Nash's turn to jeer, but Phoebus carried on, undismayed. 'The Irish are the key to everything, I tell you. They are here in great numbers, and every one of them has at least a rudimentary knowledge of the political situation. They understand their own interests and are willing to do something to achieve them. It is the best thing about the government's outrageous conduct in Ireland.'

'What do you mean?' asked Crosby-Nash, grudgingly.

'Why, the law that allows Irish magistrates to send any man suspected of Republican activities to the fleet! Not *convicted*, mind you, but merely *suspected*. It is rank tyranny, of course, but it has provided me with the sort of men I need.'

There was a creaking sound, as if someone had shifted in his chair. 'Rank stupidity, certainly, to expect such men to fight enthusiastically for England.'

'Precisely. And as for the rat-catcher, I do not believe that *his* operation has been particularly successful.'

'No, I—' began Crosby-Nash, before continuing more warily. 'What news do you have?'

'Only that there were definite signs of unrest, but the soldiers have failed to take the logical step to active rebellion.'

'They failed to act or they were not sufficiently encouraged to do so?'

'My men did their job, I can promise you that!'

'Well,' muttered Crosby-Nash, 'it is early days yet.' Then he added, 'I do not suppose there is a great population of *Irishmen* currently serving in the Foot Guards?'

Phoebus paused before answering, and even at her distance Mary could sense his displeasure. 'Not quite so many as are in the Navy,' he acknowledged, sullenly.

'No,' snapped Crosby-Nash, 'so we can plumb no deep well of Irish political wisdom, nor depend upon a display of righteous Irish fury. Perhaps the Guards are rather a more difficult nut to crack than your sailors?'

'Perhaps.'

'Yes, and perhaps careful coordination was even more important for this operation to succeed. Some of us were very keen that it *should* succeed.'

'As was I,' Phoebus protested. 'And something may still come of it, as you say. My men have not given up — far from it. But if my plans for the Nore bear fruit, any early . . . setbacks will be forgotten.'

'*Your* plans? Which you mean to keep to yourself, I suppose?'

'Initially, yes. Security does not flourish when a campaign is widely discussed.'

'And security, doubtless, is your motivation. I do not dispute the point,' Crosby-Nash urged, as the other man strove to defend himself. 'Not in the least. And as for your gangs of ill-used Irishmen, I admit that there is something in what you say. They are probably suited to the atmosphere you will doubtless encourage at Sheerness. For myself, I prefer passion when it is allied to calculation, but . . . perhaps that can be called upon another time.'

'You are contemplating another project?'

'Perhaps. But I shall say no more at present. Security, you know.'

Phoebus did not comment, or at least not orally, but after a short silence Crosby-Nash spoke a word — or a name — that Mary did not understand. 'Rabellay' — or it might have been 'Roblay' — was also keen that they achieve the desired results. Something in his tone, a hint of menace, caught Mary's attention, and she tried to listen more closely. 'You saw him in Town, I suppose?'

'Mm.'

Crosby-Nash chuckled. 'Did he frighten you? You needn't deny it,' he advised, as Phoebus tried to speak, 'for I can see that he did.'

'I have no wish to deny it. Of course he has been very helpful, but sometimes—'

'Sometimes you wish that you had never made his acquaintance? You ought to have known him in the old days, when his ambition extended only to himself. He used not to be keen on the reformation of society, you know, unless he could increase his profit thereby.'

'He is very greatly changed, then.'

'Indeed. But now that the two of you share the same philosophy – democracy, and equality, and the rights of the people – your relations ought to be extremely cordial.'

'They are,' Phoebus protested, 'and I have the greatest admiration for him. He has made many sacrifices – of a great fortune, it is said – only, sometimes I think that he is . . . that he goes too far.'

Crosby-Nash chuckled. 'Well, Robespierre is his model, you know. When Rabellay returned to France, the Incorruptible was at the height of his power.'

'Incorruptible he may have been,' agreed Phoebus, 'but terrible too, and in the end he paid the price for it.'

'Rabellay is too clever for that. He can sense treachery at a very great distance.'

'Oh! I did not mean to suggest—'

'Of course not,' said Crosby-Nash, his voice silkily reassuring. 'No one could accuse *you* of a lack of enthusiasm. You would do well not to disappoint him, however.'

'I do not mean to. But I am curious – you seem to know him very well, and yet you have little sympathy with his— with our cause.'

There was a pause, during which Crosby-Nash might have shrugged or shaken his head. 'We are old friends,' he replied. 'Or rather, business associates of long standing.'

'Does that mean that you are more or less afraid of him?'

'Neither. It means that we know each other's methods, and each of us understands how dangerous the other can be.'

12

Colonel Crosby-Nash was sitting at his desk, sorting his post and sipping a cup of his favourite tea. It was an idiosyncratic blend, flavoured with saffron and honey among other things, and as well as enjoying the taste, he found that it helped him to think. Not that he required any artificial stimulant. He had expected that the arrival of Phoebus would herald some new development – news, at the very least, but this had not occurred. Nothing had been disclosed about the situation in London that he had not already learned from elsewhere. *No, as usual the fellow has been a damp squib.*

He glanced quickly at a message from a local worthy – *surely Susannah can reply to this* – and tossed it aside. The next was a letter from Mr Garbett on the subject of tithes. The colonel had not realised that either the parson or his patrimony was in any way his concern. Was the living in his gift? *Why do they expect me to resolve their problems whenever I come down? Does everything in this place hang fire while I am away?*

He was replying to Mr Garbett when a sturdy knock on the door prevented a curt observation on the subject of those whom God could be expected to help. 'Yes? Come in.'

The man who entered was Lockwood, the butler. He was small, neat, and smooth-faced, with a knack for knowing when he was needed – in short, a very efficient servant. He had come down to Kent along with several other members of the

185

Scarborough House staff and, while in no way *of the country*, he had adapted effortlessly to life on the estate. 'I beg your pardon, sir, but I wonder whether I might bring something to your attention.'

Crosby-Nash set down his pen. 'Of course,' he replied. Lockwood had served him for many years, and in varied circumstances; he was unlikely to waste time with trifles.

'Thank you, sir. It's to do with George, sir. You remember, the second footman we took on some months ago?'

'Yes. A fellow with particular skills, as I recall, though I cannot say very much for his work in the . . . domestic sphere.'

'No, indeed, sir. Rather a rough customer, and I have always assigned him to somewhat menial tasks . . . away from the silver, shall we say. However, this morning he informed me of a singular incident which − if true − might have serious consequences.'

'Very well,' said Crosby-Nash. He sat back in his chair and listened to the report, carefully and distinctly presented by his subordinate. At its conclusion his face was stony. 'This could indeed be serious,' he agreed.

'Yes, sir.' Lockwood was standing in front of the desk, and he absently straightened the books that were propped in the corner nearest to him.

'What was George doing at St Stephen's? He does not strike me as a praying man.'

'Well, sir, I do not like to say,' replied the butler, diffidently, 'but I understand that Miss Garbett, the parson's daughter, is quite an attractive young person.'

'I see.'

Presently, Crosby-Nash rose and went to the window. There was Phoebus, standing within an arbour of roses and honeysuckle, oblivious to the bees flying industriously from blossom to blossom. The colonel supposed he ought to inform his guest of this latest development. Nothing had been proven, of course, but if George were correct, they would all be in danger − their plans possibly discovered and studied, and their alliances known. The very fact that Phoebus had come to Champian Hall could now constitute a danger to the rest of them.

No, no, you are making too much of this, Crosby–Nash warned himself. *Let us suppose that George is correct — that does not mean that our situation is desperate, merely that you rightly anticipated the dangers. You expected to attract attention and took the necessary steps; why should you be dismayed if the hounds have come sniffing? Let them. Let them howl, if they like.*

Without turning he said, 'Tell George to keep his eyes open, and to inform me straightaway if he discovers anything else. I shall have orders for him shortly.'

'Yes, sir.'

'And Lockwood . . . tell him also to mind his manners with Miss Garbett.'

On Saturday afternoon Phoebus departed for Sheerness. His destination was not announced, and Mary had gleaned it by hovering as nearly as she dared during the past two days, hoping for any whispered words between the two men. Now, as she stood in the stable yard with Susannah and Crosby–Nash, waving farewell to the departing carriage, she reflected on the falsity of her position. She was treating Phoebus as if he were an ordinary houseguest when she knew he was nothing of the sort, just as she knew the colonel was no ordinary host. *And I am the same*, she mused, *no true guest, bound by the laws of hospitality, but a sham, a counterfeit. We are all three playing a kind of awful game. Only Susannah is honest and genuine, and everyone condescends to regard her as a simple soul. There is something to be said for being too 'simple' for such studied deceit as the rest of us practise.*

The two men had certainly played their parts very well. Mary knew from the conversation in the library that Crosby–Nash did not like Phoebus, but nothing of this had been apparent in his public demeanour. Neither had he revealed anything of his secret activities. The colonel's steward had come to see him about the recurring problem of damp in the Champian Hall cellars, and it had been very difficult to discern in Crosby–Nash any feeling other than the anxiety of a homeowner. Outside the library, too, Phoebus had shed his sulky, diffident manner. He had made himself comfortable, and seemed to have taken a casual remark about his health so much to heart that he had done little more than walk in the garden, or try to make polite conversation with the ladies.

The exchange in the library, therefore, comprised the sum of Mary's information. *If only*, she brooded, *I could have discovered something more*. It was clear that Phoebus had been involved in the Naval mutiny at Spithead and now intended to take a hand at the Nore, but what was to be the colonel's role? He was privy to the lawyer's activities, but his own interests seemed to lie elsewhere . . . perhaps with 'the rat-catcher', who also seemed to be involved in a different scheme. Both Phoebus and the colonel were under some kind of obligation to a man called Rabellay, who sounded as if he were the most dangerous of them all. Might he be the French agent whom Mr Shy was seeking? Mary had included all of this in her report and deposited the roll of closely written paper behind the loose brick in the north wall of St Stephen's. But how helpful was any of it?

She would have liked to speak with Romney about the significance of her discoveries; partly, she admitted to herself, out of a base desire to be complimented, but more to maintain a sympathetic contact. She did not regard the grumpy tinker as a friend, exactly, but they were at least engaged in the same task. It was easy to feel isolated at Champian Hall, and Romney was experiencing the same hopes and fears. A conversation with him was dangerous, however, and not to be indulged in without some particular, pressing need. She had seen him once or twice, when she walked into the village or along the river. They never spoke, however, and an observer seeing them pass each other in the lane would not have guessed that they were in any way acquainted.

Slipper, as anyone who knew him could attest, was very enterprising. Every morning he presented himself first in the kitchens and then in the breakfast room, with the knowledge that titbits were likely to come his way by chance. He returned to his post for each subsequent meal, and in the evening he liked to go for a run out-of-doors. The latter exercise was in addition to any he managed to coax out of Mary, for he had come to realise that she was not keen on vermin hunting, or on excursions that involved getting very dirty or rolling in unpleasant substances. As all of these activities were very dear to him, therefore, he was obliged to undertake them alone.

Dusk was generally the best time for ratting, but this could not always be managed, and Slipper was on the alert for any chance. On returning from a morning walk, therefore, he dodged Mary's attempt to wipe his feet and darted back in the direction of the stables. From there, further opportunities for exploration might present themselves.

Mary called, but with little expectation that her words would have any effect. 'Oh!' she fumed. 'You are the worst, most disobedient . . .' She supposed she really ought to track him down, but he had already been so badly behaved that morning that she refused. He would doubtless return when he pleased, and if some bigger dog came along and ate him up in the meantime, it would be no more than he deserved.

She had forgotten all about him when, an hour or so later, he sought her out, apparently anxious to renew their friendship. She was sitting in the upstairs parlour, sewing a lace border onto an old collar. Her seat near the window also afforded her an excellent view of the lawn, where Crosby-Nash was studying the water level in the moat. 'So, you have come back, have you?' she asked, as Slipper sidled guiltily into the room.

Turning back towards the window, she watched as Baxter, the estate steward, joined his employer on the lawn. Baxter had a notebook, from which he was reporting. Crosby-Nash stood with his arms folded across his chest, then rubbed his chin, then began to walk up and down in a deliberate manner. Baxter displayed a greater energy, pointing down at various undulations in the ground and up at sections of the wall. His gesture took in the house itself, and Mary withdrew quickly behind the curtain.

'Oh, what *is* it?' she cried, for Slipper was pawing insistently at her ankle, and when she bent down, he scrambled onto her lap. This action surprised her; he had never before made any such demonstration of affection. Nor did affection quite seem to explain his present conduct. He was uneasy, and when she stroked him he shivered beneath her fingers.

'What is the matter, Slipper?' she asked, frowning down at him. 'Very likely you have eaten something nasty, you greedy animal.' Thinking that her lap was not the best place for him if he were going to be ill, she attempted to return him to the floor, but this caused a yelp of protest, and he snuggled more closely into her arms.

'Well, you are a funny one,' she remarked. 'You do not usually like to be held. And now you are distracting me.' A second attempt to move him produced the same result, and she was obliged to submit. He quieted after a time, and she resumed her observations. What she saw almost made her laugh. The two men were staring down into the moat, Crosby-Nash leaning so far forward that he almost tumbled in. Then they both looked up into the sky, and then just as earnestly into the water. Old Tom, the gardener, joined them, and all three performed the same ritual.

Mary expected another repetition when Lockwood, the butler, made his appearance, but either the contents of the moat held no interest for him, or he was less easily diverted from his duties. He stood slightly apart, bearing a tray and waiting to be noticed. Mary looked on more interestedly when she perceived that the tray contained several letters. Surely it was unusual for the servants to follow Colonel Crosby-Nash about the estate in order to present him with his post? Had he given special orders? Was he expecting something particularly important?

She watched as the colonel opened and perused each letter in turn, and tried to control her agitation. It was not possible to read his expression at such a distance, and he made no obvious gestures. He seemed to hesitate over one document, and her hopes rose, only to fall again when he said something to Baxter and passed him the paper. An estate matter. Another letter he

190

returned to its envelope and replaced on the tray, and the next received the same treatment. A slight breeze made Lockwood clap his hand on top of them to prevent them blowing away.

Crosby-Nash unfolded the last piece of correspondence. It was a mere note, unsealed, and apparently dashed off hastily on a page torn out of a book. He read the contents, and then glanced at the butler. 'I do not suppose there has been quite as much work for the staff as we expected when we came down to Champian Hall, has there, Lockwood?'

'No, sir, that is so. It has been a very quiet visit.'

'George, for instance. I daresay he has generally been twiddling his thumbs.'

'Well, sir, I believe Mr Baxter has occasionally found work for him in the stables, but for the most part he has had little to occupy his time.'

'Hmm, I thought so, and I doubt that mucking out the stables is precisely to his liking. Better tell him to go back to Scarborough House. I doubt we need him here.'

'Very good, sir. When shall I tell him to set off?'

'Oh, as soon as he likes . . . and I have letters for London that he can take with him. Tell him to report to the library before he leaves.'

'Yes, sir, and I am certain that George will be grateful for your consideration.'

The colonel received this compliment with the nod of a benevolent employer, and then he and Baxter resumed their estate discussions. Lockwood withdrew, and eventually Crosby-Nash came inside.

Dinner was a largely silent meal. Susannah's usual fund of small talk seemed to have been exhausted, and when neither her host nor her hostess was inclined to speak Mary felt awkward attempting to fill the breach. Crosby-Nash rose quickly from the table, saying that he wanted to have another word with Baxter. Apparently, several large branches had fallen into the moat and would have to be recovered. The drainage was being affected.

Concluding that there was nothing to be gained by remaining indoors herself, Mary decided she might as well make the most of the early evening sun. She was still feeling magnanimous towards Slipper and called to him to accompany her. He answered, but not with his usual enthusiasm. 'You will feel better once you have had a run,' she assured him. 'We shall go down to the river, and you may frighten the ducks.'

At first her confidence appeared well-founded, but as they drew closer to the river Slipper began to behave oddly. He kept close beside her, whereas usually he charged ahead, jealous of any new sight or smell. When she chided him he only gazed up at her, shivering faintly, until she was convinced that he really was unwell. 'I am certain it is your own fault,' she remarked, but her voice lacked authority.

Frowning, she turned away from Slipper and towards the water. Two men, whom she recognised from the mill, had landed their boat on this side and were lifting something out of it. Their burden looked like a sack of some kind, or a large piece of cloth with something underneath. Whatever it was, it was heavy. One of the men slipped, and then Mary saw a hand. They were carrying a body.

'Oh!' The exclamation was automatic, and the men noticed her for the first time.

'Afternoon, miss,' called one. Mary thought that his name was Henry. 'Here's a bad business.'

The sun was shining brightly, but she felt very cold. She walked towards the two men and what lay upon the blanket between them – she could see now that it was a blanket with one half turned over – hardly aware that she was doing so. How could she possibly recognise a hand? A pale, grimy hand, emerging from a bedraggled sleeve? But she knew whose it was. 'What— Who is that?'

'Old tinker feller,' replied Henry.

'Is he . . . dead?'

Dead. Dead. Dead. Of course he is dead. The words rang ominously in her head. She was quite close now, close enough to recognise Romney when the blanket was turned back, despite

192

the grey, waterlogged features and the ghastly wound to the head. There were straggling bits of weed in his hair, and green slime on the front of his jacket. She shut her eyes, her lips pressed tightly together against a wave of nausea.

Then the other man was speaking. He was called Bill. 'Old tinker feller,' he repeated. 'Bin hangin' about.'

'Yes, I know. What—' She steadied herself. 'What happened? I mean, do you know what might have happened to him?'

'Must've fell into the mill pond,' said Henry.

'Or slipped,' Bill suggested.

'That's right, fell or slipped, and got pulled under by that old wheel.'

'She's mighty strong,' Bill added. 'She did for him all right.'

'What he means, miss,' explained Henry, 'is that old wheel done give the poor chap's head a fearful crack, and that likely did for him. And then he was drownded besides,' he added, completing the grisly account.

'Yep, and drownded besides.'

Mary became aware that she had not taken a breath for a very long time. She took one now, but it provoked the strangest sensation: a roaring in her ears, and a tingling feeling in her hands and feet.

'You all right, miss?' asked Henry. 'You look terrible pale.'

The question seemed to have travelled a great distance before it reached her. Nevertheless, she replied, 'Yes, I am quite all right. It is only . . . Where are you taking him?'

'Well, we didn't rightly know *what* to do,' explained Bill, 'but we didn't dare leave him where he was, that's for certain. So we thought as we'd take him up to the church. Mr Garbett'll know what to do. He'll hafter see to him, any road.'

'He . . . he was quite an old man, really. He oughtn't to have been—'

'What's that, miss?' asked Henry.

Mary started. She had not realised that she had spoken the words aloud. 'I only . . . I hope he did not suffer. But,' she bit her lip hard, 'he must have done.'

Henry considered her dispassionately. Her colour was not of

193

the best, and he hoped she was not going to have a fit or something like that. Women did have fits, sometimes. 'You best cut along now, miss, and not think o' such things. He's out of it, poor chap. We'd see you safe home, only, we oughter take care o' this here.'

'No, no,' Mary assured them, shaking her head. 'It is very kind of you, but do carry on. I shall be quite all right.' It seemed as if it were another person speaking; she did not recognise her own voice at all.

She stood to one side, and they passed by. Henry, however, was not pleased with the situation. 'You didn't oughter have showed her, Bill, you silly buzzard. What was you thinkin' of? Showin' a poor drownded feller with his head all caved in to a young lady. I never heard o' such a thing.'

As the sound of his voice faded away, Mary sat down slowly, heedless of where their wet boots had muddied the ground. And this time when Slipper crept onto her lap she did not push him away, but hugged him in silent consolation.

Holland awoke in the middle of the night with the strong feeling that Mary Finch was in trouble and wanting him. A moment's reflection convinced him that neither of these contingencies was very likely and, after telling himself not to be a damned fool, he turned over and went back to sleep.

When he awoke a second time it was morning, and he had forgotten all about it. Instead, he was thinking about his task for the day, which had to do with rifles. A well-constructed rifle could fire further and more accurately than could a musket, and the Army was interested in expanding its use of such weapons. Or perhaps it was safer to say that some gentlemen in the Army were interested in considering the possibility of expansion, while others complained that rifles were expensive things and temperamental, while the ability to fire from extreme range would not encourage the proper degree of fortitude in the ranks. The desirability of a 'rifle policy' lay with Horse Guards and the War Office; its practicality was a matter for the

Ordnance. Could rifles of adequate quality be produced economically and in sufficient numbers?

As with most proposals of a tentative, speculative nature, no one knew the answer to this question, and Holland had been ordered to find out. He was off to London, therefore, to discuss the matter in a tentative, speculative way, with Mr Nock, Mr Manton, and Mr Baker, three of the most knowledgeable gunmakers in the capital.

'Jack of all trades, that's what you are,' Holland informed his reflection as he adjusted his stock. 'Jack of all trades and master of bloody none. Any little job they need doing, and you're for it.'

Regiment-issued shoes clattered up the stairs, followed by a swift triple knock and Drake's muffled announcement, 'Boat's at the quay, sir.'

'All right,' called Holland, trying to keep the gloom out of his voice.

Drake followed Holland down the stairs and then fell in step beside him. 'Lovely morning, sir,' he observed, conversationally. 'Ought to 'ave a nice smooth run into Town.'

Holland nodded, and Drake could not suppress a smile. Most people who travelled between Woolwich and London did so by water. There were plenty of boats making the journey, the fare was cheap, and if one were careful with the tide it was simply a question of pulling in on the rise and out on the ebb. Nothing could be simpler. Captain Holland, however, did not see it that way. He preferred to ride or travel by coach, despite the considerable time, effort, and expense involved.

And why? Drake shook his head. *Because 'im and boats don't mix, that's why. Poor old Captain Haitch. Put 'im in a boat and 'e's gone green in ten strokes. Don't matter if it's flat as a millpond – and Gawd 'elp 'im if there's a bit of a swell.*

Because Holland's first appointment today was an early one, he had decided to brave the river, although it meant arriving at his destination unwell and in a foul temper. More foul than usual.

'Got them sketches to show Mr Nock, sir?'

'Of course I've got them,' snapped Holland.

'Yes, sir.' *Already workin' 'imself into a state,* mused Drake. *Well, leastways he won't be 'eld up forever with the traffic on London Bridge, like last time. Poor bugger.*

They reached the quay, and Holland turned to Drake. 'Sorry about that.'

'Oh, don't you fret, sir.'

Holland considered the boat below. To his critical eye it seemed to be rolling a great deal. God, he hated boats – and water.

''Ere's luck to you, sir,' said Drake. 'In your discussions, I mean.'

The discussions went well, but it rained steadily throughout the return journey, so that when Holland disembarked late that afternoon he was soaked as well as queasy. Having breathed several deep, steadying breaths on solid ground, he set off quickly towards his quarters. He was eager to set his thoughts down on paper and conscious that such notes as he had taken were decidedly damp. Fortunately Drake had a fire going, and for the next two hours Holland sat at his battered deal table, gently steaming, while he sketched rifle locks, recorded stock dimensions and relative levels of recoil, and considered the efficacy of rifled pistols as compared to their smooth-bore counterparts.

Drake brought him his supper and took most of it away again, muttering that them wot sat about in wet clothes and ate no supper were asking for the influenza, just asking for it, and what use was any sort of gun against the influenza?

'Leave it, then,' replied Holland, not looking up from his work. 'I'll eat it later.'

'You can't eat food wot's meant to be 'ot after it's gone stone cold,' Drake complained from the passage, in the tone of one reciting a known dietary law. 'Ain't 'olesome.'

'Well, then get me a drink – tea, if you're so worried about influenza. But put something in it so I can get it down,' Holland added, smiling to himself.

There was no immediate answer, but presently Holland heard the sound of voices. Then Drake opened the door, his grievances apparently forgotten. 'Mr Dalton for you, sir.'

'Evening, Bob,' called Jack Dalton, entering the room and making straight for one of the elderly armchairs. 'Thought I'd check up on you before heading home. Speaking of which, we must have you to supper again. Kitty would love to see you.'

Mrs Dalton – Kitty – was an attractive, silly, feckless woman, and Holland did not care for her. He cared even less for her sister, whom Kitty was always promoting as a worthy object of his affection. As a result he rarely visited the Daltons' crowded, untidy cottage in Woolwich town, and the two men tended to see each other on occasions like as this one.

Holland dipped his pen and continued writing. 'Wait a minute – I'm almost done.'

Dalton sighed and stretched his legs in front of him. 'I've spent the entire day behind a desk, and no sooner do I close up shop, feeling pleased with myself, than I find you still toiling away. What is it?'

'Nothing. A report.' Holland gathered the sheets into a stack and placed the empty ink-bottle on top as a paperweight.

'It'll keep, then. If you finish it, they'll only give you another. Say, did you get those epaulets for me from Hetherington's?'

'No.' Holland paused and then added, 'You couldn't afford them, so I got you a pair at Davenport & Gilpin's. The gold will probably rub off, but they were half the price.'

'Ah, well, by that time I will have so distinguished myself that vast sums will be showered upon me by a grateful nation.'

Rising from his work, Holland intercepted a steaming mug from a tray carried in by the silent Drake. Then he went and stood beside the other armchair; he was tired of sitting.

'Hot tea with whisky and lemon,' mused Dalton, taking a sip. 'Well I never.'

'You ought to – it's probably your whisky.'

'Hmm, probably. I must remember to collect what you owe me before we sail.'

'Orders not changed, then?'

197

'No, *if* the Navy can find a loyal ship to take us, of course. That's the latest word. Then begins the great Western Adventure.'

While his friend joked about what the future might hold in Canada, Holland saw the next several years stretching dully before him. Not for the first time he thought of resigning his commission and returning to India. The pay would be better, and he would not have to wait another ten years for a command. The regiment was too damned slow, and there was nothing else for him in England – nothing that he would permit himself to take. True, Dalton and Kitty seemed happy enough, but that was different . . . *they* were different, or rather, the two of them were alike. No, that wasn't true either, for Kitty was surely not her husband's equal in character or intelligence. *But he can look after her*, concluded Holland. *He can trust himself to do that, and so can she.*

Getting away would certainly make things easier, and he liked India, particularly the India that he remembered. He forced himself to do so, and for a few moments he was transported to a wholly different world. Only Dalton's words, '. . . too slack – it's not good for the men,' brought him back to his dingy quarters.

'*Slack?*' Holland demanded. 'The Warren? I never see a party of men unless they're at drill.'

'Yes, infantry drill, most of them,' agreed Dalton. 'Might as well be foot-sloggers as gunners. But what do you expect with officers like Adair and Fanshawe, who take no interest in their companies and leave everything to the subalterns and the sergeants? And what is there for all of us to do, really? We're too many, and we've no prospect of a real job. No wonder the men complain, and when they go into the town they cut up worse and worse.'

'Don't remind me. But *are* they complaining?'

Dalton shrugged his shoulders. 'Mine are all right, but they know they're off soon. I wish the War Office would pull its finger out and put things on a proper footing again – some-where – and stop this mucking about. Are we at war or aren't we, for God's sake?'

'I think— Yes, what is it?' Holland called, at the sound of a respectful knock.

Drake slipped into the room. 'Sorry to bother you, sir. Colonel's compliments, and would you come along to the laboratory?'

'What the—' muttered Holland, placing his empty mug on the mantelshelf and buttoning up his waistcoat. 'There aren't any tests going at this time of night.'

'No, sir,' Drake agreed. 'It's, ahem, *'is office.'*

Holland grimaced, and Dalton laughed unsympathetically. 'I think I'll push off, Bob. Looks like you're in for a roasting from the old man, and that will doubtless take some time.' He finished his drink and handed the mug to Drake. 'Must have been neglecting your duties again.'

Holland presented himself at the office of Colonel William Congreve, comptroller and superintendent of military machines, and took a deep breath. He was conscious that he had done nothing wrong, and that he generally got on well with his chief. There was no reason why this interview, despite its unseasonable time, should cause him apprehension. He told himself this as he knocked at the door. Nevertheless, he knocked warily.

Colonel Congreve was sitting at his desk, hands folded, and flanked by a pair of shaded candles. Their light wavered as Holland stepped inside, and he took in his surroundings with a quick, sweeping glance. 'You sent for me, sir?'

'Yes, Captain Holland. Good of you to come so quickly.' Congreve nodded at the well-dressed officer sitting opposite. 'You know Major Whittington, I understand?'

'Yes, sir. Good evening, sir.' Holland kept all surprise, all familiarity, out of his voice.

'Sit down, Holland, sit down,' frowned Congreve, gesturing fussily at an empty chair. 'Major Whittington is here from Horse Guards with a rather . . . unusual request.'

'Perhaps I ought to explain, sir?' suggested Whittington. 'Captain Holland and I are friends, but he is not acquainted with the precise nature of my work.'

'Ah, no, certainly not,' Congreve agreed. 'Well, carry on.'

'Thank you, sir.' Whittington turned to Holland and smiled briefly, while keeping his expression wholly professional. 'I work for General Dundas, in the . . . confidential office. My job, just at the moment, is the investigation of certain individuals and groups in this country that pose a grave threat to our national interests.'

Holland tried not to stare at his friend. General Dundas was the quartermaster-general, the Army staff officer responsible for the movement and quartering of troops. In the nature of things, however, not all of these troops were directly involved in fighting. Some did reconnaissance work, investigative work, intelligence work – what the uninitiated might broadly describe as spying. And when supervision of these activities had not been delegated elsewhere, as sometimes happened in the field, it was the responsibility of the quartermaster-general.

'We are particularly concerned with what appears to be a plot to undermine loyalty and morale across the service,' continued Whittington. 'It is known that intriguers attempted to influence the mutiny at Spithead, and there have been other worrying developments in the Army.'

Whittington paused. With Congreve also mute, Holland felt compelled to make some contribution, however little he wished to speak. 'Developments, sir?' he asked.

'Yes. Attempts to seduce the men from their duty. Sometimes the aim seems to have been merely to dishearten our chaps – they are told what a miserable job they have and reminded of the fact that they have not been paid in months, that sort of thing. But sometimes more serious arguments have been advanced. The men are assured that a fundamental political change would improve their lot. If this country were governed according to Democratic principles, not only would liberty reign and the streets run with milk and honey, but poor fellows such as themselves would not be obliged to fight the French, who are really their brothers in the struggle for liberty.'

'Are the men listening to that sort of thing?'

Whittington shrugged. 'There have been some serious murmurings. About a fortnight ago, we learned that a mutiny would shortly take place among the Guards regiments. Fortunately, we prevented an actual outbreak, and the matter is being dealt with, but the *possibility* of such a thing, let alone its imminent prospect, is deeply troubling.'

It was more than troubling. The Guards protected London and what was of essential importance in London: the Mint, the Tower, the Houses of Parliament. If they proved unreliable, or worse, seized places on behalf of men hostile to the government, the situation would be extremely perilous. Moreover, instability in the capital could trigger unrest elsewhere. The Navy's problems had already spread from Spithead to the Nore, and a general rebellion within the armed forces did not bear thinking about. Once such a cancer became well entrenched, how would it be excised? By force? Even assuming that the loyal men could be identified, there was nothing so inimical to soldiers as an order to fire upon their own comrades.

Holland instinctively turned away from such a vague, speculative problem. 'You said "intriguers" – do you have any idea who they are?'

'Yes, and that is why I want your help.'

'*My* help?'

'My office believes that you can assist my investigations. You see, there are several individuals – those who might be described as the small fry – whose activities can be watched by the usual means, but supervision of their chief requires a different approach.'

'Supervision,' repeated Holland. 'You mean *spying*?' He glanced at Congreve. The colonel was aware that Holland had been directly involved in the Déprez affair, but they never spoke of it. No one was supposed to speak of it. 'But I don't— I've never—'

Congreve raised his eyes at last. 'I have explained to Major Whittington that espionage is not exactly our line of country, but this particular matter is apparently exceptional.'

'Quite,' agreed Whittington. 'Let me explain, sir. This man, the one we consider the chief of the operation, is Colonel Arthur Crosby-Nash.'

201

'Oh, Christ,' breathed Holland, and then he added to Congreve, 'Crosby-Nash is married to my cousin, sir.'

Congreve pursed his lips. *'Colonel?'*

'East India Company, sir.'

'I see. You have met him?'

'Yes, sir, briefly. I wouldn't say I'm *acquainted* with him at all.'

'But Captain Holland's relationship with Mrs Crosby-Nash means that he could observe her husband at close quarters without exciting suspicion,' continued Whittington. 'They are in Kent at the moment, and Holland might pay them a visit. Once on the premises . . .'

'Yes, yes, I take your point,' acknowledged Congreve, quickly, as if he did not want to have matters explained to him in any great detail.

'What is more,' added Whittington, 'I think it highly likely that my enquiries will take me shortly to Sheerness and the Navy's current problem. You may know that Sheerness is to be fortified, in the event of the situation not being swiftly resolved. The assistance of an artillery officer would be invaluable to me. He could move among the defenders without exciting suspicion – as well as lending his professional expertise to the defences, of course. Admittedly, any competent officer could perform that task, but Captain Holland's qualifications with respect to Crosby-Nash render him uniquely suitable.'

'It seems a very long shot,' grumbled Congreve, 'but . . . what do you say to all of this, Holland?' He gazed piercingly at his subordinate. 'Are you keen to go?'

It was a question, but one whose answer was clear. 'Yes, sir.'

'Very well. Major Whittington has managed to get everything signed and sealed, with orders so opaque that they do not say a damned thing, other than that I may let you go with a clear conscience. I congratulate you, Major Whittington, on your efficiency, especially as I do not strictly assume command here until tomorrow.'

'Thank you, sir. Official wheels can be made to turn faster, when necessary.'

'Being wheels, that is not surprising.'

'And you have no objections, sir?'

Congreve threw up his hands. 'It is not my place to stand in the way of great and secret undertakings. Well, gentlemen, I believe that concludes our business. Undoubtedly you will want to continue your discussions in private, and I have more mundane work that requires my attention.'

Holland and Whittington rose at this clear sign of dismissal. 'Yes, sir; good night, sir,' they chimed, and the air of formality continued until they had left the laboratory. When the door had closed behind them, however, Holland could no longer contain himself. 'All right, Dick,' he complained, as they set out across the deserted courtyard, 'what was all that about?'

'Sorry to spring it on you,' replied Whittington, 'but these inter-service affairs require careful managing. I had to act through what are known as "the proper channels", and that meant presenting my request – the request of my office – to Colonel Congreve in the first instance.'

'Of course, I know that, but what's going on? Are you really saying that Crosby-Nash is some kind of . . . *revolutionary*?'

'Yes, afraid so, old chap. A very nasty piece of work.'

'And I'm to do what, exactly? Spy on him?' Holland shook his head. 'What made you think that he'd confide in *me*, for God's sake?'

Whittington halted, his hand on Holland's harm. 'You mustn't worry about that,' he urged. 'I will explain everything in good time. It is not quite as mad as you think.'

They walked in silence past the extensions to the foundry, where the secret mortar-boring machines were housed. 'How long have you been on the QMG's staff?' asked Holland, thoughtfully.

'Oh, quite some time. We do not exactly make it a topic of general discussion, you know.' Whittington opened his watch, turning it this way and that in order to reflect the pale moonlight onto its face. 'Look, are you able to leave straightaway?'

'Yes, I suppose so.'

'Good. Collect your things and meet me at the main gate in ten minutes. I will have your horse saddled.'

'But what will we say to Crosby-Nash?' demanded Holland. 'We can't turn up in the middle of the night with no—'

'I will explain everything,' Whittington repeated. 'Only get your things. I have seen the state of your wardrobe – it oughtn't to take you very long.'

'All right, all right,' agreed Holland, turning to go.

'And Bob? Do not speak about this to anyone.'

'Well, I'm not likely to, am I? I hardly know what I'm doing myself.'

13

Holland rode silently beside Whittington. They had left the arsenal behind and joined the Maidstone road. Fortunately, conditions for travel were good, and there was little other traffic, for Holland was concentrating on more serious matters than managing his horse.

'So, you see *I* will be the one endeavouring to obtain information from Colonel Crosby-Nash,' finished Whittington.

'Christ,' Holland murmured, shaking his head. 'And he thinks you're on *his* side?'

'Yes.'

'Does he know who you work for?'

'He is aware that I have a confidential post. I have never provided him with details, other than that I have a certain influence and access to information. That is why he considers me valuable. I am his agent within the government. Using my influence and information, I suggest likely targets, help to advance such schemes as are decided upon, and report on their degree of success.'

Holland thought for a moment. 'Were you involved in the Spithead Mutiny?'

'No. I know a bit more than was published in the newspapers, but not much. My job has been with the Foot Guards. Crosby-Nash wanted something significant in London, and there was talk of a bomb or a fire, even an assassination – something that would produce real chaos. I did not like the sound of that, so I suggested an approach to the Guards instead. Crosby-Nash liked it because of the damage that would result if it succeeded, and from our point of view it was far more *controllable*. As indeed it proved to be.' Whittington smiled briefly. 'I do not say that I had no anxious moments, but in the end all that happened was that we identified a few malcontents, who will be dealt with, and the government has agreed to a wage increase for the Army as a whole. Not bad work, I think.'

'You're damned cool about it all,' said Holland. 'What if Crosby-Nash traces the failure to you?'

Whittington shrugged his shoulders. 'That is the risk, of course, but I believe it is worth taking, for the sake of the information that can be acquired.'

'But why don't you arrest him? You must have enough proof.'

'We do and we do not,' said Whittington. 'I am not privy to everything he does, unfortunately. There is a feeling in my office – and among some of the other intelligence services – that a larger scheme is in the works whose details we do not yet know. The time is not yet judged right, therefore, to move against him.'

'How do I fit into all of this?'

'You are my latest recruit, a gunnery officer with expertise in explosives and—'

'Hold on – you don't expect *me* to help him make a bomb, do you?'

'No, no, he has gone off that idea, thankfully, but your knowledge of fortifications will make you attractive – from his point of view – if he is interested in Sheerness.'

Whittington slowed his horse to a walk and pulled his watch from his waistcoat pocket to study it again. 'Ah, we are making good time. Now look, Bob, when we get to Champian Hall, follow my lead. It is always best to stick as closely as possible to the truth in these affairs.' He frowned thoughtfully. 'You and I are old friends, of course, and you are in dire financial straits. I have promised you a significant sum in return for your help – enough money to see you out of your present embarrassment. Filthy lucre will be your motive, not high-minded principles.'

Holland could feel himself reddening. 'All right.'

'And silence is golden when it comes to Crosby-Nash. Let me do the talking. All you need do is back me up. He is very clever and, well, ruthless. None of this is a game.'

Holland did not answer, and Whittington looked across, trying to judge his friend's thoughts by the quality of his silence. 'You are not very keen on all of this, are you? Sorry I got you into it?'

'No, not really. It's only . . . I know that what you're doing is important, but I don't like it – for myself, I mean. Sneaking about Crosby-Nash's country house, hobnobbing with traitors and trying to wheedle confidences out of my cousin.' Holland sighed and patted his horse's neck. 'But I suppose it must be done.'

'Yes, it must.' Whittington chirruped his horse, and Holland followed. 'Crosby-Nash is more dangerous than any cavalry charge, believe me. I think I can promise you that the next few days will at least prove interesting. That is something, surely? A bit of a change from the sulphur and smoke of Woolwich? And you will have to miss your big parade on the twenty-sixth.'

'What? Oh, yes.' Holland frowned and shook his head. 'I hate those things. All the great men in dress uniforms, playing soldiers again for the day. We had a visit from the Prince of Wurtemburg the other day, you know, and that was more than enough.'

'I thought you might feel that way, somehow.'

'One thing, Dick. I've got to ask – can't we protect Susannah at all?'

'We mustn't do anything that would compromise our standing with Crosby-Nash,' replied Whittington, 'and spiriting away the fellow's wife would certainly do that. However, I do not think you need worry. He has no reason to do her any harm, and neither do we.' Whittington paused, as something else occurred to him. Then he continued, in a neutral tone, 'No, I do not believe either of the ladies is in any real danger.'

'Damn it, Dick, do you mean to say that Charlotte is there too?'

'Char— Oh, yes, the younger sister. No, not Charlotte . . . Mary Finch.'

'*Mary Finch*?' groaned Holland. 'What is *she* doing at Champian Hall?'

'She came down with them from London,' explained Whittington, innocently. 'As a companion for Mrs Crosby-Nash. Did I not say?'

'No, you bloody well didn't.'

'Well, I am sure I meant to – it must have slipped my mind. And you needn't sound so gloomy. I should have thought the prospect of seeing Miss Finch would affect your view of our mission in quite the opposite way. The two of you can renew your common interest in poetry. The work of Pope, was it not?'

Champian Hall, when they reached it, was dark and silent. Crosby-Nash himself unbolted the door and, after a slight delay, Holland was shown to his bedchamber by a yawning, half-dressed footman. Whittington would also have liked to retire for the night. For all that he had made light of the dangers of his situation, they were very much in his thoughts. He was also aware that he was tired, and that fatigue often led to mistakes. Nevertheless, when his host suggested that they take 'a glass of something', he smiled cordially and accepted.

Once in the library, Crosby-Nash settled into his usual place behind his desk and motioned Whittington to a chair opposite. There was no fire, for the night was warm, but the curtains were drawn, and lighted candles on the desk and side tables made the room feel cosy, if slightly mysterious.

'Excellent brandy,' observed Whittington.

'Thank you.' The colonel replenished his tea from a small, delicately painted pot and closed the book that lay open on the desk in front of him. 'I presume that you did not bring my wife's cousin here merely for a social visit, but that can wait.' He sipped. 'As I have been obliged to wait. An event of some significance was planned for the twelfth – it is now the twenty-third. By anyone's calculations you have taken the devil of a time to report.'

This was not a particularly auspicious beginning, but it did not surprise Whittington. He had expected to find Crosby-Nash in a tetchy humour, and he doubted whether the substance of his report would improve matters. The question was, should he merely explain or should he attempt to defend himself?

He began to answer before he had quite made up his mind. 'I am sorry you consider yourself ill-served, but I have had other business that could not be put off without attracting attention to myself. You received my letters, I suppose?'

'Yes, and found them insufficient. What I wanted was a full report explaining the action – or rather *inaction* – and submitting recommendations as to how we might recover the position. I have heard from Phoebus – more than once – gleefully recounting his progress at the Nore. There are committees of rebellion in charge of every ship, and the men have free run of the dockyards and the fort at Sheerness.'

'I believe some of those statements are exaggerations.'

'Perhaps, but if they were even a tenth part true they would trump the Guards, and I want to know why.'

'Well, sir, I am here now and at your disposal.'

Crosby-Nash shrugged sulkily but motioned for the other to continue.

Whittington shifted in his chair, crossing one leg over the other in a gesture of casual comfort. 'The story of the Guards is easily told. As you know, their show was intended to begin on the twelfth so as to coincide with the sailors. Unfortunately, the government became aware that trouble was imminent on the eleventh. Despite a lack of detailed knowledge, ministers judged the danger sufficiently grave to warrant a meeting of the Privy Council that evening.'

'Did you attend?'

'Yes, as a sort of observer cum secretary.'

'What was your impression of the occasion?'

Whittington rubbed the back of his neck, considering. He gave a superficial account of the proceedings, naming the ministers in attendance and describing the varied representatives from Horse Guards, the London police, and the Home Office.

'What about a man named Shy, was he there?'

'He might have been. Not everyone was introduced. I remember that name, however: "Mr Shy". He was mentioned, but I could not swear that he was present.'

'Very well. What was decided?'

'To isolate any groups or individuals who appeared to be particularly ill-disposed, without causing public alarm or distressing the majority of the men. The trouble, by the way, seems to have been confined to the 1st and 3rd battalions of the 3rd Regiment, and I imagine they will shortly be re-assigned. On the fifteenth all units were paraded in St James' and Hyde Park and informed that their grievances would be heard and appropriate action taken. In the mean time, ministers hammered out a wage increase that would satisfy the average soldier and not cripple the Exchequer. The announcement will be made in the House tomorrow, which is why I took the risk of coming down.'

'There was a whisper of such an increase in the *Times* – nothing about it being precipitated by any particular trouble, however. And the figure?'

'Well, the government wanted to keep things quiet, and the *Times* was certainly not likely to let them down. When all the stoppages and allowances are taken into account, there will be an increase of two pence per day.'

'Two pence per day – hardly a sum to inspire loyalty, I should have thought. It is surprising how little it takes to satisfy most men. An interesting weakness.'

'One upon which you rely,' said Whittington. For a moment he and Crosby-Nash stared at each other, and the eyes of the older man seemed to issue a subtle challenge. Then Whittington smiled rather sheepishly and added, 'Well, most fellows need money, after all. That is how I was able to secure Holland's services, and I believe—'

'We will consider Captain Holland in a moment,' Crosby-Nash repeated. '*After* the present matter has been dealt with satisfactorily. Why did we fail to achieve our ends with respect to the Foot Guards?'

You mean, 'after you have dealt with it and I am satisfied', thought Whittington. 'As I told you – government got wind of the mutiny. Once that happened I decided it was too dangerous to go forward.'

Crosby-Nash nodded. 'You were probably right. Have you an opinion on how our plans were discovered?'

Whittington hesitated before answering. He wanted to take another swallow of brandy but decided that this would look as if he were afraid to speak. 'There are several possible explanations,' he temporised, 'the most likely being that one of the men spoke . . . unguardedly.'

'So much for military discipline.'

'Yes, but men will talk, particularly when they are off duty and have had a bit to drink. It was always a risk, and . . .'

'*And?*'

Whittington took the plunge. 'And the men Phoebus sent to . . . agitate them were probably not very discreet.'

'They were working under your orders.'

'Yes, but I would never have employed them in the first place! I told you that most of the soldiers did not need to hear all of that liberty nonsense – it only complicated matters – while the presence of known Republicans in and about military premises almost certainly attracted the attention of the authorities. But most importantly, those friends of Phoebus cannot keep their mouths shut – and they were damned careless. I saw some of those "Men of Britain" posters strewn about, and I do not suppose I am the only one.'

'I know you wanted to keep this operation entirely in your own hands,' acknowledged Crosby-Nash. 'Do you think it would have succeeded under those circumstances?'

Whittington shook his head, unwilling to be drawn. 'I can only tell you what I think *did* happen, not what *might* have happened if you had approved a different plan.'

'No, and there is no use crying over spilt milk.' Crosby-Nash sighed thoughtfully. 'It was an opportunity, however.' He sat back in his chair and ran his finger along the rim of the teacup. Then, in a different tone of voice he continued, 'We have had a bit of excitement here at Champian Hall, you know. A government agent has been prowling about the place.'

Whittington started. 'An *agent*? Are you certain?'

'Yes. Elderly fellow, dressed as a tinker. He called himself Romney. One of my servants recognised him.'

'How did your *servant*—'

'The term is but loosely applied – perhaps I ought to describe him as a man in my employ, hired for particular skills. In any event, he had come across this tinker at an earlier stage in their respective careers. Apparently, the old fellow had worked for the Home Office, and elsewhere, in his time, in a confidential capacity. Have you heard of him?'

Whittington's mind was racing – what did this mean? How should he respond? What the devil was the Home Office doing? 'No, but that is not surprising if he worked in one or other of the civilian services. We have little to do with them, as a rule. But what happened? Where is he now?'

'Now? Awaiting burial,' replied Crosby-Nash. 'He met with an accident, I am afraid. I cannot give you the precise details, but he was fished out of the river yesterday with a fatally damaged skull.'

Whittington blew out his breath in an angry gust. 'Of all the—'

'It was not, perhaps, the most prudent course,' Crosby-Nash agreed, 'but the event itself was well-handled, and the only other person privy to the affair is safely returned to Scarborough House.'

'But—'

'The coroner is a man of moderate powers, and I am confident that he will bring in a verdict of death by misadventure.'

'To hell with the coroner! A verdict of misadventure will not satisfy the Home Office! Not if one of their men has been killed.'

'No, I did not imagine that it would.' Crosby-Nash lit himself a cigar, pausing until it was drawing well, and gazed thoughtfully at Whittington through the smoke. 'And then there is the fact that they were sufficiently interested in me to send a man down here in the first place. I do not suppose that you would know anything about that?'

The question, casually posed, created a sudden, cold fear in the pit of Whittington's stomach. '*Me?*' he demanded. 'How dare you! *I* am no traitor—'

'Indeed? I thought that rather unflattering term described you quite accurately.'

'You know what I mean,' Whittington insisted. He felt as if he had been plunged into deep water and must fight his way to the surface. 'Of course I do not express myself clearly – how can I, if you make that sort of . . . outrageous accusation against me?'

'It was merely a question. It was not my intention to startle you.'

Whittington glowered at his host. *You have intended little else since we began.* 'Well then, this is merely my answer. No. I did not have anything to do with it. If you suspect disloyalty, I suggest you look for it elsewhere. Why on earth would I do such a thing? You know the dangers of my situation. The risks for me are increased tenfold if one of the other services has become involved.'

'So much as that?' asked Crosby-Nash in apparent surprise. 'But I take your point – of course I do. You must not be so sensitive.'

'How can I not be sensitive?' complained Whittington. He tried to project a truculent irritation that would mask his actual feelings. 'And I do not understand why you came down here. Leaving Town – it was certain to draw attention to yourself. What does—' he began, but failed to complete the question.

'I came because I wanted a change of scene,' Crosby-Nash replied, 'and because I do not choose to order my private affairs to suit the authorities. They are most welcome to observe me, if it pleases them. They will see that I live the life of a country gentleman – one who is perfectly content to entertain his friends and relations. Which brings us to Captain Holland.'

'Er, yes, Holland.' Whittington had not expected Crosby-Nash to change topics so quickly, but he was not ungrateful. Indeed, he felt as if he had reached shallow water after a long, difficult swim. From somewhere behind him a clock sounded the hour in dull, ponderous tones.

Crosby-Nash smiled and pushed the decanter across the desk in Whittington's direction. 'You are tired, I know,' he remarked sympathetically. 'I will not keep you much longer, but I would like to hear about him. And I am forgetting my manners. Do have one of these cigars.'

Before seeing Champian Hall, Holland had been prepared to dislike it as something belonging to Crosby-Nash. Once he *had* seen it, his dislike increased. He hated the gaudy decoration – not what he associated with 'proper' Indian furnishings at all – and the remnants of Tudor opulence did not improve matters. Mary had likened the Hall to an Indian palace; to Holland it conjured up a very different image.

His memory of the place was clear, although more than five years had passed since he had left India. Perhaps it had once belonged to a prince, but in Holland's time it was known as 'Missie Amber's House', and its residents – 'the little sisters' – dispensed hospitality to gentlemen of the European community in Madras. Missie Amber actually hailed from Shoreditch and had come out to India as a naive young girl attached, more or less, to a minor functionary in the East India Company. At some point he had faded from the scene and, lacking the means and the inclination to return to England, she had gone into business for herself. In the years that followed, her desire to create a vision of the Arabian Nights (her knowledge of geography was somewhat lax), and her inability to pass up a bargain had resulted in her 'House' becoming a strange amalgamation of East and West.

The respectable female section of Madras society had strongly disapproved of Missie Amber and her little sisters, and had thought that her House ought to be closed down. Holland, who had been a young subaltern at the time, had certainly not

214

shared this view. However, he did not now like the idea of Susannah living in a place that reminded him of it so vividly, even though it was not a comparison that she would ever draw. He felt awkward and embarrassed, as if Susannah – and Mary Finch too, for God's sake – had somehow wandered into a place where they ought not to be, and his own presence made it worse.

This particular feeling of uneasiness disturbed him as he came down to breakfast, and when the two ladies joined him his spirits sank further. Susannah maintained a flow of undemanding small talk, but as soon as Holland started explaining his appearance at Champian Hall he found the casual lies, and Susannah's unquestioning acceptance of them, deeply depressing. Mary said almost nothing, but her silence was equally painful. She looked distracted, even troubled, and as she was sitting across from him, he could not help but see her whenever he lifted his eyes from his food.

They were surrounded by the incongruous decorations that everywhere characterised Champian Hall. On one side was an ornately carved sideboard of dark oak graced by two massive copper ewers. A rosewood chair with embroidered seat cushion stood in the window bay, and from this vantage a spectator might observe the breakfast arrangements: a mahogany table set with plates bearing an heraldic device and ebony-handled cutlery. The morning sunlight streamed in through a roundel of stained glass, but otherwise the walls were fitted with leather panels, painted and varnished to represent an exotic garden of twining branches laden with fruit and flowers, while above the fireplace hung a painting of a voluptuous, but no doubt penitent, Magdalene. Nothing he could see encouraged Holland to prolong his stay. On the contrary, he ate quickly and rose from the table with a brief excuse, Susannah's half-heard reply still hanging in the air as he closed the door behind him.

Mary breathed a private sigh of relief. Holland's unexpected visit had thrown her into confusion, and seeing him again, at close quarters, had done little to restore her mental balance. The cool, distant manner he had displayed at the ball was

215

obviously unchanged, but she had never seen him out of uniform, and the plain tan coat and brown breeches made him look even more a stranger, less a person in whom she might confide. Yet confide in him she must − or at least speak with him, but how to do so? Ought she to go after him? *No, that would seem . . . and yet, what is the good in waiting? I am letting 'I dare not' wait upon 'I would',* she brooded, *but what an unlucky quotation!*

Susannah lingered over her correspondence, but there was nothing so tedious, in Mary's current state of mind, as listening to snippets of information about someone else's circle of acquaintances. Pleading a slight headache, therefore, which was close to the truth, she left her friend musing over the competing attractions of the cabriolet and the Chinese bonnet for summer wear.

The great hall was empty. Mary stood before the fireplace, pondering her course. It was not as if she were *afraid* of Captain Holland, she told herself, but perhaps it would be wise to rehearse again what she proposed to say to him. An invigorating walk, therefore, would do her good, and she crossed the hall and passed through the entrance chamber at the front of the house. She rarely chose this direction when in need of exercise, but since Romney's death the sight of the mill, and even the intervening fields, made her uneasy.

Striding purposefully across the front lawn, Mary was brought up short by an unexpected sight. There was Holland, just visible through the gatehouse arch. He was on the stone bridge, forearms resting on the low wall and gazing into the water below. He appeared to be absorbed in his own thoughts, and if she could only slip aside, out of view . . .

The possibility of escape was immediately lost when Holland turned and saw her. It seemed to Mary as though a look of apprehension passed across his face, but if this were so he quickly composed himself. 'Ah, Miss Finch,' he said, straightening up so that now he was facing her, with one hand resting on the top of the wall. She did not answer, and he added, 'I would like to speak with you, if you don't mind.'

216

She approached him slowly, and he thought she was going to refuse, or even pass by without speaking. 'Yes,' she answered, 'but − first *I* must say something.'

When they were standing together the difference in their heights was significant. He was conscious of the light, graceful way she stood, almost on tiptoe, and the curve of her neck, and her upturned face. 'Of course,' he agreed, feeling big and clumsy. 'I—'

'Please, let us go into the lane,' she urged, glancing about. 'We can be more private there.'

Having made her request she set off like a confident general, not waiting to see whether her subordinate would follow and, strangely, despite her earlier uncertainty, she *did* feel confident. She knew precisely what she meant to say, and she had some faith that it would succeed.

Holland soon caught her up, but such was her energy that he remained passive even as he walked at her side. He had been thinking about her on the bridge, perhaps that was why he had turned, but his thoughts had reached no firmer conclusion than that, of all the damned bad luck that had brought him to Champian Hall, finding her there was the worst of it.

They turned right-handed into the lane that connected with the main drive. It was narrow, only accommodating vehicles with careful manoeuvring, and overhung by ivy-covered trees. Here and there wildflowers sprang up along the grass verge, and butterflies darted in and out of the dappled sunshine. Apart from the songs of the birds in the ivy, which stilled at their approach, the only sounds were their footfalls on the hard ground.

Mary stopped when she reached a carved figure in yellow stone. He wore what looked to be a bow across his shoulders, although the top had been broken off, and he was kneeling in a patch of violets. Facing Holland, Mary took a deep breath. 'Captain Holland, you must leave Champian Hall immediately.'

14

The announcement was so unexpected that Holland stared back in surprise and something like bemusement. Then, frowning, he managed, *'What?'*

'You have made a terrible mistake, but it is not too late! Only you must stop now, before there is real trouble.' Mary gazed at him earnestly and, lifting her chin, continued in the same, dogged fashion. 'You ought to have told me that you were in such straits. Regardless of your decision about . . . I would have given you the money – whatever you needed. I will now, only—'

He still did not understand her, but the mention of finances touched a raw nerve. 'What are you talking about?' he snapped. 'I don't want money – not from you or anyone.'

'Please, it is no good blustering, for I know all about it. That . . . *Major Whittington* has convinced you to do something terrible!'

'But how do you— Oh, my God,' Holland breathed, staring first up at the sky and then down at her. 'Did you hear him talking to Crosby-Nash last night? Did he say something about me?'

She nodded solemnly. 'Major Whittington said that you had a great knowledge of weapons, and . . . that you were terribly in debt. He told Colonel Crosby-Nash that if he would pay you, you would give him all sorts of valuable information about bombs, and equipment, and . . .'

Her voice trailed off. Of all the responses that her words might provoke, the one she had least anticipated was laughter. Yet Holland was laughing. It was not a particularly happy sound, but it effectively halted Mary's flow. What was happening? Had she somehow made a mistake? She experienced a strange, vulnerable feeling, as if she had missed the final step on a staircase without a banister.

'Miss Finch,' he said at last, with an ironical smile, 'I'm afraid you've got hold of the wrong end of the stick. Dick – Major Whittington – isn't quite what he seems, and he doesn't always say quite what he means. He has a secret job in the Army. I never knew it until yesterday, when he asked me to come down here and help him *stop* Crosby-Nash. Whatever he said about me was just part of the tale he is spinning.'

'Oh.'

'In fact, he's working to undermine Crosby-Nash while pretending to be part of his gang, which is no easy trick.'

Relief flooded over her. 'He is a spy! Oh, thank goodness!'

'What?'

'Thank goodness,' she repeated. 'Then all is well! I am so very—' She smiled at him. 'You do not know how I worried! You will say I have been a great fool to have been taken in, but *Major Whittington* . . . he does not seem a very likely agent. I would never have imagined—'

Holland could not understand Mary's breezy response. 'Of course you wouldn't. Don't be daft.'

She bit her lip and stared down at the statue. There was a patch of moss on the top of his head, and she rubbed it off. 'It is not *quite* daft, for you see—'

'And if he *did* seem likely, it would mean he wasn't very good at his job. But never mind that now,' urged Holland, his glance moving from the patches of rose on her cheeks to her green fingertips. 'How did you find out what Dick said?'

'Well, you see,' Mary repeated, 'I made a point of listening to them, because . . . I am a kind of spy myself.'

If her first announcement had been surprising, this one left Holland dumbfounded, and now he listened in silence as Mary explained how she had become associated with Cuthbert Shy, and all that had happened since her arrival at Champian Hall. Her account was not altogether coherent; such was her relief at being able to confide in someone, and perhaps in Holland particularly. 'Monday was the most dreadful day,' she admitted in a low voice. 'Finding poor Mr Romney and thinking that were it not for me, he would still be alive . . . and then I was frightened that Colonel Crosby-Nash had discovered that I knew Romney and—'

'There is no way anyone could connect you with him, is there?'

'No, I do not think so, but I could not help worrying that somehow— Then the colonel mentioned that someone was coming – a visitor – and I thought that it might be important, like when Phoebus came. I waited and waited, and then last night . . .' Mary shuddered as she remembered her feelings as she had huddled in the priest's hole and had heard Holland's name mentioned. Shock, dread, and then a numb despair. She had struggled to listen to the rest of the interview, and afterwards, she had been unable to sleep. 'I expect that is why I made a muddle of things today.'

Holland shook his head irritably. 'You weren't to know, but why the devil did you agree to do any of this? Creeping about in secret passages and passing notes. And in this . . . place! All because this fellow Shy asked you?'

'But Sir John said—'

'What,' scoffed Holland, 'that the government had *confidence* in Shy? So much confidence that the attorney general keeps his distance, and no one will acknowledge that he even exists!'

'But he was right about Colonel Crosby-Nash, and I am certain that the government would support whatever—'

'The government won't do a damned thing unless it suits them. Whatever understanding they have with Shy won't mean bug— I mean, it won't stop them from dropping him. Then where will you be? Where are you now, for that matter?' He stopped abruptly. Then he sighed and stood for a moment, not looking at her, his fisted hand tapping against his lips.

Although Mary fervently disagreed with Holland – never having met Mr Shy Holland could not hope to understand him – his words gave her pause. Might it have been foolish to come to Champian Hall, with no one but Romney to help her? It certainly seemed so now. She waited for Holland to regain his temper and continue, but when he did not speak she asked, tentatively, 'What do you think I ought to do?'

He glanced at her. '*I* think you ought to pack this in and go back to Suffolk double quick, but I suppose it's not my decision to make.'

'Oh, yes, I was forgetting. We must consult with Major Whittington, and I may still be of some use here.'

'I didn't mean that, only we don't want to ruin his plans. *You've* got to keep your head down – to the devil with Shy and the rest of them.'

'But what—' began Mary, before remembering that there were some situations when Captain Holland simply would not be convinced, either by logic or intuition. This was probably one of them, as evidenced by his bad language. Swiftly she changed course. 'What about Susannah?'

It was a well-chosen move, for Susannah was something upon which they could agree. No, he did not imagine that she knew anything of her husband's activities, and yes, she ought not to be left solely to his dubious protection. When Holland had acknowledged these points, Mary urged, gently, 'Then, you see, whatever else happens, I must remain.'

He shrugged irritably. 'Well, perhaps. But looking after Susannah is one thing, and spying on Crosby–Nash is another.'

Mary did not challenge this, and instead asked Holland if he would tell her Major Whittington's plans.

'I don't think he has any, other than waiting for Crosby-Nash to tell us what to do, agreeing to it, and then doing the opposite,' said Holland, gloomily. 'I understand that we must learn what he's up to and try to stop him, but I wish there were some better way. I don't like the idea of promising to help a man and then stabbing him in the back. If he's a bas— a villain, I'd rather tell him to his face and have done with it.'

'Yes.' Mary was surprised by the strength of feeling that his words inspired, and she felt compelled to explain her own difficulties, or to attempt an explanation. 'I feel as you do. I thought I would not mind it, but being here makes me feel treacherous, even though Colonel Crosby-Nash certainly does not deserve anyone's loyalty. Then when Mr Romney . . . that frightened me terribly. But at the same time it convinced me that the colonel must be stopped, and I must . . . remain at my post. Only, I did not know how best to do it, on my own.'

Mary had clasped her hands together as she spoke, and now she spread them in a gesture that conveyed both dismay and resolution. She looked so appealing at that moment, her courage making her more beautiful than any ball gown, that Holland felt an almost overwhelming surge of confused tenderness. He wanted to hold her in his arms, to protect her, and to stand with her against any danger. *No, no, that's not the way to help her!* And aloud he said, gruffly, 'Well, you're not on your own now. I— I mean, Dick will know what to do. He generally does.'

'I hope so. It is so wonderful that the two of you have come.'

They lapsed into silence. It seemed to Mary that there had never been a conversation in which so much had changed from start to finish. She supposed that they *had* finished, but she felt worn out and did not want to move. On the other side of the statue, unnoticed in the tall grass until that moment, was the stump of a tree, and she sat down upon it. Holland had retreated a step, and now he stood with his arms crossed, scuffing a stone that was embedded in the path with the toe of his boot.

Mary watched him. '*Dick* Whittington. Of course. He must be "the rat-catcher". That is what Phoebus called him,' she explained, in response to Holland's quizzical look. 'Have you . . . known each other a very long time?'

'Mm.' Holland dislodged the stone and kicked it across the path. 'Since before I went to India.'

'How did you meet?'

Holland glanced at her and then at the ground. A small bird fluttered into the undergrowth at the edge of the path and then, greatly daring, hopped into the open to retrieve a seed. It stared at him and then flew away. 'The first time I ever saw Dick he was having dinner. He was just like he is now, ordering all sorts of special dishes, and he sent the wine back twice. As we were the only officers present – I was a cadet, actually, and he was newly commissioned – he asked me to join him.'

Mary was looking up at him, her hand shielding her eyes against the sun, and she nodded politely. 'That was very generous of him.'

'It was,' Holland agreed, 'except that . . . except that neither of us had the money to pay the bill.'

'Oh.' Mary flinched with embarrassment. Of all the unfortunate topics! But she must not let his statement hang in the air between them. Lowering her gaze she murmured, 'What did you do?'

'Dick huffed and puffed. His father is a viscount, and Dick must have thought they would be grateful for his custom – but they weren't. They threatened to lock us up until someone responsible came along and paid the bill, but we managed to talk them out of that. In the end I gave them every penny I had, and Dick left his watch as security for the rest. I walked back to Woolwich, I remember, and was barely in time for morning parade.'

'Oh, dear.'

'It was worse for Dick, really. He was mortally offended when they wouldn't take his note of hand.' Holland smiled briefly. 'And we've been friends ever since.'

'A friendship founded in adversity.'

'That's right.' Holland glanced back in the direction of Champian Hall. 'I think the others will be up and about by now, and we don't want to attract any attention.'

'No,' agreed Mary, rising to her feet. 'You know, whatever I thought about Major Whittington I would still have told you everything. Why I was here, I mean.'

'And if Dick and I *had* been in Crosby-Nash's pay?'

'I thought I could convince you to stop . . . though perhaps I was not so sure about Major Whittington.' They were walking

223

side by side, and she smiled up at him timidly. '*You* might have had to speak to him.'

'Ah. I'm glad I don't have to.'

'I am sure you would have succeeded . . . but I must have sounded terribly foolish.'

'No, you didn't.'

'And what I said about . . . money,' she continued, dropping her voice at the final word. 'I beg your pardon for implying— I hope you were not offended.'

'No,' he assured her. 'Don't think about that anymore.' But he did, long after they had parted.

It was not immediately possible to discuss matters with Dick Whittington. When they returned to the Hall he was closeted with their host, and when he emerged the presence of Susannah rendered all private communication impossible. In the afternoon Holland was summoned to the library in his turn. Chafing at the continual delay, Mary resolved to take matters into her own hands, and she asked Whittington whether he would care to take a turn with her in the garden.

At first he seemed distracted and not wholly listening to what she said. Something in her tone, however, or the fixity of her glance, gained his attention. Having assured himself that Susannah was not watching them, he flashed Mary a knowing smile and said he would be delighted. There was nothing he liked so much as a well-kept garden.

His attitude was still buoyant when they stepped outside. While Mary attempted to prepare herself for what might be an even more awkward conversation, Whittington drew her arm confidently through his and led her along the path towards the sundial. 'Ah,' he cried, 'and what have we here? An interesting motto, I daresay.'

'I— I believe it is Marvell,' stammered Mary. '"*Time's winged chariot*".'

Whittington nodded. 'Yes, Marvell – capital poet, I have always thought. "*The grave's a fine and private place, But none, I think do there embrace.*"' He smiled at her and decided that she was really very pretty, especially when she blushed, and he did not generally care for redheads.

'No, indeed. Certainly not. Major Whittington, I must tell you—'

'Yes, it is *mea culpa*, I am afraid,' he laughed. 'But do say you are not too displeased.'

'Displeased?'

'With me – with Holland – with seeing him again. It is my fault that he is here, you know.'

'Yes— I mean, *no*, I am not displeased.' Mary frowned, considerably flustered at this surprising announcement. 'But I—'

'Good. I would not upset you for the world, you know, and neither would he.'

'No, of course not, but— Oh, this is *not* what I wanted to speak to you about!'

'It isn't?'

'No.' She slid her arm free and stood facing him. 'It is something much more important. It is,' and she lowered her voice, 'to do with why *you* are here.'

Whittington's smile remained, but the light behind it dimmed. 'Why *I* am here?' he repeated, airily, but he blinked twice, as if disconcerted.

She nodded, and in the moments that followed their positions reversed, as with every word he grew more astonished and she more confident. She began with an explanation of her own position. After this, Holland's disclosure of his and Whittington's activities would seem more natural, and less like a breach of confidence on Holland's part. She could not have said why that point was important to her, but it was.

Whittington, however, let it pass without comment. He was more interested in Cuthbert Shy. 'Well, God bless my soul. You have actually met the old bogle! What is he like?'

'I could not really say,' she admitted. 'You do not feel quite at your ease with him, but he is . . . You want him to think well of you – or at least *I* did.'

'The best generals are like that,' Whittington agreed, 'and I suppose he is a sort of general to his agents. Crosby-Nash asked about him last night.'

'Yes, I remember, and it frightened me. Do you think he suspects that Romney was working for Mr Shy?'

'He has no reason to – his question was probably asked out of curiosity. We are all curious about Shy, you know, those of us who have never met him. When you are in the priest's hole, can you hear *everything* that is said in the library?'

'Yes, so long as whoever it is speaks up.'

'Well, I am sorry I gave you a fright,' said Whittington with a thin smile, 'plotting away with Crosby-Nash, but you have had your revenge. Now, let us continue our walk and, if you will be so kind, I should like to know what else you have discovered about our host.'

Whittington listened attentively, and his incisive, prompting questions impressed Mary. Clearly, he was not so frivolous as her earlier meeting with him had suggested, although he liked to present himself in that light. His explanation of 'Rabellay', which he corrected to 'Rabelais', focussed on his having once read a very scandalous book by an author of that name. 'My tutor was a broad-minded fellow, and apparently this Rabelais was a great Humanist who tweaked the noses of the Sorbonne, and the Catholic Church, and everyone else who was stuck in the old ways of thinking. I am afraid the philosophical side of the book was lost on me at the time, but I had never read anything so . . . well, peppery. Made quite an impression on me.'

Mary did not quite understand the reference to peppery literature, but decided not to enquire further. 'But who is *our* Rabelais?'

'I have never had the pleasure of meeting him, I am afraid, but he is the spider in the web. Phoebus and Crosby-Nash set plans in motion, but only with his approval. I wish I knew more. I have tried to sound Crosby-Nash, but you seem to have learned something of him yourself.'

'Well, he is French, I believe,' said Mary. 'I guessed that from what the colonel told Mr Phoebus, and now that you say that the *real* Rabelais was a Frenchman, it must be so. And besides that—'

'It is difficult to imagine treachery on this scale, involving all our armed forces, and the French *not* taking a hand,' finished Whittington.

'Yes.'

'I would like to know how the colonel became entangled with an admirer of Robespierre. Phoebus is easy to explain, but I could have sworn that Crosby-Nash cared neither for republic nor monarchy, except as they allowed him to make money and spend it without losing his head.'

'That is exactly what the colonel said about Rabelais!' cried Mary, 'that he used not to care for anything but making money. They were business associates, apparently, which seems rather odd. I had understood the colonel to have made a fortune in India, somehow, but could a Frenchman have worked for the East India Company?'

'No, very likely not,' replied Whittington, thoughtfully, 'but I know something about the colonel's career that might throw some light on the matter. His commission was in the Bengal army, and for some time he was stationed near a place called Chandernagar.'

'Yes, he has spoken of it — apparently there is very good tiger hunting in the neighbourhood of Chandernagar.'

'I daresay that was not its only attraction. As you may know, the French were pretty much thrown out of India in the last war, but they were permitted to retain a few trade centres in the Carnatic and Bengal. Chandernagar was one of them.'

'Perhaps Rabelais was one of the Frenchmen doing business there, and he and Colonel Crosby-Nash joined forces to . . . do what?' Mary caught Whittington's arch expression. '*Defraud* the East India Company?'

'Well, such things are not unknown. It is rather a long shot, but it would explain the connection between the two of them, although not why Crosby-Nash has put in with Rabelais now.'

'Perhaps out of friendship?' asked Mary, dubiously.

'Well, possibly,' said Whittington. 'If there were also money involved . . . but perhaps there is.' He shrugged and smiled. 'I am afraid I am rather better at spending money than acquiring it.'

'Yes,' agreed Mary, absently. 'Perhaps there is money involved. And what about Phoebus? Do you know anything more about him?'

Whittington's smile broadened. 'Ah, the dismal Phoebus,' he laughed. 'Not quite one's image of the sun god, I think. What did you say he called me? "Rat-catcher"? The fellow has a cheek! He organised the political side of my little venture – handbills, speeches, political songs – he and his friends. I gather that they do most of the fieldwork as he fancies his own skin too much to expose it to danger very often. He refused to attend the Scarborough House ball, you know, though it made things very inconvenient for the rest of us. We did quite a lot of business that night.'

They stopped in the far corner of the garden and admired a climbing rose whose blossoms were the colour of butter.

'Yes, I thought so,' said Mary. 'Not actually during the ball, I mean, but it occurred to me afterwards.'

'*Afterwards*,' repeated Whittington. 'Well, I am glad to hear that, at least! I would not like to think that our manoeuvres were transparent to innocent damsels, who ought to have been thinking only about their dancing partners. Now, what you tell me of the Naval mutinies is very interesting.'

'But I think they concern only Phoebus . . . and Rabelais. I did not understand that the colonel had a particular interest there.'

'Perhaps not to begin with, but remember what he said about Phoebus – bragging of his success at the Nore. I doubt Crosby-Nash can resist playing a part. He will want to score off Phoebus somehow, especially after the less than satisfactory result with the Guards. If I can convince him to send Holland and myself to Sheerness, we might make something of it for our side. That is my idea, you see.'

'Yes, I see.' Mary fingered one of the roses, whose petals fell softly to the ground in a golden shower, and she frowned.

'I wish that Mr Shy had known about all of this — that you were working against Colonel Crosby-Nash, and your guesses about Rabelais.'

'All confidential information for the quartermaster-general's department, I am afraid,' said Whittington. 'I cannot go about hawking what I know to all and sundry.'

'Mr Shy is not "all and sundry",' Mary protested.

'No, but we do not generally have much to do with any of the other official services — we occasionally talk to the Navy, but rarely to the Home Office or the Foreign Office — and Shy is not even acknowledged to exist!'

Mary could almost hear Holland's exasperated condemnation of Mr Shy, but she refused to listen. 'No, but you know very well that he *does* exist, and the government relies upon him a great deal. It seems to me a matter of common sense that, when you are working on the same problem, to achieve the same end, you ought to work together.'

'Common sense has very little to do with it, I am afraid,' admitted Whittington. 'Perhaps it would be better if the different services worked more closely together, but,' he shrugged, 'that is not how the game is played.'

After further unflattering observations on the subject of Phoebus, Whittington turned the discussion to Mary and the future. 'Clearly, your people may send another agent to replace Romney, and then all will be as before. But if they do not, how will you pass on your information? Do you know how Romney was communicating with Shy?'

Mary did not know, and Whittington considered the possibilities. There might be another of Shy's men somewhere nearby. If so, he would probably try to contact her when he realised that something had gone wrong — if he and Romney had a regular rendezvous, and that date passed without Romney turning up. Of course, the contact might not work that way.

Somehow, Mary did not think it did work that way. So profound had been her sense of isolation that she could not imagine other agents operating in the vicinity. She was in Kent, and Shy was in London, and something would have to be done to bridge that gap. One means of doing so had already occurred to her – a letter like the one she had received, in which the real message was concealed among innocuous information. The only problem, she said, lay in not knowing whether such a letter would actually be passed on, if she sent it to Coutts Bank.

That she was willing to remain at Champian Hall and did not blanch at the prospect of drafting such a letter impressed Whittington. She was certainly a brave girl, as well as a clever one. It was no wonder Shy had recruited her. 'If a letter could be carefully composed,' he mused, 'that plan would be a good one. I think that there is some channel of communication, undoubtedly obscure, little used, and never mentioned, but available when required. But be careful! Do not be tempted to tell the fellow at Coutts that you have been reading Rabelais, for example, on rainy afternoons. If the letter were to fall into the wrong hands, *that* observation would certainly arouse suspicion!'

'Too peppery?' asked Mary, smiling.

Whittington took her arm again. 'Precisely.'

If she had been keeping a diary, Mary would have described that evening as another of those odd periods during her stay at Champian Hall when she entered a kind of dreamy reality in which deceit and treachery did not exist. Crosby-Nash was simply a doting husband and convivial host, his wife was untroubled, and his visitors were nothing but friendly, appreciative guests. So, it was not surprising that, after a well-cooked dinner, Holland and the colonel should exchange anecdotes about India, and Whittington turn the pages for Susannah while she played the pianoforte. The major had a very pleasing baritone, and the only anxious moment occurred when he tried to coax Mary into singing a duet. She declined the invitation, despite teasing from her host and hostess, and at last placated them by offering to sketch the portraits of the company.

She drew quickly, and so produced her sketches in quick succession. They were not true likenesses, but she had the knack of capturing her subject in a few strokes and, as her portrayals were frequently of a humorous nature, they were received with a mixture of acclaim and laughing protest. 'Do not tell me that I convey such an air of conceit when I am singing.' 'No more so than when you're speaking, Dick.' 'Oh, no, Major Whittington; your voice is splendid, but Mary, dear, I think your portrayal of me is rather too fond.' 'Nonsense, my dear, and I have never heard the Gambarini played so delightfully.'

Mary agreed; the music and singing were delightful, but she was particularly captivated by the stories of India. So captivated, in fact, that she was tempted into an anecdote of her own, which her watchfulness in the everyday world of Champian Hall would have prevented her from revealing. 'The gods and heroes you mention sound so interesting,' she sighed. 'Rama and Krishna . . . although I believe Kali is rather horrid. I know a bit about the ancient Assyrian gods, and those of the Philistines and Moabites, but I would like to know more about the Indian ones.'

Everyone but Holland stared at her. 'Indeed, Miss Finch,' said Crosby-Nash, slowly. 'I am astonished that you should have made such a study of mythological personages.'

'Oh, I have not done so, really,' Mary admitted. 'Only, we swore by them, for a time, at Mrs Bunbury's school.'

'*Swore by them?*' breathed Susannah, while the gentlemen made an effort to hide their smiles.

'Well, yes,' said Mary. 'You see, Miss Trent was adamant that the girls – our students – mustn't even *slightly* take the Lord's name in vain, and she hit upon the idea of encouraging them to use the names of heathen gods whenever they were particularly vexed. There are quite a few of them mentioned in the Bible, you know.'

Whittington gave up the struggle and began to laugh. 'Did you look them up?' he demanded.

'Well, we needn't have done so, for Miss Trent knew them all, but we thought it might also make Bible lessons more interesting. Some of the books are rather . . . Well then, for a time we adopted her plan, and said things like, "by Nisroch, I shall not stand for such nonsense". Or we might say "Dagon" or "Tammuz"' – here she was obliged to raise her voice, because even Colonel Crosby-Nash was chuckling unrestrainedly – 'if a teapot was broken or someone ran a needle into her finger.'

'"By Nisroch",' echoed the colonel. 'Pray, where is this extraordinary school, Miss Finch?'

'St Ives,' said Holland. 'In Huntingdonshire.'

'If you are contemplating a visit, Colonel, I will accompany you,' laughed Whittington. 'I would like to see these priestesses of Baal.'

Mary frowned at him. 'We were nothing of the kind, and we did not adhere to the plan for very long . . . generally for the reason that you have suggested. We wondered if, by mentioning those gods we might be seen to be . . . *invoking* them in some way.'

Whittington said that it certainly sounded like the darkest witchcraft to him, and Crosby-Nash added, with mock seriousness, that he had not appreciated the excitement that was to be found in rural Huntingdonshire.

'It does seem an absurd thing to have done, looking back on it,' Mary admitted, 'and really, we never imagined . . . But poor Miss Trent – I believe the experience ruined the story of the golden calf for her. That was Baal, you know.'

'Indeed,' said Whittington. He nodded gravely, despite the fact that he and the story of the golden calf were practically strangers.

'I daresay there was nothing really *wrong* in what you were doing,' said Susannah, frowning slightly, 'and certainly among ourselves . . . but I would not mention it to Mr Garbett.'

'Oh, no,' agreed Mary.

'More to the point, don't tell Charlotte,' advised Holland, dryly.

'Or Mrs Tipton!'

Mary flashed a smile in his direction, but almost as quickly looked away. Holland was the least animated of the group that evening, but for various reasons Mary found her thoughts tending in his direction. Their interview that morning had been highly unusual, and she did not now understand where they stood as a result of it. There had been moments when he had either teased or scolded her in his old manner, only to assume a chilly reserve that undermined any suggestion of intimacy. Nor, when she examined them, were her own feelings any less confused than his appeared to be. Perhaps the safest course was to communicate only on a professional level, as their common business with Colonel Crosby-Nash dictated.

For his part, Holland found the evening tedious at best. He endured the falsity of his situation, but without the skill or, he suspected, the relish of Crosby-Nash. He was disturbed rather than impressed that the same man who had asked about smuggling a bomb into Horse Guards could now attend his wife with a lover's devotion. And Dick Whittington was no better. When he made an indecent allusion to an exclusive London brothel, which fortunately neither of the ladies understood, Holland dreaded that Missie Amber's would somehow come into the conversation. Meanwhile, there was Mary Finch, darting glances at him from across the room. It seemed to Holland that she was the worst problem of the lot. What was he to do, ignore her for the rest of his time at Champian Hall? He was not very good at that, not when she was near. But perhaps it wasn't the best way to proceed after all.

'Miss Finch, I wonder if I might speak with you.'

The question, and Holland's shadow falling across her book, made her look up. It was the following afternoon, and Mary was reading in the garden. Moreover, she had thought herself alone, for Crosby-Nash and Susannah were taking tea with their neighbour, Mrs Cathcart, and the two gentlemen had gone for a ride.

'You remember that I mentioned it, yesterday.'

'Yes, of course,' said Mary, brushing back a rebellious curl. In fact, she had forgotten the beginning of their last conversation, recalling only the revelations that had followed, but it seemed rude to point this out. Unaccountably, the legal expression 'right of pre-audience' occurred to her at that moment, but she decided not to mention that either. Such flourishes belonged to another, increasingly distant, period of their association.

'It doesn't really matter,' Holland continued, 'if you don't mean to continue your . . . investigation after we've gone. Dick sees no harm in it, but—'

She answered automatically. 'I believe I will be all right.'

Holland looked as if he wanted to protest, but with an effort he replied, 'Of course . . . it's not for me to give the orders. But if you *do* stay, would you . . . object to doing something for me?'

She glanced up at him, cautious, but not wanting to refuse. 'Can you tell me what it is?'

'Yes, but not here.'

Something in his manner made her curious. That, and the attraction that still stretched between them, tipped the balance and she consented.

They left the Hall and gardens behind and set off across an expanse of open, undulating ground known as 'the pleasance'. Holland indicated a hill approximately half a mile distant, on which a previous owner of Champian Hall had planted a stand of ornamental trees, as their destination. When they reached it, he guided her to a stone bench that afforded a view of the ornamental trees as well as the surrounding countryside.

Scenery, however, was not his object as he handed her an oblong, mahogany box. 'Right. If you're determined to carry on, you'll need this. Go on, open it.'

'Oh, my,' breathed Mary, as she lifted the lid to reveal an elegant pistol of walnut and brass, together with several wads, a ramrod, a number of lead balls, two spare flints, and several cleaning tools, all neatly arranged on a bed of green baize.

It was one of Henry Nock's finest, Holland explained. Rather on the small side perhaps, but it ought to be about right for her. He lifted the weapon out of its case, felt the weight, and then handed it to her.

Mary had no idea what she ought to say. How did one compliment a pistol? 'It is very . . . handsome. But I cannot— Do you mean to teach me how to fire it?'

'Well, I don't see how else you'll learn. It's very easy, really. Are you game?'

Game, she thought would be stating it too strongly, but she agreed to try, and even to hear an explanation of the mechanism.

He sat down, with the case on the bench between them. Perhaps because of the unusual subject matter, it proved a highly successful tête-à-tête. The anonymous principles of flash ignition, recoil, and trajectory could be explained without the slightest diffidence on Holland's part, and his relaxed manner helped to ease Mary's lingering anxieties about him. On the other hand, she *was* apprehensive about actually loading and firing the weapon herself, so she listened with a degree of attention that Holland found endearing. Her willingness to undertake a task with which she was not comfortable, moreover, always impressed him.

'If this were a musket, you would have a cartridge,' he noted, his hands moving confidently through each step of the loading process, 'with powder, ball, and wadding all together.'

'And that would be much easier than having each ingredient – each part – separate?'

'Yes, but then you'd have to bite through the cartridge, to get at the powder and ball, and that's not very nice. I once saw an old fellow lose his false teeth trying to do it.'

'Oh, you never did,' she laughed.

'On my honour,' he protested. 'Out they came, straight into the mud.'

'Did he put them in again?'

'Of course – he had to make a second shot. Now we're primed, loaded, and ready to fire.' Holland stood up. 'If I mean to use only one hand, I stand side on to the target, extend my arm, look down the barrel, and pull the trigger steadily. If I mean to use both hands – and that's what you'll do – I stand square on to the target. I still hold the pistol in my right hand, but I use my left as an extra support to keep my aim true – like this. All right?'

'Yes. What shall be our target?'

'Well, we have a range of about thirty yards—'

'And you mustn't undermine your authority as an instructor by *missing*.'

'That's right – it's bad for discipline. How about the tree with the forked trunk?'

'The little one? Very well, but your authority hangs in the balance.'

Mary had willed herself not to be startled when the gun went off, but the sound was louder than she had imagined it would be, and she did jump, just a little. She attempted to disguise this with an appreciative remark. 'Oh— Well shot,' she affirmed.

He cocked an ironic eyebrow. 'Discipline's maintained, at least. Now it's your turn. I'll load for you. We'll reduce the charge until you're used to the recoil.'

Mary nodded nervously. In what seemed like a matter of seconds, the pistol was loaded and in her hands. It felt very heavy and extremely dangerous.

'Make ready to fire,' he said, calmly, 'but don't pull the trigger until I say. Aim at something closer . . . the cedar.'

'Very well.' She attempted to imitate his stance, but her concentration was interrupted when he asked whether she wished to *hit* the tree. If she did, he advised against closing her eyes.

'Keep looking along the barrel at your target – that's right. The pistol will jump a bit in your hands when you fire, so be ready for that, and the bang. Squeeze the trigger . . . steady . . .'

There was a puff of smoke and a loud report – much louder, surely, than when Holland had fired. The recoil surprised her, despite his warning, but she managed not to drop the pistol, and turned to him in triumph.

'Well done,' he said, nodding judicially. 'Very good.'

Mary agreed with him wholeheartedly, but modesty required her to ask, 'Do you think so? I did not hit anything.'

'Practice makes perfect,' he reminded her. 'You load it this time, and what do you say to a full charge?'

Her elation was diminished somewhat by these suggestions, and she immediately began thinking of the various mistakes in loading that might cause the weapon to misfire or explode. Fortunately, her technique was sound. The second shot was wide, but she creased the bark with the third, and the fourth hit the tree square on. 'Hooray!' she cried. 'That was as straight as yours, I think. And I suppose you are quite a good shot?'

'Tolerable.'

'Well, then if I keep practising, I shall soon be an expert.'

'If you keep practising, you'll soon be out of ammunition,' remarked Holland. 'I don't have any balls that will fit this pistol apart from these in the box, and you cannot ask Crosby-Nash for spare powder.'

'No, very likely not.' She laughed, then, as if this were a joke between them, and handed him the weapon. Still smiling, she gazed out over the pleasance. Her hands were smeared with gunpowder, but she did not mind that, and she breathed in the acrid scent that hung in the air. There was something called 'grapeshot', and she wondered if it had a different smell. 'Is this your own special pistol?' she asked, liking the idea that it might be.

'Not particularly.' Holland cleaned the weapon as he replied. 'I bought it in London just before I came down here, as it happens. The fellow who'd ordered it was— He didn't need it, so I got it for a good price.'

It did not occur to Mary to consider why a man who had ordered a pistol might no longer need it. One often changed one's mind about purchases, after all. 'I did not think that I would enjoy shooting,' she confessed, rejoining him on the bench. 'Indeed, I do not believe I have ever thought about it, but it is really very exhilarating, especially when one hits the target.'

'Yes, it's good fun, usually. But suppose you were shooting at something other than a tree?'

The change in his voice caused Mary to glance across at him. He was holding the pistol by the muzzle and made as if to hand it to her. 'Well,' she acknowledged, 'the gentlemen of

Suffolk seem to shoot birds with great enthusiasm, but I do not believe I would care for that.'

'Ah, the gentlemen of Suffolk,' said Holland, with a hint of scorn. 'I expect the ducks and the pheasants provide them with excellent sport, and the ladies – those who don't choose to join them in the field – are told of their exploits over dinner.'

Mary nodded. She considered a tart rejoinder dismissing both exploits and the accounts thereof, but Holland's tone of voice prevented her from uttering it. She did not understand this latest humour, but she knew that it did not include levity. 'It is the fashion, you know,' she reminded him. 'I daresay Sir William Armitage had shooting parties at Storey's Court.'

'Very likely,' Holland replied. The words, 'And so will you, or your husband will,' were on the tip of his tongue. Before they could escape he remarked, 'But that's not what I meant when I asked you.'

'No, and that is not why you taught me how to fire this pistol,' she agreed and gazed down at her hands. Suddenly she wished that she had a handkerchief. 'You want to know, how should I like to shoot a man? Naturally, I should not like it at all.'

'But could you do it?'

He was still holding out the pistol to her, and she took it. 'I suppose . . . if I were obliged to – if I were in mortal danger. Or if I had to protect someone else,' she added, thinking about Susannah.

'Good,' said Holland, nodding, 'I'd expect that of you. See that you don't forget it so long as you're here. But shooting Crosby-Nash or one of his sort wouldn't be so difficult.' He stood up and folded his arms. 'Suppose it was someone that you cared for – or thought you did – and who . . . cared for you? Could you shoot *that* man?'

'But why— I do not understand you,' cried Mary, as a sudden chill ran down her spine and settled in the pit of her stomach. She rose and tried to return the pistol, but he stepped back and would not take it. 'What do you mean? Why would I ever do such a terrible thing?'

Holland shrugged and walked away from her. 'Because he beat you, or he drank too much, and you were afraid of him. Or because marrying him had been a mistake, just as everyone had said it would be. He had dragged you down, and you hated him for it.'

Mary was stricken by his words, and when he turned towards her again they stared at each other. 'That's what I wanted to tell you,' he explained. 'About myself – my family. I should have done it before, but . . . well, now you know.'

'But what— Do you mean . . . Is *that* what happened to your parents?' asked Mary in confusion and horror. 'Charlotte said—'

'Lottie doesn't know anything about it. No one does, apart from Quincy, the lawyer, and now you.' Holland watched as the colour blossomed and faded across Mary's face, leaving her pale. *She is sickened by this*, he thought. *She has always lived among decent people, and nothing like this has ever touched her. Now she will feel sorry for me.* In a hard, emotionless voice he continued, 'Sir William was very fond of my mother. He took care of her, afterwards, and kept everything quiet so that there was no scandal and no trial. He could do things like that when he was in government.'

'No trial,' breathed Mary.

'For murder.' Holland was still looking at her, and when she flinched he continued remorselessly. 'You know about the law, so you know what that means. Though I suppose they might not have hanged her, as she was with child at the time.'

'No.' Mary answered in a small voice. 'You learned the secret last year, at Sir William's funeral.' Suddenly things that she had never understood about Holland's conduct, which had never quite made sense, began to fall into place. The pieces made a terrible picture.

'That's right. Sir William had meant to tell me, Quincy said, but he never managed it.'

'But—' Mary hesitated, not wishing to press him, but unable to remain silent in the face of this bleak, bald account of his mother's crime. It was so terrible – to have *killed* her husband

– there had to be an explanation beyond Holland's forbidding hints. 'Do you know why she . . . It was not because they were poor, surely. Did he . . . ?'

'Beat her?' finished Holland. His tone was bitter. 'He probably did. It doesn't sound as if there was much good in him. And her family cut her off without a penny, you know – that part of the story is true. Maybe after a time it was too hard for her, living with him, and knowing that things weren't going to get any better. It had cost her everything to marry him, everything that was important.'

'I am sorry—'

'Don't be,' he snapped, and then sighed. 'I mean . . . it's good of you, but . . .'

Mary returned the pistol to its box and softly closed the lid. 'I wish that Sir William had told you,' she murmured. 'He might have helped you to understand.'

'I'm glad that he didn't,' Holland replied, and now his voice was merely dull. 'There was nothing to be done, and it would have been hard on him. He was fond of her, and I look just like my father.'

15

Holland opened his eyes early the next morning to the sound of rain lashing against his bedroom window. As he considered the grey half-light and the billowing draperies where he had neglected to fasten the casement properly, he became aware of another, more insistent tapping, coming from the passage. Before he could acknowledge it, the door opened and Dick Whittington strode into the room, dressed in a worn, faded suit of clothes, and displaying less than his usual calm.

'What's happened?' Holland demanded, sitting up.

Whittington frowned at him from the foot of the bed. 'Trouble, I am afraid. A mutiny at Woolwich, and it is going to start today.'

'Christ!' Holland flung back the bedclothes and sprang to his feet. As he struggled into his breeches and out of his nightshirt he fired questions at Whittington. Was the mutiny widespread? What were the details? Was it Crosby-Nash? Of course it was, but how many men were involved? 'We— I must get back.'

'Steady,' advised Whittington, 'and I will tell you what I know. You are correct in thinking that it is our friend's latest venture. He has a particular fondness for stirring up trouble in the military, it seems. God knows how long he has been planning it – he informed *me* a short while ago, over a cup of tea! He says that approaches have been made to at least five companies at Woolwich, and these have been very favourably received.'

'Five companies gone to the bad? I don't believe it.'

Whittington shrugged his shoulders. 'Perhaps it is exaggerated, but there must be some truth in the story. And you know very well that a small spark can trigger a very large conflagration.'

'You're damned right I know it,' Holland snapped. 'That's why I must leave straightaway. What do we tell Crosby-Nash?'

'Fortunately, we need tell him nothing apart from "yes, sir". He wants us to go. I am to play my usual, behind-the-scenes role, and he fancies that you will be of considerable assistance inside the Warren – which is correct, but not in quite the way that he expects, eh?'

Holland nodded. 'Do you know who is there now? Who is actually stirring things up?'

'No,' said Whittington, glumly, 'or I *may* do. I am not certain, and I could not press Crosby-Nash for details.'

'Why not?'

'Well . . .' Whittington struggled to explain. 'He was very evasive . . . as well as being far too proud of himself. He wanted admiration, not interrogation. And only telling me at the last moment . . . it made me wonder whether he was starting to mistrust me, because of the Guards' failure. But if that is so, why send us to Woolwich?' He shook his head. 'I do not enjoy being puzzled by a fellow like Crosby-Nash.'

The rain also woke Mary that morning, first invading and then interrupting her dream about Sophia Holland. It was a very disturbing vision, in which the frail, lovely young woman, whose portrait Mary had seen at Storey's Court, walked calmly down a long, wide passage. She was beautifully dressed, and the passage too seemed to belong to a house in which no expense had been spared. At the end of the passage stood a man, but his face was averted. Sophia called to him, but before he could turn she shot him, twice, and he fell sideways into a glass-fronted cabinet, filled with jewels. The woman – it was no longer clear whether she was Sophia or Mary herself – continued walking, and she entered a small, meanly furnished room, in which the only light came from a smoky coal fire. A man sat on a stool before the

242

hearth, holding something on his lap – a portrait of Sophia in an elaborate gilt frame. While the woman behind him watched, he sliced through the canvas with a knife and slowly twisted the frame into pieces. Then he fed both wood and canvas into the flames. As he did so the sound of burning grew steadily, from hissing crackles to a dull, pounding roar, until Mary opened her eyes and saw the rain beating upon the window ledge.

The images of her dream and what they might mean were so troubling that Mary could not immediately rise and dress. Even after she had done so, their vividness remained. The sound of pistol shots seemed to echo in the passage as she made her way to the stairs, and she could almost smell something burning in the empty fireplace in the great hall. When she encountered Susannah in the breakfast room, she almost spoke of the episode (intending to omit any mention of Sophia), but Susannah's own news forestalled her. Holland and Whittington were leaving.

'Oh? Indeed?' remarked Mary, surprising herself by her ability to pour out tea with a completely steady hand. 'Have you spoken to them?'

'No, the colonel told me. Poor Bobs – I do not know *why* he must dash back to Woolwich in this dreadful weather—'

'*Woolwich?*' demanded Mary, as her cup overflowed, 'did you say he was going to *Woolwich*? To the Warren, do you mean?'

'Why, yes, I imagine so,' replied Susannah. 'Is there another military . . . something or other in Woolwich with which Bobs has to do?' She handed Mary the basket of rolls.

'Thank you. No, I do not believe so.' Mary's thoughts leapt from spectral murders to entirely mortal concerns. *To Woolwich and not to Sheerness, as Major Whittington expected. What can have provoked the change of plan? Has Phoebus communicated with Colonel Crosby-Nash? Or perhaps the sailors have returned to their duty as happened at Portsmouth?* She forced back a feigned yawn and mopped up the tea in her saucer. 'I think . . . ah, I am not quite awake yet.'

'Did you sleep badly? The wind was very strong last night, and I believe I heard thunder – perhaps it bothered you. It really is bad luck all round.'

'Oh, no, you mustn't mind me. I am quite well.' *Captain Holland has certainly not been enthusiastic about his mission here, but if he is hurrying back to Woolwich, perhaps that means . . .*

Mary left the breakfast room as soon as she decently could, darting across the yard and into the stables. The sound of masculine voices encouraged her, and she crept along the row of stalls, their inhabitants gazing at her speculatively as she passed. In the last but one, Holland heaved a saddle onto the back of a large black horse with white stockings. Bending to fasten the buckle he called, 'If you're not happy, change the damned things!' He turned. 'It's not worth— Oh, sorry. I thought you were Dick.'

'No, I . . .' Mary faltered. Holland had done little more than tumble into his clothes that morning, and he looked rough and dishevelled. More than that, he seemed to exude tension. His hastily packed gear was piled in a corner with a cloak flung over it, and he was clearly not waiting for a groom to prepare his mount. It had seemed so important to speak with him, and now she felt foolish, an intruder. He wanted nothing more than to set off as soon as he could, and she was delaying him. She could think of nothing sensible to say. 'You have been called back to Woolwich?' she asked hopefully.

Holland shook his head and replied in a low voice. 'We're going, but on Crosby-Nash's orders.'

He explained that there was going to be trouble at the Warren – it might have begun already.

'*Trouble?* Do you mean a mutiny?'

'So we've been told by Crosby-Nash.'

Mary had once visited the Woolwich Warren, and in her mind's eye she saw the buildings wrecked and the officers' quarters in flames. 'And you— Of course, you must go and set things to rights,' she acknowledged. 'But what if— I mean, please be careful.'

Holland frowned and rolled down his shirtsleeves. His expression was partly an attempt to dismiss her fears and partly a check on the feelings that her presence inspired. He did not want her to worry about him – or rather, he *did*, but he knew he ought not. 'It may turn out to be nothing, you know. A few hotheads, or men who've let the drink speak for them.'

'Perhaps, but the Naval mutinies have not been such tame affairs.'

'Ah, but those are sailors, not gunners. I don't know about the Navy, but the first thing we teach our men is to look after their officers.'

'But . . .'

Holland shrugged into his jacket and buttoned up his collar, so that he began to look more officer-like, and his gaze became speculative as he tied his stock. 'You're a sort of artilleryman as well, now that you've had proper firing instructions on a piece of ordnance.'

She was conscious that he was trying to reassure her, and although not reassured, she felt obliged to follow his lead. She mustn't be a coward – or worse, let him see that she was frightened. 'Does that mean I am required to obey your orders?' she demanded quizzically, and her chin lifted in the way that he knew so well.

'It does.'

'Well?' He was smiling now, and she could not help responding. 'I do not say that I agree, mind you, but I am willing to listen.'

Damn, damn, damn, thought Holland, as his heart turned over. *What is the point of speaking to her like this? As if nothing has changed and some things are still possible?* There was no help for it, however, but to continue as he had begun. 'Your orders are to look after yourself, to do nothing reckless, and to give up a position if it becomes indefensible.'

Mary had forgotten how blue his eyes were. It was the coat, of course, and she could almost hear Miss Marchmont's warnings about scarlet fever. *Oh, the blue coats are worse by far,* she silently informed the shade of Miss Marchmont, *but how can I let him go, without—*

'Here I am, ready at la— Oh! Miss Finch!' cried Whittington, halting abruptly in the doorway. 'Ah. Yes. I shall just—' He turned and started to withdraw.

'No, it's all right,' said Holland. 'Goodbye, Miss Finch.'

He held out his hand, and she took it. She did not understand what he intended by the gesture, or even what she meant to convey by her own close, answering clasp. Then they both let go, awkwardly, and neither looked at the other.

'Sorry,' Whittington muttered as Holland pushed past him, leading his horse into the stable yard. Then he shrugged at Mary and had the satisfaction of watching her blush rosily in reply. 'I have made our farewells to the colonel,' he continued, raising his voice to Holland, 'and he wishes us a pleasant journey.'

Holland eyed the low ceiling of murky, grey clouds and patted his horse's neck. 'That's good of him.'

Mary remained under cover just inside the stable door as the two men made their final preparations. A gust of rain made her shiver. That Captain Holland and Major Whittington were riding into danger was unquestionable, and the fact that its particulars were unknown only increased her sense of foreboding. If she had been going with them she could have borne it better. Remaining behind, with nothing but her imagination to console her, would be much more difficult.

Whittington swung into the saddle and flashed her a winning smile. 'Goodbye, Lucasta, we are off to the wars. I have vastly enjoyed our brief acquaintance and trust we shall meet again soon in more pleasant circumstances.'

Mary nodded. 'Yes, I hope so.' She looked beyond him to Holland, but he had already turned his horse. 'Good luck,' she murmured, more to herself than to either of the men.

When they passed out of sight Mary returned to the house, trying to gather her thoughts and reduce them to some kind of order. A mutiny at Woolwich – the soldiers casting off all restraint and sense of duty, and Captain Holland riding straight into the fray! *Hold hard; it is not known what he will encounter. The sailors have not offered violence to their officers— Or have they? In any case, Captain Holland doubtless knows his men. It is pointless to imagine the worst.* The departure of her friends would also create a void at Champian Hall – she would be thrown once more upon her own resources, with no one in whom she could confide. *Yes, but the situation here is not so very insecure, and there is the chance of re-establishing contact with Mr Shy. I need not be completely alone.* Then there was Sophia Holland, not the subject of a confused dream, but the real woman who had been driven to do a terrible thing. Sophia was the key, Mary felt, to whatever the future might hold for herself and Captain Holland. *But I fear that she is too difficult a problem, just at the moment, and must wait upon less hectic times.*

As she stood in the chilly entrance chamber, reminding herself of this final imperative and absently shaking the dampness from her skirt, she became aware of voices conversing in the great hall. One belonged to Crosby-Nash, and when she inched open the connecting door she could overhear both sides of the conversation. She relaxed as she realised that the other voice belonged to Lockwood, the butler, and they were discussing the likelihood of the rain abating and the colonel being able to call on one of the neighbouring gentry. Here, at least, was a normal, one might almost say *wholesome* problem, and she continued to listen for that reason.

Suddenly she realised that the two men were coming nearer, and she straightened abruptly. There was no place to hide in that empty room — they would see her at once, and how on earth could she explain what she was doing there? She glanced up at the portrait of the elephant god; in the pale light he seemed to be grinning at her.

'Well, I had better have a word with Walters about that,' said Crosby-Nash, his hand on the heavy brass doorknob.

'Yes, sir, I daresay he'll know what's best.'

'And if the weather will cooperate— Why, Miss Finch, you gave me a start, I must say.' As Crosby-Nash and Lockwood opened the inner door and entered the chamber, the outer door opened to admit Mary, looking suitably damp and windblown.

Mary also started in surprise. 'Oh, colonel! I beg your pardon. I did not expect—'

She paused, looking flustered, and he quickly intervened.

'I shall be coming in to breakfast directly, Lockwood – if you would let them know . . .'

The butler stared fixedly at his employer, apparently not having noticed Mary, and backed out of the room. 'Certainly, sir.'

'I should not advocate outdoor exercise in this weather,' remarked Crosby-Nash when they were alone.

'No, that is to say, I have been, well, you know that Captain Holland and Major Whittington are leaving, and I . . . I wanted to say goodbye.' She dropped her eyes demurely.

'Ah, yes, of course.' He started to reach past her. 'Are they still here?'

'Alas, no,' she sighed, moving away from the door.

'What a pity. I would have liked a final word.' Then he smiled sympathetically. 'But I expect they preferred the proxy.'

She smiled in return. In a less genteel young lady it might have been called a smirk. 'Oh, I do not know . . . I daresay he— And the wind is so strong. What a sight I must be!'

She made as if to tidy her hair, and he assured her that it was not necessary; she looked charming. 'But if you will excuse me, I must have a word with my groom. You, er, did not notice him in the stables, I imagine?'

She pondered this. 'I cannot call him to mind, I am afraid. But I expect he is somewhere about.'

'Yes, quite.'

Mary closed the inner door behind her and maintained her somewhat roguish expression until she had crossed the great hall and entered the passage beyond. Finding this empty, she collapsed against the panelled wall and exhaled deeply, thankful for a narrow escape.

The rain kept her indoors for the rest of the morning, but she was far from idle. After several false starts she drafted a letter to her bankers, which also contained a message to Mr Cuthbert Shy. This message, she hoped, would inform him that her work was not proceeding smoothly, but would also pass undetected if read by anyone else.

Champian Hall
near Maidstone
Kent

Mr William Herbert,
Thos Coutts & Co.,
59 Strand
London

26th May 1797

Dear Mr Herbert,
Thank you for your letter of the 9th of this month, which reached me shortly before I departed London. Since coming into Kent I have had ample opportunity for considering your advice with regard to Indian investments, and I am happy to continue along the lines you suggested. Thank you too for the curious Spanish trinket you sent me. As you know, I am very interested in baubles of this sort, and it was kind of you to remember me in this way.
At our London meeting you suggested that I might wish to retain a reliable agent to oversee my investments on a more regular basis, naming Mr Marsh as most qualified to perform this service. I have since communicated with Mr Marsh, but unfortunately he is unable to continue the commission. Are you able to propose an alternative candidate? Certainly one such as myself, unused to matters of business, would benefit from regular, experienced guidance, and I believe I might easily find myself in financial difficulties were I to continue to act largely on my own. I would be most grateful for your assistance in this matter.
Yours sincerely,
Mary Finch

It was, admittedly, very abrupt, but surely there were sufficient hints to alert Mr Shy? He was very clever, and he probably received cryptic messages from his agents on a regular basis. Even as Mary assured herself on these points, she could not quite stifle other, nagging doubts. What proof was there that he would actually receive the letter? Major Whittington had been

249

fairly confident that a secret channel of communication existed through Coutts bank, but what if he were mistaken? Perhaps her own letter had had nothing to do with the bank, but had come directly from Mr Shy. It would not have been impossible to obtain Coutts' stationery, after all. Any letter *she* sent might very well go no farther than its ostensible recipient, and how would Mr Herbert receive such a strange communication?

She smiled ruefully as she contemplated the likely discussion between the officers of the bank on the subject of her sanity, but a misdirected communication was no laughing matter. If Mr Shy did not learn of her situation, what ought she to do? Remain at Champian Hall, possibly in danger and unable to communicate any important information that she discovered? Phrased that way it certainly sounded foolish. *It is foolish,* she could hear Holland telling her.

Yes, but what choice have I? If I do nothing I am in precisely the same position of . . . not knowing. Not doing and not knowing; that was an intolerable combination, particularly now, when important things were happening all around her. The letter, therefore, must be sent. *And yet . . .* She dreaded doing anything that might draw attention to herself, especially now that she was alone again. Perhaps she ought to wait. She could send the letter tomorrow, or wait until the colonel went out. *No, no. Why should I not post a letter if I choose? There is nothing suspicious in that. And what could he suspect, after all?*

Taking up her pen she recopied the letter, substituting 'advisor' for 'agent', and carefully sealed it.

Holland urged his horse into a brisk trot, and Whittington did the same. The rain had abated slightly since their departure from Champian Hall, but it was still falling steadily. They would be soaked long before they reached Woolwich.

Whittington mopped his face with his handkerchief, realised that this was a particularly useless action, and replaced the sodden article in his pocket. He wanted to talk, but everything about Holland seemed to discourage conversation at that moment, so he desisted and they rode in silence. Presently, however, his natural effusiveness obliged him to make the attempt. 'I have been thinking about Miss Finch,' he announced.

Holland nodded. 'She's a fool to stay there.'

'She is resourceful,' Whittington corrected, 'and this Cuthbert Shy fellow is very sharp. I am sure you are worrying un-necessarily. No, I was thinking about another aspect of the situation. Does it occur to you that your curt farewell might *not* have been the best way of parting from her?'

'Does it occur to you to mind your own damned business?'

Whittington chuckled. 'If it did I would hardly be in my present job. Besides, as your friend and advisor I consider it my business to intercede when you are making a hash of things.'

'Is that what you think I'm doing?'

'Certainly. This . . . hanging about is utter madness. You will lose her if you do not take better care, and that would be a pity.' Whittington observed Holland's stony profile and continued, 'She is good-looking, she has a considerable fortune, she is intelligent – although her attraction to you must call the last point into question. If I were in your place—'

'Which you're not.'

'No, but if I *were*, I would certainly have a go. Her fortune *is* sound, is it not? Reasonably secure?'

'*I* don't know.'

'Well, you ought to find out. A bit of money would do you a world of good. You might buy yourself a new uniform, for a start, and something decent to give your friends to drink when they come to call. Hospitality, don't you know. I can tell you one thing, the necklace she was wearing at the Scarborough House ball cost a pretty penny, and then there is the Suffolk property, probably some other investments . . .'

'Let's say she's rich and be done with it, shall we?'

'One oughtn't to appear grasping, I grant you. But I fail to understand why you hold back. What more do you want? I gather the two of you had some sort of disagreement, but that is easily mended. Believe me, the only thing women like better than a virtuous lover is one who strays and must be redeemed

251

and forgiven. Throw yourself on her mercy, and I am sure she will let you off.'

'I don't want to be let off. You talked before about marrying a rich girl and giving her a title. That's all well and good, but what can *I* offer Mary Finch? Nothing, and I'm damned if I'm going to live on her money.'

'Well but surely you ought to let her decide, I mean, she will not see it that way.'

'I don't care *how* she sees it, and besides . . .' Holland looked down at his hands. The wet had turned an old scar at the base of his thumb red, as if he had been burned. 'My mother married a man with nothing. He was . . . He was a right bastard and . . . she had to get away from him. And maybe—'

'Ah, I see. Unfortunate precedent. But dash it all, you are not your father,' argued Whittington, 'and Miss Finch is not your mother, I am happy to say! That would make things awkward, what? Like that fellow – what was his name? Odysseus – no, Oedipus. By God, but the Greeks certainly took the biscuit for complicated domestic relations.'

Holland dismissed the allusion with a shrug. 'No, I know that, but it doesn't matter. It's my responsibility, and I know what I'm doing.'

'But—'

'Damn it, Dick, let it go!'

For a few minutes the only sounds were the patter of rain and the muffled tread of the horses' hooves. Then Holland asked, 'Who is Lucasta?'

Whittington had fallen into a reverie, and the question surprised him. 'What? Oh, she is the object of an exceedingly romantic poem, in which her lover tears himself from her fond embrace to meet his destiny on the gory field. "*I could not love thee, dear, so much, loved I not honour more.*" To be recited with a full helping of sighs, you understand.'

'What a lot of nonsense.'

'Romantic nonsense,' agreed Whittington. 'Exactly the sort of thing that ought to appeal to you.'

By late afternoon the two officers were on the outskirts of

Woolwich. Now the horses were jaded, however, and they showed little enthusiasm for the climb up Shooter's Hill. Their riders dismounted and led them forward. The rain had stopped in the previous hour, and here the ground was actually dry, but the boots of the two men squelched as they walked, and their damp travelling-cloaks flapped against their legs.

From a military perspective, Woolwich had three distinct components. Firstly, there was the Warren, the main production and storage facility for government-manufactured weaponry. It also housed the military academy and the laboratory. Secondly, there was Woolwich Common. Between twelve and fifteen artillery companies were typically quartered in Woolwich, and they could not all be accommodated inside the Warren. The majority had been put into new barracks built on the Common. And finally, there was the dockyard.

'What is the real danger?' asked Whittington. 'If you wished to cause the most trouble, what would you do?'

Holland considered. 'That would depend. If I wanted to disrupt the regiment, I'd make a broad approach to the men. I'd concentrate on the Common because there are more men there, and they would be the easiest to approach without their officers knowing. But if I wanted to damage the capacity of the Army generally, then I'd concentrate on the Warren – destroy everything I could get my hands on, including the laboratory. That would badly reduce our ability to manufacture the necessary ordnance, and we would lose the benefit of the advances that we've made.'

'Ah, secret weapons.'

'Up to a point,' Holland agreed, 'but losing all the dull, routine work we've done with regard to powder, gun-boring, sights, carriages – that would be worse.'

'So the attitude of the men on the Common is crucial,' said Whittington, 'and may indicate Crosby-Nash's objectives. What about the dockyard?'

Holland shrugged. 'I can't help you much there. The Admiralty runs the dockyard – or the Admiralty and the Ordnance together. I suppose the biggest danger would be a mutiny by any of the ships in for repairs, which could spread to the workers on shore.'

Whittington lapsed into a thoughtful silence. 'I think,' he said, slowly, 'that perhaps we ought to divide our forces. I will go to the dockyard and have a look round, while you find out about the artillery side of things.'

'Agreed,' said Holland, who did not really care what Whittington did. The closer they came to Woolwich, the more he felt that this was a situation, however awkward, in which he did not need an outsider's help.

They halted at the top of the hill beside a curious, triangular tower. Holland stared down at the Common and beyond it to Woolwich town. 'Everything looks quiet,' he murmured.

'What is this thing?' asked Whittington, looking up at the tower. 'The number of times I have ridden past it, and I have never—'

'It's a memorial to a man called Sir William James,' replied Holland, without turning. 'There's an inscription. Look, Dick, I'll turn off here, and you'd better carry on till you come to the Charlton turning. Then you can double back to the dockyard.'

'Ah,' nodded Whittington, 'I see. "*To record the conquest of the castle of Severndroog, on the coast of Malabar, which fell to his superior valour and able conduct on the second day of April 1755.*" I did not realise that the capture – I beg his pardon – the *conquest* of . . . Severndroog was such an historic event.'

'His widow built it.' Holland remounted as a further encouragement to departure.

'Just so,' agreed Whittington, retreating several paces so as to take in the whole of the structure. 'And a tower . . . a proper wifely sentiment.' He removed his hat and began to fan himself with it.

'What about arranging a time and place for a meeting?'

Whittington shook his head. 'Best not to plan anything until we see the lie of the land. I note that Sir William James was an officer of the East India Company – like our gallant Colonel Crosby-Nash.'

'Yes, just like him. Look, if there's been trouble, you may find it hard getting into the Warren, especially after dark. But if you *do* hear of anything in the town—'

'Rest assured that I shall find you if I need to communicate anything important,' said Whittington, turning at last to his friend. 'Very well. I know you want to be off. Good luck to you.'

'And to you.'

Whittington's smile faded as he watched Holland's horse pick his way diffidently down the hill and then break into a trot when he reached the flat. 'Well, that is one of us who is eager to take on this job. I wish I felt the same.'

16

The sight of Colonel Crosby-Nash comfortably ensconced in the upstairs parlour was so wholly unexpected that it brought Mary up sharply on the threshold. True, it was nearly half past four, and this was where Susannah usually took tea, but the colonel so rarely joined his wife that his presence today seemed almost sinister.

Mary had rehearsed her plan of campaign – a few simple, inconsequential remarks, followed by a brief, unremarkable absence – but the shock of seeing Crosby-Nash drove this completely from her mind. Before she could remember what she had intended to say, Susannah executed a rescue of sorts. She had been frowning blankly at her needlepoint, but now she noticed Mary's hat and remarked, 'Oh, my dear, you do not mean to out in this weather, do you?'

'Ye-es, I thought I would. The . . . the rain stopped hours ago, you know.'

'Did it? But it is still so gloomy, and the ground,' she yawned behind her hand, 'will be terribly damp.'

'Oh, well, I shan't mind that,' said Mary, trying to sound as if muddy walks on grey, chilly afternoons were among her favourite activities. Casting about for inspiration, her gaze fell upon Slipper dozing at his master's feet. 'I thought I might take Slipper for a run.'

Even as she spoke these words they seemed to her highly

dubious, but at least they convinced Slipper. At the sound of his name he raised his head and thumped his stubby tail enthusiastically against the floor.

'Ah,' said Crosby-Nash, lowering his newspaper. 'Do you know, I was about to propose the same thing myself.'

'Oh.' The colonel's company was the last thing Mary desired.

He observed Slipper's antics with a tolerant smile. 'But you go ahead, if you are so inclined. No doubt you are more indulgent with him than I am.'

His smile and observation, the latter delivered with a patronising edge to his voice, added to Mary's discomfort. 'Well, if you— Come along then, Slipper,' she urged, and he, needing no further encouragement, scrabbled to his feet and began barking. She knelt down, partly to calm him and partly to steady her own nerves. In neither task was she wholly successful.

'Will you be going into Saxonhurst, do you think?' asked Susannah. Her voice was placid, but she winced as if Slipper's barking made her head ache.

'Well, perhaps,' Mary admitted. 'I might do.' As she stood up it seemed that the colonel was watching her with a particular intentness, but why should that be? Surely there were many reasons why a person might choose to walk into the village – or there might be none at all. She knew she was imagining things, yet she felt that somehow her letter was known to him – that he could see it peeking out of her reticule.

Susannah's enquiry broke the spell. 'If you *do* go, might you buy that spool of green cotton for me at Mrs Humphreys'? I have been meaning to do so, and something always distracts me. It is such a nuisance.'

'Yes, of course. I . . . I must fetch Slipper's lead.'

On Mary's departure, Susannah and Crosby-Nash resumed their solitary occupations. After a few minutes, however, Susannah roused herself. 'I forgot to warn Mary about leaving Slipper outside when she buys the cotton.' She turned to her husband with greater animation. 'You remember how he growled at Mrs Humphreys when he saw her in the lane?'

'No, but it would not surprise me to learn that he had done so.'

'Well, he did, and I am so afraid he may not behave himself in the shop.'

'Very likely not.'

'Perhaps I ought to go with her.'

'I expect that Miss Finch is quite capable of managing Slipper. However, if you wish to become as wet and bedraggled as she will make herself—'

'I was not thinking so much of Slipper,' Susannah admitted, 'but only that Mary oughtn't to ramble about on her own. I daresay she does not think of such things, but I would not want her to be the subject of gossip, especially while she is under our care. Walking out alone, in such unseasonable weather, might be considered the conduct of a . . . person of disreputable character or situation. Unless you disagree, I mean.'

Crosby-Nash smiled complacently as his own words came back to him. 'No, you are quite right.'

'And we shall be very careful to avoid becoming bedraggled.'

'I am certain that you shall.' He lowered his newspaper a second time. 'Tell me, my dear, what is the nature of the connection between Miss Finch and Captain Holland?'

Susannah had risen, but she halted on her husband's words. '*Connection*?' she queried.

'Not in any formal sense, of course. I merely meant . . . they were acquainted with each other before his visit.'

Susannah nodded. 'Oh, yes. And they are great friends, I daresay, although perhaps that is not quite the right word either. They met in very peculiar circumstances, you know.'

Crosby-Nash did not know, nor did Susannah, in fact, but she explained that when Mary inherited White Ladies she had become entangled with some very dangerous highwaymen, or they might have been smugglers – criminals of some kind, desperate men. It had been perfectly dreadful, but somehow Bobs had rescued her, defeated the villains, and generally behaved very heroically.

258

Crosby-Nash thought it odd that Holland should have been available to perform heroics of any kind in Suffolk, but perhaps these events had occurred before his tenure at Woolwich had begun? On this point, however, Susannah was more informative. Bobs had been stationed or attached – she could not recall the precise term – to Woolwich upon his return from India, but he had been given a special job in the regiment that involved travelling about a great deal. He was very clever about guns and things. Everybody said so.

'And enterprising, to rescue a young lady from smugglers,' agreed Crosby-Nash. 'Such heroism would, of course, endear him to Miss Finch.'

'Yes, I expect so, but she never speaks of it.' A sudden thought occurred to Susannah. 'Perhaps it is because of the money.'

Crosby-Nash raised his eyebrows. 'My dear, the course of your logic defeats me.'

'Well, if she loved him, she would naturally want to marry him, but *that* would never do, for dear Bobs is awfully poor – much too poor for someone like Mary. And she would not want to think about how heroic he had been, for that would only make things worse.'

'Ah, yes, I see what you mean. Hurry along, now, if you wish to catch her.'

Susannah did hurry, and intercepted Mary and Slipper before they had left the main grounds of the house. This was a notable achievement, for Susannah had been obliged to strap on a pair of wooden pattens over her slippers (her outdoor boots having disappeared), and then totter, somewhat clumsily, after her friend.

'Oh,' she complained, laughing, as she caught her breath, 'That gravel – I was like a cow on ice.'

The idea that Susannah could ever conform to such an ungainly image made Mary smile, that and the mere fact of her company. It was much easier to pretend that there was nothing unusual in the outing – certainly nothing secret or mysterious – when Susannah was one of the party; somehow Mary even *felt* more ordinary. *What could be more innocent than that two ladies should walk into Saxonhurst of an afternoon?* she asked herself, while aloud she observed, nodding at Susannah's umbrella, 'I do not think it is likely to rain again.'

'Neither do I,' Susannah agreed, 'but the colonel thought it might, and I would not like to be caught out.' Had Susannah but known it, this remark caused Mary's heart to jump; fortunately her next was more reassuring. 'Besides, have you never noticed that arming oneself against rain is the surest way to prevent it falling? Rather like a charm against evil influences. Not that rain is evil, of course.'

'Oh, no,' said Mary with a wan smile. 'But it is as well to use a charm, if you have one.'

They emerged triumphantly from Mrs Humphreys' shop some time later, having obtained a selection of cottons in various shades of green, as well as a milk jug and a packet of hairpins. Neither considered herself fond of shopping, and both found it remarkable how often the search for one item could inspire several apparently unrelated purchases, sometimes with the original errand quite forgotten. After laughing over this phenomenon, they hurried across the street and into the Queen's Head, the small tavern cum hostelry (fortunately empty at that hour), which also collected the post for the neighbourhood. Slipper, who had been tied up at a safe distance, begged most plaintively for his freedom, but was ignored.

Inside the Queen's Head they encountered an obstacle. The proprietor, Mr Neville, seemed incapable of concluding Mary's business speedily. The letter had first to be weighed, which required a search not merely for the scales but also the weights, several of which had apparently been lost on the preceding Tuesday. Mary's inability to produce the exact change called for a digression on the surprising want of copper coins, particularly since the start of the war. The ladies bore this with a moderate good humour until Mr Neville turned his attention to the letter itself. He was surprised, he said, that they should have brought it, rather than entrusting it to the Champian Hall footman who usually performed that task. Even this oblique suggestion that she might have been responsible for upsetting the usual routine seemed to disturb Susannah, but she recovered when he quipped that Mary's letter might have justified a personal delivery.

'Reckon this here mighter been somethin' special, eh, miss?' he chuckled, winking at her. 'One o' them love letters, p'rhaps?'

'Indeed, sir,' cried Susannah, drawing herself up. 'Your expression is irregular. I must ask you not to speak so to my friend.'

Mary blushed and this, coupled with the fact that Susannah was not Mrs Tipton, caused the unrepentant Neville to offer nothing more than a casual, 'Well, well,' by way of apology. Then, having made a more careful scrutiny of the address, he remarked, 'Ah, bankers, is it? Well, they do say as high finance is more important than love. More valuable, maybe. The heart is lighter when the purse is full?'

'If you *please*,' said Mary, stonily, 'might I ask when the post is collected?'

'Oh, aye,' he replied tossing the envelope into the cubby hole in the wall behind him. 'Let's see, now, it's Friday today . . . that makes it tomorrow afternoon she's off.'

'Thank you.' She nodded, and Susannah said, 'Good afternoon,' in what was for her a very marked manner.

Outside again, Mary wondered if it were possible to attract any more attention to her letter. *Well, what is done is done*, she told herself, and then smiled as Susannah whispered, 'We ought to have let Slipper bite him.'

Woolwich Common was very quiet for a spring afternoon, but otherwise the scene appeared unremarkable. The union flag, rather than the red banner of mutiny, fluttered above the barracks at the north end of the Common, while the barracks itself, a long, three-storied brick building, seemed undisturbed. At the edge of the parade ground a party of men stood huddled around a 12-pounder cannon, while their sergeant, an enormous Irishman who had the distinction of being the best boxer in the regiment, reminded them of the consequences of failing to swab out the barrel after firing.

'Now then, Kennedy, what would happen if you was to

forget what I've said and ram home the next charge regardless, and you peerin' down the mouth of the barrel like it was
a jar of rum?'

'The charge would blow me head off.'

'"The charge would blow me head off," *Sergeant O'Dwyer.*
Here would be you, and there would be yer head, and that
would be the shame of the world, so it would, and a terrible
sadness for Mrs Kennedy.'

'Kennedy ain't married,' complained one of his mates.

'Don't I know it,' O'Dwyer replied, 'and him still in petti-
coats last month? To be sure, I was thinkin' of his mother, the
poor woman.'

Holland was about to hail the sergeant when the sound of
raised voices from inside the barracks attracted his attention. It
was a dispute of some kind, but impossible to interpret at that
distance. Another voice, deadly in its ferocity, quickly restored
order, and then there was a more temperate exchange. Whatever
the storm, it seemed to have passed over without breaking.
Holland was conscious that the men at drill were watching
him covertly, having lost interest in their instruction. Then a
door three quarters of the way along the front of the barracks
opened and Jack Dalton appeared. He stood for a moment,
collecting himself, and then hurried across the parade ground
when he recognised Holland.

'What's going on, Jack?' demanded Holland, swiftly
dismounting and returning his friend's handshake. He noted
that Dalton was wearing his dress uniform and that neither the
men nor their sergeant had saluted him as he passed.

'Trouble, but no one knows how bad it is yet. You'd better
come with me. I'm going back to the Warren with a list of
the men's demands.'

'*Demands*?'

'Shh. "Complaints", if you like that word better. I'll explain
as we go.'

Holland nodded, and when they had left the barracks behind
them, asked, 'What was the meaning of that back there?'

'The gun drill? Probably intended to show that they can get

along without us.' Dalton shrugged. 'Or perhaps they mean to use it.'

'When did the trouble start?'

'This morning. I can hardly believe it, even now,' Dalton admitted. 'Everything was all right to begin with, apart from the usual bother whenever there's something special on.'

'Of course, I forgot – it's the twenty-sixth. What a time for the men to kick over the traces.' It was indeed. The twenty-sixth of May was the anniversary of the foundation of the regiment, the date on which gunners everywhere, but particularly at Woolwich, paraded in formal recognition of that fact.

'Exactly. Colonel Congreve was on edge, what with the master general beside him and it being his first big parade. He gave the order to dismiss, and none of the men moved. I've never seen anything like it. The order was repeated, and still no response. Then a delegation of sergeants left the parade and addressed the reviewing party – as if it were part of the programme. The sergeants said that the men respectfully declined to obey any orders coming from an officer at the present time.'

'Bloody hell,' breathed Holland. 'Are they holding the Warren against us?'

'Not precisely – Congreve and MacLeod are there now. The sergeants—'

'Bugger the sergeants!'

'No, it isn't quite like that. It seems that some of them were approached by the men who didn't want trouble but were afraid to hang back. The sergeants talked it out among them-selves and decided that it would be better if they took charge and stopped things from getting out of hand. A few may have their own ideas, of course . . .'

'But who started it?'

'I don't know. Some of the men *are* unhappy – I've known that for months – but God knows what brought it to a head.'

'Well, go on,' Holland urged. 'What happened next?'

'Lord Cornwallis asked the sergeants whether *they* would continue to obey orders, and they said yes, but that they hoped they wouldn't be ordered to do anything that made things

263

worse. There was a bit of a conference, and it was agreed that the sergeants would take responsibility for the men for the time being. The officers, apart from those with special duties such as yours truly, have been sent into Woolwich town, and we've been warned against doing anything that would provoke a confrontation.'

'But the sergeants are in charge?'

'For the moment there's a kind of . . . accommodation between them and Congreve.'

Holland fell silent, but as they approached the main gate of the Warren he checked Dalton with a hand on his arm. A brief argument ensued, but the result was that the list of demands was handed over, and Dalton was the one to retire. Holland did not often pull rank on his friend, but he had no intention of cooling his heels in Woolwich town. Yes, Colonel Congreve had ordered his officers away from the Warren, but Holland had worked closely with Congreve long enough to feel that this did not necessarily apply to him. At any rate, he wanted to give his chief the option of using him if he so desired.

The atmosphere inside the Warren confirmed to Holland that something unusual was happening. As a rule it was a noisy, bustling place, with civilian workers moving freely about the grounds. Today it was largely deserted, and the loudest sound came from a pair of strident gulls that squawked and called to each other as they circled the empty forecourt. Yet not quite empty, for there was Gunner Drake, advancing quickly from the direction of the barracks and officers' quarters.

He sidled up to Holland and took the reins from his hands. 'I'll see to this 'ere animal, sir,' he muttered, 'and your gear.'

Drake would have led the horse away, but Holland stopped him. He knew that they ought not to be seen talking, and that officers' servants were in a particularly awkward position whenever there was a breakdown of the normal hierarchy. Drake looked as if he had already discovered this; the side of his jaw was swollen and discoloured. 'You all right?' Holland demanded in a low voice.

Drake smiled, despite the bruising. 'Oh, this 'ere's nothin', sir. Some ignorant buggers 'as to learn to keep their traps shut, is all. Nothin' I can't 'andle.'

'Well, don't do anything foolish.'

'No, sir.'

They parted, and Holland advised, over his shoulder, 'Get yourself a poultice.'

'I'll do that, sir.'

Holland proceeded down the tree-lined avenue that divided the main block of workshops and storehouses from the laboratory. Under normal circumstances, this was where he would have expected to find Colonel Congreve. Today, however, the laboratory was closed, with guards posted at the doors. The colonel, he learned, had shifted his office to the Shop for the time being. The decision to close the laboratory was a sensible one, but Holland could not like the idea of the commandant being obliged to vacate the premises like a clerk whose office was being painted.

The Shop was actually the Royal Military Academy building, where cadets hoping to receive commissions in the Royal Artillery or the Royal Engineers were taught the rudiments of their profession. It was generally the province of raucous schoolboys and their harassed instructors, but instead of the usual habitués, Holland found the front steps blocked by armed men. From their general demeanour it was unclear whether they were protecting their commanding officer or holding him in custody. Their attitude towards Holland was more openly hostile. The blank looks, belying the fact that more than one knew him, and the surly tone of the man who received his name and asked him to wait, suggested that they would not back down from a confrontation – perhaps they were half-hoping for one.

After a short while he was allowed inside and told to proceed to the main lecture room. There he found the new commandant of Woolwich, Colonel Congreve, and Major MacLeod, the regiment's adjutant general.

'Holland,' said Congreve, looking up from his papers. 'Good, I am glad to see you. I gather that you know something of the mess we are in?'

'Yes, sir. I met Captain-Lieutenant Dalton on the Common. Here are the . . . complaints that he collected.'

'Ah, yes. MacLeod, have a look at them. Assuming that the men have not said that they want our heads, my judgment is that while things are not good, they could be much worse – just ask the Navy. Our task now is to make sure things do not *become* worse here. We cannot risk a spark.'

'No, sir.'

'The trouble started with a rumour, you know, that the government was going to increase the pay of the Army and militia, but that we would be left out. Now, the first part is true and the second is not, but it stirred everyone up. Then the barrack-room lawyers weighed in with a lot of silly demands, and fellows who never wanted to join the regiment in the first place let us know it.'

'What about outside agitators?'

'I daresay there have been a few of those. We cannot prevent the men from going into the town, and there are plenty of civilians who come into the Warren. But we also have our own bad apples, I am afraid.'

'Of the fourteen companies and detachments stationed here, three are in a bad way,' explained MacLeod. 'They have been poorly led and have taken on a large number of convicts and quota men. These companies are unsettled and contain trouble-makers. Thus far they have complied with all orders given them, but they must be watched carefully.'

'And those are not the only dangers,' said Congreve. 'Lord Cornwallis is a man of sense, but if he hears that we are in a dangerous state he will want to intervene. I expect he will come down again – he ought to come, by God – but I do not want him breathing fire and *provoking* a riot.'

'No, sir.'

'So, you see that it is important for a variety of reasons that Woolwich remains quiet tonight,' urged MacLeod. 'We need time to remind everyone that we are gunners, after all, and we do not go off half-cocked.' It was an ancient joke, but it made all of them smile.

Although he did not say so, Congreve considered Holland's arrival fortuitous. It had been agreed that two officers would remain in the Warren until the mutiny was resolved. Congreve had expected to perform this task himself, along with Major MacLeod, but now he perceived that the adjutant and Holland would be better suited to it. He disliked the idea of leaving his post, but he had great confidence in his subordinates – the first as a manager of men, and the second as having the nerve for situations when management did not suffice. There was no point in turning their heads, however, so he simply announced that he would be retiring to his house in Charlton. Major MacLeod would be in charge in the Warren, and Captain Holland would render any assistance as was necessary.

To MacLeod and Holland the colonel's decision made good sense. From Charlton he would be best placed to confer with Lord Cornwallis and to direct any response to trouble. Moreover, if the worst came to the worst, it was important that the commandant could not be harmed or made a hostage. Neither of the men who were to remain in the Warren mentioned this, however.

17

Mary retired early to her room that evening, tired by the day's events and the role they had obliged her to play. That role and her situation at Champian Hall were becoming increasingly difficult.

And how would it all end? With the colonel . . . arrested? It was certainly hard to feel much sympathy for him, but what would happen to Susannah if he were revealed as a traitor? She did not seem to *love* her husband, but she would undoubtedly feel some loyalty towards him, and how would she bear the humiliation of his disgrace? Would she ever forgive Mary for her part in his unmasking? Mary thought again of Sophia Holland. Sophia had married an unsuitable man and suffered humiliation in consequence. The cases were otherwise different, but she and Susannah were both Armitages. Might there be similarities in their characters? Sophia had died young, perhaps worn out and defeated by the burdens she had borne. If Crosby-Nash were made to stand his trial, would Susannah be any more resilient?

Mary walked slowly up and down the room as she considered these matters, although not so distractedly that she forgot to avoid the loose board, which squeaked alarmingly when one stepped on it. Her course, therefore, was not a straight one, and it took her to the edge of the writing desk. The pile of her open correspondence caught her attention, and she sat down to peruse it – not because the observations of Miss Trent and Miss Marchmont were particularly interesting, but because they were a world away from espionage and double-dealing. Charlotte's letter in particular made her smile, being written in that young lady's breathless style. Why, she wanted to know, could the Princess Royal not have had her wedding a few weeks earlier, when *they* had been in London? 'It would have been so exciting to see her pass by, or at least to see her carriage, for I do not believe she is particularly handsome. Do you think that "Wurtemberg" sounds like a very odd place to be princess of? I do, but Mama says not.'

I really oughtn't to leave these lying about, where anyone might read them, thought Mary, imagining the exchange between Charlotte and Lady Armitage. *There is nothing important, but the colonel . . .* She cajoled herself for the suggestion that her host might come into her bedchamber and rifle her letters. *No, I am the only one hereabouts likely to stoop to such a thing. Still, it is better to be care—*

Suddenly she sat up in her chair, and the smile faded from her lips. A thought, or the germ of an idea, occurred to her and began to grow, and with it came a nagging fear. Her last report to Romney, the one detailing the departure of Phoebus, had been deposited in the hiding-place in St Stephen's church shortly before the tinker's death. She had promptly retrieved her coin, but she had never checked to see whether Romney had collected that final message. He probably had done so, for she had left it on Thursday and he had very likely been killed on Sunday. But if he had not . . . *then it is still there, behind the loose brick, waiting to be found . . .*

Her stomach tightened even as her mind began to whirl with possibilities. *Romney was very efficient, therefore, it is not in the church, and if it is, it is well hidden. Why should anyone find it – or even think to look for it? Unless that is where they attacked Romney – in St Stephen's – perhaps the killer . . . perhaps he followed him there.* She shuddered at the image of Romney being struck down, perhaps even as he bent to remove the brick. *Horrible!*

But even if someone were to find the message, it would not betray

269

me . . . would it? She tried to remember what she had written. Might it be possible to compare the handwriting with hers? *Perhaps . . . but after all, there is no reason to believe that any of this happened. I am only frightening myself, imagining such horrors. The most likely case is that Romney collected the message, or it is still in its hiding place because no one knows about it!*

She rose from her chair and went to the window. The weather had cleared, but the air was still cool and fragrant with the earthy smells that followed rain. Could she possibly go to the church now and . . . make certain? She pictured the journey. It would be possible, but the more she thought about it the more implausible seemed the problem that prompted it. Surely, if the message was still in its hiding place – *and it probably is not, because Romney removed it* – its discovery by anyone else that very night was extremely improbable. *One might almost say, impossible.* It would lie in perfect safety behind the loose brick for years and years, unknown to all save an inquisitive mouse or beetle. *It really is a very inconspicuous brick.*

Telling herself that it was just like her to stir up a great deal of trouble over nothing, she closed the window and drew the curtain, thus shutting her mind resolutely against disturbing thoughts. When she climbed into bed she re-read her letters, smiling over Miss Trent's account of a tea party at Lindham Hall and how everyone complimented Mary and longed for the return of Miss Trent's umbrella, or perhaps it was the other way round. *I will examine the hiding place tomorrow morning, to be absolutely certain,* she resolved as she blew out the candle.

She sank into a dreamless sleep and never heard the respectful knocking at the front door of Champian Hall or, a few minutes later, the deferential voice of Lockwood reporting to his master that Mr Neville from the village would like a word, if convenient.

Holland returned to the academy building a little after nine o'clock, having spent a tedious evening in the Warren gate-house. He found Major MacLeod in one of the smaller lecture rooms, reading. 'Ah, you're back, I see,' remarked the latter, rubbing his eyes. He looked tired. 'Any news?'

'Yes, sir, and it's much as you'd expect. Lord Cornwallis has come down – I met him just now at the gate, and he's gone to see the colonel. He said that the Seventh Light Dragoons are being sent to Lewisham, in case we have need of them.'

'Ah, well, that is a comfort, although Lewisham is not quite on our doorstep.' MacLeod closed his book and surveyed Holland through the gloomy lantern light. 'So for now it's just us, then, holding the Warren for His Majesty.'

'Is that what we're doing?' asked Holland, wryly. 'Do the men know that?'

'I hope the point will not occur to them. Everything in order when you passed through?'

'Yes, sir, very quiet. The place seems a bit on edge, I think, but maybe that's just me.'

'No, I think we are all feeling the strain.' MacLeod sighed thoughtfully. 'Sometimes men lose their nerve at night, when everything is quiet and they have time to think, and sometimes the stillness fires them up. Well, I am going to finish this chapter and then turn in, and I advise you to do the same. They have put you across the way. Doubtless if anything *does* happen, we shall be the first to hear about it.'

When Holland looked in on his own accommodation he immediately recognised the influence of Gunner Drake. Not only had a cot been made up in proper regimental fashion, but also several items had been retrieved from Holland's rooms, including his razor and a clean shirt. Even more welcome were the plate of sandwiches and the half bottle of brandy.

He felt pleasantly weary after he had eaten, but not yet ready for sleep. Taking the bottle with him, he walked out into the night. Without really thinking about his destination, he headed for the river, but instead of turning left to the main wharf he walked towards the tree-lined path behind the sea wall on the right, the area that had once been known as Prince Rupert's Walk. It was a cool, moonless night, but the brandy and Holland's

271

own thoughts kept him warm. He was thinking about Woolwich, Dick Whittington, Horse Guards, and Mary Finch, although not in that particular order. *What is Mary doing?* he wondered. She would have gone to bed by now, but had sleep come easily? Might she be lying awake, thinking of what he had told her? The possibility made him flush, and instead he pictured her face at their parting; she had been worried about him. *Damn it, when she's the one in danger, in that bloody house, with no one to help her.* He longed to do something, but what? As long as the mutiny lasted he was practically a prisoner himself.

It was probably a mistake to sit down beside the edge of the wall, with his back against a tree. The tide had turned, but there was still an expanse of black, greasy mud between the water and the shore. A breeze carried the several odours of the Thames, some of them unpleasant, but they also reminded Holland of spring rain, and growing things, and the sea. He could hear the wavelets trickling and gurgling below him, coming closer, as the river returned to its bed. *The river . . . London . . . What if . . . But London might as well be a hundred miles away, and at this time of night . . .*

He might have dozed for a few minutes, but he was perfectly aware of the sound of approaching footsteps. He had been expecting them, in fact, ever since wandering into this secluded area. When the steps drew closer he remarked in a low, conversational voice, 'Thanks for the grub.'

A voice grunted an acknowledgement. 'Thought you might not've 'ad time for much today.'

'No, I haven't.'

Drake squatted down beside him, and Holland passed the bottle. Drake took a brief swig and handed it back. For a few minutes neither spoke, and Holland gazed out over the dark, shimmering expanse. Finally Drake began, rather diffidently. 'About this 'ere, sir . . . Are we buggered?'

'The men, do you mean?'

Drake shrugged uncomfortably. 'Mm . . . But I was thinkin' more . . . of heverything.'

272

'I don't know. Horse Guards doesn't like mutinies – especially not just now.'

'Too bad they *'ad* to 'ear about it,' Drake grumbled. 'I mean, if things could've been patched up just amongst ourselves.'

'Woolwich is too important for that. Any trouble here was bound to bring in the Army. Whosever idea this was should have thought of that before he decided to make the regiment look like a pack of idiots.'

'I know, but . . .'

Holland glanced across. 'I'm not asking you to give anyone away, but now the colonel's got to hold the ring between our men and any the Army sends, and that's no easy job.'

'Wot's likely to 'appen, d'you think?'

'If nothing changes, we'll be made to stand down and the trouble-makers dealt with – but if the men act up now there'll be hell to pay for everyone. Any sign of that?'

'Well, there's a few bright sparks – or them wot thinks of 'emselves as such – but I don't know as they can do much 'arm.' Drake considered this for a moment. 'Not on their own.'

'Good. Then maybe it will all blow over.'

'Aye, maybe.'

The silence between them grew until Drake thought Holland had fallen asleep, but when he cast a speculative glance in Holland's direction, Drake saw that his eyes were open. More than that, he was fully alert and listening to something. Then Drake heard it too, or rather, felt it: a soft, stealthy presence somewhere nearby.

Holland returned the glance, a warning finger against his lips, and they both rose cautiously. The sound resolved itself into footsteps; they were coming from the direction of the carpenter's shop at the end of this section of the wall, close by the old arsenal boundary. Holland weighed up the likely possibilities – a gunner who did not fancy a long stint on guard duty? A convict escaping from one of the hulks anchored outside the new wharf? An intruder bent on thievery or . . . something worse? Whoever he was, he was certainly trying to keep his presence a secret.

Drake moved slowly to one side, so that whoever it was would have to pass between them. He had no weapon apart from the brandy bottle, but he grasped this by the neck as a makeshift club. *Oh, Jesus,* he fretted as Holland too began to move. *Stay where you are, sir, for Gawd's sake. Let the bugger come to you.*

Then the footsteps stopped, as if their owner sensed that he was not alone. A moment of silent speculation followed, and then Holland moved slowly forward again. Reassured, or at least not put off by the confirmation of Holland's presence, the footsteps resumed, and a voice whispered, tentatively, *'Major?'*

'Yes,' Holland answered, also keeping his voice low and advancing a few more steps. He was fairly close now, and could make out the other man's dark silhouette; he looked to be dressed in civilian clothes. 'Here I am.'

But this was apparently not the correct reply, and the man drew back. Something in his posture sent an immediate warning to Drake. 'Knife!' he hissed and, abandoning all pretence of silence, smashed the bottle against a tree trunk to create a jagged edge.

He could give no tangible aid, however, for suddenly the other two men sprang at each other. There was a scuffle, the sound of blows exchanged, and then they were on the ground, a twisting, struggling mass. Drake could only look on, or rather, stand by, for he could hardly distinguish between them, and he certainly could not intervene without putting Holland in greater danger. 'Jesus, sir, look out!' he urged, helplessly.

The combatants were on their feet again. The stranger struck out wildly, like a frenzied animal; Holland dodged, and again. He grasped his opponent's flailing arm, cursed, and stepped aside. The other man started, dropping his guard, and Holland delivered a hard blow to his midsection that robbed him of breath. He stumbled and was disarmed.

Drake heard, rather than saw, the knife fall to the ground, and he fished it out of the grass. It was a wicked thing, a clasp knife whose blade flicked open at a touch. Drake ran his finger along the serrated edge. Was it wet?

As its former owner was hauled upright, still gasping, Holland wrenched the man's arms behind him and held him fast. 'Hold still,' he ordered, enforcing his wishes with a further wrench. 'Search him, Drake.'

Drake found something long and round, like a tube of some kind, in the man's coat, and tossed it at Holland's feet. 'You all right, sir?' he asked. 'Did 'e cut you?'

'Yes. A little.' The admission, however, stoked Holland's anger, and having transferred control of his opponent to Drake, he demanded, 'Who are you, damn it? What's your name?'

'Smith,' came the halting reply. He was a slight man, and in his shabbily decent suit he looked like a clerk who had been caught up in a mêlée against his will. His furious glare, however, belied the passive image. Although he was breathing hard, if Drake had freed his hands he would have sprung at Holland again with neither hesitation nor mercy.

'Well, Smith, what the bloody hell are you doing here? Who let you in?' Holland knelt and retrieved the tube, which proved to be a sheaf of papers, tightly rolled and tied with a piece of string. 'Starting your own revolution, eh?'

'Reckon 'e ain't got breath for it just now,' advised Drake, tightening his grip and effectively lifting Smith onto his toes. 'What should we do with 'im?'

The slash on Holland's arm was starting to sting. He shook a handkerchief out of his pocket and wound it over the torn place on his sleeve. *God, I'm shaking*, he marvelled, and consciously took a steadying breath before he replied. 'Take him to the Shop. MacLeod will want to hear about this straight-away . . . without a lot of noise.'

'Right you are,' nodded Drake, but he hesitated when he perceived that Holland was not coming too.

'I'm going to have a look round,' Holland explained. 'Make sure that we don't have any other visitors.'

'But wot if—'

'Stop jawing.' Holland gestured angrily. 'Or aren't you taking orders any more either?'

'Well, all right,' allowed Drake, grudgingly, 'but if you see anything, don't tackle it on your own!' Shaking his head, he conducted Smith back along the path towards the academy. 'And just you behave yourself, *Mr* Smith,' he warned, his voice a low growl. 'Try anything funny and I'll gut you like a fish.'

Holland watched them depart and then set off towards the main gate, walking purposefully but not too quickly. There was no point startling the sentries, and he had not quite made up his mind what to do. Smith's papers had given him an idea, and it was a good one, so long as he had the nerve for it. *And if you're right about the men*, he added to himself, *for it all depends on them*. Was the Warren a powder keg, waiting for Smith to light the fuse? Was that what his coming signified – that they were ready for him? Or did the moderation they had displayed thus far mean that the wilder calls for rebellion had been ignored, and the agitators were trying one last throw?

What Holland proposed would answer those questions, one way or the other. If successful it would help to convince the men that they could trust their officers. Of course, it would also give any hothead the chance to succeed where Smith had failed, but if the mutiny were to turn violent, two lightly armed officers were unlikely to survive for very long in any case. With that contrast before him, he made his decision and turned to the left in the direction of the barracks. As he expected, lights were burning inside the nearer building. A simple relaxation in normal discipline or did the men inside have a particular reason for being awake? He could hear voices, but nothing out of the ordinary. 'Well, here we go,' he muttered, knocked firmly at the door, and entered.

So surprised were the men by his sudden appearance that no one spoke, and only a few rose haltingly to their feet. Chairs scraped, and there was a dull clank as something metal fell over. The room smelled of sweat and pipe smoke, and the boiled cabbage that had been served for dinner. Holland scanned the faces gazing back at him, pale or shadowed by the candlelight. Many were strangers to him, and he could not immediately interpret the situation. These men were off duty, yet most were still dressed. Some were gathered round a table; they might have been playing cards, but bunks had also been moved as if to clear space for a meeting.

'Evening, men.' He stepped deeper into the room, conscious that he would have no clear line of retreat. 'I wouldn't ordinarily intrude here, only I've had some news, and I thought you'd be interested to hear it.' He paused. 'A civilian by the name of Smith got into the Warren tonight . . . probably over the east wall.'

An anxious murmur greeted Holland's words, but this was his chance and he must take it. 'So, I don't think he came with the blessing of any of the sergeants, but just on his own authority. He brought some papers' – the tension that had faded slightly with the previous sentence flared up again with that word – 'that I think he wanted you to see.' He unrolled the sheets and held them up.

Some of the men stared at Holland – in disbelief, in fear – while others looked away. A voice spoke guardedly out of the shadows. 'What do they say?'

'I don't know,' Holland replied; he could not find the speaker. 'Do you want to read them?'

'It's a trap,' cautioned a sallow-faced man to Holland's right. He was leaning back in his chair, legs outstretched, his tunic unbuttoned. 'He'll take down the names of anyone who even touches 'em.'

'Don't be a fool, Curtis,' complained a balding man on the other side of the room. 'Paper and ink can't hurt you.'

'Paper be damned,' snapped the other. He sat up slowly in his chair, but did not take his eyes off Holland. 'Reckon they've got spies watchin' at the window . . . or in here amongst us.'

Other voices joined the argument, and Holland had to intervene. His heart was pounding and he knew that his authority was precarious, but he had to assert it. 'I'm not here to spy or to take down names,' he called. 'I don't think any civilian can tell you what's right or wrong in the regiment, and that's what Smith meant to try. And I think that letting outsiders stir you

277

up will only cause trouble for all of us – worse trouble than we have already. But I don't say you shouldn't look at these papers. I think you *should* look and then make up your own minds, without someone like Smith driving you.'

Holland attempted to pass the documents, which he now perceived to be roughly printed handbills, to the men standing nearest to him, but they shrank back as if he were offering them a poisonous snake. They, in turn, were shoved forward by men behind them who cried, 'Take one, Joe, you old woman' or 'Let me have a look'. A few handbills thus made their way to the back of the room or onto the floor. Most remained in Holland's hand, however, and now he was uncertain. He could not very well force the men to read the damned things, but if they simply held back out of fear the real issue remained doubtful.

Then a calm, reasonable voice suggested that Captain Holland read the paper aloud. 'That way we'll all know the truth of it with no man singled out as one thing or the other. And you can't say fairer than that.' It was Sergeant O'Dwyer, leaning casually against one of the bunks in a shadowy corner.

'How do we know he'll read 'em honest?' demanded someone, but more heads were nodding in support of the sergeant's suggestion, and Holland said, 'All right, I'll read it, and any man among you can stop me if I change a word or leave anything out.'

'Not you, Roberts,' complained one of the men at the table. 'You couldn't read to save your life.'

'That's how come he joined up,' agreed his neighbour. 'Only signed the 'listment oath cause he thought he was buying a lottery ticket.'

'Well, you can read it for him,' Holland urged. He handed papers to both men and set down the rest at the empty place at the table. Then he asked for another candle. Its light shone onto his face as he began to read, and if the exercise made him nervous, neither his expression nor his tone made this obvious.

'To the British Army. Comrades! Are we not men? Is it not high time we should prove that we know ourselves to be such? Are we anywhere respected as men, and why are we not? Have not wrong notions of discipline led us to our present despised condition? Is there a man among us who does not wish to defend his country and who would not willingly do it without being subject to the insolence and cruelty of effeminate puppies?'

'Who's a puppy, then?'
'He means the captain.'
'Pipe down!'

'Were not the sailors like us mocked for want of thought, though not so much despised for poverty as we are? Have they not proved that they can think and act for themselves and preserve every useful point of discipline, full as well, or better, than when under the tyranny of their officers?'

'Oh, aye.'
'Pipe down, Roberts! Let him finish!'

'What makes this difference between a commissioned officer and a private or non-commissioned? Are they better men? You must laugh at the thought. Do they have discipline half so well as our sergeants? Don't they owe their promotions to their connections with placemen and pensioners and a mock parliament which pretends to represent the people?

When we think of the people ought not each of us to think of a father or brother as a part of them? Can you think a parliament speaking like fathers and brothers would treat us as we are treated?

Would they mock us with a pretended addition to our pay, and then lock us up in barracks to cheat us and keep us in ignorance? Would they not rather consider the price of everything wanting for our families and at least double our pay?

279

Are we so well clothed as soldiers ought to be? Ask the old pensioners of your regiment. Ask them too if it was useful when there were fewer regiments for colonels to make a profit out of soldiers' clothes. Don't colonels now draw half their incomes from what we ought to have but of which we are robbed?

These, COMRADES, are a few of our grievances, and but a few. WHAT SHALL WE DO? The tyranny of what is falsely called discipline prevents us from acting like other men. We cannot even join in petition for that which common honesty would freely have given us long ago. WE HAVE ONLY TWO CHOICES, either to submit to the present impositions or to demand the treatment proper to men.

THE POWER IS ALL OUR OWN! The regiments which send you this are willing to do their part. They will show their countrymen they can be soldiers without being slaves, and will make their demands as soon as they know you will not draw trigger against them. Of this we will judge as soon as we know that you have distributed this BILL not only among your comrades, but to every soldier whom you know in any part of the country. BE SOBER! BE READY!'

Holland looked at his audience. 'That's the end.' There was silence, and then he added, 'Whoever wrote that doesn't know much about the regiment. We've no bought commissions and no special benefits for officers that haven't been earned.'

'What about the sergeants?' demanded the gunner named Curtis, who was now leaning forward, elbows on knees. 'Paper's right about them. They know their business better 'n any officer.'

Holland forced himself to answer lightly, and his query, 'Is that because Sergeant O'Dwyer has got you under his eye?' won a laughing admission from another quarter. Pressing his advantage, he continued, 'It's the sergeants' business to teach you your drill and to keep the guns firing when enemy shot is coming in, and that's damned important. But do you think it's the whole work of the regiment?'

280

'It's all *I* ever seen,' complained someone else. 'Drill and nothing but.'

'That's because you've never been away from Woolwich — never seen real fighting. Once you've been in a scrape, you'll know that it takes more than loading and firing to win it. Who has to site the guns so that they hit the enemy hardest? Who has to decide whether to use mortars or cannons to bombard a city or bring down a wall? The officers who have studied and learned all those things and more — first here at the Warren and then in the field.'

'Aye, and where'd *you* learn?'

'India,' replied O'Dwyer, before Holland could speak. 'Where there's tigers, and the sun's so hot it'll burn you black as yer boots, and the natives like to strangle you in yer bed. "Thuggees", they call 'em. They'll have a drink and pass the time o' day, as free as the feller you meet on the road to Templemore, and then squeeze the life out of you with their little scarves, so they will. I only mention it, Plumb, in case you're thinkin' of makin' a change.'

Laughter greeted this remark, too, and someone cried that they didn't have a complaint against Captain Holland, nor against Colonel Congreve. But others . . .

'There are bad apples in every barrel,' Holland admitted. 'Bad officers, bad sergeants, and bad gunners. But not many, and the good of the regiment is stronger than the bad. That's why the colonel has put his faith in the sergeants, and why you're still following their orders. That's why the colonel asked you to set down your complaints in a petition — a petition that this paper says you can't make.'

'We goin' to get what we asked for?'

'Very likely you will,' said Holland, 'if you don't ask for the moon, and if you keep calm. If you lose your heads, like . . . like a crowd of Frenchmen, then you'll have the rest of the Army down here, and that will be the end of anything reasonable. Look, I know you'd like to be off fighting the Frogs — so would I — but until orders come through for that we've got to be patient.'

'What about our pay?'

'You'll get an increase, the same as every other man in the Army. It was agreed in Parliament days ago. Anyone who says different is a liar.'

This assertion, and the confidence with which Holland uttered it, seemed to win general support, but a few men asked for Sergeant O'Dwyer's opinion. What did he think?

The big sergeant straightened, but he still spoke with the same, placid lilt. 'Well, lads, if it was a choice between the word of a man that's known the regiment all his life and a civilian, an outsider that couldn't tell you the difference between a rampart and a ravelin – which even young Evans, there, could do – I know where I'd be putting my trust.'

The unfortunate Evans, who was one of the dullest men in his company, was prodded and teased, and the feeling in the room seemed to lighten. Men smiled at Holland who had avoided his glance, and he heard the word 'sir' for the first time. Sensing that this might be the time to retire, he asked whether anyone had anything else to say. No one did, so he wished them a curt good night and executed his manoeuvre – in good order and taking the papers with him.

Outside he felt the tension slide from his shoulders and permitted himself a sigh of relief. He had taken a chance, a hell of a chance, perhaps, but it had paid off. *Thank God*, he thought, feelingly. *Thank God and Sergeant O'Dwyer.*

The lesser of those two beings loomed up beside him. 'That was well done, sir, if you don't mind me saying,' he murmured.

The two men moved away from the building. 'I'm grateful for your support, sergeant. Everything all right in there now?'

'As right as rain, sir.'

'Do I need to go along to the other barracks?'

'I don't think so. I'll maybe have a little look and a word, just to steady 'em, but they're good lads, and I don't think they'll be needin' it. This is where the trouble was going to start – *if* it started. That's why I was keepin' an eye on 'em. But they'll settle down now.'

'I'll leave you to it, then.'

'Yes sir. That Smith fellow, now – I heard him oratin' in the town once, and I couldn't think much of him. He was like one of those little popguns. The bang can give you a bit of a fright, but you soon see that there's no iron in it at all. It's often the way with your Englishmen . . . saving your presence.'

'Good night, sergeant.'

'And to you, sir.'

The air felt fresher and the pavement more solid beneath his feet as Holland walked away. The darkness was no longer a gloomy threat, but merely the natural way of things. He was still smiling at O'Dwyer's remark as he turned the corner. Then a figure stepped out of the shadows and whispered his name: *'Captain 'Olland, sir!'*

'Damn it, Drake, you nearly killed me that time.'

'Aye, and you nearly done the same fer me! I seen you come out of that barracks and I thought – wot was you doin' in there?'

'Nothing, just having a chat. What happened with Smith?'

'The major and Sergeant Mitchell 'ad a go at him, but 'e kept 'is mouth shut, so 'e's been put in the cells to think it over.' Smith's knife had somehow not been confiscated, and Drake turned this over to Holland. 'Arm all right, sir?'

Holland surveyed the weapon and handed it back. 'Yes.' Then he smiled. 'But I wish you hadn't broken that bottle.'

Drake grinned in reply. 'So do I, sir. 'Specially as I borrowed it off of Mr Dalton, and I bet you 'e says I owes 'im an 'ole one back.'

18

'Holland! Wake up!'

The urgent tone and the awareness of being in unfamiliar surroundings triggered a sense of danger. Holland opened his eyes and rolled over onto his elbow, fully awake and reaching for his sword. Above him loomed Major MacLeod in night-shirt and uniform coat, and Holland relaxed. 'What is it, sir?' he murmured. 'What's happened?'

'Nothing *here*,' MacLeod replied in a similar tone, 'but we've had some news, and Horse Guards ought to be informed of it. Get dressed and come across. Quick as you can.'

Having slept in his shirt and breeches, it only took Holland a moment to pull on his boots. His coat required more care; the left sleeve was stiff where the blood had dried, and he had to ease it over the bandage on his forearm. A pale twilight shone in at the window, and beyond the shot yard the Thames looked grey and cold. He consulted his watch – not quite four.

MacLeod was writing when Holland entered, hastily tying his stock. 'Right,' he said, 'here is the position. Word has just come through that His Majesty's Ship *Lancaster*, currently at anchor in the Long Reach, has mutinied.'

The rebelliousness of one more Navy vessel was of little general interest to Holland, but he immediately saw the signifi-cance of this particular announcement. 'Can her guns fire on the Purfleet magazine?' he asked.

'No, apparently not. However, apprehending the possible danger, Captain Nesbitt has his men drawn out, and they have orders to fire on anyone attempting to approach the magazine. However, that is a very ticklish situation, as you are well aware. We mustn't have any shooting there if we can help it, with all that powder liable to go up. Nesbitt has a garrison of eighty men, but he needs reinforcements, if any can be found, in case the mutineers decide to come ashore.'

MacLeod placed his hand on the papers they had taken from Smith. 'What is more, Mr Smith's friends have been active elsewhere. Apparently documents of a similar kind have appeared in Canterbury among our horse troops – where I am pleased to say they received a very frosty reception. I trust that Nesbitt will have no difficulties with *his* men, but that is another reason why it is important that he receives reinforcements straightaway.

'You are to ride to Charlton and inform Colonel Congreve and Lord Cornwallis – if he is still there – of the situation. I expect they will send you on to London. You ought to have a clear run at this time of day. Better give Woolwich town a miss though. Smith's friends may be making mischief there, too.'

As MacLeod had predicted, Holland made only a brief stop in Charlton and then set off again. On arriving in the capital he sought out Captain Parrish, Lord Cornwallis's aide-de-camp, on the grounds that no one deserved to learn of his chief's wishes via a sharply worded note from headquarters. Parrish, in turn, advised that they take the news straight to Sir William Fawcett, the Army's adjutant general, on the grounds that there would be no one awake at Horse Guards at half past five in the morning, and Sir William would never forgive them if they did not notify him first – whatever the hour.

The general received them in his dressing gown and questioned Holland closely, while Parrish wrote to his dictation. He then sent them off to Horse Guards with a string of orders for the East London and Warwickshire militias and the Coldstream Guards. There was little for Holland to do in all of this, and it occurred to him that he might undertake some business of his own. Again he conferred with Captain Parrish, whose London contacts were extensive and who was still feeling grateful.

'I doubt if he is likely to be anywhere but in bed at this hour,' said Parrish, in response to Holland's question, 'and if you do not care to visit him at home—'

'No, I don't think so.'

Parrish attempted to disguise his curiosity. These gunners were clearly not quite the dull dogs that everyone thought them. Who would have thought they would concern themselves with high politics? 'Well, then, I believe the attorney general's chambers are in Lincoln's Inn.'

Even the most energetic government lawyer was unlikely to be in his chambers before eight o'clock on a Saturday morning; therefore, Holland decided to walk to Lincoln's Inn. Two faces of London society greeted him as he turned north into Whitehall; clerks hurrying towards their offices climbed over the prostrated forms of last night's revellers, while women bearing baskets and calling 'mackerel, new mackerel, four for a shilling' and 'primroses, all a-growing, all a-blowing' took up positions on corners only just surrendered by those with other commodities on offer. Holland was propositioned by more than one of the weary prostitutes lingering outside the gin shops at Charing Cross. Unshaven and haphazardly dressed, he too seemed to belong to the city's night-time world.

This would also have been the view of the highly respectable denizens of Lincoln's Inn, if any of them had been stirring. All was quiet, however, when Holland passed through the gatehouse in Chancery Lane, and in New Court the only sound was the faint splashing of the fountain. He sat down to wait on the steps of number eleven, and to eat the spicy meat pie he had purchased from one of the stalls outside Horse Guards. They were called 'bow-wow pies', but Holland, like many a soldier before him, was too phlegmatic to worry about the possible implications of this choice of name.

286

As he waited, his thoughts turned to the attorney general. He had met Sir John Scott once before. Like Mary, Holland had been obliged to submit himself to questioning by various representatives of government following the Déprez affair, and the attorney general had been among them. That experience had confirmed Holland's view that lawyers were worse than senior officers for saying one thing, meaning another, and doing something else.

Sir John Scott appeared at nine o'clock, accompanied by his clerk. If he was surprised by his visitor there was little indication of this in his greeting, apart from his observation that Captain Holland looked as if he could do with a cup of coffee, and would Peters be so good as to call round at Serle's for one? And then he shepherded Holland inside.

'Now, sir, to what do I owe the pleasure of this meeting?' asked Sir John, having settled himself at his desk. He produced a pen and paper. 'It is a matter of some importance, I presume? Do, please, sit down.'

'Yes, sir, it is. It's Cuthbert Shy. I've got to find him.'

Sir John set down his pen. 'Ah, Mr Shy.' Then he leaned back in his chair and smiled blandly. 'The man of mystery. Fancy your making enquiries about him to me. I do not like to disappoint you, sir, but I fear you have made a wasted journey. The government, and myself in particular, has no knowledge of Mr Shy – or even whether he exists.'

Holland bit back a sharp reply. This was exactly the kind of quibbling he had expected, and there was nothing to be gained by losing his temper. Nevertheless, he stared implacably at the attorney general. 'You knew about Shy when you sent Mary Finch to see him.'

Sir John's expression changed in an instant. 'Mary Finch?'

'That's right. Does *she* exist?'

'Indeed, sir—'

'You can save all that,' Holland advised. 'I've been to Champian Hall – where Shy sent her to spy on Colonel Crosby-Nash – and she needs help.'

★   ★   ★

Holland's encounter with Cuthbert Shy was even less straight-forward than Mary's had been. He too was bundled in and out of cabs by the dutiful Peters, but his journey terminated, not at a small, private residence, but at Montagu House, the repository for the treasures of the British Museum. Furthermore, partway through the journey, Peters' place was taken by a middle-aged man in a plain, smoke-coloured suit and tie wig. With small spectacles pushed up on his forehead and a gold watch chain stretched across his waistcoat, he looked like a reasonably prosperous tradesman. His only concession to fashion – if it could be called that – was an elaborately carved walking-stick, which, he explained, was actually a club used by warriors of the South Seas. The furious, two-faced top warded off evil spirits, and the rows of sharp points projecting at the bottom were useful against an earthly enemy.

The club, the journey, and the man himself aroused all of Holland's prejudices against 'spies and trickery', nor were these dispelled when they reached their destination. The museum was closed, but Holland's companion brushed that detail aside – he was a trustee and could come and go as he pleased. Private viewings, moreover, were so much more peaceful. 'Of course, they know me here under a different name,' he added, as the porter passed them through. Once inside the main building he continued to act as if he were conducting Holland on such a private tour, pointing out the 'marvellous disorder' of the entrance hall and asking Holland's opinion of the painted ceiling. At the top of the great staircase he bowed to the terracotta bust of a gentleman in a frilled collar and large, old-fashioned wig – his invariable custom, he said, in honour of the Great Man. As no other identification was provided, the source of this greatness escaped Holland, and he trailed after his conductor in a growing state of suspicious mystification.

In the saloon, however, his opinion began to change. Mr Shy, for it was he, proved to be both a keen and a penetrating questioner. He immediately appreciated what Holland had to tell him, and he pressed for details that Holland had not realised that he knew. On the other hand, he continued to weave observations on the museum specimens into his 'official' enquiries. Their conversation proceeded, therefore, along interesting, if unpredictable lines.

As concerned the affair of the Birchin Lane jewellers, for example.

'Miss Finch has never spoken to you about the shop?' 'No, sir, only how the woman there bested her.' 'Ah, the device of the bent fastening. What of the shop itself, do you recognise the name or the address?' 'I know the street, sir. The offices of Tinker and Taylor – two gunpowder-makers – are in Birchin Lane.' 'That is interesting . . . Gunpowder . . . hmm, rather brings Parliament to mind. An act of Parliament created the museum, you know. A jeweller would have connections abroad, of course, with Antwerp and Amsterdam . . . you are aware that diamonds come from India, I daresay, Captain Holland?' 'Yes, sir, like the Pitt Diamond.' 'Indeed, the French have it now, unfortunately. Gems make a very efficient means of transporting large sums of money, which most conspiracies need, eventually.'

And the men known as Rabelais and Phoebus.

'This Greek vase, they tell me, represents the apotheosis of Homer, which is quite an achievement for a poet. I wish we were in a position to unite this "Rabelais" with his eternal reward. An associate from the colonel's time in India, you say?' 'That's what Miss Finch and Major Whittington believe.' 'And a devotee of Robespierre . . . nasty fellow. What do you say to this display, sir? The Lethieullier mummy. Is it not astonishing? The fellow was in the colonel's line of work, I believe – Lethieullier, I mean, served in the East India Company Army – I cannot speak for the mummy. The lawyer Phoebus I consider less interesting; there was a painting of Apollo and Phaeton in the antechamber at the top of the stairs – I daresay you noticed it?' 'Yes, sir; you pointed it out.' 'Different story, of course. Our information on him will be communicated to the Admiralty. "*Do unto others*", you know, Captain Holland. They will like to be informed that he is stirring the pot at Sheerness, and that business is rather more than I can take on at this stage. Rabelais, on the other hand . . . I believe we must strain every sinew in his direction.'

On the topic that concerned him most, however, Holland was disappointed.

'Will you tell Miss Finch to leave Champian Hall, sir?' '*Tell her?* Oh, no, no. She knows the situation best and must make her own decision. One must always trust the man – or woman – on the scene.' 'Will you send another agent, at least, to keep an eye on her?' 'Perhaps, perhaps, but do you see that stuffed beast in the cabinet? It is a kangaroo, and a curious beast if ever there was one.' 'Very curious, sir.' 'Curious beasts attract attention, especially if someone with a particular interest in the species is on the lookout for them, and attention of that sort is often dangerous. Dangerous to all concerned, as a matter of fact.' 'Yes, sir, I see your point.' 'Splendid. I thought that you would.'

Morning sunshine, particularly after a day of rain, generally raised Mary's spirits. As she approached Champian Hall, however, the fine spring weather had no perceptible effect upon her, for she was deep in thought. She had visited St Stephen's and opened the secret hiding place. There she had found . . . nothing; the scrap of paper containing her final report to Romney was gone.

There was nothing sinister in its absence. Romney had had plenty of time to retrieve the paper, and he had undoubtedly done so. It was pointless – silly, really – to imagine that some unknown person could have located the hiding place since his death. She told herself this more than once as she retraced her steps from the church, and she was frowning as she crossed the lawn.

The great hall was pleasantly cool, particularly for someone who had forgotten her hat. Moreover, as Mary closed the door behind her, she heard the tail-end of an exchange that entirely changed her frame of mind. Lockwood was scolding one of the footmen, who stood before him bearing a loaded tray. 'No, no, you blockhead, not here. The gentlemen will want their coffee in the library. And see that you don't dawdle.'

He offered a few more remarks on punctuality, listening to

instructions the first time, and avoiding spills, but these passed Mary by. *The gentlemen will want their coffee in the library.* The colonel had a visitor, and if she had not returned at that moment, she might not have known! Of course, it was not certain that the visitor was related to her work, but she thought it very likely. Why else would he have been spirited away to the library, rather than being presented to Susannah or at least entertained in one of the more public rooms? *And Lockwood called him a gentleman, so he has not come on estate business . . .* No sooner had the butler retired in the direction of the kitchens, shaking his head, than she was racing up the stairs towards the storeroom.

As she gently opened the trapdoor and descended into the narrow passage, she congratulated herself on fulfilling Mr Shy's expectations of her. Yes, and very soon she would be able to communicate her findings to him again. This feeling of satisfaction grew as she heard the stranger speak through the library wall. He had an unusual accent, and this strengthened her conviction that his appearance at Champian Hall was important. Foreigners very likely meant trouble. Then she heard another voice, but it did not sound quite like the colonel's. Was something muffling the sound? She drew nearer to the wall of her compartment, her hand pressed against the rough surface as if this might help her to sympathise more directly with her quarry.

The voices sounded odd again, as if two people were speaking at once . . . but now she was more certain that she heard the colonel . . . and the oddly accented voice . . . and now a third. *Ah, he has two visitors,* Mary concluded. *Lockwood did say 'gentlemen', after all. Well, I must simply listen more carefully.*

The wall behind her had a shallow indentation just above waist height, and by standing on tiptoes and using the wall in front for leverage, she could raise herself onto this narrow ledge and let her feet hang down. It was much more comfortable than standing, especially if she had to remain at her post for any length of time. She carefully executed the manoeuvre and prepared to be patient.

Patience and a comfortable seat soon proved necessary. The three men must have moved away from the desk and sofa, for their conversation was no longer perfectly intelligible. Mary pictured them standing in front of the windows, perhaps, or studying something at the large table on the other side of the room. Yes, perhaps that was it. She could pick out individual words, occasionally phrases, and these suggested that the men were looking at a map.

'Yes, I . . . Erith,' remarked Crosby-Nash. 'The activities . . . Nore mutineers . . . difficult for you.'

'Difficult,' complained the Foreign Voice, 'these villainous fellows . . . to ruin me!'

The Other Voice explained, 'Mr Rangan's ship . . . to sail, . . . captain . . . dare to leave port . . . mutinous vessels in the Long Reach . . . guns at Tilbury and Sheerness . . . out of the water, no sensible man . . . the gauntlet.'

Colonel Crosby-Nash said that he quite agreed. 'No one . . . employer's interests at heart . . . such a risk.'

'. . . other captains, I assure you, sir. We are . . . hostage . . . pistol . . . to our heads.' The Foreign Voice had a light, faintly singsong quality to it, and this became more pronounced as he strove to make his point. 'Why does . . . government . . . this wickedness? . . . livelihoods of honest men?'

Mary leaned back on her makeshift seat. As the conversation continued, she gradually put the pieces together to construct a coherent whole. Mr Rangan – the Foreign Voice – was responsible for a ship stuck somewhere on the Thames between London and the sea, whose departure was being disrupted by the Nore Mutiny. In consequence of this disruption he had been obliged to trespass on the hospitality of his friend, the Other Voice. *He* was definitely English, and seemed to be a neighbour or acquaintance of the colonel's. Given the colonel's own Indian connections, the visit appeared to have been designed either to divert Mr Rangan's thoughts to more pleasant topics or to provide him with a sympathetic audience.

As it became clear that neither Mr Rangan nor the other gentleman (his name might have been Ponsonby) had any sinister purpose in coming to Champian Hall, Mary naturally lost interest in their conversation. Even a reference to Woolwich – Mr Rangan had heard that there was trouble at the Warren – proved a false alarm, for when pressed he admitted that he had no actual information about the mutiny and mentioned it only as further evidence of his dire situation. 'I am absolutely between Scylla and Charybdis!' he lamented.

For some unaccountable reason, Scylla and Charbydis made Mary think of Captain Holland. Perhaps the mention of Woolwich had brought him to mind. She was wondering what was the true state of affairs in the Warren when she became aware of a strange noise . . . no, it was not strange at all; she knew precisely what it was – *Slipper*. He must have accompanied his master into the library. He had become bored, or the conversation had disturbed him, and now . . . now he was scratching at the floorboards very close to her hiding place.

Mary recoiled in silent horror as her sometime companion did his best to make her presence known. *Go away, Slipper, go away.* He stopped for a moment, as if considering this request, and then growled menacingly. Something . . . a smell, or a sound, or a sense that all was not right had aroused his curiosity, and now he was determined to satisfy it.

She could feel the perspiration gathering at her temples; the atmosphere had become close and stifling, but at the same time she felt terribly exposed to the men on the other side of the wall. Were they still talking? Had anyone noticed Slipper? Perhaps . . .

'Slipper!' called Crosby-Nash irritably, 'stop that. What are you doing, you wretched animal?'

'He has seen something,' affirmed Mr Ponsonby, his voice suddenly louder. 'A mouse, perhaps, or a rat. What is behind that wall?'

Oh, no, thought Mary. *Please, no!*

'Nothing – only a small sitting-room. Very likely there is a bird come down the chimney – they often do. I hear them – pigeons especially.'

Mr Rangan said something about the use of snakes to deal

with vermin, but no doubt the gentleman's little dog was also very industrious in that occupation.

'That is enough, Slipper,' ordered Crosby-Nash, 'come away from there.'

Mary held her breath as she heard footsteps approaching, then Slipper's nails scrabbling as he was dragged away. *Am I safe?* She forced herself to relax. Slipper was so badly behaved; surely no one would be made suspicious by any action of *his*. They would probably— A sharp tap on the wall only inches from her face made her gasp, and she instantly clapped her hands over her mouth in a useless attempt to recapture the sound. *Have they heard me? Did the wall sound hollow? Is there another way in?*

Mary could not see Crosby-Nash, but she was keenly aware that he was staring hard at the wall that separated them. Would he also sense her presence? He might even hear her heart, it was beating so loudly! What would happen when she took another breath?

There was an intense silence, and as it lengthened Mary felt a perverse desire to move or cough or even cry out, or rather, she began to doubt whether she could stop herself from doing one or other of these dangerous things. Her gown was sticking to her back, and the dust from the inner wall had become grit on the palms of her hands.

Someone ran his fingers along the panelling, and then Ponsonby announced that it all looked sound, but one could not be too careful. Rats were the devil to root out, once they had become well established.

'Oh yes, they are the worst sort of devils, both on land and at sea,' agreed Rangan, and now it seemed to Mary that all three men must be within a foot of her.

'Better have a look at the panelling in the room next door,' suggested Ponsonby. 'That may give you a clue.'

'Mm. Perhaps you are right.' Mary could tell from the sound of Crosby-Nash's voice, now slightly muffled, that he was no longer looking at the wall, and she permitted herself a measured exhalation. 'It is this way,' he added.

The footsteps moved again, crossing floor, then carpet, then floor, and a door opened. Slipper started barking and scrambled after them. As the door closed, Mary heard Ponsonby observe, 'Old Masefield . . . rats. Before your time, of course. Had to use poison in the end, and then the stink!' He grunted feelingly.

Mary collapsed with relief when they had gone. Safe! Yes, safe for the moment, but what was the condition of the wall on the other side? And Slipper had gone with them – what if he could still smell her, or they decided to remove the panelling? She listened intently and heard nothing, but perhaps because they were doing the same? Was this her chance to escape? She knew that it was, but she could not will herself to move.

Although she was now free to do so, she discovered that it was becoming increasingly difficult to breathe – had the air somehow grown foul? No, of course not, but the possibility and Ponsonby's mention of poison spurred her to action. She must not faint in that place, whatever happened! Even as the library door opened a second time and Slipper pushed past the three men, she was climbing the steps. Her fingers found the latch, and she lifted the cover.

A welcome draught of cool air greeted her as she paused, then lifted herself free of the cavity and lowered the trap door soundlessly into place. Ah, she had done it! She permitted herself a moment to recover – but only a moment. She would not really be safe until she was back in her own chamber. Then she could wash her hands and face and . . . think about what to do. As she rose to her feet she felt a sudden wave of dizziness, and she closed her eyes until it passed. When she opened them the implacable features of the goddess Durga caught her glance. *Yes, yes, madam*, she thought, *I am leaving!*

Holland returned to Woolwich in the early afternoon and went straight to bed. Fortunately, he was one of those men who could fall asleep almost immediately, but it seemed as if his head had only just touched the pillow when he was being told to get up again. For a moment he imagined he was back in

Champian Hall, for when he opened his eyes there was Dick Whittington, standing at the foot of his cot and peering down at him.

'What's the matter?' Holland demanded, still half asleep.

'Nothing is the matter. It is three o'clock and all is well, although you look rather a mess. What happened to your hand?'

Holland sat up and swung his legs round and onto the floor. 'Someone tried to get in here last night, hoping to stir things up, but he ran into Drake and me instead. And it's not my hand, it's my arm.' He ended his report with a mighty yawn.

'Ah yes, Smith,' said Whittington. 'I warned him that it was folly to try selling revolution to your gunners. You are all too hard-hearted for political idealism – either that or the guns have deafened you. But it was no use.'

'*I* would have liked a warning that he was coming.'

'And I would have liked to send you one, but unfortunately, that was not possible. I could not go in and out of this place whenever I liked, you know.' Whittington glanced around the room; it was where the Ordnance Board met and, apart from Holland's cot, the furniture comprised a long, leather-topped table and several uncomfortable-looking chairs. He commented on these, and then on the fact that things seem to have settled down. The dockyard was quiet, and the three worst-affected artillery companies were to be assigned duties away from Woolwich. Doubtless they would learn to behave themselves in Berwick-upon-Tweed, or some such interesting place.

'Doubtless. Smith was looking for you, you know. He called me "Major" when he thought I was a friend. That was before he tried to stick his knife in me.'

'Ah, and I am the only officer of that rank in Woolwich, obviously.' Whittington considered his friend for a moment. 'But you may be right – he may have been hoping to meet me. Wishful thinking on his part, of course, and hence his dis-appointment. Perhaps a knife *was* a bit excessive, but then he has always been rather excitable. That is what comes of reading – and writing – incendiary pamphlets. One must make allowances. And what is this I hear about your rushing to London in the small hours? It sounds exhausting, and I find Horse Guards unpleasant at the best of times. No wonder you are in such a bad humour.'

Holland answered with more than his usual terseness. He did not want to talk about the knife fight or his business in London. 'Your people in the QMG's department say you're to go to Sheerness. I don't have written orders, but I said I expected to see you and would let you know.'

'No, they never put orders on paper if they can help it,' said Whittington, frowning. He would have liked to hear more about his superiors' view of recent events, but Holland's reticence discouraged further questions. 'Well, I am quite happy to leave. You know what I think about Woolwich – hardly the place one would chose to spend one's time.' He produced a handkerchief and mopped his face. 'This heat is appalling.'

Holland sat silently, observing Whittington's nervous gestures and wondering how much more he would say. Dick was always happiest when he was talking, even when there did not seem much point in it. When he lapsed into silence, therefore, Holland did not attempt to fill the void. Finally he rose and suggested they go outside. It would be cooler there.

It was cooler, with a light breeze moderating the bright spring sunshine. As he had done on the previous evening, Holland turned towards the river and Prince Rupert's Walk. Whittington trailed after him, saying something about the row of trees that lined the passage. Holland let him carry on for a while, scarcely listening, but at last even his friend's tone of voice became irritating. He turned impatiently. 'You knew all about it, didn't you?'

Whittington blinked enquiringly. 'I beg your pardon? Knew about the history of tree planting at Bamfield? Yes, to a degree—'

'Is it likely I'm asking about your bloody trees?' Holland demanded. 'You knew there was going to be a mutiny here at Woolwich.'

'I *knew*— Do not be ridiculous,' scoffed Whittington.

'I oughtn't to have woken you, obviously. You are not thinking clearly.'

'But it isn't ridiculous, is it? I think that you planned the whole thing and then made as if it was a complete surprise.'

'Indeed. What has prompted this . . . astonishing determination, may I ask?'

The superior tone, the refusal to consider the substance of the charge – these sounded more like the Whittington that Holland knew; yet there was also an edginess that rendered the performance ineffectual. More than that, it snapped the final cord on Holland's temper. 'Hell, Dick, you knew exactly when we would be most vulnerable – a big occasion, with all the officers in one place and the men able to act together, and a new, untested commandant. You knew about the twenty-sixth of May and about Congreve assuming command. You even said that I would miss the parade, when we went down to Champian Hall.'

'You have quite a good memory, I see.'

'And those handbills – Smith had a supply of them in his pocket. They hadn't been written for us, so I suppose they were left over from the Guards' show?'

Whittington tried to reply, but for once Holland refused to give way. 'A mutiny here was just as big as anything involving the Guards. Both would have occurred to you, and that was your job, wasn't it, suggesting likely military targets to Crosby-Nash and then sorting out the details for him?'

While Holland was speaking Whittington turned away and gazed across the river as if he found something on the opposite shore of particular interest. He even shaded his eyes. Finally he replied, still staring outwards. 'You must think you are very clever.'

'No, but I'd have to be a fool not to put things together. Now I want to know what it's all about.'

Whittington sighed and turned to face Holland. The breeze had died completely, and the sun cast a shimmering glare upon the surface of the river. 'Things worked out satisfactorily, you know. In a few days the trouble-makers will be removed, and the rest of you will be as before.'

'Is that what you thought would happen?'

'Not quite,' Whittington admitted. 'I thought there was a risk, but I did not know enough about the Warren to defuse a mutiny here, nor could I jeopardise my position with Crosby-Nash – not after the failure with the Guards. It was simply too dangerous to be personally involved on the day, one way or the other.'

'So you thought you'd do nothing?' demanded Holland, his voice steely. 'No warning, just sit back and see how we got on?'

'Yes,' Whittington snapped, 'sometimes one has to make decisions of that kind in my line of work. Damn it, you are an officer – and I do not know what you mean by "we". I got *you* out of it, or tried to.'

'*Got me out of it?* What are you talking about? Do you mean— What you said about needing my help— All of that was to get me away from Woolwich?'

Holland's startled, sputtering response reassured Whittington, and his own voice grew in confidence. He said that he had known full well that Holland would have been in the thick of it if he had been present when trouble had broken out. 'That sort of heroism reads very well in the regimental history, but things might have turned ugly, and jumping in with both feet might not have been the best way to stay alive. So, remembering how long we have been friends, I decided not to give you the chance of being killed by your own side.'

Now it was Holland's turn to hesitate, and Whittington continued, breezily, 'Of course, we were obliged to return, despite my best intentions. Whittington proposes, but Crosby-Nash disposes. Still, as I said, everything seems to have come right in the end.'

Holland did not answer immediately, and then he supposed that he ought to be grateful, in a way. Even to him the admission sounded grudging, truculent.

A slight lifting of the eyebrows suggested that Whittington thought so too. 'Well, yes, you might be,' he replied.

The tension between them seemed to relax with that remark,

and Whittington was glad of it. He resented having to explain himself and considered it all rather embarrassing, but if Holland was going to be so damned officious, he deserved to be taken down a peg or two.

'You've managed things pretty well with Crosby-Nash, what with one thing and another,' acknowledged Holland.

Whittington shrugged, but to himself he affirmed that this was rather better – a recognition of his superior abilities, and under difficult circumstances. 'It has been rather tricky, you know, deciding exactly how much information to give him – to convince him that the arrangement was worth while.'

'Mm.' Holland nodded. 'Has that been your only concern? I mean,' he added, as Whittington frowned a question, 'your arrangement with him. It's a financial one, isn't it? Filthy lucre?'

'Yes, if you wish to put it like that. What are you trying to say?'

'This,' said Holland, and now Whittington perceived that the dogged expression remained in the other's eyes. 'You've needed money for as long as I've known you, but lately you've had plenty for smart uniforms and new horses. Has that come from Crosby-Nash?'

'What if it has?' demanded Whittington. 'What does it matter to you?'

'It doesn't, so long as it hasn't made you forget which side you belong to.'

'It has not.'

'Then tell me, what do your people at Horse Guards think about all of this? Do they know that you collect . . . what, double your pay from Crosby-Nash? Or is it more than that?'

Whittington did not reply immediately, and then he muttered, 'What did you say to them when you were in London?'

'Never mind what *I* said,' Holland warned, 'what are you going to do in Sheerness? Try and stop the mutiny or help it along? Those are your orders from Crosby-Nash, aren't they? You undermine the fort while that . . . Phoebus makes speeches and circulates handbills?'

300

'For God's sake, Bob, you said you were not a fool, and now you are behaving like an idiot. Do you think I am really *working* for Crosby-Nash?' Without intending to, Whittington stepped back a pace and gazed at his friend. What he saw caused him to fold his arms slowly across his chest, and he answered in a clipped, brittle voice. 'And what do you propose to do? Stop me?'

'If I have to.'

'Well, you are wrong. I am *not* working for him – not the way you think. I admit I have taken money from him – rather a lot, in fact – but I had debts to settle and . . . and I had not met the Honourable Mrs Whittington.' He finished the sentence with a wan smile.

'And now you're in that bastard's pocket!'

'Not quite,' Whittington argued, 'as a matter of fact, not at all! At first I thought I would be obliged to become his creature, and I *was* rather upset about that. Not quite what one expects of oneself. But then I decided that, instead of racking myself over what I could not help, if I simply made the best of things, they could actually work to my advantage. I have given him trifling bits of information – nothing really important – and so long as the QMG's department believe I am working for *them*, and Crosby-Nash believes I am working for *him*, I can keep them both reasonably satisfied and work for myself.'

'What does that mean?'

'It means that I will be safe, whichever of them comes out on top. Of course, I would prefer that to be the Army, but why should I be made to choose between two sides, when I have neither the information to judge which is the stronger nor the capacity to determine how they behave? Any choice on my part would be folly. It would not *be* a choice, and yet I might lose everything.'

Holland could not speak. What was the point of mentioning words like 'honour', and 'loyalty'? They wouldn't fit the kind of logic Dick was using – they wouldn't mean a damned thing.

Whittington stared back at him condescendingly. 'I thought of bringing you in at one stage, when I thought that I could trust you to see things practically. God knows you could use the money, but now that you take such a romantic view of every—'

For a moment Holland felt as if his heart had stopped beating—

And then it pounded double time. 'God damn you, Dick!' he cried, gripping Whittington's forearm like an iron band, 'did you give her up to him? By God, I'll kill you if you've given her up.'

The question also shocked Whittington out of his languid superiority. '*Given her up?* Of course I did not give her up. To Crosby-Nash? How dare you even suggest it!'

They glared at each other, and then Holland's hand dropped away, and Whittington continued in something like his usual tone of voice. 'No, I would never do that. Although I do not mind telling you that when I heard Cuthbert Shy was also on Crosby-Nash's trail, and that one of his agents had been killed, I was greatly displeased. It is bad enough dealing with one's own people, but if the civilians are going to shove their oar in as well—'

Holland shook his head. 'Stow it, will you? Does Crosby-Nash suspect Mary?'

'I do not think so. Believe me, if I had thought her to be in danger I would have told you.'

Holland observed Whittington closely. He still *looked* like the old Dick Whittington, but he had changed utterly; he was like a stranger. 'What are you going to do now?'

'Why, proceed to Sheerness, of course. I have my orders and, contrary to what you think, Crosby-Nash would not be so displeased if Phoebus were to fall on his face. Quite the reverse, in fact. So, there is nothing to worry about . . . unless you do not trust me.'

'I don't know that I do.'

'Well, then you can perform an act of heroism and stop me.'

'There wouldn't be anything heroic about it.'

'Informing against one of your oldest friends?' Whittington gibed. 'No, perhaps not. But you would not do that. I believe

302

you would opt for the direct approach. Are you armed, by any chance?'

'No. Are you?'

Whittington shook his head. 'But then I did not anticipate this conversation, whereas you have clearly been brooding about it for some time.' The sight of Holland's strained expression afforded Whittington a perverse pleasure. He did not enjoy confessing his sins. While confident that he had done the right thing – the clever thing, certainly – as regards Crosby-Nash, he was all too aware that Holland did not see it that way. Of course, Bob had a very limited perspective, but to have afforded him this moral advantage ran counter to the whole tenor of their friendship. He smiled scornfully. 'And now I really think I ought to be going. Ah, here is Drake come to look for us like a faithful hound – what a surprise. Good afternoon, Drake.'

'Afternoon, sir.'

'I do not suppose you could have a horse saddled for me, could you? Would that run counter to the current regime? I am off to Sheerness and need a fresh animal for the journey. I will leave mine, of course.'

Without looking at either of them, Holland could sense Drake's question and Whittington's amusement. God, he felt such a fool! 'Tell me,' he said, 'do you know anything more about Crosby-Nash?'

Whittington lifted an eyebrow. 'Oh, a great deal more, I should think, but nothing that would be of particular interest to you. You have thwarted him most effectively.'

'You're sure that he's finished here . . . he won't try anything else?'

'My good fellow, I cannot predict the future!' complained Whittington, 'but so far as I know, there were no contingency plans to harass Woolwich if the initial attempt failed. In my opinion, the next focus of attention is the disturbance at the Nore, which is why I wish to go to *Sheerness*.'

Whittington's emphasis on the last word made Holland grimace. At last he turned to Drake, who had been watching the exchange with a not-very-well-disguised interest. 'It's all right – get him his horse,' he muttered. 'You'd better go with him,' he added to Whittington.

He heard the sound of their retreating footsteps, and then he was alone. As they walked, Whittington began speaking to Drake about something or other in his familiar, blithe tone, but Holland had stopped listening.

19

Mary and Susannah were taking tea that evening when Crosby-Nash joined them. His expression, coupled with the fact that he often preferred his own company after dinner, warned Mary even before he spoke. His face was flushed, and his eyes sparkled; Mary wondered whether he had been drinking, although this would have been most unusual for him. She set down her cup, untasted. Something out of the ordinary had happened, or was going to happen, and she must be ready for it.

Despite this injunction, she felt her heart contract when he announced that a secret passage had been found. 'A "priest's hole", I believe it is called,' he continued in an eager voice, 'behind the library panelling.'

Susannah nodded dutifully at the news. It was a warm, almost sultry evening, and she was fanning herself. 'Oh, how very interesting, my dear.'

'How did you come to look for such a thing, sir?' asked Mary, her expression registering a confidence that she did not feel.

'Well, I have been noticing some odd noises, and I asked Baxter to undertake an investigation. He has only now given me the news.'

'A *priest's* hole,' repeated Susannah, as if she were not sure she had heard correctly. 'But what can have been making the noises?'

'Probably rats, my dear, not secretive clergymen,' and in response to his wife's look of alarm he added, 'or perhaps it was merely the wind rustling through the passage. But Baxter will take the necessary steps to remove any, ahem, *visitors* that are discovered.'

'It all sounds very exciting,' said Mary. 'Not the rats, of course, but the passage itself. The presence of a priest's hole suggests an interesting chapter in the history of Champian Hall,' she concluded, making her voice sound as pompous as possible.

Crosby-Nash nodded. 'Yes, indeed. We shall have to make a thorough investigation, of course, but I would guess the construction dates from the middle of the last century. I am going now to have a look. Would you like to come along, Miss Finch?'

Despite her preparation Mary went cold at the innocently phrased question. But was it innocent? Was there something *knowing* in that smile? How ought she to respond? 'Is there much to be seen?' she asked, forcing herself to meet his gaze steadily. 'Has the panelling been removed?'

'Oh no, that seemed to me both excessive and likely to result in damage, and in any case it will not prove necessary. That enterprising fellow Baxter has found the entrance to the passage! It is in one of the upper rooms.'

Mary tried to weigh the advantages and disadvantages of complying. After two near discoveries she was on edge, but she must not lose her nerve. He could not possibly suspect her. 'I see,' she affirmed. 'Yes, I should very much like to see it, if I may. As I believe Susannah informed you on our arrival, I am fond of old things.'

'Shall we do so now?' asked Crosby-Nash, rising to his feet.

Mary did likewise. 'Certainly, if you wish.' Her voice wobbled slightly. 'Susannah?'

Crosby-Nash turned to his wife. 'My dear, I presume that you do not choose to accompany us, but you would be most welcome—'

'Oh, no,' she replied, settling herself more comfortably in her chair, 'I shall stay here. I cannot think where you get your energy in this heat, Mary – I can scarcely move. But do go ahead and . . . tell me what it is like.'

As they departed the room Susannah made a final request. 'If you *do* find any rats, I would rather not know about *them*.'

Mary and Crosby-Nash climbed the stairs together. It seemed to her even warmer on the first floor, but this might have been caused by the growing sense that she was making a mistake – that she had accepted a dangerous, and not very worthwhile challenge. Feeling obliged to continue speaking as proof of her interest, she enthused, 'What a marvellous discovery this is, colonel. *A secret passage.* How very exciting.'

'They are not uncommon in old houses, I believe. Have you such a thing at White Ladies?'

'No— Or I should say, not that has been discovered. Priests came and went freely when the Cistercians were in residence – every convent had its own father confessor – and after the Reformation the property was placed in the hands of very staunch Protestants, who had very little to say to the old religion.'

'Ah.'

Mary's anxiety continued to build. It was hardly conceivable that Crosby-Nash could associate her with the storeroom, but when she stepped across the threshold she half-expected to discover one of her own hats or a pair of gloves, something to show that she had been there before. In fact there was nothing more alarming than the bluff, weathered features of Baxter, the colonel's steward. He was kneeling on the floor beside the open trap door, and he rose to greet them.

'Are these more of your Indian things, colonel? Oh, good evening, Baxter.' Mary smiled, and perceiving her young friend the under-gardener, added, 'Good evening, Tom.'

'Evening, sir, evening, miss,' replied Baxter. 'Just tidying up me things. We'll be finished directly minute, and outer your way.'

'Not at all,' Crosby-Nash assured him, 'take your time. And if you have your lantern handy, you might light it again so that we can see into the passage.'

'Right you are, sir. Gi'us a light, will you, Tom?'

The lantern was produced, lit, and lowered into the dark hole. Mary leaned forward, and Crosby-Nash offered her his outstretched arm to balance against. She managed to take it without flinching. 'Oh my,' she breathed.

'Yes,' Crosby-Nash admitted, 'very interesting, but to appreciate it fully I think one must venture inside.'

Mary's shiver was not lacking in authenticity. 'Do you think so?'

Her host smiled tolerantly. 'Oh yes. Even at this remove of time I expect it would convey the sense of being closely confined, perhaps for hours or even days, and all the while knowing that discovery would mean imprisonment or even death. You . . . would not like to try it, I suppose, as a student of history?'

She could not decipher his tone. Was he challenging her? What did he expect her to say? He was standing very close to her, but she did not dare to let go of his arm. She peered again into the hole, this time more nervously. 'No, sir,' she replied. 'My interest in the historical does not extend so far.'

'No, of course not.'

'I am sure it will be very thrilling for *you*, however,' she added, in recognition of his superior fortitude. 'Thank you so much for showing it to me.' She glanced up at him; was he sneering at her? Had her compliment sounded forced?

'It has been my pleasure to do so. Thank you, Baxter. You may close it up now.'

'Right you are, sir.'

Crosby-Nash gestured back towards the passage, and Mary obligingly followed the unspoken suggestion. She waited while he closed the door behind them, and then risked a question. 'Is there nothing at all to be seen in the library? No evidence of the passage, or another means of entry?'

'No, I believe not. But the passage ends quite close behind the library wall – one can determine the place from the hollow sound of the panelling. Shall I show you?'

She swallowed hastily. 'Mm, yes, please.'

As the sound of their voices trailed away, Baxter returned to his work. He replaced the trap door and polished it and the surrounding area of floor with a waxy cloth. 'That's us done, Tom,' he decreed, tossing the cloth into his bag. 'If you'll get a move on, that is, and put away them things like I told you.'

'Oh, aye,' Tom agreed, but apparently oblivious to his superior's observation. 'Mr Baxter?'

'Reach me that bit o' rope.'

Tom coiled the item in question and handed it over. 'Funny thing, this old cubbyhole, ain't it?'

Baxter shrugged indifferently. 'S'pose it is. But they did all manner o' queer things, in olden times.'

'Mm. Mr Baxter?'

'Well, what is it?'

'What I can't make out is, didn't you say that the colonel'd already seen it? Before today, I mean.'

'Aye, showed him meself when we fixed the chimbley, last year.'

'Then why'd he want you to open it up again?'

Having rightly concluded that he could finish clearing up more quickly himself, the steward did so before he answered. 'Daresay he wanted to show it to the young lady. Bit of fun, you know. Mysteries and such.'

The next day was Sunday, which meant that Mary attended the morning service with Susannah. Mr Garbett preached authoritatively on the parable of the talents, but Mary could not concentrate on the sermon. More than once she found her thoughts drifting to Colonel Crosby-Nash. She felt reasonably confident that she had acquitted herself ably with respect to the priest's hole. The very idea that the colonel could suspect her to have hidden in that passage was so unlikely that she relaxed and even chuckled when Mr Garbett made a mild witticism about separating the sheep from the goats. He really was not such a bad speaker. Soon, however, he had lost her again. Secure once more in her position, she began to think more critically about the conversation between the colonel and his visitors. Had she been too quick to dismiss it?

A bee buzzed loudly against the window, trying to find a way out. One of the smaller panes at the top of the frame was missing, but he persisted in bumping against those at the bottom, and then walked dejectedly along the sill. Was it not suspicious that the colonel should have had a private conversation touching on both the Woolwich and Naval mutinies? Perhaps Mr Rangan's remarks *had* been innocent, but that did not mean that the same could be said for the colonel's. He might have been drawing the other man out, trying to gain information that only Mr Rangan knew, while feigning mere interest. The devil could cite Scripture for his purpose, and was this not something like? Mr Ponsonby might even have been part of the scheme. He had brought Mr Rangan to Champian Hall, after all, and she had not liked his insistence on rats and poison.

But what had they actually discussed? She had not always been able to hear them, and the details could be all-important. *Woolwich and the progress of the mutiny there.* She felt an uneasy shiver at the thought of what that might mean, but reminded herself that Mr Rangan had known nothing about it, and perhaps the trouble at the Warren had already been resolved. *No, he was mostly concerned about the ships that were anchored in the Thames, unable to sail because of the sailors' mutiny. What was the place he mentioned? Ear . . . something. Mr Rangan's was not the only ship delayed, and the colonel was very interested in that.*

Susannah thanked Mr Garbett as they stepped out of the vestibule and into the sunshine, as did Mary, although she felt rather hypocritical in doing so. *Still, I daresay it was a good sermon.* They set off for Champian Hall, both apparently content with their experiences of the past hour, but when they were out of earshot, Susannah admitted that, despite Mr Garbett's words, she felt sorry for the third servant.

'What?' asked Mary, with a slight sense of alarm. 'I mean, I beg your pardon?'

'The third servant,' Susannah repeated. 'The one who was given a single talent.'

310

'Oh, yes.' Mary could not quite remember how the parable ended, and so she answered guardedly.

'He did not lose his master's money, after all,' continued Susannah, 'but only failed to think of a clever way of adding to it, and yet he was cast into outer darkness. Perhaps things were different in Biblical times, but investing money is very difficult, it seems to me, and people are as likely to lose as to gain by it.'

Mary agreed that this was so, but when her opinion on the Bible story amounted to little more than a suggestion that the third servant probably had a bad character, Susannah's suspicions were aroused. She had been picking wildflowers as they walked, and now she raised her eyes questioningly. 'You were not listening to the sermon at all, were you?'

'Well, I—'

'I had my doubts when you laughed at the account of the goats getting loose in the parsonage garden. I was not precisely certain of the parallel that Mr Garbett was attempting to draw, but I do not think it was meant to be humorous.'

'Oh, is *that*— I thought it was something else,' cried Mary, aghast. 'Do you think that anyone else noticed? Did it look *very* odd?'

'*Very*.' Susannah tried to assume a discouraging expression, failed, and then they both burst into laughter. 'Poor Mr Garbett, and he was trying so hard! You are as bad as Charlotte.'

'Not that bad, surely,' Mary complained, still laughing.

'Yes, indeed. Do you know, when we were small Papa had to bribe Charlotte with sweets to keep still in church, and she was not allowed to sit beside our cousin Robert. It all began one Sunday when there was a special collection for the poor, and Lottie made a fuss about the shilling she had put into the bag – she said that she wanted change!'

Susannah smiled at the memory of her sister's piping explanation, delivered at full volume during a period of quiet reflection. How she missed Lottie, and Bobs; if only they were not so far away! But then she sobered, as if in punishment for that traitorous thought. A married woman, after all, ought to need no companionship apart from her husband, and she certainly ought not to hearken back to childish pranks.

'Was she allowed?' laughed Mary. 'To break her shilling, I mean.'

'I beg your pardon? Yes, I think that she was. The poor man taking the collection was so startled, I daresay he did not think to stop her, and Charlotte, of course, was never one to hold back. It all ended badly, however, when we returned home. One hundred lines and no cake for tea.'

'That was hard. But you were not all three punished, were you?'

'Well,' said Susannah, fondly, 'Bobs *had* laughed at the shilling – it may even have been his idea – and it would not have been fair to abandon Lottie to her fate. I do not think I would have liked my cake without her.'

They parted on their arrival at Champian Hall. Susannah, it must be said, was still suffering from a certain lowness of spirits, while Mary's condition was just the opposite. This had something to do with the mention of Captain Holland in Susannah's story – indeed, she would have pressed her friend for further accounts of his youth if she had dared – but the more potent source of her present keenness was the sight of Colonel Crosby-Nash crossing the lawn in front of them, accompanied by a delighted Slipper. Mary knew the dog's preferences well enough to know that if they were departing on a ramble, which appeared likely, he would insist upon a very lengthy one. That would guarantee the colonel's absence for at least an hour, which would be plenty of time to execute her latest plan.

There had not been time to think through exactly what she meant to achieve, but this was too fortunate an opportunity to be missed. She hurried to her bedchamber, therefore, stopping only to remove her hat and to retrieve Romney's pair of skeleton keys from the small carrying case at the back of the wardrobe. Then she descended the stairs and advanced cautiously to the library. She paused on the threshold. Was it safe to proceed? Yes.

Her first task, because it might be awkward, was to examine the colonel's desk, and she chided herself that she had not reviewed his papers more recently. Perhaps there were all sorts of incriminating letters and memoranda here, waiting to be discovered, while she had been doing what, precisely? Listening out for the odd word, no doubt, *eavesdropping*, but neglecting this important aspect of her work!

She quickly surveyed the papers on the desktop and in each of the drawers, but the harvest thus gained was not a bountiful one. Most of what she found was routine – estate records and newspapers that revealed nothing new. Two notes from Mr Garbett made her frown, but not on account of any clandestine information. The colonel, it seemed, had no great sympathy for the proposed village school, and Mary foresaw an awkward conflict when Susannah came to square her social conscience with her duty to her husband. The contents of the locked drawer looked to have been re-arranged, as Slipper's collar was now on top of the foreign documents, but what could be made of that? The colonel was unlikely to use the collar as a means of communication while he was in Kent. *The very fact that Slipper is without it this morning speaks against that*, she told herself.

A note from Mr Ponsonby, introducing Mr Rangan and proposing a visit, reminded her of her other task. Having re-locked the drawer and restored the neat arrangements of documents elsewhere in and upon the desk, she moved to the long, marble-topped table in front of the windows. In addition to a wooden candlestick and a bronze statue of a four-armed figure, poised elegantly within a circle of flame, the table was notable for its collection of maps. There were maps of India, of France, and several of England, but the uppermost attracted her attention – a detailed map of the Thames, from London to the sea.

Champian Hall was too far south to be included, but she identified several landmarks: Woolwich, of course, but also Dartford, Gravesend, Tilbury and, finally, the curiously named Isle of Grain, which did not seem to be an island at all. Erith, which she supposed was the place that the colonel and his visitors had mentioned, looked to be a rather nondescript spot, just north of Dartford. Might it have any significance other than as the anchorage for Mr Rangan's ship? It was impossible to tell. Some stretches of the river also bore particular designations – Gallions Reach or Tipcock Reach – but these meant nothing to Mary.

She leaned over the map, tracing the curves of the river as it rose and fell and gradually widened until it was no longer a river but the open sea. The marble was cool under her hands and contributed to the image in her mind of fresh, flowing water, but her analysis advanced no further. The map might be important, but she could not say for certain, and even if it were, what could she do about it? There was no one to whom she could communicate her suspicions, nor would there be until Mr Shy received her letter. If only she could speak with Captain Holland or Major Whittington! That seemed impossible, but perhaps she ought to compose a second letter for Coutts Bank . . .

A movement – light flickering at the top of her field of vision – caused her to look up, and she saw a man standing on the lawn. She stepped back from the table, her heart racing. One of the gardeners. Had he seen her? *No,* she reasoned, *the sun is shining on the lawn, and this room is in shadow.* Nevertheless, it was difficult to calm herself. Was the room really so dark to someone outside? *Yes, probably, but the light may have changed!* How long had she been standing here? *Not long, surely, not very long . . . and besides, why should a gardener care if he saw me looking at a map?*

Then something infinitely worse occurred; she could hear voices in the corridor! Not Colonel Crosby-Nash, thank heaven, but the butler, Lockwood, and . . . a woman's voice. *Susannah? No, then it must be one of the maids. They must be coming to tidy the room, or —* Mary was paralysed as the voices drew near. Should she conceal herself or bluff it out? She had explained away her presence once before in Lockwood's presence, he might not believe it a second time. But where could she hide? The furniture afforded very little shelter, and even the curtains did not quite reach the floor. The desk? In desperation she seized the uppermost volume from a stack and darted to the wall of books just as the door opened.

'I beg your pardon, miss – I hope I do not disturb you.'

Mary turned, smilingly. 'Not at all, Lockwood. I am changing my book.' She held it up, praying that it was not an almanac or gazetteer, which no one was likely to read for pleasure, or at least that the title was illegible at that distance.

'Yes, miss.'

She stole a glance at the spine, it was Selden's *Table Talk*, and felt the tension between her shoulders ease slightly. *This* would not get her into trouble, at least. The maidservant was a stranger to her; a plump, expressionless woman, and Mary decided to ignore her. Lockwood was the important person to reassure, and she directed her remarks to him. 'I never use the library when Colonel Crosby-Nash is at home,' she admitted, ingenuously, 'I do not like to disturb him.'

'No, miss.'

'This is really his study, I believe, and the books more for ornamentation. I daresay he will not mind my borrowing one.'

'Just as you say, miss, though I believe the colonel has read a great number of them.'

Mary nodded. 'I am sure he has. He is a very knowledgeable gentleman.' She made as if to resume her perusal of the bookcase, and then turned questioningly to Lockwood a second time. 'Oh, have you work to do here? Ought I to go?'

'Not at all, miss,' urged Lockwood, both his tone and posture signalling deference, a willingness to wait upon her convenience. 'Do choose your book.'

She smiled at him and, with a conscious effort, selected a volume, leafed through it, repeated the exercise with another on a different shelf, and finally settled upon a third – a traveller's account. 'This looks interesting,' she affirmed.

Lockwood said that he hoped it was a pleasant book, and she said that she was certain it would be. She had always longed to travel, and being at Champian Hall had undoubtedly whetted her appetite more keenly. All of the colonel's wonderful foreign things . . .

While she spoke she was glancing along the shelves, looking for the place where *Table Talk* belonged. It would not do to leave it on the desk, and yet there did not seem to be a gap.

'May I help you, miss?'

'No, no, I—' There was no reason why she should remember where the book belonged, but not being able to perform the simple action was making her feel uneasy. He was looking at her, and now she wanted very much to leave the room. 'Ah, here is the place.' The book slid smoothly into the gap on one of the lower shelves; very likely it *did* belong there.

Lockwood thanked her, and the anonymous maidservant curt-seyed as Mary passed. In the passage Mary stood for a little while, listening to the resumed conversation. The door was ajar, and she could hear every word. Its very banality helped to restore her confidence. Whatever had brought them to the library, it had not been a suspicious sighting of someone lurking at the window, and her explanation of her presence had been accepted – she was certain of it. It had been a close-run thing, however, and as she made her way back to her bedchamber she could not be certain that it had been worth the risk.

Colonel Congreve received some awkward instructions that morning, so awkward that he brooded over them for a good half an hour before summoning his adjutant. The official view of the Naval mutiny had apparently clarified, and Horse Guards wanted to position guns at strategic points along the Thames estuary to fire on the ships at the Nore if the government deemed this necessary. The Royal Artillery, therefore, was required to provide the necessary men and equipment, and to transport both to appropriate sites on the North Kentish coast.

Congreve did not like the sound of it. He questioned whether heavy guns could be sited effectively on the marshy east side of the Isle of Grain, and he doubted the wisdom of threat-ening to bombard the sailors back to their duty, especially when his gunners must do the bombarding. The situation at Woolwich was settling down, but it was by no means back to normal, and orders like these were unlikely to sit well with the men.

MacLeod agreed, but he tried to temper his commander's anger by reminding him that the project was a complex one that could not be undertaken straightaway. As a first step, a competent officer must make a survey and report on local conditions. Until that report established that it *was* actually feasible to site the guns appropriately, the men need not be distressed by a purely hypothetical deployment. Indeed, MacLeod advised strict confidentiality as regards the entire matter. In the meantime, the Naval mutiny might well resolve itself, such that intervention by the gunners would prove unnecessary.

Congreve was largely placated by these suggestions, and he proposed that Captain Holland undertake the survey. Holland was on the spot, and he could be depended upon to keep his mouth shut about what he was doing. Besides, he had been haring about on behalf of the quartermaster general's office – he could jolly well do something for the regiment. MacLeod thought that Holland had lately done quite a bit for the regiment, but he refrained from saying so and merely agreed that Holland was the man for the job.

Some of this was conveyed to Holland along with his orders, and if the expression 'jack of all trades' occurred to him, he also kept it to himself. It was something, after all, to be doing proper regimental work again, although the context was disturbing. Like his seniors, he opposed the idea of firing on the sailors – certainly as anything other than a last resort. More than that, a mission connected with the Naval mutiny kept his other recent difficulties at the forefront of his mind. Had he made a mistake letting Whittington go to Sheerness? And what about Mary Finch?

Holland's thoughts continued to distract him as he packed his gear in preparation for departure. Drake would never have allowed such a haphazard performance but he, for some reason, was absent. Holland did not mind carrying out the job himself; on the contrary, he was happy to be spared Drake's sceptical remarks, which usually became more pointed if anything remotely interesting was in prospect, and he knew he was going to be left behind. Drake could be a damned nuisance about some things.

A quick triple knock announced the return of the nuisance.

317

'Scuse me, sir,' he announced, casting a dubious eye at Holland's half-packed satchel, ''ere's a chap says 'e's got a message for you. Says 'is name's . . .'

'I did not give my name,' finished a voice from the doorway.

Then a youngish man of middling height stepped into the room. He was in all ways unremarkable, with mousey brown hair and wearing a nondescript suit, but somehow he seemed vaguely familiar. 'Have you come from Champian Hall?' Holland demanded, dropping a notebook on the table. He strode past Drake and confronted the newcomer.

The other man shook his head and motioned to Drake to close the door. 'No sir, I have come from a friend of yours – Mr Lethieullier.' He paused, letting the name register, and then continued. 'He has uncovered what he considers some very important information, but he would like your opinion on it before he takes further steps.'

Holland's surprise showed in the tone of his reply. *Lethieullier . . . what the devil could Shy want with me? And if this hasn't to do with Mary . . .* 'My opinion? I . . . Very well, sir. Please sit down.'

The agent crossed to one of the dilapidated armchairs in front of the fireplace, but he remained standing. 'I beg your pardon,' he said, 'but my orders are to disclose this information only to Captain Holland, and I wonder...?'

The question, together with the glance in Drake's direction, made Holland smile, and his amusement grew as Drake choked down his outrage in a muttered growl. 'When we're in the museum we follow Mr . . . Lethieullier's rules. When we're in the Warren we follow mine. Let's hear what you have to say.'

'As you please. To come to the point, then, we strongly believe that enemy forces intend to blow up the Royal Gunpowder Magazine at Purfleet.'

Holland stared at the other man, the smile fading from his face; from somewhere behind he could hear Drake shuffle his feet. The awful possibility of an explosion at the government's largest storage facility was certainly not new, but this cool announcement of a plot caused his heart to beat faster.

Nevertheless, he answered cautiously. His opinion of Shy was not wholly negative, but he had no intention of falling in straightaway with the gentleman's every suggestion. 'Purfleet is not unprotected, you know. Troops are stationed there, and the buildings themselves were designed to be as safe as possible. The walls are five feet thick, and the roofs are specially constructed.'

'Yes, sir, it is a formidable target, but I think you will agree that it is comparable to the recent outrages that have been planned – both of them in or near London. The destruction of Purfleet would cause tremendous damage – disruption on the Thames, injury and loss of life, not to mention the obvious destruction of valuable military supplies.'

'You don't have to convince me of the danger,' observed Holland, dryly, 'only the plan. How do you say the explosion will come about?'

'As the result of a waterborne assault.'

The words made Holland relax slightly. 'That's not very likely. There is only one mutinous ship in the Long Reach, and she is not in a position to fire on Purfleet. In fact, at the last report she was trying to sail down river, towards Sheerness.'

Shy's agent shook his head. 'The assault will not come from the *Lancaster*, but from up river – probably from Barking Creek.'

'*Barking Creek?*' queried Holland, and now his apprehension resumed. Several of the private gunpowder manufacturers stored their property in warehouses at Barking Creek, and from there it was transported to Purfleet by boat. 'I think you had better tell me all you know.'

'Gladly.' Carefully, but somewhat circuitously, the agent made his report. Information had been obtained from the Hardy & Son's jewellers, as well as from other persons and places, relating to the following: the tide tables for the lower Thames, the warehouse records of Mssrs Taylor, Bridges, Hill, and Pigou, and a diagram of the magazine buildings with an explanation of the daily routine.

'You've seen all these things yourself?' demanded Holland. 'Actual papers?'

'Yes, sir, or received detailed descriptions. We know that these materials exist, and that some were in use as late as last night.'

'And your idea is that the enemy forces will approach Purfleet pretending to be delivering powder. They will be allowed to land and attack?'

'Yes, possibly aided by sympathisers from within.'

Holland stood thoughtfully, his arms crossed. 'Pigou's mill is on the Darent – he warehouses at Dartford. It would be too risky to bring boats up river to Purfleet. No one would try it – Pigou wouldn't try it, I mean. The others, though, use Barking Creek or warehouses on this side of the river at the bottom of Tipcock Reach. A delivery down river to Purfleet from any of those *might* not seem unusual. You mentioned you had tide tables – have they been marked up at all?'

'No, but we also know that the sunset has been calculated for all of this week. If the raiders planned to make their assault at dusk, they would have the benefit of the tide and their appearance – their falsity – would be less easily detected by loyal forces inside Purfleet.'

'Mm, I see.'

'And do you agree that it is feasible?'

'Yes,' said Holland, slowly, 'if the men are daring and have an escape plan.' He was silent for a short while, and then asked, 'When do you think they're likely to try it?'

'Well, it *is* possible that our actions have caused them to give it up entirely. We made things rather uncomfortable last night for Mr Rabelais and his friends.'

'Rabelais!' cried Holland. 'Did you catch him?'

'No, I regret to say, but we have thrown everything into confusion. However, Mr Lethieullier believes that Rabelais will make an attempt tonight, in the hope of succeeding before we have fully deciphered his plans.'

'That makes sense to me. And *your* plan, I take it, is to prevent the boats from leaving the warehouses?'

'Exactly that. I understand that more troops are being sent to Purfleet, which is a comfort, but it must be preferable to avoid any sort of confrontation at the magazine.'

320

'We're in agreement there,' said Holland. 'About your own forces – have you enough men for the job? It won't be easy, and you've got to be careful at those warehouses. They have nothing like so much powder as Purfleet, but we don't want any accidents.'

'Er, yes sir, indeed. As respects our forces, they ought to be sufficient. Stealth and quickness take precedence in an affair like this one.' The agent rose and offered his hand to Holland. 'I am most grateful to you for your assistance – and your discretion. As you can imagine, this is not the sort of problem that one can pose officially to the military, but we were most anxious for an expert opinion.'

Holland shook the agent's hand and frowned thoughtfully. 'You were at Sir William Armitage's funeral, weren't you?'

The agent bowed. 'You have a good memory, captain.'

'Have you been watching Crosby-Nash as long as that?'

'Longer.'

Holland breathed a condemnation of the colonel and shook his head. 'Well, good luck to you, and now we'd better get you away again.' He turned to Drake. 'You can fix up a cab without any fuss, can't you?'

'Course I can,' Drake complained, as if the question were a ridiculous one.

'Good luck,' Holland repeated and, stepping back, he nodded curtly at his subordinate. 'Quick as you like, then, Drake. I want this gentleman on the London road in a quarter of an hour, and I *don't* want anyone else to know about it.'

'Right you are, sir.'

When Drake returned, pleased at having met the deadline with a good three minutes to spare, he found Holland seated at the rough deal table that passed for a desk, poring over a sketch he had drawn.

'Sorted?' asked Holland, without looking up.

'Yes, sir, sorted.' Drake paused. 'Wot 'e said about Purfleet . . . it sounds bad.'

Holland nodded. Two thousand tons, that was the amount of gunpowder stored at the Purfleet magazine. *God, what an*

321

explosion that would make. The magazine destroyed and everyone inside killed, and river traffic within five miles blown apart and sunk. That's the likely damage done by the powder alone. He had not mentioned this to Shy's agent, but a shipment of mortar shells was also being stored – temporarily – at Purfleet. That they were there at all was madness and completely against the rules of the magazine, but madness happened in wartime, and cockups were even more commonplace. No one had expected that the shells would remain at Purfleet for more than a few days, but once the mutinous sailors had started impeding traffic on the lower Thames, it had been judged safer to leave them where they were.

Drake listened in silence as Holland explained the situation in more detail. He was less impressed by the elastic force liberated by fifty-two thousand barrels of powder and perhaps one hundred mortar shells than by the fact that his officer was alarmed by the prospect. Captain Haitch, he knew, was first rate when it came to machines and devices of all sorts, and he didn't generally lay it on thick. Drake's own concerns were purely practical. 'When do we start, sir?'

'What do you mean?'

'We ain't leavin' it all to them London chaps, are we?'

'That would be the safest,' Holland confessed, 'if everything were stopped at the warehouse.'

'Course it would, but wot if they can't manage it? There's an 'undred things could go wrong, and 'ere's all of us at Woolwich who are that much closer, tho' on the wrong side o' the river I grant you, not doin' a blessed thing.'

Holland shook his head. 'I don't know that that would help matters. We can't exactly bombard any suspicious-looking boats on the Thames every afternoon until sunset, and we don't want to cause a panic here at Woolwich, not after what's been happening.'

'No,' admitted Drake, slowly.

'And don't forget, some of these . . . radicals may be about still. If they learned that we were on to their plan, God knows what else they might stir up, here, to distract us.'

322

Drake pondered all of this, and then his expression cleared. 'But there's somethin' else, I reckon. You wasn't laying all your cards on the table with that chap – I could see it plain as day.'

'It isn't quite like that.' Holland sighed and sat back in the chair. 'He may be absolutely right about what's likely to happen – what Rabelais has in mind – but I'm not so sure. As far as I can tell, it's expected that he'll make a direct assault on the magazine. Now, he must have quite a good idea of how strong those buildings are, so he cannot expect to blow them in any usual way and survive. Rabelais may be desperate, but it still doesn't sound right to me.'

'But there's a way wot *does* sound right,' prompted Drake, and when Holland nodded, he added, 'and you've got a way of stoppin' it that won't cause the other trouble.'

Holland had watched the play of emotions across his sub-ordinate's face, from worry to gloom to reassurance, and he could not help smiling at the confidence that his own ability apparently inspired. 'I have got an *idea*,' he admitted, 'but it might not work. Very likely it would not work.' He shrugged and explained briefly what he had in mind, using the sketch to illustrate the relevant details. 'Of course, we could all be wrong about how Rabelais is planning to do it in the first place.'

'But if that's so, then your London chaps won't be much good, and they'll need reinforcements on the spot,' Drake reminded him.

'Yes, that's what I thought.'

Drake continued to study the map. 'Maybe another pair of 'ands wouldn't go amiss?' he asked. 'I was thinkin' of Mr Dalton. You know 'e'd be game.'

'No,' said Holland, shaking his head. 'He's got a family. Better leave him out of it.'

Drake nodded. 'Yes, sir. I was forgettin' the little uns. Then it'll just be the two of us, but that's all right.'

Holland glanced across questioningly, but before he could speak Drake continued, 'You're not goin' without me, that's fer certain. You'd never manage it on your own, but with two of us, there might be a chance.'

'God knows I could use your help, Drake,' Holland acknowledged, 'but—'

'Reckon it's like you said before, sir. Wot with the lads at Purfleet dead, and everything from Woolwich to Gravesend knocked to 'ell if that magazine *does* go up, it don't look like we've got a choice.'

'Well, thanks. And what do you think of my idea?'

Drake shook his head. 'Oh, I think it's mad, sir, same as you do. But as we ain't got another, I reckon we'd better give it a go.'

20

'What do you ladies say to a game of cards?'

The three of them had been sitting together silently for the last half hour or so, Susannah working on her needle-point, Mary pretending to read Mr Keate's *Account of the Pelew Islands*, and Colonel Crosby-Nash apparently engrossed in his newspaper, so that this suggestion came as something of a surprise.

Susannah looked up from her work. 'Certainly, my dear, that sounds a lovely suggestion.'

'Well, one does one's best, you know,' acknowledged her husband. 'What do you say, Miss Finch?'

'Oh, yes,' Mary agreed, closing her book. The memory of her earlier distress had faded to an odd lethargy, and now she gazed placidly at her host. 'We used to play a few simple games with the girls at Mrs Bunbury's.'

'What an advanced sort of school it must have been,' said Susannah, 'to have allowed— But I was forgetting about Nisroch. Of course, it was *very* advanced. Mama did not approve of card games of any sort – apart from Pope Joan.'

'Ah, well, perhaps we might venture slightly beyond that,' suggested Crosby-Nash. 'Do we all know Casino?'

They all did know it and, while Crosby-Nash went to look for a deck of cards, Mary arranged a table and chairs. Very soon they had lapsed into silence again, but this time it was focused on a common object, and it was broken occasionally by such observations as 'building queens', or 'eights again'.

As might have been expected, Susannah was the weakest player. Lacking a sense of guile, she was forever leading with her smaller cards, which greatly increased the likelihood that her opponents would build upon them to their own advantage. Crosby-Nash, on the other hand, was extremely adept, within the limits of the game, while Mary simply tried to take as many tricks as she could. As play continued, Mary found that she was enjoying herself, possibly for the first time since Holland and Whittington had departed. She felt almost grateful to Crosby-Nash for suggesting the entertainment.

'Last,' announced the colonel, as he dealt the final hand of that round. They played it out and counted their points. Mary was the surprising leader – or at least it was a surprise to her – with Crosby-Nash a close second. 'Well played, Miss Finch,' he said. 'You managed to steal both the Good Ten and the Good Two, I noticed.'

'Thank you, sir,' Mary replied, 'but I fancy it was more a question of luck than of skill.'

He pursed his lips in disagreement. 'The skilful player makes use of his opportunities. Now, ladies, having begun so well, what do you say to a little wager to maintain our interest?'

'Oh, should we *bet*, do you mean?' asked Susannah. *'For money?'*

'Well, that is the usual currency.'

'I told you I would not agree to gamble for White Ladies,' Mary reminded him.

'No, no, certainly not,' laughed Crosby-Nash. 'I did not mean to suggest anything so extravagant, merely a few pennies. It is not the amount wagered that creates the interest, I find, but the fact that one has taken a risk, and is willing to act upon it. And, as an indication of my magnanimity, I shall provide the stakes.' Passing the cards to Mary, he reached into his coat pocket and produced a handful of coins. 'I have a good deal of loose change,' he admitted, 'which is perfect for our purposes. There you go, my dear, and Miss Finch, and I shall keep the rest.'

Mary shuffled the cards conscientiously, if not very well. 'I am making rather a mess,' she laughed, 'not like the colonel's neat pile. I must watch him more carefully next time, and see how he manages it. We surely cannot wager on each *hand*, can we?'

'No, I had thought on each round.'

'Yes, of course.' Mary nodded, and started to deal – four cards to each of them, and four cards face up in the centre of the table. Did they have a particular name? Were they the 'kitty' or the 'pool'? Neither sounded quite right, but cards and card games used such odd expressions. Was there not even a card that was called the 'Curse of Scotland'? As an afterthought, she added two of her coins to those being wagered by Crosby-Nash.

The sound of Susannah's voice drifted vaguely into Mary's rumination on the subject of gambling terminology. 'Oh, what an odd-looking coin you have given me, my dear – pray, what is it?' Immediately Mary experienced a sinking, shuddering feeling. She dared not raise her eyes, but forced herself to study her cards – king of spades, eight of hearts, three of hearts, ten of clubs – and now Crosby-Nash was answering, in that same bland tone of his. 'Ah yes, that is a very interesting thing. Not really a coin at all, you know, more of a token that some of the City banks are accepting.'

Mary swallowed awkwardly, her throat suddenly dry, as Susannah acknowledged, 'It is quite pretty, in a sort of way, but if it is not real money . . .' She regarded the coin sceptically, as if she mistrusted it.

Oh God, where did he get that? What does it mean? Has he . . . Can he somehow have found my coin? What shall I do? As these thoughts raced through Mary's brain she stared at the droopy-eyed king of spades as if hoping for assistance. Forcing herself to assume a smile that she was very far from feeling, she folded up her cards and looked attentively at the coin that Susannah still held in her hand. 'Yes, it *is* interesting,' she affirmed. It is a . . . a bank token, you say?' Then came the more frightening task – to look at Crosby-Nash himself. What would she see when she met his gaze?

327

His expression was decidedly cool; it acknowledged nothing and made no obvious accusation. But was it also calculating? 'Yes,' he explained. 'If you look closely you will see that it is actually a Spanish dollar that has been re-stamped.'

His remark gave her the opportunity to look away, back at the coin. For some reason she did not want to touch it, and she drew Susannah's hand closer instead. 'Yes,' she nodded. 'It certainly does look . . . foreign.' It was the best she could manage, and she strove to achieve the same tone of detachment that he had employed. 'Are you going to wager it, Susannah?'

'I suppose so, if nobody minds.'

'Of course not, my dear. It is only for fun, you know.'

The coin sat staring at Mary from on top of the pile of wagered coins throughout that round; a round without a winner, for she and Crosby-Nash each scored four points to Susannah's three, so there it remained. Somehow she managed to marshal her concentration sufficiently to win the next round; either that or she simply had a pronounced run of luck, but that meant the coin came to her, which seemed worse. She knew that it made no difference, but she did not want the coin near her, or in any way associated with her. What was it people said about the corpse of a murdered man bleeding when the murderer was close by? *But I did not— Oh God. What if he actually struck Romney down? Murdered him and then discovered this coin?*

The image of Colonel Crosby-Nash bending over the still warm body of the tinker and calmly searching through his pockets was sickening, and it heightened her dread of the coin and the colonel. She felt her face becoming hot. *Oh – am I blushing? What if Susannah notices and says something? Of all things, I must not appear uneasy.*

She included the coin in her next wager and made a determined effort to ignore it and concentrate entirely on the game, but it was a difficult task. When Susannah announced that she was building fours, Mary found herself thinking *four shillings; they are worth four shillings and nine pence*, and then wondered, fearfully, if she had spoken the words out loud. She was almost

328

relieved when Crosby-Nash won that round and collected his winnings, only to do precisely what she had done and use the coin in his next wager.

Mary told herself that Crosby-Nash knew nothing; perhaps this *was* Romney's coin but there was nothing to connect it with her. *Her* coin was safe at the bottom of her travelling trunk . . . Of course it was; it had to be.

The deal had come back to Mary again. 'Things are becoming exciting,' said the colonel, who was keeping track of the score. 'This ought to be the deciding round, so you had better play very carefully.'

Oh, what a thing to say! Mary silently raged, and in the next instant, *Keep your head; remember what Major Whittington said — the colonel likes to make people feel off balance.* She frowned, thinking how right that assessment had been, and added an ace to Crosby-Nash's build of seven, remarking, 'Eights,' in a confident voice.

The next few hands passed in a kind of dream for Mary, and then it was over. Crosby-Nash added up the final scores. 'We have a winner,' he announced. 'Susannah, my dear, you have a total of twelve, which is very creditable for someone who cut her teeth on Pope Joan. I am on eighteen, and Miss Finch has claimed a triumphant twenty-five.'

'Oh, congratulations, Mary,' cried Susannah. 'How well you have played.'

'Yes, indeed,' Crosby-Nash agreed. 'A most inspired performance. I do not think I should venture a serious wager with you, Miss Finch. But this homely game poses no risks and promises nothing but enjoyment. Shall we play again? Susannah, I believe it is your deal.'

Woolwich was sufficiently tranquil for Holland and Drake to leave the Warren without any untoward questions being asked. In fact, the two men on the gate considered it evidence that things were returning to normal. Captain Holland was forever going somewhere or other with his notebooks and his fancy equipment, though he didn't usually go kitted out like a civilian. Or with that old bugger Drake tagging along; worse than an officer, with his airs and graces and his Sunday afternoon coat. A regular Pontius Pilate he was, and just as if he'd be doing anything but making the bloody tea.

Holland did have a notebook as well as his surveying equipment, because he hoped eventually to fulfil his orders regarding the Isle of Grain. His immediate destination, however, was the village of Erith, about two and a half miles upstream from Purfleet. Little more than a street of cottages and warehouses leading down to the Thames, Erith was nevertheless a busy place, on account of it being the regular anchorage for Indiamen sailing up and down river. Incoming vessels were frequently lightened there before proceeding to London, while outbound ones often acquired passengers or visitors. The presence of two more strangers, therefore, would excite little interest. More importantly, East India Company captains had a habit of giving their ships a quasi-naval appearance, and this was likely to prove helpful for the execution of Holland's idea.

The idea might not actually *need* to be executed – and they reminded each other of this point more than once – but they must have a boat for it to be possible, and Drake undertook to find one. He had spent his boyhood in Wapping and, as he explained to Holland, he knew something about small craft. They both appreciated that in this case 'have' meant 'steal', but as this was only a small complication to what was already a complex and highly dubious undertaking, there did not seem any point in discussing it.

'And she's got to look like a proper Navy boat,' Drake insisted. 'It don't matter if she's small – jolly boat or the like – but she's got to look like she's come off of a King's ship, or they'll smoke us directly. If we 'as to do it, that is.'

'They'll smoke us directly.' The phrase came back to Holland as he waited for Drake in the village's only pub, an establishment that seemed to be called the Happy Return, although the sign bearing that name and a ship under sail had fallen down. He had taken a room, and there he had deposited his bag of instruments and made what changes were possible to his appearance. These were not very great, but he hoped that

330

an old shirt and breeches, bare legs, buckled shoes, and brown flannel waistcoat would at least render him inconspicuous. As he sipped a mug of beer in the deserted taproom he rehearsed again the various contingencies that might occur in the next few hours.

There were two ways by which Purfleet might be destroyed – sabotage from within and assault from without. During the day both methods were possible. Powder was received and dispatched all the time, and the magazine doors were kept open as the powder men trundled the lethal barrels in and out. After sunset, however, the internal threat was greatly reduced. It was not possible to work in the magazine after dark, for no one in his right mind would countenance the use of lanterns or candles, so the entire area was shut up, locked, and guarded.

That left an external assault as the most likely, and Holland thought he knew how this could be accomplished without costing the lives of the attackers. Late-arriving barges were not permitted to remain at the Purfleet wharf overnight. They were, however, allowed to anchor in mid-river, suitably buoyed and lit, in the charge of their own crew. It was not a very wise practice as regards the barges, for there was always the chance of an accident that might prove fatal to the crew. The magazine buildings themselves were presumed to be safe, with their thick walls and massive, arched roofs, but because an explosion had never occurred, that presumption was untested. Suppose the barge crew rigged a long fuse, set it alight, and rowed quietly away? If a fully laden barge exploded, might that not blow the magazine as well, despite its bomb-proof construction? *Eight hundred barrels – that's how much a Thames powder barge can carry – would make a bloody great bomb.*

It made sense and, more importantly, it corresponded with what Cuthbert Shy had learned. The barge would come from one of the warehouses that regularly delivered powder to Purfleet. The only difference this time was that the vessel would be in the hands of dedicated bombers instead of the regular crew. No one at Purfleet would notice anything amiss, because the barge would arrive too late to be unloaded. So, the bombers would anchor and light up, set the charge, and clear off before everything blew.

Holland worked through the various logistical factors as nearly as he could guess them – the speed of the tide, the barge's rate of sailing, and her planned time of arrival at Purfleet. *Late, but not too late*, Holland concluded. *Not so late as would look suspicious.* Relying on fairly conservative estimates and on how he himself would conduct an operation of this kind, he came up with an answer. Half past seven. The barge would aim to reach Purfleet at half past seven in the evening.

Where and when should he and Drake try to intercept the barge? Of course, they might not need to do it. Very likely the barge would not appear; it would be stopped before it sailed from Barking Creek. There was plenty of time for Shy's plan to work; he would appreciate the necessity of a quick stroke, and his men would carry it off. Holland's watch said a quarter past six. *Where is Drake? We should have been on the river by now.*

Drake slid through the half-opened door at the front of the pub and motioned for Holland to join him outside. Amazingly, he had managed to dress himself in a checked shirt and a pair of the wide-legged trousers that seamen called 'slops', and he was carrying a blue jacket over his arm.

'Have you got it?' asked Holland, frowning in the evening sunshine.

'Aye, sir, I've got 'er all right,' Drake replied. 'She's in the marsh, close to shore.'

'Good. Let's go.'

As they moved towards the river, Drake continued in a conversational voice, 'Now I got this 'ere jacket, which I figure looks near enough to a sailor's, and you could maybe wear it.' He held up the garment for inspection.

'Thanks. I won't ask where you got it . . . and the rest of that rig.'

'No, sir, best not.'

They lapsed into silence, and then Holland asked, 'What sort of boat is it?'

'She's wot you might call a skiff, sir,' Drake explained. 'We've a pair of oars, and there's a sail if only we'd get a bit of air.'

'Well, I'll row and leave the rest to you.'

'Arm all right?'

Holland nodded, flexing his left hand, and, in answer to the unspoken question, added, 'I learned to row when I was a lad. The motion didn't bother me so much then, and I think it's harder to be sick when you're doing something. Not a lump in the bottom of the boat.'

'Daresay you're right, sir.'

The boat had been hidden in a reed bed. They climbed aboard, and Drake punted them out into the river. Then they shifted places – Drake at the tiller and Holland at the oars.

'Shall we drift down river a bit, sir, and maybe 'ave a look at Purfleet?' asked Drake.

Upstream or down? thought Holland. *Meet the barge as far away from Purfleet as possible, or waste time rowing in the wrong direction?* Against the possibility that he was wrong about the entire scheme came the more frightening vision of the barge already having reached the magazine. What then?

Suddenly Drake cried, 'There she is, sir! In the stream, about 'alf a mile back.'

He swung the tiller over hard, trying to turn the boat, but Holland muttered, 'Ease off, I'll spin her.' Alternately backing and rowing, he spun the boat quickly and then sent it off in the direction of the barge. He acknowledged Drake's surprised expression with a nod. 'I told you I knew how to do it.'

The combination of Holland's nervous energy and the now sluggish tide brought the two vessels together in a matter of minutes. Holland glanced over his shoulder to check his course and observe their quarry. There was no mistaking it. Large and broad, with overhanging sides that curved inward at both ends; the sort of vessel commonly used to transport goods up and down the Thames. The sails had been taken in as useless on such a still, close evening, and the red flag, warning that explosives were on board, hung limply at the mast.

The greater height of the barge made its crew largely

invisible to those in the skiff. The captain seemed to be alone in the stern, standing at the tiller, but how many others might be crouching on deck or resting in the tiny cabin?

Holland spun the skiff a second time and took up station on the larger boat's starboard side, like a terrier trotting beside a carthorse. Then he nodded at Drake, who cupped his hands and bawled across the water, 'Where you goin', mate?'

The captain glanced down at them uninterestedly. 'What's that to you?'

'Well, I'll tell you,' Drake replied, in a strong but placid tone, 'we've come up from the Nore, and we've been put in charge o' this bit o' river. We don't mean you no 'arm − if you're honest − but we got to keep a close watch on things 'ereabouts, along of they've got it in fer us.'

'*Who's* got it in for you?'

'Why, the government a course, you dozy bugger. Don't you know nothin'?'

'We're never the British government, and we haven't a bad word for any man who takes a stand against 'em,' another voice assured them from somewhere farther forward.

'Oh aye, and 'ow's that?' Drake wanted to know.

'Why, because we're for liberty, of course, and freedom. We gave the lads at the Nore a cheer when we heard they'd risen.'

Drake considered this. 'Ain't no outsiders been doin' much cheering, Paddy, not so's we've 'eard. But we'll 'ave our own back, see if we don't. Ain't that so, Bob?'

'It is,' Holland agreed. 'How's the war to be fought without us, I'd like to know.'

'Can't be done,' said Drake, 'simple as that. And we'll see 'ow they like it when we sets sail for France. Not much, I reckon!'

The captain attempted to cut short the two men's grievances. 'Look here,' he urged, 'we've business down river − important business − so just you clear off and leave us to it, eh?' He nodded and turned away, as if the conversation had ended and he now intended to concentrate on steering.

It was not difficult to keep abreast of the barge, and with a few powerful strokes the skiff shot forward. Drake steered across the other's bows and resumed his place on the opposite side, so that now the skiff lay between the barge and the Essex shore – and between the barge and Purfleet.

'You damned fool! What the hell are you playing at?' bellowed the captain. He had steered wide as soon as the skiff had darted ahead, and now he steadied his boat back on course, trying to keep to the middle of the stream where the current was strongest.

'It's you tryin' to make a joke of it,' said Drake, 'and it's us ain't 'aving none. I tell ye, nobody passes without we say so. There's more lads in the Long Reach and some of 'em bad-tempered, so if you don't want worse trouble you'll say where you're goin' and wot's on board.'

There was a pause, and then the sound of an urgent conversation could be heard between the captain and another, unseen speaker, both of whom seemed to exercise authority on board. Holland thought he could discern at least one other voice.

A slim, dark-haired man appeared forward of the cabin and stared keenly down at them. His dress, as much as could be seen, was sober and correct, although he had removed his neck cloth, and his shirt hung open above his waistcoat. After a moment he spoke in a low, urgent voice. 'Gentlemen, we do not desire any trouble with you, but we have our own work to perform, and it must not be halted. You say the government has got it in for the mutineers, and I believe that is so, but what proofs do you have that *you* are of that party?'

Drake seemed surprised at the question. 'Why else'd we be 'ere, mate? I'm captain's steward, and Bob 'ere's a quarter gunner – or was, till he was broke for fightin' with the carpenter's mate, who was a right bastard and drunk besides.'

'What is your ship?' queried the dark-haired man.

'*Sandwich,*' replied Drake, proudly, 'wot was the first to make a stand.'

'Have you signed articles?'

'We 'ave.'

A third figure loomed up beside the dark-haired man. He was taller and more simply dressed in a canvas smock and striped breeches, his brawny arms and legs bare. When he spoke it was clear that it was he who had claimed to admire the mutineers. 'Have you now? Let's hear your pledge.'

Drake's demeanour changed as he considered this request. His tone became knowing, even slightly confiding. 'It weren't none of your mad Irish talk, Paddy, about the cockcrow and the branch in me 'and. Just plain words wot everyone could understand. But we're true fer all that. True blue, through and through.'

'Are you sober?' demanded the Irishman.

'Aye, we're sober,' Holland replied. 'And we're ready.'

'And who has the power to make a change?'

'The power is all our own.' Holland took a deep breath. He could not remember any more of Smith's handbill, and that document constituted his entire store of radical rhetoric.

'And what—'

'All right, James,' nodded the dark-haired man, his hand upon his companion's arm. Then, gazing down into the skiff, he continued, 'We are true as well, my friends, and tonight we have a very important task before us. One that will astonish the British government and may help you as well. So you will not wish to hinder us.'

'We're bound for a place called Purfleet,' added the man called James.

'Purfleet,' said Drake, 'you don't say you're . . .' He stared up at the barge, 'You don't say you're goin' fer the magazine?'

'How do you know about that?' demanded James.

''Ell's bells,' Drake scoffed. 'Ain't we been sent up river fer powder more times'n you've washed your neck? Chap said you was on a big job at Purfleet. Wot else'd you be after? What d'you mean to do with the powder once you get it, Paddy?'

'Not a thing. We're going to blow the whole place to Kingdom come.'

'*Wot? Blow it?*' Drake shook his head, although there was admiration in his smile. 'You'll never do it, mate,' he pronounced. 'They don't let outsiders near them buildings.'

'We'll get close enough, never you fear,' the Irishman assured them. 'We've only got to anchor and set the fuse.'

'Oh, aye,' nodded Drake, chuckling. 'All you've got to do is set the fuse. And wot poor sod 'ave you found to do it, eh? Make sure 'e says 'is prayers good and proper. I think that's our signal to weigh, Bob, old son. I don't mean to see 'eaven just yet.'

'*Heaven?* More like the other place for you, mate,' replied Holland.

He obediently made as if to draw away when the barge captain hailed them. 'Hold on,' he called. 'What do you mean about saying prayers?'

'I mean you'll be needin' 'em,' called Drake. '"*Lo, though I walk through the valley o' the shadow o' death . . .*" That's wot the Book says. It's the river o' death for you lot.'

Holland allowed the distance between the two vessels to widen again. 'Handy with fuses, are you?' he called up to the barge.

'I am,' said James. 'I've set them before.'

'Long ones? Half an hour? An hour?'

'No, but—'

'That's how long you'll need, unless you want to go up with the rest. You want to be right careful if you mean to set off a bargeload of powder and live to tell about it.' Holland took another stroke and then turned speculatively to Drake. 'What do you say, a couple of weeks with the militia? He's no sapper, and I doubt if he's seen the inside of a mine.'

'I think you're right, Bob – a spell in the militia and someone let 'im fire off a musket once for a bit of a laugh. A first-class hexpert, 'e is.'

'I know what I'm about,' James insisted, but then he was drawn into another conference with the barge captain and the dark-haired man. Holland took a half stroke, but held up when the captain called, 'Hold on, there,' a second time, and the two boats drifted on the tide.

The conversation on board the barge continued for a few minutes, while Drake stared vacantly across the water. Then he noticed that Holland had begun to grow pale, even slightly greenish. *Oh Christ,* he groaned, *that's all we need; Captain Haitch 'eavin' 'is guts over the side.* Aloud he urged, 'Keep us off 'em, Bob. Couple o' strokes.' The exertion produced a healthier colour, and Drake relaxed again. 'That's it.'

At last the dark-haired man leaned down to them and enquired, 'Do you know much about such things as fuses, then?' in a conversational tone.

'Bob 'ere does,' replied Drake. 'I told you, 'e was a quarter gunner until—'

'We've heard all that,' snapped James. 'The point is—'

'The point is,' continued the dark-haired man, calmly, 'that you may be right. It might be best if we had help with the fuses. The timing is essential to the success of our plan, and if you could be of assistance, we would be much obliged to you.'

Drake rubbed his chin and eyed Holland questioningly. 'I don't know . . . What do you reckon, Bob? Should we give 'em an 'and?'

'I don't mind,' said Holland, shrugging, 'but it'll have to be one hell of a long fuse. Have they got the stuff on board?'

'Oh, aye, we've got plenty of fuse,' nodded the captain, 'but some of it might have to be spliced together.'

Drake rolled his eyes. 'You do need 'elp, mate, that's fer sure. Come on, Bob.'

Holland backed his oars, and the skiff crept close to the barge. Drake coiled the painter and prepared to toss it up to the captain. Suddenly James cried, 'Say, if you know so much about powder, why didn't you know straight off we were carrying it?'

'Anybody can 'oist a red flag,' replied Drake, coolly. 'It don't mean nothin'.

'Aye, and any black thief can talk like an honest man, so he can,' James agreed. 'It works both ways, you know.'

'That it does, mate. Now just you catch 'old o' this rope, and we'll come aboard and show you 'ow much *we* know.'

The evening passed slowly for Mary. It had been impossible to resist the colonel's suggestion that they play another round of

338

cards, and even when it was finished she did not dare to be the first to retire. Never since coming to Champian Hall had she felt so keenly that she was playing a part, and that she must maintain her character for as long as was necessary. Doing so was very difficult. Thankfully, no new surprises occurred either to shock or frighten her, but she longed to make some acknowledgement of her earlier distress. The atmosphere of the room also seemed heavy, even ominous. They were sitting in the great hall, and their candles heightened the darkness rather than banished it. From the shadows above their heads the hostile, snarling faces of the stuffed animals could be glimpsed, while the body of the hall, beyond the pools of light, was a black, mysterious void.

You must stop this, Mary commanded, *nothing good can come of these . . . fancies,* and as if in answer Susannah wondered whether a storm was likely. Crosby-Nash agreed, remarking upon the distant rumble of thunder, and privately Mary tried to reassure herself that the atmosphere she felt, of something dangerous and imminent, had a wholly natural basis. Animals were generally sensitive to changes in the weather, after all, and poor Slipper was panting so loudly that the sound was almost an additional presence in the room. And thunder, well, *that* was certainly not a fancy.

At the stroke of nine o'clock, Susannah announced her intention of going to bed, and Mary was at last able to make good her escape. Abandoning Mr Keate's *Account,* she closed the book and placed it on the table beside her chair, taking up a candle instead. It was still important not to seem too eager, however, and she purposely followed her regular routine of cajoling Slipper into the pantry, where he was obliged to pass his nights. His compliance was not more than usually dubious, in that he refrained from snapping at her but attempted to escape when she locked him in. Afterwards she wearily climbed the stairs to her bedchamber, thinking that *she* would not so disdain her sanctuary. No, she longed for quiet, solitude, and perhaps even sleep.

Mary took three steps into the bedchamber and stopped

short – there before her was Colonel Crosby-Nash. He was leaning against her writing desk, his back to the curtained window.

She immediately raised her guard, like a practised fencer, as she tried to calculate what his presence might mean. 'Why, colonel,' she cried, permitting her surprise – her innocent surprise – to show through. 'Whatever are you doing here? Is something the matter?'

He did not reply immediately, and for Mary it was the longest moment of her life. She was intensely conscious of every detail of the room – the ivory muslin bedspread shot with threads of gold, the woven rug with tassels at both ends, the glass of water on her bedside table, the open door behind her.

'Spare me your outraged modesty,' he said at last. His face was in shadow, but the contempt was evident in his voice. 'You ask what is the matter? *You* are the matter, and have been since you came to Champian Hall – perhaps even before.'

Oh God!

'Tell me,' he continued, moving towards her – she tried to retreat, but he grasped her firmly by the arm. With his other hand he closed the door. She heard it click. 'Tell me, for how long have you been spying upon me? Since the night of the ball at Scarborough House? Since you came to London?'

Fear and shock at his words confused her, and the feel of his hand seemed to spread a deadening poison through her veins. *I am lost – what shall I do?* Her lips were stiff, and she struggled to speak. 'I do not know what you mean.' She swallowed. 'I am not a spy.'

With an effort she shook free of him and stepped away – not towards the door, but sideways, as though she wished only to put down her candle, which was dripping wax onto the floor. She did so, all the while thinking hard. *He is guessing – he has no evidence – keep calm and do not let him see that you are afraid.* 'I think you have made a mistake, sir, and now I must ask you—'

'To do what?' he snarled. 'Leave you in peace, I suppose? I shall do so, after you have answered my questions.'

'But your questions make no sense,' Mary urged. She let her shawl slide from her shoulders and folded it in half; doing so helped to keep her hands from shaking. 'I am not a spy, and I fear that you are . . . unwell to make such an accusation.'

Crosby-Nash watched her manoeuvres with a hard smile. 'You are very cool,' he acknowledged, 'with your steady gaze and your chin in the air. How shall you like this?' Slipping his fingers into the pocket of his waistcoat he withdrew a coin. Without looking, Mary knew what it was.

He caught the flicker in her gaze and chuckled mirthlessly. 'Ah, that makes you blink, I see, though you were composed enough during our game. Yes, it belonged to your friend Romney – at least, it was found in his keeping.' He dropped the coin onto her bed. 'And where do you suppose is its mate? In the bottom of your wardrobe, perhaps? I suppose you might carry it with you . . . That would have been sensible while Romney was alive. Did you use it to communicate with him, by the way, or only to identify yourself as a friend?'

The sight of that coin brought Mary's fears flooding back, but she replied doggedly. She could think of nothing, no strategy apart from refusing to give in. 'I . . . do not know what you mean,' she repeated, knowing that she sounded desperate. 'I have never seen that coin before.'

'Oh, come now,' complained the colonel, 'let us end this performance, interesting as it may be.' He produced a second coin, and she knew immediately that it was hers. *Her* coin. *And he knows . . . he must know everything.* After tossing it in the air and catching it, he held it between thumb and forefinger as if studying it. 'A curious Spanish trinket,' he mused, 'or so I have heard it described.'

'You— My letter,' gasped Mary, unable to help herself. 'How did—'

'I come to know what it said? I intercepted it, of course. Do you think that was very bad of me? You should have thought of that – and of all the other bad things that could happen before you started playing hide and seek with me. Now that the game is over, you can tell me for whom are you have been working. Is it the Home Office? That was Romney's usual employer, I believe.'

Mary shook her head, and he affected not to care whether the gesture signified a negative or a refusal to answer. 'You still do not consider yourself beaten? Well, it makes little difference, now that you have no one with whom you can communicate. I read your letter carefully, you see.'

That taunt, and the knowledge that her position had been utterly ruined, gave Mary a strange sense of power. Without knowing why, she was suddenly unafraid. 'You are a coward,' she scorned, 'and a traitor.'

'As are you. Having been welcomed into my house, you have betrayed every obligation incumbent upon a guest. Unfortunately for you, the penalty for breaching the laws of hospitality at Champian Hall is severe.'

Mary's eyes blazed with anger; she advanced a pace towards him. 'Are you threatening me?'

Her opponent regarded her with unmasked disdain. 'Not in the least. I am merely reminding you that you are in *my* house, where I answer to no one, and where an accident would provoke not a single untoward question.'

'You would not dare to harm me, sir, not in front of Susannah or the servants. I wager that some of them, at least, are honest.'

'Susannah,' he scoffed. 'Do not pin your hopes on my wife's powers, and as for the servants, they hear and see . . . and *act* according to my instructions.'

In spite of her anger, the colour drained from Mary's face with those words, and Crosby-Nash pressed his advantage. Drawing near to her, he had the satisfaction of feeling her shiver, and now he spoke softly, but with a deep malevolence. 'My business is drawing to a close, and then I will deal with you. But if you try to cross me again, by God, I will kill you without the slightest hesitation.'

He smiled scornfully and then turned his back on her, as if

she were a minor inconvenience not worth further consideration. Mary watched him leave, still without a backwards glance, and heard the door close firmly behind him. A key turned in the lock, footsteps moved steadily down the passage, and then all was quiet.

21

While the shadows were lengthening around Mary, Susannah, and Crosby-Nash in the great hall, Holland was adjusting fuses. The barge had reached Purfleet at half past seven and, following the decision of the magazine foreman to delay unloading until morning, had anchored at a moderate distance from shore. There the crew and its two supernumeraries had waited for full darkness. Ostensibly, the plan was for Holland to set fuses that would blow the powder at approximately nine o'clock, with the barge to be evacuated half an hour earlier. Holland and Drake, however, had other ideas. Ideally, they would retake the barge before any explosives could be rigged, but as this might prove impossible, Holland would also perform an act of sabotage.

He intended to fix the fuses so that they would fail after a couple of minutes. The crew, seeing the charge successfully lighted, would row away, thinking that all was well. They would probably have fled from the scene before they realised that something had gone wrong, but even if their suspicions were aroused more promptly, Holland doubted that any of them would have the courage to come back on board. He and Drake, by contrast, would only make a show of escaping, and would return secretly to secure the barge. So long as their true identities were not discovered in the meantime, the plan seemed marginally less dangerous than a direct assault on the crew.

It was delicate work, made more difficult by the fact that the moment of departure was nearing, and everyone on board knew this. In addition to the captain, the crew consisted of three men: the stern, dark-haired man; James, the Irishman; and a hulking fellow called Chabot. He had an expression both brutal and simple, but he seemed to know his way around boats. None of the conspirators looked to be wholly in control of his nerves, and each time that one of them looked over Holland's shoulder, asking whether he had nearly finished, the likelihood increased that the deceit would be discovered. As the darkness deepened, the lantern illuminating the work on the fuses seemed to draw spectators like moths.

'Are you sure that splice will hold, now?' demanded James. He was the most dangerous bystander, both because he knew something about explosives and because he resented having been supplanted. His tone alternated between genuine, even deferential interest, and surly disdain. 'This is how *I* would have done it,' he continued, and he cut a spare length of fuse to illustrate his technique.

'I understood what you meant before,' said Holland curtly, without looking up. 'That way's all right, but this is more secure.'

James displayed the partially completed splice and then lowered it, frowning. 'Well . . . then hurry, if you know the way of it. We don't mean to pass the night through on this barge, you know,' to which remark his large, dull colleague urged, 'Let us be going.'

During the exchange Drake had kept his eyes on the barge captain. Since arriving at their destination he had seemed particularly tense, sweating and tugging the grimy handkerchief that was knotted about his neck, and so when he urged James not to interfere, Drake swiftly concurred. ''E's goin' as fast as 'e can, is Bob, and you oughtn't to rush a chap when 'e's got a tricky job on.'

'But this part isn't dangerous, is it?' asked the captain anxiously.

'No, but if it ain't done right, she don't blow. And I reckon none of us would fancy comin' back on board, after the fuse is lit, to see if maybe it's come apart somewheres?' Drake smiled. 'Or maybe the fuse is fine, and it's only the timing's wrong.'

'God no.'

'I'd have had it all finished by now, and us away and drinking a pint of the Bull's finest,' James complained.

'Almost done,' Holland announced, shifting so that the other man's view was obscured. 'Have you got the boats ready?'

'Aye,' murmured the barge captain, while the one they called Chabot jerked his head and added, 'À tribord.'

Drake turned to the Irishman companionably. 'You fixin' to make for Dartford, mate? I'd give it a wide berth, if I was you. When this place blows, you can bet your life the Dartford mills'll go up as well.'

'Do you think so?'

'Stands to reason. It's what they call "concussion" . . . a sort of pressure, and there's enough powder at Dartford—'

'Never mind where we are going,' advised the dark-haired man. 'We have made our arrangements – you may depend upon it.'

'That's the idea,' Drake agreed. 'I seen a frigate once, catch fire and blow – Jesus, wot a sight. Bits o' wood, and rope . . . bits o' the crew, even. There was one poor bugger, all was left of 'im was 'is 'ead floatin' about in the water, just grinnin', like, and heverything ablaze.' He shuddered with the memory. 'Orrible it was, and that's nothin' to wot this'll be.'

'Maybe we'd better shove off now,' suggested the captain, and he glanced about, as if to discover whether anyone thought him cowardly. 'I mean, well, it doesn't take all of us to light a fuse.'

'That's so,' said the Irishman with a crafty smile, 'and who were ye thinkin' might be the feller to do the honours in that department?'

'Why not him?' The captain motioned towards Holland. 'He knows what he's about, and the rest of us are only . . . delaying things with our talk and getting in the way.'

Holland rose slowly to his feet and stepped back from the coiled fuse. 'I don't mind,' he said with a shrug. This was precisely the chance for which he and Drake had been hoping, but he had to be careful. Any enthusiasm on his part must seem suspicious.

Indeed, the black-haired man was observing him carefully, but then he nodded. 'Thank you.'

'Well that's grand,' agreed the Irishman, and he shook Holland's hand. 'Don't scrimp on the length of the fuse, now, and good luck and the Lord's blessing on us all.'

He and the rest of the barge crew moved forward and across the deck, and Drake followed them. From behind he heard another voice. 'I shall light the fuse, young fellow, if you have no objection.'

As Holland knelt again he felt a hand on his arm. The voice was a new one – had there been another man below deck? He looked up, and in the gloom perceived a short, slight man, with grizzled hair cut close to the scalp, as though he usually wore a wig.

'Just as you like,' said Holland. 'Half a second, and I'll hold the light.'

'I am much obliged to you.'

Holland raised the lantern shade, and the other man bent forward. As the light shone on both their faces they recognised each other. The tilt of Holland's head, the other man's pale blue eyes – although their only other meeting had been brief, in the crowded entrance hall of Scarborough House.

For the space of a heartbeat neither man moved, and then chaos erupted across the barge. Holland swung the lantern away and scrabbled on the deck for his knife. 'Ah! I know you, sir!' hissed the other man, springing backwards and drawing his pistol in the same instant. The Irishman stumbled forward with a cry that he had been killed; the others rushed at Drake, who held a knife over their comrade's body. 'Christ Almighty!' The barge captain gasped at the sight of the pistol and even tried to draw it towards himself in his terror. 'Don't fire into the powder!' The stranger flung away the restraining hand and, for an instant, seemed to turn on the barge captain. 'To hell with the powder,' he snarled. 'These men are traitors, they have betrayed us!' Holland lunged at him, and the pistol fired.

347

The captain stared for a moment in disbelief at the red stain that streamed across his chest, and then fell against Holland, clutching his arm and shirtfront, and wresting the lantern from him as he hit the deck. A blow from behind brought Drake down. He was up again straightaway, but before he could regain his balance he was caught in Chabot's killing embrace. A lucky misstep won him his freedom, and he stumbled against something. A second pistol appeared out of nowhere and, without thinking, he thrust the muzzle downwards as it went off.

A smothered cry revealed that the bullet had hit home, but before Drake could consider who was down, Chabot had seized him a second time, the powerful hands knotting around his neck. The stranger had almost retrieved the lantern from beneath the captain's body when Holland thrust him aside, and he fell awkwardly against a powder barrel. Drake could not free himself; his throat was being crushed, and the blood was pounding furiously against his temples. Suddenly he was free. Even as he lost consciousness someone else cannoned into him. He drew breath and fell.

The shock of their contact sent Holland and Chabot over the side and into the river, and they struggled, thrashing and flailing. They were half-blinded by the water and the darkness, Holland's knife against Chabot's powerful grip. Holland was the better swimmer, and he snarled at his opponent to 'Come on, come on, you bastard!' but more than once he had to dive to avoid the wild, enveloping surges, as Chabot launched himself forward, bent only upon attack and heedless of any danger. 'You do not hide from me,' he growled, '*je te noyerai comme un chiot.*'

The barge itself was dark, for Holland had thrown the lantern overboard, and the stranger crept towards the sound of someone crying. 'André?' he whispered. 'Where are you?' He found his comrade, felt his bloody leg, and suddenly became aware of lights and voices from the shore. The wounded man gasped, 'Citizen Patron, we are finished!'

Drake came to his senses in time to see a figure climbing clumsily over the side and dropping into one of the waiting boats. He also became aware of the lights and voices on shore, and he stumbled in their direction, waving and calling in a harsh, strained voice. 'Over 'ere! This way!' he cried, before rushing across the deck towards the fleeing boat. But was it fleeing? He could not tell. Below and some distance away he could hear thrashing, and now other voices were calling from mid-river. 'Chabot! Come! Leave him!'

'*Je viens, Patron!*' called Chabot, but he lunged again at Holland, and this time managed to seize his arm. Holland slashed him, gasping as he was drawn inexorably into the larger man's hold. They wrestled together in a heaving, furious melee, and Chabot cried, 'Ah, little dog!' They sank together, still struggling.

From across the water the order was repeated, 'Chabot! Come now!' but it was Holland who flailed upwards to the surface, and answered when Drake called, cautiously, 'Captain Haitch?' Drake leaned over the side and waved in the direction of Holland's splashes. ''Ere, sir,' he continued. 'Can you see me?' Presently he was rewarded by the sound of Holland's voice, directly below him. 'Toss me a line, can you?'

Somehow Holland scrambled back on board, and for several minutes he could do little more than rest, panting, on the deck. 'You all right?' he gasped.

'Aye, sir, don't you fret about me, but I think two of them buggers is getting away!'

Holland got to his feet and stared blindly into the night. Yes, he could hear the sound of oars. 'Who is it?'

'The old chap, for sure,' said Drake, 'and maybe the other one – not the Paddy – and I think I may 'ave clipped 'im.'

'Damn!' spat Holland. 'One of them must be Rabelais!' He grasped the gunwale as if about to leap down into the second boat and give chase.

'Should we go after 'em?' asked Drake, dubiously.

Holland relaxed as common sense returned. Swearing under his breath he shook his head. It was pointless to go haring off in the darkness, leaving behind what was still a highly dangerous bomb. 'We won't catch them now,' he complained.

His last words were interrupted by a hail from the shore.

'You there! Show a light and identify yourselves! If you do not identify yourselves immediately, I shall order my men to fire.'

'Oh, hold on, can't you?' demanded Drake. 'We ain't the henemy!'

The order and its response made Holland smile. 'I think we had better try to arrange a parley. We seem to have roused the Purfleet garrison, and if we don't answer their challenge they're likely to do Rabelais' business for him.'

Alone now, Mary sat on the edge of her bed, clutching the two Spanish coins. She had been obliged to sit down. As long as Crosby-Nash had been present, even when threatening her, she had faced him without failing, but when he departed he had somehow taken her strength with him. Her legs had folded beneath her, and if no piece of furniture had been close by she would have collapsed onto the floor. Collapsed. That word described her situation in every way. *You are lost – alone in this house and at his mercy.*

At first her mind could not escape this terrible conclusion. She could think of nothing other than that she had failed; she had played a game for high stakes and had lost everything. *You are alone in this house and at his mercy.* Slowly, however, she began to consider alternatives, however unlikely. Was every chance truly gone?

She tossed the coins aside, then rose from the bed and knelt beside it. It was large – nearly six feet across – and when she thrust her arm between the mattress and the frame she could just feel the smooth edge of a wooden box. Her pistol. She had it still, and as she drew forth the box a profound, immense relief spread through her.

Presently, she considered what the pistol meant – not as a symbol of freedom but as an actual weapon. *Precisely what do you mean to do with this?* she asked herself. *Kill him? Could you really do that?* She had told Holland that she could, and the memory of her own anger, her fury when the colonel had taunted her, gave her pause. *Perhaps I could . . . if he threatens me again, or if he tries to hurt me, but could I kill him as he sits at his* desk in the library? As he watches me? Or from behind, like an assassin? Her stomach crawled at the thought of shooting someone, even Colonel Crosby-Nash, in cold blood.

Nevertheless, the realisation that she was not completely helpless encouraged her to keep thinking. *This house is his stronghold; he has all the advantages . . . But might it be possible to escape?* Her heart began to pound as she imagined being free, out of danger. And the danger was real . . . and terrible. The colonel's promise had been no idle threat; Romney's death proved that. If only she could only get away!

But that would mean . . . She tried to imagine bringing Susannah into her confidence. Could she explain everything in a manner that Susannah would understand and accept? *And quickly, too! We would never manage a leisurely chat!* Well, what if she were to leave Susannah behind? Not for long, of course, only until she could reach London and inform Mr Shy. Or she might try for Woolwich; that was closer, and Captain Holland would know what to do. *Yes, if he is still at Woolwich, and if the Warren is not in a state of mutiny!* For herself, it seemed a risk worth taking, but would Susannah be in danger? Who could say what the colonel might do if he were threatened with capture? Or, if he escaped, what if he took Susannah with him?

It is pointless to worry about what might happen to Susannah in your absence if you cannot manage to escape, Mary reminded herself. And escape, short of by violent means, seemed unlikely. She might be let out of her room in the morning, but how would that improve matters? She was sure to be kept under watch, and Colonel Crosby-Nash would have had time to consider whatever he was going to do. The fact that he had simply imprisoned her meant that he had not yet decided, but by the morning . . . If she could escape now, she would have a head start against any pursuit.

A head start, and she must travel as swiftly as possible, so on horseback. This realisation brought new fears. Mary did not baulk at the notion of stealing a horse, particularly from Colonel Crosby-Nash, but the practical difficulties of such a scheme immediately assailed her. She did not know any of the colonel's horses – what if they would not obey her, or were wild? And then there were the mysteries of saddling, which she had observed, but never actually performed. Was it possible to ride without a saddle? *Well, never mind any of that now, first things first. How are you going to get out of this room?*

With the door locked from the outside, the only other means of egress was the window. Her room had a large, mullioned window in three panels, the centre of which opened, above a wide stone sill. To the right of the window a vine of some sort grew, supported by a wooden trellis. Surveying vine and trellis by candlelight from the open casement, Mary wondered whether, together, they would hold her weight. She was not very heavy, after all, and even if they did not support her for very long, she could probably descend a few feet by that means, and then jump the rest of the way. At least, she hoped so. Her candle did not illuminate the ground below, but it could not be so very far.

She drew back into the room, which seemed very bright and cheery in contrast to the darkness outside. The thought of descending, perhaps jumping, into darkness was rather unnerving, and she wondered whether she ought to wait until it was light. *No, even if the colonel does not rise at dawn, the servants will be up and about, and it will be much more difficult to get away unseen.* Despite that warning, she stepped away from the window and tried the chamber door one more time. Unsurprisingly, the lock still held. Still, it was better to be certain, particularly as one might easily break one's leg falling – or jumping – from a first-floor window. *Why do you insist upon imagining such things?*

She consulted her watch – not quite midnight – and decided to wait until one o'clock before setting out. Baxter and his keepers made their rounds at half past, she knew, and it would not do to run into them. Besides, she did not feel quite comfortable being out alone during '*the witching time of night*'. Of course, she did not believe in ghosts, but, well, one oughtn't to invite trouble. *There is no harm in being careful.* That was Captain Holland's expression, and Mary smiled as she thought of it and of him. The captain would no doubt scorn all mention of ghosts *and* tell her that she must not climb out of the window. *Which is just like him,* she mused, *for he seems to have done it frequently when he was a boy.*

While she waited for the time of departure, she dressed herself in the closest thing she had to a riding habit – an old, full-skirted bodice and petticoat, and her disreputable boots. A dark cloak would complete her ensemble. It was not hooded, unfortunately, but if she covered her hair with a large, dark handkerchief she thought she would not look too extraordinary to anyone who encountered her – although hopefully these would be few. Then she remembered something else. She would need both hands for climbing and riding, so she wound her shawl tightly around her waist like a sash and thrust the pistol into it. Her petticoat, thankfully, had pockets, so she put the powder flask in one and the handful of pistol balls and other necessaries in the other. She felt laden down and rather foolish, but carrying a reticule would be even worse, and the pistol might prove valuable. Even if she did not actually fire at anyone, it might be necessary to threaten them.

At a little after one o'clock she went to the window and tossed her cloak, which she had tied into a neat package with the handkerchief, down to the ground. Then, heart pounding, she climbed out onto the sill and stood up. The first thing that happened was the pistol slipped to an awkward angle, and she was obliged to reposition it and tighten her sash. Although initially terrifying, the fact that she could perform such a manoeuvre while standing on a windowsill gave her confidence, and after only a few deep breaths she edged carefully sideways until she reached the trellis, her back pressed firmly against the leaded glass.

Now that she was close to it, the vine felt dangerously thin, and the trellis moved slightly against the wall when she tested it. Resisting the temptation to look down, she tried to plan her next move. It was quite straightforward, but her stomach fluttered at the prospect of performing it. She must turn and then, grasping the trellis with her right hand, lean forward into nothingness and grasp the vine with her left. At the same time

353

she must find a foothold; from there she could climb down. At least, she hoped she could. If only it were possible to see what she was doing, but the light from her window was behind her; she could see the near edge of the trellis and vine, but little beyond that. *Of course there will be handholds,* she commanded. *Stop thinking and do it.*

Taking another deep breath, she turned, leaned into space, and reached. She grasped a coil of ivy and landed with her foot on a branch that bent ominously. *Oh, please God!* Then she secured a better foothold on the right side. Something cracked, but now she was descending, swiftly, swiftly, and jumped the last few feet.

Simple, solid ground, albeit wet with dew, had never felt so pleasant. She had done it! She was free! Her heart was still pounding; she felt giddy with excitement. *Steady now, you must be sensible; there is still a great deal to do. And you had better carry on, now, straightaway,* she advised herself. *You will not be truly free until you are away from this place and on the road to Woolwich.* Woolwich! How distant that seemed. After adjusting her pistol a second time, she looked up at her window and was pleased to see that the traverse and descent looked very impressive from that angle. Her cloak was located after a brief search, and she put it on. Then, with another deep breath, she made her way towards the stables.

This next task proved quite straightforward. Mary stealthily entered the low, brick building and exited in the same manner not very long afterwards, leading a mare whose nameplate identified her as 'Sita'. The animal's hooves sounded terribly loud on the flagstones, but the sound provoked no response from the servants' quarters, and Mary hurriedly, if inelegantly, climbed into the saddle. The mare showed a flash of temper at the first tap from the ineligible boots, but when the command was repeated she stepped forward in a brisk walk, as though she thought nothing of late-night rides by the dark of the moon.

As Sita picked her way onto the path and raised her pace to a trot, Mary considered luck and confidence. She had feared that the horses would all be asleep and difficult to rouse, or that, having been awakened, they might make loud noises. Sita, however, had simply opened her eyes when Mary appeared in her stall with a shaded lantern; nor had she misbehaved when Mary cautiously presented her with bit and saddle, but had opened her mouth for the first and waited obediently while the second was settled upon her back and fastened. One of the particularly friendly, agreeable Hindu goddesses was also named Sita, and the mare's temperament seemed to reflect this.

Perhaps good luck makes one confident, thought Mary. She had relaxed, and was riding more easily, in sympathy with her horse's motion. Sita was the smallest of the animals in the Champian Hall stables and, in addition to the auspicious name, Mary had chosen her for that reason. Gradually, her other merits were revealed. She was sure-footed and had an easy, contained gait, the sort that would remain comfortable for many miles. Which was just as well, for it must be thirty miles to Woolwich, by far the greatest distance that Mary had ever ridden. The first part of the journey would be relatively simple. The lane had taken them to a slightly wider track, which Mary knew would eventually lead to the London road. Although it rose and fell, and wound through hamlets and around fields, so long as they remained on it, they would not go wrong. The London road might prove more difficult, but Mary told herself that there would surely be signs to Woolwich. As for other travellers, she would prefer *not* to encounter any, but if she did, well, she would simply have to come up with a plausible story. She would not even consider the possibility of . . . highwaymen.

Presently it began to rain, not hard, but enough to cool the air and muffle the other night-time noises. Sita halted while Mary fastened her cloak more securely and tied the handkerchief under her chin, and then they set off again. They passed a lone house, set back from the road, at the end of a footpath edged with white stones. Gleaming dimly in the pale starlight, they looked rather eerie, and the house itself mysterious. A lamp shone at the window, and Mary wondered what it might signify. *Is someone ill inside, or a late visitor expected from afar? Might there be another adventure behind that very door?* Then a dog

355

barked, and Mary acknowledged that most probably the master was simply reading in bed, never imagining that anyone would consider his house in the least fantastic.

At last they reached the main road. There was no obvious sign, but Mary knew she must turn left, for that was west; to the right lay Maidstone and eventually the Kentish coast. She turned left, accordingly, and now the road seemed to be heading north as well, but that was all right. Her only means of navigation was the North Star, which Cuff had taught her to identify, and she decided that so long as she kept that in front of her, or on her right-hand side, she would not worry. *And there is only one road, after all.* She would have liked to see a clear signpost stating *LONDON*, and preferably *WOOLWICH*, but no doubt she would do so, when it began to grow light.

No sooner had she convinced herself that her journey was well in hand than she thought that she saw something odd – a light flickering some distance ahead of her. It went out, and then appeared again, and now . . . was it coming towards her? Mary glanced down at Sita and saw that the mare had pricked her ears. *She* had certainly seen something, or perhaps— Mary pulled her up, and now she could hear the sound of approaching hooves; it was a carriage then, or some kind of vehicle, and it was bearing a shaded lantern. *A perfectly ordinary traveller, no doubt,* she concluded as she guided Sita to the far side of the road. Concealment would be difficult, however, as the vehicle neared.

'You there, girl!'

It was a gentleman's voice, and she did not know quite how to answer. 'Yes . . . sir?'

'Please, I do not mean to alarm you, only, can you help me?' The light fluttered and then grew steady; the lantern had been opened and placed on a pole, creating a wider pool of illumination.

Politeness or curiosity drew Mary nearer. It was hardly likely that this man posed any danger, and she could always ride away from him. 'What is it?' she cautiously replied.

As she approached the vehicle she could see it and its occupant more clearly. He was an older gentleman, although the state of his dress made that designation questionable, for his neck cloth was undone, and his coat had been torn at the shoulder. He was driving an open chaise, or cart, which also looked to have endured some rough handling. All this she took in with a single glance, along with the gentleman's keen eyes and closely cropped head. Did not the lack of a wig made him look faintly . . . sinister?

'I am looking for a house, which I believe is somewhere in this neighbourhood, called Champian Hall. Do you know it?'

'Cham— No, I— I have *heard* of it,' Mary stuttered. *Champian Hall!*

'Is it very far?'

Mary's thoughts were tumbling though her head – *Who is this man? Why is he here?* – so that she hardly knew what answer to give. 'I do not . . . that is to say—'

Before she could finish she heard a sound, a moan, coming from the rear of the cart. '*Le fusible, Patron!*' and then, more urgently, '*Allumez la poudre!*'

Fire? thought Mary, *and did he say 'fuse'?* The speaker was invisible; she could discern only a dark shape, moving vaguely. *He spoke French! Frenchmen are coming to Champian Hall!*

'Do not be frightened,' urged the driver. 'My friend is ill – he is talking nonsense. That is why I must proceed with haste. There has been an accident, you see. Is the Hall far from here?'

The realisation that this man, indeed, both of them, must be confederates of Colonel Crosby-Nash, struck Mary with a sharp stab of panic. Friends of the colonel's – from whom she had just escaped! She feared suddenly that she would be recognised, seized. 'No, not far,' she urged. 'Take the next turning on the right – only a little farther; that will take you to the drive of the house.'

She backed Sita as she spoke; was the driver looking oddly at her? Did he suspect something? 'The next turning on the right,' she repeated.

'Thank you,' murmured the driver. 'I am very grateful for your assistance.'

He raised his whip in acknowledgement and then flicked it across his horse's shoulders. Mary turned Sita more sharply as the cart rolled forward, and they were parted. The light moved away from her, and then dimmed as the lantern shade was fastened again.

Listening to the fading sound of the hooves and thankful for a fortunate escape, Mary was confronted by a wave of new fears. Frenchmen coming to Champian Hall, and one of them injured, what did that mean? Was one of them *the* Frenchman, the agent whom Mr Shy was seeking? Neither question was answerable, but they threw her own plans into turmoil. Ought she to continue her flight when strange, important things seemed to be happening at Champian Hall? Would Mr Shy want her to turn back? *No, that would be impossible, far better that you get help. In fact, help is even more important, now that—* *Oh, but why did you not think to misdirect them? What a fool! You were given a chance – the best chance – to thwart the colonel, and you failed to do it!*

Susannah was not a heavy sleeper, and the sound of low, urgent voices awakened her. All was dark in her chamber, but she could see a gleam of light along the floor. Shrugging quickly into her dressing-gown, she opened the door and saw her husband bearing a lighted candlestick, and behind him the butler, Lockwood, supporting a young, dark-haired man, who seemed in considerable distress. All three were in a state of disarray; Crosby-Nash and the butler were half-dressed, while the stranger was in his shirtsleeves with his waistcoat hanging open. The dancing candlelight, moreover, revealed his pale, drawn features.

The tableau fixed her in the doorway. 'What has happened?' she cried.

'An accident, my dear,' replied Crosby-Nash, in a tone both brusque and soothing. 'One of these gentlemen has had an accident.'

'But—'

'I apologise most sincerely for the intrusion, madam,' said

another voice, and a second stranger emerged from the darkness. He was an older man and, from what she could discern, he had also suffered an accident. But what accident could have drawn these men to Champian Hall? She longed to know more, but something in the speaker's manner, or perhaps his voice, checked her, and she replied with even more than her usual politeness.

'Not at all, sir, you are most welcome, you and your friend.' She turned to Crosby-Nash. 'Has the doctor been called?'

'Yes, my dear, and he will probably be here directly. In the meantime Mr . . . what did you say your name was, sir?'

'Thompson.'

'Mr Thompson and I can do what is necessary to make him comfortable. Please go back to bed now − everything is in hand.'

Susannah wavered. 'Well, I . . . I would not like to be in the way.'

'Not at all, madam,' urged Mr Thompson. 'Your interest is commendable, but I believe we shall manage. Please, do not distress yourself.'

'No . . . well, good night,' said Susannah. The words made her feel foolish, but she clearly was not wanted. What more could she do?

When Susannah had retreated and closed her door, Crosby-Nash led the way to the empty chamber at the end of the passage. Inside, he lighted more candles and drew the curtains, while Lockwood helped the wounded man onto the bed. 'Mr Thompson' stood in the doorway. 'What is to be done?' he demanded.

Crosby-Nash stopped short at the foot of the bed, even as his mind was racing. Fears, suspicions, and counter-arguments occurred to him, and he wanted to stop, to retrace his steps and think things out, but he had not that luxury. He was correct when he said that he could do what was necessary until the doctor arrived. Indeed, he had no intention of calling one. *A doctor to treat a Frenchman with a gunshot wound in the middle of the night! By God, Rabelais is pushing things too far.* Turning to

Lockwood he said, 'Fetch the bag with my medical equipment – you know the one – a basin of water, a strong dose, and a pair of scissors.'

When the butler had departed the other two man faced each other across the bed. The stranger gestured down at his wounded companion. 'He will be all right?'

'I will know better when I have had a closer look,' said Crosby-Nash. 'The journey has not done him any good.' He paused, and then complained, 'And I wish that my wife had not seen him . . . or you.'

'So do I,' Rabelais agreed, 'but neither could be avoided.' He placed his hand upon the injured man's forehead; his own expression was one of deep concern. '*Mon pauvre camarade*,' he murmured, before raising his eyes to Crosby-Nash. 'You will do your best for him, I know, and we will not trouble you for a moment longer than is necessary.'

When Lockwood returned he laid out the instruments on the bed and administered the dose – whatever it was – in a small drinking glass. 'It will not hurt him,' Crosby-Nash assured Rabelais. 'It will only put him to sleep while I probe for the ball.'

The colonel washed his hands and turned back his cuffs in preparation to examining the wounded leg, with Lockwood standing by as his assistant. Rabelais was urged to remove himself to the other side of the room, but he remained at the head of the bed, watching his friend's face for signs of suffering. The other two worked quickly and efficiently; each seemed to know what the other wanted with only the occasional nod or word. Crosby-Nash inserted a probe and nodded at Rabelais. 'There it is – I do not think it will trouble him much longer.'

'Ah,' sighed Rabelais, as Crosby-Nash dropped something into Lockwood's hand. 'You have it?'

'Yes, sir,' replied the butler, and he displayed a small, gory object for examination. 'And a nice clean wound. The ball was hard up against the bone, but doesn't seem to have harmed it.'

'The shot must have come from an unusual angle,' said

Crosby-Nash, 'as often happens when pistols discharge accidentally.' He dropped his probe onto the bed and began wiping his hands on a cloth.

Rabelais nodded. 'Yes, certainly.'

After Crosby-Nash had dressed the wound, he and Rabelais withdrew to the library. Rabelais sat down wearily on the sofa and leaned back, his eyes closed. He opened them when Crosby-Nash pressed a glass of brandy into his hand, and nodded his thanks. 'Ah, that goes better,' he sighed, after taking a swallow.

Crosby-Nash studied the other man anxiously. This sudden appearance, and the manner of it, had been very off-putting, and being in the library did not sooth his nerves. He had led the retreat to that room without thinking, but now the book-lined walls and heavy curtains made the atmosphere close, even threatening. Although the door to the priest's hole had been securely fastened with long iron nails, he could not banish the image of someone – of Mary Finch – crouching in the secret passage and listening to all that was said. He wanted to question Rabelais but could not bring himself to begin. Glancing once at the traitorous fireplace he observed, sympathetically, 'You are tired.'

'Indeed.' Rabelais answered dryly and took another sip. 'You do not join me? *À chacun son goût.*' He shrugged, and with that gesture his benign, if troubled, demeanour faded. Now his voice was grim, and the expression in his eyes implacable. 'We have been betrayed to that devil, Shy,' he muttered. 'The shop in Birchin Lane was rifled, other friends of ours seized or their houses broken into.'

Crosby-Nash stared, aghast at this disastrous litany. 'When? How much has been lost?'

'Last night, when all good Englishmen should have been tucked up in bed. As for losses, I would say almost everything has been upset, but immediately the position is not so clear. I managed to burn some papers, and it will take time – even for Shy – to understand the rest.'

'But what of ourselves? Is it known that you have left London?'

'Ourselves? Do not worry,' Rabelais urged with a wry smile. 'I have not brought the wolves to your door. Of course, whoever has sold my organisation may well have sold you too.'

Crosby-Nash agreed, and privately his thoughts were even more uncomfortable. Not for the first time he wished that he had never agreed to help Rabelais. 'You suspect an actual betrayal?'

'I do more than suspect it. There can be no other explanation for what has occurred. And when I discover the traitor, I will deal with him in the usual way, whatever else happens. I owe that to André and to the others.'

Rabelais briefly explained the failure of the Purfleet mission, and Crosby-Nash became increasingly alarmed. The carefully laid plans – at least that was how Rabelais had boasted of them – were in ruins. Everything – their very lives were at risk! 'What do you mean to do now?' he demanded. 'You cannot stay in England, surely?'

'No, we are for the coast, for Dover, as soon as André can safely travel.'

Crosby-Nash perceived the question in Rabelais' remark, and he shrugged. 'The wound is not serious, but he lost a great deal of blood. It would perhaps have been better . . . You know that he will hold you back.'

Rabelais shook his head and took another swallow of brandy. 'No, for without him I do not go at all. I cannot . . . Chabot was killed, you know.'

'Killed or captured.'

'He is dead. Chabot would never suffer himself to be taken alive. I could not have left him, but for that knowledge of his character. He had a good heart, but he ought to have listened to me and come when I called.'

The late Monsieur Chabot's good heart had never made much of an impression on Crosby-Nash, but he nodded. 'André should rest for twenty-four hours.'

'*Bon*. I am very grateful for what you have done for him. Such services were certainly not part of our bargain, and I would not have troubled you, only it was imperative that André

362

receive proper treatment, and I remembered your skills in that regard.'

Crosby-Nash acknowledged the compliment with a nod. 'I do not act only out of financial considerations, you know.'

'No,' chuckled Rabelais, 'but they are usually not far to seek. The terms of our agreement remain in force, of course. Whatever my situation, I shall not return to India and the old life. I shall leave that business wholly in your hands.' He paused and regarded Crosby-Nash more sharply. 'Unless you wish to come with us to France? You would be welcomed, and there would be some meaning to your life.'

Rabelais' change of expression did not escape the colonel, but he was not certain as to its meaning. Concern for André's condition, or even Crosby-Nash's own safety? They had been colleagues for many years, after all, and Rabelais had a keen sense of loyalty. *Yes, but loyalty to France and the French cause means more than anything to him now, and if he is not certain about me . . .* 'I think I would only be welcomed if I could speak better French than I do,' he said with a smile. 'And my dear wife is no traveller.'

'Ah, now I see the true motivation,' laughed Rabelais. 'A very charming lady. I should like to make her acquaintance more properly. Twenty-four hours, you say?'

'Yes, and you ought to be safe here for that long,' said Crosby-Nash, as smoothly as he could. He considered a teasing comment on the subject of flirtation but rejected it. Rabelais' temper was too hard to judge, and a mistake might be dangerous. 'Lockwood will say nothing, and we are very quiet here, very retired.'

'Indeed,' said Rabelais, 'such is the seclusion of Champian Hall that I had considerable difficulty finding it. A gypsy girl gave me directions. You do not have much trouble with horse thieves hereabouts, I suppose?'

'Hmm? Oh, no.'

'No – only she was riding quite a good horse, if I am any judge of such things. It is of no matter, however. I believe that gypsies have a particular way with horses.'

'Yes.' Crosby-Nash watched Rabelais roll his glass slowly between his hands, warming the liquid. He wanted to ask, 'Whom do you suspect of betraying you?' but he did not dare. *He cannot suspect me*, the colonel told himself. *He would never have come here if he did not believe it to be safe.*

'Your own security, you are content with it?'

The question came out of nowhere. 'My security? Why, yes.'

'Naturally, I am concerned because of what happened in London,' explained Rabelais. 'I am for Dover, but you may yet find yourself in difficulties hereafter, if you remain.'

If I remain . . . Does he mean to press me to go with him? 'I have taken every precaution possible,' replied Crosby-Nash. He spoke firmly, watching Rabelais all the while to see whether a more cautious approach was warranted. The other man's expression did not change, but the colonel nevertheless added, reluctantly, 'Of course, one can never be absolutely certain that one's trust is justified.'

'No, indeed not,' Rabelais agreed, 'and from small lapses great damage may be done. Since tonight's adventure one thing has puzzled me, but perhaps here is the explanation.'

Crosby-Nash felt suddenly cold. He blinked and struggled to maintain his normal tone of voice. 'What do you mean?'

'The surprising fact that the man on the barge – he who betrayed us – I met him at your house.' Rabelais shrugged. 'The small lapse.'

22

It seemed impossible that one could feel both fearful and drowsy; the fear ought to do away with any chance of sleep. Nevertheless, Mary realised that she was tiring, and that even the fervent wish to press on, and the dread that she would miss the turning to Woolwich, could not prevent her eyes from growing heavy. Sita, sensing her rider's lack of urgency, slowed to a walk, and the slow, plodding rhythm felt almost soothing.

Ten paces with my eyes closed, thought Mary, with the fuddled logic of the half-asleep. *Ten paces, and then ten with my eyes opened. That way I will rest and wake alternately. One, two, three . . .*

Her head snapped forward. She had forgotten to count beyond eight, but something else had disturbed her – the sound of someone approaching. She could hear horses' hooves and a man's voice. It sounded like a question, so he must have a companion – perhaps more than one – and now she was wide awake.

The sky had begun to lighten so that the darkness was grey rather than black, but a curve in the road hid the men from view. Trees grew on either side, and Mary urged Sita into those on the right, dismounting to avoid the lower branches. She gasped as she tried to walk. Her stiff muscles would not obey her, and she stumbled over the uneven ground, as much leaning against the dutiful Sita as leading her.

'Oh, hush,' she whispered, as a twig snapped under one or

other of their feet, and crept into a thicket of hazel trees. From there she had a good view of the road but would not be immediately visible to anyone who was not scanning the undergrowth. The clip-clopping was becoming louder now, and Mary saw them – two men, bareheaded and roughly dressed. She moved forward to get a better look, and the movement made Sita's bridle jingle as she also advanced a pace. One of the men turned, and his expression of disbelief equalled that of the person staring back at him.

'Captain Holland!'

'Well I'm damned.' Holland slid from the saddle and strode into the thicket, moving more easily than Mary had done. 'What are you doing here?'

'I— I have escaped!' she cried, and if she had been unsteady before, now she felt as if she could fly. 'Oh, thank heaven you are here!'

Then he was beside her, his hands on her shoulders, and she thought he was going to— well, she did not know quite what she thought, but he merely stood, his expression flickering between dismay and fierce happiness. Then he stepped back, his hands falling to his sides. 'What do you mean "escaped"? From Champian Hall? What's happened?'

Mary quickly explained what had led to her flight, and as she spoke she also became aware of Holland's condition. She had seen him in a bad state once before, but never looking so tired and so filthy. His shirt and breeches were damp and spattered with mud, and his face was pale beneath the stubble of a day-old beard. A ragged, blood-stained bandage was wound around his left forearm. She took in all of these things and was frightened by them. Had things gone so badly at Woolwich? Where was he going?

She had no chance to ask questions, however, for the mention of the Frenchmen had raised Holland's interest in her story to an even higher pitch. 'Damn it,' he muttered, 'that must be the two from the barge! When did you meet them?'

'Some time ago – I am not certain. What barge?' she asked. 'At Woolwich?'

'No. But you left the Hall at one o'clock, and it must be . . .' He frowned at the sky, which had become a faint pink. 'It must be past four.' Seizing Sita's bridle he dragged her back onto the road, calling to Mary over his shoulder. 'Where's your watch?'

She struggled after him. 'I left it in my bedchamber. I thought there might be— I did not want anything to happen to it.'

'Not worried about what might've happened to *you*,' Holland chided, 'but your *watch*, of course that's a different matter. But you were right to get away from there. That was my advice from the start, if you remember.'

'Yes, I remember – you mentioned it quite often. But if I had left earlier, as you suggested, we would not know all that we do.'

They were on the road again, and Holland was checking Sita's saddle and bridle. 'That's true,' he admitted, shaking his head over the haphazard arrangement of buckles and fastenings. 'Did you hear that, Drake? Rabelais and his friend have gone to Champian Hall.'

'Well, glory be,' murmured Drake, 'if this ain't the night for it. And Miss Finch besides. Evening, miss.'

'Rabelais!' cried Mary. 'Oh, Drake – good evening. I did not recognise you.' He was also unshaven and had a bandage wrapped clumsily around his head. 'Are you hurt?'

He winked at her. 'Just 'ad me intellects shook up a bit, miss.'

'Fortunately, he's got a hard head,' said Holland. 'If the older chap isn't Rabelais, I'll be very surprised. I didn't think we'd catch him, but perhaps we have a chance.' He stroked Sita's neck thoughtfully and then turned to Mary. 'If there were a safe place to leave you, I wouldn't take you back there, but—'

'Oh, of course I will go back,' she assured him. 'I always meant to do so, after I had found you.'

'We must hurry. I don't want to hang about.'

'Neither do I.'

Holland considered her upraised face. This was the Mary Finch he knew – *his* Mary: brave, determined, exasperating. 'Well . . . your horse is a good one, judging by the fact that she didn't unseat you after the mess you made of her bridle.'

'I did *not*—' Mary's complaint ended in a groan as Holland lifted her into the saddle. *Oh, heavens.* She never wanted to ride a horse again, but when Holland asked if she was all right to go on, she straightened her back and nodded. 'Yes, of course.'

'Good girl.' He smiled up at her and handed over the reins.

They rode for a while in silence. Mary felt somewhat constrained between the two men. Their horses were much bigger than Sita, for one thing, and seemed to loom over her. They were also, she had to admit, rather better riders than she was – certainly they were more confident, and they urged their animals more forcefully than Mary would have done. She did not feel quite comfortable cantering . . . at least not for more than a brief period.

Holland glanced across, taking in her tense expression and the rigid set of her shoulders. 'Just how did you expect to find me?' he asked, as if their conversation had not been interrupted.

'Hm?' Mary did not want to take her eyes off of the road, and she replied tersely. 'Oh, why, I would have gone to the Warren, of course.'

'In the middle of the night?' asked Holland. 'That was taking a chance.'

'Yes,' Mary acknowledged, thinking of cutthroats and other malefactors who might have been lying in wait for her, perhaps around the next bend in the road, 'but what else—'

'I doubt the men on duty would have let you in.'

She started. 'I beg your pardon?'

'Well, the regiment has its standards, you know.'

Mary risked a look at him. 'Of course,' she replied, 'I had almost forgotten the first principle of the regiment, that the men should look after their officers and keep them from harm. But I should not have asked for *you*, Captain Holland,' she continued, trying to keep her voice sober.

'No?'

'Oh, no. I should have asked for Drake. You would have vouched for me, I am sure, Drake, would you not?' She turned to him.

'Eh, wot was that, miss?' Drake was not sure what to make

of this conversation, but a glance at his officer enlightened him somewhat. 'Oh, aye, miss, certainly I would.'

'I daresay that is what happens whenever Captain Holland has any dangerous visitors,' Mary continued. 'One cannot be too careful, after all.'

'Exactly,' Holland agreed, smiling. 'Now, ask the mare to change foot.'

'Change . . . Whatever do you mean?'

Holland explained that Sita would be more comfortable leading with her left leg for a while, but she needed encouragement to make the change. Mary hardly knew what she was doing, but under Holland's instruction she managed to achieve the desired end. Sita gave a little skip, changed legs, and immediately her motion became easier.

'Well done,' said Holland. 'She'll do anything you ask her. Open your fingers a trifle, that's the way.'

'She is lovely,' Mary agreed, as one of the uncomfortable places in her back ceased to complain quite so much.

All was quiet when they reached Champian Hall. The day was still young and, apart from the birds singing in the hedgerows, there were few signs of activity, either natural or man-made. Curtains remained drawn at the Hall windows, and no wisp of smoke rose from the kitchen chimney. The cart, which Mary identified as the one used by the Frenchmen, stood in the stable yard.

'Good,' said Holland. 'Looks like they're still here.' Nevertheless, after tying up their horses in the orchard, out of sight, he and Drake made a cautious circuit of the property, while Mary waited in the gardener's shed.

Alone, she wondered how they were going to proceed. Having heard a terse account of the foiled attack against Purfleet, she was frightened of what might be about to happen. Colonel Crosby-Nash was bad enough, but Rabelais had been willing to cause an explosion that would have killed . . . heaven knows how many people. Nor had he shrunk from setting off the charge in such a way that everyone on the barge would have perished, even himself! In her imagination he became a strange, unnatural person, to whom ordinary rules of conduct did not apply.

And how did she know that other men of the same ilk had not arrived? Perhaps Rabelais' gang, disturbed from their London hiding places, had gathered at Champian Hall!

Holland returned first. 'All quiet,' he said.

Her fears found expression in her reply. 'We mustn't do anything that would endanger Susannah,' she reminded him. 'Do you think that Mr Shy will be sending men?' Ought we to wait for them?'

'He might be,' Holland allowed, 'but I wouldn't bet on it. His men weren't able to stop the barge from sailing, and he may not know yet what's happened.'

'Then there are only the three of us,' said Mary.

No, the two of us, Holland amended, privately. Drake joined them at that moment, and Holland asked, 'Everything quiet on the other side of the house?'

'As a tomb,' replied Drake, with great complacency. 'I don't reckon anything's moved since them Frenchies turned up.' Then he and Holland looked at each other. 'Wot was that?'

'Horse,' said Holland. Motioning the others to remain where they were, he stole round the shed towards the stand of lime trees that had replaced the tumbled outer wall on the east side of the property.

Drake drew a knife from inside his jacket; it had a large blade with a jagged edge. Mary touched his arm and gestured towards her pistol, but he declined. Which was just as well, she realised, since the weapon was not loaded, and she would have been obliged to dig out the necessary bits from the jumble in her pocket to render it serviceable. Then she had a brighter thought. *A horse, did he say? Might Captain Holland be wrong, and Mr Shy has sent help after all?*

They waited, but nothing seemed to be happening, neither within the Hall nor without. The silence grew, and Mary shifted to a more comfortable position. Where was Captain Holland, and was everything all right? If Drake had not been beside her she might have crept outside to explore. Perhaps sensing

370

her impatience he smiled reassuringly and put down his knife. 'Don't you worry, miss. Captain Haitch generally knows what 'e's about.'

Mary nodded, and she felt obliged to show Drake that she was *not* worried – at least not excessively so. 'Did he . . . *meet* Mr Shy?'

'I never 'eard 'is name,' confessed Drake, 'but a rum sort o' chap turned up yesterday at the Warren. That's 'ow we 'eard about the big show on the Thames. Course, it were the captain as figured out 'ow that Rabelais bugger – I beg your pardon, miss – how 'e planned to blow the magazine, and not them others.'

Mary smiled at Drake's expressions of confidence in Holland, but hearing them also made her feel proud. 'And . . . he did not really fall into the river, did he?'

'Well, miss . . .' Drake hesitated. Holland had told Mary about the confrontation with the powder barge, but his account had skimmed lightly, even humorously, over any violent aspects. Drake's own natural inclination was to err in the opposite direction, and while he appreciated that the young lady oughtn't to be alarmed by the captain's narrow escape from a watery grave, old habits were hard to break. 'It was awful dark, you know, and I didn't see exactly,' he temporised. 'E weren't shy, though. Captain Haitch'd never leave off of a scrap . . . if one should 'appen to come along, that is.'

'Oh, no,' said Mary in a tone that made him regret the omission of Chabot's monstrous grip (*paralysin', it was, like Death 'imself*). 'He must have been furious – you both must have been – when Rabelais escaped in the boat.'

'Oh, we were that. If we'd a got 'old of 'em we'd a been like—'

'And you went after them,' said Mary. 'But when we met . . . Surely Captain Holland had not guessed that Rabelais would come to Champian Hall?'

Now it was Drake's turn to smile. 'I don't think it was no Frenchman 'e was worried about. No sooner 'ad we sorted out that bloody barge – beg your pardon again – than 'e got

371

it into 'is 'ead that there might be trouble down 'ere. *I* thought there'd be trouble with us goin' back to Erith fer them 'orses, on account of the boat we borrowed, but we 'ad the luck last night, that's fer certain. And 'e can be that stubborn, when 'e gets 'old o' something. 'E's like— I mean, nothing'll shake 'im.'

Holland appeared in the doorway. 'No, nothing will shake him,' he agreed as he moved to crouch beside Mary. She turned to him, a question on her lips, but it remained unasked as Dick Whittington likewise slipped into the shed, on Drake's other side. He was far tidier than the other two men, and not as disreputably dressed.

'Good morning, Drake. Are you surprised to see me?'

'Yes, sir, I am.'

'Well, not more than I am to see you, after hearing about your exploits. I would offer you my hand, if I thought you would take it.'

Disapproval moderated to suspicion, and then Drake accepted the compliment with an embarrassed shrug. 'It's . . . good you've come, sir.'

'Any reinforcements welcome at this stage, eh? And Lucasta, you are looking as charming as ever. Climbing out of windows at the dead of night appears to agree with you.' He observed Mary briefly, concluded that she had learned nothing to his discredit, and continued in the same, effortless tone. '*I* have not been doing anything particularly exciting, I am sorry to say. In fact, things were so dull in Sheerness that I decided to see how you were getting on.'

Holland frowned his impatience with this badinage. 'Dick thinks we should go for them in the Hall, now,' he announced.

Whittington laughed at him, but said, 'Yes, exactly. Only a couple of gunners would opt for a siege with our limited forces. Far better the bold stroke, before they have a chance to gather themselves.'

'If Rabelais comes out, thinking no evil, he won't have gathered *anything*,' Holland replied, 'but I agree that the odds against us are likely to increase once the servants are up and stirring. If we can get inside without anyone raising the alarm . . .'

He turned to Mary for information on how and where Rabelais and his friend were likely to have been accommodated. She thought there were two sets of chambers on the first floor in addition to those that Holland and Whittington had used, but only a single set on the second floor.

'Good. That's easy enough; I'm glad this place is no bigger. So, if I were to climb back up into Mary's room and—'

Drake shook his head. 'Best if we try the back way. There's a door that don't look too sturdy.'

'I know the one you mean,' chimed Mary, 'it is just here, close to the kitchen garden. I think that a good shove would probably force the lock. My chamber would be no help at all, because the door was locked on the outside, and it is much stronger.'

'All right,' Holland acknowledged. 'What about you, Dick?'

'I shall enter by the front door, of course. I have no taste for heroic entrances or for shoving, and besides, a straightforward, normal summons will distract the servants.'

'You expect them to let you in?' demanded Holland, 'just like that?'

'Certainly. I am Crosby-Nash's comrade-in-arms, after all, his confederate. Why should I not be admitted?'

'What if he suspects something?' asked Mary.

'What would he suspect? He has no reason to connect me with you.'

'No, but . . .' Mary frowned. 'If *I* were the colonel, I would suspect *everyone*, after what has happened.'

Whittington considered this. 'There may be something in what you say, and I will bluff it out with him if necessary. It will not be the first time that I have talked my way out of an awkward situation.'

'But—'

Holland drew her hand away from Whittington's arm. 'No,' he ordered, 'let him try it,' and to his friend he added, 'Give us time to get inside first, and we can take them between two fires if necessary.'

'Very well.'

The men rose to their feet and Mary did likewise. 'And what should I do?' she asked, immediately feeling small and easily dispensed with, like a toddler whom the older children occasionally tolerated in their games. She did not like the idea of re-entering the Hall, but neither did she want to be left behind.

'*Do?*' demanded Holland, a wealth of exasperation in the single syllable. 'You're going to wait here and not move until it's over.'

'But you are still only three against . . . we do not know how many,' she urged, 'and Drake has been hit on the head. I could—'

'Ain't nothing wrong with me 'ead,' sputtered Drake.

'May I ask how you came by this?' queried Whittington, pointing at her pistol. 'Have you the key to the colonel's gunroom?'

'No, Captain Holland gave it to me.'

'Just so, and very thoughtful of him.' Whittington traded glances with Holland, the one amused, the other irritated, before turning to Mary. 'I suggest that you take up a position in the near gatehouse tower. That way, without exposing yourself to any shots from within, you will be in a position to fire at anyone who comes out. Not us, of course, but villains.'

Holland started to object and then changed his mind. 'All right,' he agreed, 'go ahead, if you must, but—' He grasped Mary's arm. 'Be careful, and don't try anything foolish.'

She felt the imprint of his hand even as she hurried towards the front of the house with Whittington. When they reached it he crept forward, studied the lawn, and then they both ran lightly across to the gatehouse. Mary's heart was beating so fiercely she thought it would burst. She sat down beneath a window, her back against the wall, while Whittington surveyed the scene.

Presently he turned to her. She was breathing fast, her lips pressed together. 'You know how to load and fire, I suppose?'

This practical question reminded her of her duty, and she sat up immediately. 'Of course I do. Captain Holland showed me. It will not take me a moment to be ready.' She drew her pistol and began fishing in her pockets for the rest of her equipment.

'Nothing may happen, you know,' he reminded her, as she spread her shawl on the ground and laid out the various items. 'Who was it said that discretion was the better part of valour?'

Mary thought about it. 'Falstaff.'

'Ah, well he ought to know.' Whittington drew his own weapon and examined it. 'I am going now, Hippolyte, so keep your head down and remember what Holland said. He would never forgive me if anything happened to you.'

He pressed her shoulder, and she whispered, 'Good luck.'

'Thanks,' he replied, smiling, while to himself he added, 'And if Colonel Crosby-Nash condescends to open his own door, so much the better.'

Mary finished loading and knelt before the window. From there she could see Whittington approach the front door with no obvious stealthiness, but concealing his pistol behind his back. She rested her own upon the sill, so that, if anything happened she might fire without needing to steady the weapon. Whittington climbed the steps and stood just out of sight, but she could hear the iron knocker falling heavily against the door. Presently the knocks were repeated. *That door squeaks,* she thought, *and when it opens, I will know.*

She heard the familiar creak, and the sound of Whittington's voice, and then silence. And more silence. The absence of sound − of gunfire − was a good thing, but what was happening? Against her will she began imagining all sorts of silent calamities. Could the Frenchman have discerned their presence and sprung a trap? What if Captain Holland and Drake had not been able to enter through the rear door? Major Whittington would be captured and— *Stop!* she told herself, *do your part and do not worry about things that have not − that may not have occurred.* Inside the gatehouse it was damp and cool, but that might not have been why she shivered.

How long ought she to wait? She did not know the answer, but presently she began to feel foolish, crouching there in the gloom, on guard against a threat that did not exist. Cautiously she crept out of the gatehouse and approached the house. The door was ajar, and she slipped through and into the entrance chamber. Two conflicting images of what she might discover made her pause with her hand on the door to the great hall: the enemy disarmed and herself forgotten, or Rabelais and Crosby-Nash holding her friends at gunpoint and waiting to make her their final captive. Gripping her pistol as steadily as she could in one hand, she pressed the handle and pushed open the door with the other.

The great hall was empty, but from the top of the stairs she could hear voices, and she raced towards them. 'I don't know, I tell you!' cried someone, and another – it sounded like Holland, demanded, 'Which is her room?' Then Mary was running along the passage, passing rooms whose doors had been flung open, and finally to Susannah's bedchamber. Drake was planted in the doorway, and she pushed past him. Inside she found the butler, Lockwood, cowering before Dick Whittington, and Holland bending over the bed. Susannah's maid, still in her nightdress and clutching Susannah's dressing-gown, hovered nearby. The curtains had been drawn back, but the pasty light from the windows made the room look dismal and cheerless.

'It was only tea,' cried Lockwood, wringing his hands. 'The colonel often drinks it last thing at night; he finds it soothing.'

'*They* certainly did,' snapped Whittington. 'What was in it, damn you?'

'I don't know!'

Holland tasted the dregs in the cup on the bedside table and then spat them out. 'Opium,' he said. He pulled Susannah into an upright position. She was like a rag doll and lolled help-lessly against the headboard. 'Christ,' muttered Holland, and he shook his cousin by the shoulders. 'Wake up, Susannah! Open your eyes!'

'What has happened?' cried Mary turning to Drake. 'Where is the colonel?'

'Not here,' growled Whittington, without turning, and Drake added, 'Looks like 'e poisoned the others and scarpered.'

'*Poisoned?* Are they dead?'

'One's gone, and the other near to it. In a coma, Captain Haitch says.'

'And Susannah?' Mary set down her pistol and started forward, but Whittington stopped her before she could reach the bed. Susannah was not responding to Holland's orders, and Mary gasped as he reinforced them with a slap.

'Open your eyes!' he repeated, and after the second blow Susannah uttered a vague murmur. 'More! Come on, Suz, open your eyes and look at me.' He shook her again.

'My dear fellow—' began Whittington, still with his hand on Mary's shoulder, but Holland cut him off.

'I know what I'm doing. Suz! Help me get her on her feet, Dick. Mary, bring me that jug of water and have another filled – two more. And you,' he gestured at Lockwood, 'is there any coffee in this damned house?'

'Yes, sir.'

'Brew as much as you can – strong – and bring it up here on the double. Drake, make sure that he understands me. We must keep her properly awake. If she carries on dozing, she'll slip away like the others.'

Holland in this temper was not to be gainsaid, and everyone sprang to fulfil his orders. After the maid had swathed the dressing-gown round Susannah, Holland emptied the water jug over her head and then thrust it back into Mary's hands. 'More water,' he said.

Mary withdrew from the chamber, and was confronted by the open doors of the other rooms. There would be water jugs in the bedchambers, she knew, but the prospect of seeing their other occupants made her hesitate. *Poisoned – the colonel has poisoned them and they are either dead or dying.* The words made her skin crawl, but she managed to hurry into the nearest chamber, grasp the jug from the dresser, and retreat. Then the sound of slow, shallow breathing drew her forward again, and there in the bed she saw Rabelais. The tumbled blankets and the pillow fallen to the floor gave proof of the attempts to rouse him, but he lay pale and motionless, apparently serene. She stared at him a moment longer and then fled.

Susannah was awake when she received the second dousing, but she did not seem to be aware of her surroundings. The third time looked to be the charm, for she nodded when Holland spoke to her, and even ventured to speak. At the sound of her mistress's voice the maid bounded forward, thanking Holland with fervent, tearful cries.

'We're not finished,' he warned, frowning at the woman. He had seen her often enough at Storey's Court in the days before Susannah's marriage, but he could not now remember her name.

'It's Cassie, sir, and if you'll tell me what to do – anything – I'll do it. Oh, my poor dear lady!'

Holland nodded. 'Would you be able to hold her, like this? Good. In a minute I'll ask you to walk her up and down, along with this gentleman, but where is that bloody coffee?'

'Ere it is, sir!' called Drake, and he strode into the room, bearing a large silver pot and a tankard. He poured out, and the room was immediately filled with the bracing aroma of freshly brewed coffee. 'Might be too 'ot to drink straight off,' he warned.

'I'll give it her, sir, just as soon as she's able,' said Cassie. 'And that'll save her?'

'That and keeping her awake,' said Holland. 'We'll need another pot, probably more. I hope that fellow—'

'Oh, 'e knows all right,' said Drake, smiling grimly.

'Good.' Holland lifted Susannah's chin and smiled at her through her sodden, tangled curls. 'I've ruined your hair, Suz – do you forgive me?'

'My . . . hair . . . Bobs,' she murmured, and then blinked drowsily.

'That's right, I'm here. Now, you're going to go for a walk with Major Whittington and Cassie, and you must do everything they tell you. You're under their orders. All right?'

'Bobs . . . so sleepy.'

'Yes, I know you are, but you're not allowed to sleep now. You must walk instead, and you'll soon feel better.' He transferred his cousin to the willing Cassie and explained, 'Walk her up and down this room – and get her to talk if you can. Ask

378

her questions, or make her count to a hundred, and don't let her sit down or doze off again.'

'I won't, sir,' vowed the maid.

'Come along, then, Mrs Crosby-Nash,' urged Whittington from her other side. 'I don't know about you, but I am starting to feel chilly in all this wet, and a bracing march will set us both right again.'

Holland watched carefully as Whittington, Cassie, and Susannah slowly walked the length of the room. Mary passed him the tankard, and after the return journey he motioned for them to pause, and obliged Susannah to drink. She did so, in small, complaining sips, but he was not satisfied until she had drained the vessel. 'Good girl,' he urged. 'Now off you go.'

When they had accomplished ten lengths and Susannah had recited the alphabet and the months of the year, Lockwood returned with a second pot of coffee. He would have crept away again, but Holland checked his retreat. 'Tell me everything you know about Crosby-Nash. When he left, any instructions he gave, everything.'

'But, sir, I know nothing of my master's departure,' insisted Lockwood.

'You helped administer this damned stuff, and at least one man is dead,' said Whittington. 'If you want to avoid hanging for his murder, I advise you to help us find Crosby-Nash.'

Lockwood paled at these words, but said only that he had not seen his master leave the Hall, and the mystery was as baffling to him as it was to anyone. After having brought up tea to the visiting gentlemen – on the colonel's orders and not having the least suspicion of anything wrong – he had gone to bed and not awakened until morning.

'You did not bring any tea to Mrs Crosby-Nash?'

'No, sir, on account of her having retired earlier. I didn't see the need.'

Holland thought for a moment. 'I suppose Crosby-Nash *might* have come to her room last night and left the tea himself, but she didn't drink it until later.'

'Why do you say that?' asked Mary.

'Because she isn't as far gone as the others. But that doesn't prove when he left it . . . and maybe the dose was different.'

'I see where you are heading,' said Whittington. 'If we knew when he gave her the tea, we would have an idea when he left the Hall and how far away he might be now. When did you arrive, Bob?'

Holland shrugged. 'Not long before you.'

'No one passed me on the Maidstone road,' Whittington continued, 'and that would be his route if he were heading for Dover.' He paused. 'Here is an interesting question, has anyone—'

'Oh, bugger,' muttered Drake, and in a louder voice, 'I didn't think, sir, wot with the cart still 'ere. I'll check the stables right away.'

He returned in a very few minutes, having pelted up the stairs and along the passage, to confirm, panting, that all of the colonel's horses were in their stalls, apart from Sita. However, the horse that had drawn the Frenchmen's cart – which none of the grooms could describe properly – was missing.

'But why would he . . .' Holland turned to Lockwood. 'Did you put up that horse?'

The butler admitted that he had done so, but when asked to describe it could say no more than that it was brown, of a medium height, and that he might not have secured it properly. Stabling animals was not his usual duty. He had only done so on this occasion because of the lateness of the hour.

'And because everything was to be kept quiet,' added Holland, 'with as few told as possible.'

'You are placing the rope very firmly around your neck, my friend,' Whittington observed. 'But we are wasting time.' Motioning to Drake to take his place at Susannah's side, he headed for the door. 'Are you coming, Bob?'

'Wait! How do you know—' began Mary, but Holland was already nodding in answer to Whittington.

'Keep her walking,' he advised Cassie, 'and give her another tankard of that coffee.'

'I'll do that, sir.'

'Wait for me!' cried Mary, and hurried after them.

They made their way along the passage, choked now with curious servants. Holland instructed two of the most reliable, on Mary's recommendation, to sit outside the chambers of the unfortunate Frenchmen. 'I doubt he will give you any trouble,' Holland instructed the one who was to guard Rabelais' door, 'but if anything happens, or if you hear anything, sing out.'

Mary voiced her suspicions as they descended to the great hall. Did it not seem strange that the colonel should have fled on a horse that was not his own? A horse that was tired when he might have taken a fresh one?

'If it means that he is still near at hand, I shall not complain,' said Whittington, over his shoulder as he headed towards the stables.

'Yes, but—' She grasped Holland's arm at the bottom of the stairs. 'What if this is a trick? What if the colonel has not really escaped, but is hiding somewhere close by?'

'Why would he do such a thing?' Holland demanded. He was frowning, but he did not free himself.

'Because it is clever. He knows that we will assume that he has fled, because flight is so *likely*. It is what *we* would do. But the colonel is not a man of action – not in that way – and he likes to show how cool and unruffled he is in the face of difficulties.'

'So you think that he means to hide somewhere, until things quieten down, and then leave the country at his leisure?'

'Yes. And he has sacrificed Rabelais, remember. He may think that such a prize will content us.'

'But if he *has* escaped, even on a tired horse, and we don't pursue him,' warned Holland, 'we will have lost him.'

'If you *do* pursue him and he is in hiding,' Mary countered, 'he will emerge in your absence and escape in the other direction.'

'You think we should search the house?'

'Yes, and the grounds.'

Holland's expression was sceptical, but he nodded. 'We'll never hold Dick back,' he warned, 'but that may be for the best. He can set off as he likes, and I'll organise a search here.' He started towards the door and then halted. 'And *you* can go back upstairs and keep an eye on Susannah.'

Everything happened as Holland had ordered. From Susannah's window Mary saw Whittington ride away, and observed Baxter giving orders to those of the outdoor servants who had not come down from London and so might be trusted. In a little while she heard Holland and another group clumping along the passage, opening doors and investigating cupboards and closets. The sound was annoying. How she wished she were with the searchers! Why must she be put to one side, cut off, when search had been her idea?

'Mary?'

The soft, slightly confused query put a stop to her griev-ances and dissolved her sense of ill use. With a sigh she turned her attention to the real drama being played out in the room behind her, and she cajoled herself for having forgotten it, whatever the distraction. 'Yes, Susannah?' she replied, moving to take her friend's hand.

'I have had the most . . . curious dream,' murmured Susannah. 'Walking . . . in the rain – must have forgotten the . . . charm. So very . . . sleepy.'

'Yes, dear, I know, but you mustn't go to sleep again for a good long while. You will feel better directly, but you must keep walking.'

Mary offered to relieve the other attendants, but neither Drake nor Cassie was willing to surrender their place. Between them they walked Susannah up and down the room, Drake insisting upon a smart, soldierly turn, and Cassie dutifully pressing her mistress to recite the names of the kings and queens of England, which Susannah had been trying to learn. 'Henry the Fourth, Henry the Fifth, Henry the Sixth, Edward the . . . First—' 'No, we've had him already, my lady.'

The most that Mary could do was to send Lockwood for another pot of coffee. She did not like him hanging about the sickroom; she did not trust him, and he ought to be about his business if he could not be more helpful. 'And when you have brought the coffee, please go and see that breakfast is prepared for all the men who are searching,' she told him.

'Yes, miss.'

When the coffee appeared, Mary interrupted the royal recitation with a steaming draught, which was just as well since both Susannah and Cassie had been content to crown a second Elizabeth. Presently, however, she began to feel restless. She was not really needed there; perhaps if she went outside she might find out whether anything had been discovered. A clue . . . or someone might have seen something and not realised that it was important. That would not be joining the search, exactly, but merely observing. And besides, Captain Holland was probably somewhere near the top of the house by now – too far away to complain that his instructions were being got round.

So she picked up her pistol – not because she thought she would need it, but because . . . well, there was no point leaving it behind – and walked quickly out of the chamber. To the left, near the end of the passage, were the two servants standing guard, and Mary shivered as she thought of Rabelais lying on the bed. *And there might have been a third. A third sleeper who would never awaken.* She turned instead to the right, and the stairs that would take her down to the great hall and thence to the front lawn.

From the top of the stairs it was clear that the great hall was empty, but when Mary had descended partway she was not so certain. At the far end of the hall she thought she recognised something pressed against the bottom of the panelling. She stared hard, thinking, *Of course, of course!* before the sound of a door opening made her spring back.

Lockwood came striding into the room, a linen dishcloth over his shoulder. He leaned forward and grabbed Slipper by the scruff of the neck. 'Come away from there, you.'

Slipper yelped, struggled unsuccessfully to bite his captor, and was dragged away to the sound of violent protest.

'You oughtn't to be in here,' Lockwood scolded, as he walked, bent over, towards the door to the entrance chamber. 'Why don't you go out and play, like a good dog for once.'

Mary shrank back against the wall, and fortunately Slipper's antics – he had splayed all four legs and managed to ruck up and trap a small carpet beneath him – occupied all of the butler's attention. The inner and then the front door closed behind Slipper, and Lockwood returned, shaking his head. He straightened the carpet and re-arranged a bowl of flowers on one of the side tables, and then retired to the pantry. From outside, Slipper's views on his dismissal could still be heard.

Mary waited a little while longer and then hurried down the stairs. She might be wrong, of course; Slipper was so badly behaved that it was probably not wise to rely on him. And yet, there was only one thing that he could definitely *do*, and why else should Lockwood have bothered about him?

She scanned the section of panelling where Slipper had been lying, studying it carefully from floor to eye height. It was thickly painted, like all the panelling in that room, and she could see no obvious edge or distortion that might indicate a door. *A second secret door – well, why should there not be more than one? In fact, having two was probably eminently sensible. It would throw any priest-finders off the track.* She placed her pistol on the nearby trunk so that she could run both hands gently along the surface of the panelling. *Yes, but where is it?*

The thought that Colonel Crosby-Nash might be only a few feet away, perhaps even aware of her presence, made her suddenly fearful, and she retreated a pace. What if he sprang out at her? What if— Then another thought occurred. Might it be the floor, and not the panelling that was suspect? She knelt down to make an examination of the wide oak planks, but could discern nothing amiss. Some of the planks, moreover, stretched almost the width of the floor. And yet there must be something. Slipper did not generally lie there, it was too near the tiger skin for his liking. *He must have done so this morning for a reason.*

As she stood up something caught her eye – the smallest gleam, as from metal when its painted surface has been chipped. She looked closely, and her heart skipped; it was a keyhole. Now, when she stepped back, the door was obvious. It was not a small, narrow portal, concealed within the carved linen folds and swags

384

of fruit, but an entire section of panelling, quite four feet across. The hinges must be hidden behind the lip of moulding.

'Can I help you, miss?'

She started at the sound of the voice behind her – Lockwood's voice – and turned to face him. He was staring at her, his eyes cold and his expression a world away from that of the cringing, helpless fellow who had protested his innocence upstairs. She was conscious that her pistol was just out of reach, and she edged towards it.

'Would you be wanting more coffee, perhaps?' His tone was pointed, but his quick glance showed that he knew precisely what she was doing, and he moved to intercept her.

They were standing close together now, and she scowled at him. 'Give me the key to that door.'

'Key, miss? I don't know what you mean.'

'I *mean* that Colonel Crosby-Nash is hiding behind a door in this panelling, and I want the key to lock him in. If you do not give it to me, I shall—'

Holland was descending from the second floor when he heard a shout and a smash of breaking glass. 'Help! Captain Holland!' The sound sent him racing along the passage. From the top of the stairs he saw Mary grappling with two men. One was Lockwood, and with a desperate shove she flung him backwards. He fell against one of the giant ivory tusks, and it crashed to the floor with a loud crack. The other man was Crosby-Nash, and he was trying to wrench her hands behind her back.

Leaping down the stairs, Holland drew his pistol. Mary saw him and managed to free one arm, gasping as the other was drawn upwards in a painful grip. She was slipping on pieces of glass and wet flowers from the bowl that had been upset in the struggle, and all the while she reached towards the trunk.

'Let her go,' Holland ordered. He took aim as he advanced. 'Let her go or I'll blow your brains out.'

Crosby-Nash turned quickly. He too was armed, and he aimed the muzzle of his weapon at Mary. 'Lower your pistol and stand back,' he snarled in his turn. 'Or we shall see how you like the sight of *her* brains.'

Suddenly Lockwood sprang to his feet, armed with a jagged piece of ivory. Drake appeared at the top of the stairs, bellowing, 'Look out!' as Holland ducked to avoid the butler's sweeping blow. A pistol fired, and Holland spun towards Crosby-Nash.

The colonel flinched as the ball whizzed past him, and staggered backwards in shock. Somehow Mary had managed to grasp her pistol and pull the trigger, and the recoil sent the weapon skidding across the trunk. 'You little bitch!' he cried, even as Holland's shot struck him. He gripped Mary convulsively, then fell against the panelling, and then slid down, crumpling onto the floor.

'I've a second barrel, if you want it,' Holland warned, but Lockwood abandoned the fight when he saw his master fall. He dropped his ivory shard and did not struggle when Drake flung him face down against the oak table and bound his hands with a length of silken rope used to tie back the curtains.

The air was heavy with smoke and the sharp tang of gunpowder, and Mary felt deafened by the shots and stunned by the sudden explosion of violence. She sat on the floor, dazedly staring at the colonel's booted feet. She barely felt Holland's arms around her, or heard his voice, asking if she were hurt, but she shook her head and pressed his hand. 'I am all right. He did not . . . is it over?' she asked.

'Yes,' Holland replied, gently against her hair. 'It's all over, and we're both here.'

He smoothed a curl away from her face and kissed her, and held her in his arms. His shirt was filthy but beneath it his heart was beating strongly, and she began to feel safe for the first time since coming to Champian Hall. Presently, she became aware of other people nearby – Drake and Baxter. A door opened, and the air began to clear. Slipper growled at Captain Holland and crept into her lap.

23

Mary played little part in the events of the rest of that day, and she was never clear exactly what happened following Colonel Crosby-Nash's death. She was bundled upstairs and put to bed, and the combination of lack of sleep, the constant strain of the previous days, and a healthy dose of brandy did the trick.

While she slept Champian Hall was 'put to rights' and several matters were drawn to a close. The colonel was laid out as tactfully as possible in a parlour to which Mr Baxter held the key. Rabelais died at a little past one o'clock, and the doors to his and André's bedchambers were also closed and locked. The dead ought to be left in peace, it was felt, whatever might have been their due in life.

Some time afterwards Mr Shy's agent arrived – 'the friend o' that Mr What's 'is name' as Drake called him. He was surprised, pleased, and dismayed in roughly equal measure by what he found, but he swiftly took charge of the situation. He would arrange for the three burials and close Champian Hall with as little fanfare as possible. Upon hearing Holland's diagnosis, he agreed that Susannah could return to London by easy stages after a night's rest, with Cassie to look after her and Mary to ensure that any awkward questions were deflected in a manner that did not cause upset. Likewise, he deemed that Scarborough House would be insufficiently restful for Mrs Crosby-Nash; she should instead take up residence at 10

Cavendish Square. Drake would accompany the ladies. As Holland said, 'They both know Drake, and he'll bully them into being comfortable.'

In exchange for all this, the agent wanted to know more about what had happened during the previous night. Holland complied, and while he was no storyteller, the effect upon his audience was considerable. 'My God,' breathed the agent, and he regarded the scruffy, bedraggled individual opposite him with a marked respect. 'You are damned cool, sir, if you will forgive me. But how did they avoid us on the river? My fellows arrived at the warehouses on Barking Creek in good time, and I could have sworn that no barge got away.'

'None did, but that's because they had already stolen it,' explained Holland. 'The barge had been moved to a hidden spot farther down river and stocked with powder. The crew were waiting for the signal to go – which Rabelais gave them when your lot stirred things up.'

'I was mightily relieved when I saw that vessel safely tied up at Purfleet today,' the agent admitted. 'And now, hearing what happened, I am almost minded to forgive you for not telling me your plans in the first place.'

'I wasn't at all sure about that – it was more of a feeling. What you were doing made far more sense.'

'Well, since you took all the risks, I oughtn't to complain, and especially after what happened here.'

'You must have had a feeling yourself that something was wrong, to have come down,' said Holland.

The agent smiled with mock dismay. 'I cannot even claim credit for that, unfortunately. I reported to Mr Lethieullier that the mission had been a success, but before returning to London I had made enquiries about you in Woolwich, and no one had seemed to know where you were. That struck me as odd, but Mr Lethieullier said that you were probably at Champian Hall. He said that he knew the way your mind worked.'

Their immediate obligations discharged or delegated, Holland and Whittington departed late that afternoon. Both had gone to Champian Hall on their own authority, and had deviated from their stated orders to do so. A certain degree of explaining, therefore, would be necessary to placate their superiors, and this ought to be undertaken without further delay. As their actions had been successful, they were not precisely *worried* about the ultimate reception that they would receive at the Warren and Horse Guards, respectively, but neither were they particularly looking forward to the experience.

They travelled the first part of the journey together, and it occurred to Holland that they had ridden towards Woolwich only a few days earlier, but under very different circumstances. He was tired now and his arm ached, but he was less troubled than he had been then. Of course he was. Woolwich was safe; Crosby-Nash and Rabelais had been defeated. He really had nothing to complain about, but he wished that Dick would be quiet for once.

Whittington, as was his habit, had a great deal to say, and not all of it about himself. 'If there is one constant, one thing that can be relied upon in military life,' he complained, 'it is paperwork. I envy the Navy in this respect. I imagine that they frequently lose records and dockets, and simply report "ship sunk", whereas if I wrote, "Crosby-Nash dead" I should be invited to think again.'

'I thought you didn't write anything down in the confidential office,' said Holland, smiling in spite of himself.

'A myth,' replied Whittington, 'an absolute myth, I am sorry to say. Not only are we obliged to write reports in extraordinary detail, but the fellows in charge take great delight in reading them. If you are the least careless, or dash off something in a hurry — I speak from bitter experience — you can find yourself in rather a tricky situation.'

He seemed to brood about this possibility, and after a few minutes Holland asked, 'Did you go to Champian Hall in order to kill Crosby-Nash?'

Whittington looked sideways at his friend before answering. Dusk had fallen, and it was difficult to gauge Holland's attitude either from his voice or his shadowed profile. There had been no opportunity to discuss the Woolwich revelations, and Whittington was not certain how to respond. Ought he to offer an apology of some kind or pretend that nothing had happened? Would it be possible to slide back into their old friendship again? He sensed that what might be called the 'professional side' of their falling out was more easily mended than the personal side. Holland was a loyal officer, but he would not betray Whittington to his superiors – at least, not unless another infraction on Dick's part occurred. A past sin against the king could be forgiven. One's friend, however, could sometimes be held to a stricter standard. In fact, this was frequently the case if the friendship mattered.

Whittington acknowledged to himself that their friendship *did* matter, but few men are courageous in every situation, and he had to work his way up to this one. 'Sheerness was dull, as I told you,' he protested, 'and I began to wonder about Miss Finch. You had not revealed that she was armed to the teeth and ready to defend herself against all foes. Trust you to give the girl a pistol! I suppose that is standard drill for a gunner paying court to a girl but—'

'I was *not* paying court to her.'

'Hmm, so you say. But as well as that, I also began to wonder what would happen if my chief decided to move against Crosby-Nash, and he were apprehended alive. *He* would not have kept quiet about my . . . indiscretions, and things might have been rather awkward for me. They *would* have been, of a certainty.'

'Yes.'

That word, flatly stated, did nothing to make Whittington more comfortable. He could even feel himself blushing, a thing that had not happened to him in years. Then another thought occurred to him. 'Is that why you let me go after him alone?'

Holland shrugged. 'That was part of it. I thought you deserved your chance, and so did he.'

'*And so did he?*' demanded Whittington.

'If I had found him I think I would have shot him straight off,' Holland explained. 'Whereas your way would have taken longer . . . talking him to death.'

Whittington started, caught Holland's smile, and began to laugh. 'Of all the cheek! Some people would do very well if they listened to me occasionally.'

Holland found returning to Woolwich that night a strange experience. Everything seemed so familiar and normal, from the quiet, cobbled road outside the main gate to the sleepy guards who admitted him. It was clear that the mutiny, or 'bit of bother', as Colonel Congreve had described it, was over. Making his way towards the officers' quarters and receiving the occasional salute or more casual greeting, Holland perceived that his own reappearance was also not considered in any way remarkable. If his absence had been noted at all, it had probably been put down to one of his ordinary jobs, which frequently took him away from the Warren. Given that his 'job' had been far from ordinary, Holland might have found the lack of interest galling or humbling. Instead, he merely shrugged his shoulders and reflected that the fewer people to whom he had to explain himself, the better.

He had his arm dressed a second time by the regimental surgeon, a taciturn man who also practised his profession with an astringent proficiency. On this occasion he commented sharply upon the folly of patients who did not keep wounds clean and dry, but the discomfort caused by his actual ministrations banished other irritants to the back of Holland's mind. Afterwards he climbed the stairs to his rooms slowly, as he generally did after a long day, adjusting his tread to avoid the stair that squeaked. Those of his belongings that had been taken to the academy during the mutiny had been returned, but only piled up on a chair in his sitting-room. That pile struck the only incongruous note, for Drake would never have tolerated it. Holland stood for a moment, idly fingering the cover of Muller's book on fortifications. When he became aware that he was doing this, he pushed the book aside and walked into his bedroom.

The day's events had given him a great deal to think about, but he was also tired, and he knew that his thoughts were likely to be confused. That did not stop him, however, from turning over ideas about himself, Mary Finch, and what was either possible or likely between them. Some were not even proper ideas, but rather hopes or expectations, and he twisted them round in his head, as though he could make everything fit together coherently if he only tried hard enough. But the need for sleep was like a flowing tide, not to be resisted. He lay down as he was, another thing that Drake would not have allowed.

Holland reported the following morning to Colonel Congreve, still looking rather the worse for wear and without having gained any information about the north Kentish marshes. Under ordinary circumstances Congreve would certainly have commented – if not worse – on these failings, but this morning the information that Holland *did* have was too interesting. The colonel took notes while Holland was speaking, and at the conclusion set down his pen and remarked, 'So you and Drake seized the barge and made it safe, disposing of several rene- gades in the process.'

'That's right, sir.'

'Bit of a surprise when that fellow recognised you,' Congreve barked. 'Let it be a lesson to you to keep better company.'

'Yes, sir. I'll remember that.'

'Must have been the devil of a scramble, the two of you against five of them and all that powder lying about. Well, well. And then, afterwards, you went down to a place near Maidstone?'

'Yes, sir. We had to convince the officers at Purfleet that we weren't dangerous, but that was soon sorted, and I . . . The other matter had to do with the business that Major Whittington came about.'

'Er, yes. Are you finished with all of that?'

'I think so, sir, more or less.'

'Good.' Congreve paused, as if to clear the air of secret matters, and then continued, 'Now as regards Purfleet, I will say straight off that you did a damned good job. You will have to wear your laurel leaves in private, however. I do not want this talked about; neither here nor anywhere else. It would be just the sort of thing to frighten people, knowing that there was all that gunpowder ready to go up, and only a couple of damn fool gunners to stop it. It frightens me, by God! And we do not want to give ideas to any other revolutionaries who may be hanging about with nothing to do.'

'No, sir.'

'Arm all right?'

'Oh, yes, sir,' said Holland. 'It's nothing, really.'

'Hmm, well, I think it has earned you a let-off from that surveying job.'

'Thank you, sir.'

'Nothing to thank me for,' Congreve protested. 'Simply a matter of dexterity – nimbleness of the fingers and so forth. And I suppose that the, er, powers that be may wish to speak to you more formally about the . . . other matter.'

'Yes, sir, I expect I'll have to go up to London – I mean, if I am not needed here straightaway.'

'Well, I believe we can spare you, and you might bring that fellow Drake back. If he thinks that what has happened means that he may come and go as he pleases, I shall take great pleasure in disabusing him of that notion.'

Holland maintained a scrupulously correct expression. 'No, sir. I'll make sure that he understands, sir.'

It was decided, by the earnest gentlemen in government whose business it was to consider What Ought to be Said, that Colonel Crosby-Nash had died as a result of a duel, fought with Major Whittington following a disagreement of an unspecified nature. Whittington had not objected to being designated the villain of the little drama; in fact he had suggested it. The consequences for him would be much less severe than for Holland, who might otherwise find Storey's Court and certain establishments in rural Suffolk closed to him, were he to be regarded as a duellist. 'Of course, that is always assuming that the story is generally credited,' Whittington warned the earnest gentlemen. 'Captain Holland has a far more sanguinary disposition, and frequently threatens violence against persons of his acquaintance, whereas I long for the quiet life.'

393

About Mr Rabelais and his associate, very little was said by anyone. There was certainly nothing to link them – whoever they were – to the unfortunate business at Purfleet, in which the crew of a late-arriving barge had, regrettably, become embarrassed by drink and had caused a disturbance. Fortunately, the officers and men of the magazine had acted in the best traditions of the service to resolve that situation, which, while not in the least dangerous, might have become troublesome.

Susannah was questioned very delicately. She had only a confused memory of Rabelais' arrival at Champian Hall and almost nothing of what had happened thereafter, and this greatly facilitated matters. Mary twisted the facts of the other Frenchman's injury into an account of the duel, and Susannah either believed it or said that she did. She was sorry for Major Whittington and hoped he would not get into any trouble over what had happened, and she expressed a desire to go home – to Storey's Court – as soon as possible. Whatever she thought about her late husband she kept to herself, although she did tell Mary that it was possible to aim too high and wish for too many things, and that peace and quiet, among people with whom one felt comfortable, was perhaps the wisest aspiration.

Mary thought about wishes, both lofty and mundane, when she returned to Suffolk. What sorts of things ought *she* to wish for, and might even the best wishes be dangerous if they came true? *Like King Midas*, she mused, and then decided that he did not really count, because anyone could see that the desire to turn things to gold was bound to end badly. People in fairy tales, too, generally wished for foolish things . . . but perhaps it was difficult to see the foolishness until afterwards, when one was old and wise. *Yes, old and wise, but what about in the meantime?* Had things turned out badly for her? Well, that was difficult to say. In what might be called the 'wider sphere', the results of her Adventure had been very fine indeed. She had received congratulations from various important gentlemen, and even Sir John Scott had spoken very highly of her work (not that he knew any details, of course). But in the narrower, personal sphere she was less certain, both of what she had done, and of what might yet come of it.

Such gloom, however, did not wholly characterise Mary's thoughts during those first weeks of June, and when dejection threatened it was often dispelled by the genuine pleasure of reunion with her friends, and of being at White Ladies again. As she had expected, Miss Marchmont and Miss Trent wanted to fuss over her, and there was something very comforting about being in a small, cosy world, where no one had ever heard of opium poisoning, and everyone wondered whether St Swithin's Day would be wet or fine. It was surprising how easily one could fall back into such a world, almost as if Adventures had never happened.

She received word that Susannah was recovering from her ordeal, which particularly lifted Mary's spirits. It would take some time before Susannah was whole and strong again, but traces of her old spirit were already emerging in the peaceful atmosphere of Storey's Court. Lady Armitage had settled upon a gentle regime for the invalid, in which rest and mild enter-tainments were given more weight than the strict and somewhat stultifying conventions of mourning. Perhaps more significantly, Susannah was being encouraged to make decisions for herself and to have confidence in them – to be, in fact, not quite so persuadable. Mary learned of these things, first from Susannah herself, in a carefully penned letter, and then via Charlotte's dashing missive, in which she professed a desire to make a second visit to London 'as soon as may be' and a great admiration for Major Whittington. *I hope that those two things are not related*, thought Mary, upon reading Charlotte's ill-spelled scrawl.

Charlotte also proposed making a visit to Suffolk, for she was certain that Mary was finding life terribly dull at White Ladies and in need of entertainment. 'Dull' was not the word that Mary would have used, but she warmly seconded the proposal, which was swiftly transformed into an invitation for the first week in July. Miss Marchmont and Miss Trent were, as they said, 'game for anything', although they privately rejoiced that the range of shops in Lindham would preclude any very arduous shopping expeditions, and they longed to hear the latest gossip from Norfolk.

It might have been the prospect of news, for she would have scorned any other word, that also brought Mrs Tipton to White Ladies on the morning of Charlotte's arrival. She claimed to be interested in a recipe for restorative jelly, but she also positioned herself in the sitting-room so as to command the best view of the courtyard. Not only did she make the first sighting of the Armitage carriage, but she was also able to confirm that Charlotte and her maid were not its only occupants. 'That man is here again,' she announced.

'Oh, who?' cried Miss Marchmont and Miss Trent, both springing to the window and blocking the view. They waved to Charlotte and chattered among themselves. 'Is that Captain Holland?' 'I believe it must be – how tall he looks.' 'I do not remember him being quite so tall. Might he have grown?'

'I am astonished that his duties are of such a trivial nature that he can career about the country, as he seems frequently to do,' Mrs Tipton observed. She spoke pointedly, and with a significant glance at Mary, who stood motionless in the doorway. 'There is a war on, after all.'

Mary found her voice and managed to reply temperately, even as her heart pounded and she resolved to throttle Charlotte for not mentioning this exciting, frightening development. Would there be time, even now, to dash upstairs and change her gown for something more flattering? 'I am certain he does not neglect his duties, ma'am. He must have been visiting the family and . . . Lady Armitage probably asked him to accompany Charlotte.'

It was hard to object to such a reasonable interpretation and, besides this, Mrs Tipton's lack of mobility meant that she was somewhat excluded from the next stage of the proceedings. This consisted of greetings in the courtyard, the unloading of Charlotte's many trunks, and the decision that some should be carried upstairs and others left in the passage – for Charlotte had several presents to deliver, and she could not immediately remember where she had put them. When everyone assembled in the sitting-room, however, and refreshments handed round, the normal order of things was restored. Mrs Tipton had shifted to the large wooden chair that had once belonged to the prioress of White Ladies, while the others encircled her on lesser pieces of furniture, her dependents for tea as well as for conversation. Mary was suddenly struck by the utter femininity of the room, and Captain Holland looked so uncomfortable that she wanted to laugh, and quite forgot that she had not done something more stylish with her hair.

'I understand that there was a commotion of some kind among the soldiers at Woolwich,' said Mrs Tipton, fixing Holland with a beady eye. 'One of these lamentable descents into anarchy that are so much the fashion nowadays. What do you have to say about it, sir?'

'Well, ma'am,' he replied, 'we did have a bit of trouble, but it was soon sorted.'

'*We,* Captain Holland?' demanded Miss Marchmont. 'Do I understand it that you were involved in the mutiny? In putting it down, I mean.' Both she and Miss Trent were much more intrigued with Holland – Miss Trent thought he was very dashing – but neither felt able to exhibit outright admiration in Mrs Tipton's presence. Their contributions, therefore, wavered uneasily between expressions of interest and disapproval.

'Well, I—'

'He certainly was,' piped Charlotte. 'Bobs had to fight a man – not a gunner, but a rotten civilian who was up to no good. And that was the key to everything!'

'Oh, my,' cried Miss Trent. 'The key to everything! But what do you mean by "gunner"?'

'That's what we call the men – the ordinary soldiers – in the Royal Artillery, ma'am. You know the saying, "the cobbler to his last and gunner to his linstock".'

Miss Marchmont nodded. 'Ah, yes. Mary has told us of a person called Gunner Drake. I thought "gunner" might be a sort of fanciful term, you know.'

'Or perhaps a person from Scandinavia,' added Miss Trent.

'No, no,' scoffed Mrs Tipton, as Mary looked away, biting her lip, 'that would be a different pronunciation entirely. *Gu*-nner,' she explained, 'like *Gu*-nner Pedersen, the sea captain who married Louisa Faraday's niece. Not a very good match, but then she was a headstrong girl and very ill-advised.'

Mrs Tipton shook her head, and Miss Marchmont added, 'I know the man you mean. Yellow whiskers.'

'Yes, although now that I come to think of it, he might be Gu-*nnar*.'

'And Bobs was terribly wounded in the struggle,' Charlotte continued, undeterred by Scandinavians of whatever pronunciation. 'Blood was spilled, and Drake said that Bobs' arm was laid open *to the very bone*.'

Even Mrs Tipton contributed to the collective, 'Ohh' which greeted that grisly announcement, after which all eyes turned to Holland. There being no obvious evidence of his grievous injury, however, lips were pursed and questioning expressions assumed.

Charlotte explained that the wound had been much worse a little while ago, but Holland frowned at her, and said that he was afraid that Drake tended to exaggerate. 'Like someone else I know.' He continued to look at his cousin meaningfully, but his glance conveyed a message that Mary did not understand.

'I have seen the scar,' Charlotte reported, with what sounded to Mary like defiance. 'It had to be *stitched* . . . like a torn shirt.'

'Good heavens,' breathed Miss Trent.

Mrs Tipton thought that they had heard quite enough about Captain Holland, and she debated whether turning the conversation to White Ladies might be a good idea. It would illustrate the immense distance between Mary and himself, but it might also give him ideas. She plumped for the former, and for the next quarter of an hour Holland was regaled with stories of how the roof had been re-leaded and the damp in the kitchen quite done away with, and he was invited to admire an extensive range of soft furnishings.

Charlotte was not very interested in such things, but she announced that Mary would also shortly have an addition to her stables. Susannah had decided to make her a present of the mare called Sita, and the animal was to be sent up directly from Kent. 'Which is just as well,' Charlotte added, 'for Mary's other horses are the saddest old things – quite in the grandfatherly class.'

Mary was surprised and touched by the news, particularly as she had her own suspicions about it. While Susannah would willingly have made such a gift, she knew nothing of Mary's interest in Sita. The suggestion, therefore, must have come from elsewhere. 'It was terribly kind of Susannah,' she said, smiling. 'I must write straightaway and thank her.' In fact she wanted to speak with Captain Holland even more urgently, but how on earth was that to be achieved? She could feel the others looking at her, which was quite uncomfortable, and in any case she could not very well raise any of the matters that she wished to in front of them.

The mention of Susannah seemed to Mrs Tipton an admirable means of directing everyone's thoughts to the eligible members of the Armitage family. Before she could do so, however, an interruption occurred. Slipper came barrelling into the room, barking and growling at the visitors. Miss Trent and Miss Marchmont immediately lifted their feet onto footstools. They did not dislike the little dog and had raised no objections when Mary brought him home with her, but Slipper had a habit of darting forward and administering a quick nip to anyone whom he did not trust, and ankles were his favourite target.

Naturally, he had never dared to bite Mrs Tipton, but she frowned at him and then at Mary. 'That animal of yours is incorrigible,' she decreed. 'Yet another example of the lack of discipline in the modern world. Dogs were properly trained when I was a girl.'

'I like him,' said Charlotte, and not for the first time Mary wondered what would be the result in a contest of wills between Charlotte and Mrs Tipton. 'Is he a good ratter, Mary?'

'Yes, when he feels like it.'

Charlotte stood up. 'Perhaps we ought to take him for a run now, Mary . . . and you too, Bobs.'

Her remark sparked a flurry of objections (as well as commentary from Slipper), but Charlotte saw them off by enlarging upon the planned outing in terms that would discourage interference. In addition to rats, she expressed an interest in snakes, and she fancied that it would be warm enough to paddle in the ocean, although the wind was rather strong. They could easily climb the dunes to the shore.

Mrs Tipton appreciated that she had been outmanoeuvred, for Miss Marchmont was known to draw the line at sand dunes, and Miss Trent would inevitably give way before snakes. Her subordinates, therefore, were as broken reeds in this crisis. Mary was also aware of what was occurring, but she resisted the temptation to make this obvious. Instead, she contented herself with the observation that Slipper was fond of hunting for crabs on the beach and rolling in dead fish.

'Well, see that you keep walking at all times,' said Mrs Tipton, sourly, 'and you had better take a shawl, Mary – or better still, a pelisse.'

Holland, Charlotte, and Mary were all laughing by the time they were outside, and Slipper was straining at his lead. Mary had decided against the all-enveloping pelisse, but she was carrying her linen shawl, and she saw that Holland also recognised it. He started to speak, but stopped short when Charlotte demanded to know where were the rats, particularly?

The question took Mary aback. She had thought that she understood Charlotte's strategy, but now she was uncertain. 'What do you mean, "particularly"? White Ladies is not infested, you know.'

'No, but that is where we are going, Slipper and I,' Charlotte replied. 'Later, we may go down to the shore. You may join us,' she added, loftily, 'if you want to . . .'

'All right, shrimp,' warned Holland. 'Run round to the stables, and we'll follow you.'

'You had better go the other way, to the garden,' Charlotte advised. 'I expect they are very romantic and—' she dodged Holland's swipe and ran away, laughing, 'they will not be able to see you from the house!'

'Sorry about that,' muttered Holland, when they were alone. 'She's an imp, not a shrimp . . . but I wanted to talk to you.'

'Yes, and I wanted to speak with *you*,' said Mary. 'And she was probably right about them watching.'

'I'm surprised that Mrs Tipton didn't advise you to take your pistol.'

'She might have done, if she had known of its existence.'

They strolled through the garden and beyond to the rough lawn and stunted trees that led down to the sea. To begin with their conversation was tentative. Holland remarked that she had changed things quite a bit since her uncle's time, and she agreed. The garden took rather a battering in bad weather, but the line of trees should provide a windbreak.

Mary risked a glance up at Holland; his profile was stony, and she wondered again at his intentions. He seemed so stern, so remote, but he *had* come, and she remembered how he had kissed her at Champian Hall. It would have been difficult to forget *that*. 'Thank you for Sita,' she murmured.

Holland shrugged. 'Apart from what's tied up by the marriage settlement, almost all of Crosby-Nash's property is going to his sister. She isn't much interested in Champian Hall, not surprisingly, so I thought I would try to get the mare for you. Besides,' he added, 'Susannah thinks that she's in your debt, for taking Slipper off her hands.'

'Oh, he is not such a bad dog,' Mary laughed. 'Well, perhaps he is, but he was also extremely helpful. If it had not been for him—'

'Yes, I know.'

Holland had wanted to find out how things stood between himself and Mary – how things really stood, and not only when one or other of them was in danger of death – but now he was not sure that he could do it. The burden of his unhappy conviction, built up over the past year, was not easily cast aside. He was relieved, therefore, when the mention of Slipper turned Mary's thoughts to the Adventure, proper. They talked for a time about Colonel Crosby-Nash and Rabelais, and tried to resolve Mary's unanswered questions. For example, it was clear that, ultimately, the colonel had mistrusted his friend, but why had Rabelais come to Champian Hall in the first place? Had he merely been seeking help, or had he meant to accuse? Had he blamed the colonel for the failure of their schemes?

'He might have done,' said Holland. 'He didn't know about you, but he recognised me, and he could have tied me to Crosby-Nash, if he'd thought about it. Perhaps he needed help *and* wanted an explanation, but in the end he got neither. I can't say that I feel much sympathy for any of them, and I expect that Mr Shy will uncover more when he finishes with all the papers and things he found.'

'Very likely,' Mary agreed. 'He is terribly clever. I know that you do not like him but—'

'I wouldn't say that, exactly, or perhaps I'm willing to revise my opinion. I think he's a bit mad, but I suppose that's not surprising, given his line of work.' Holland revealed that, in addition to Shy, he had also met one of Dick Whittington's chiefs. Both were rather odd, secretive men, who were like misers when it came to information.

'I would have liked to hear from Mr Shy when we returned to London,' Mary admitted, 'you know, to draw things to a close. Coutts bank sent me a ring, which was a sort of message, because it came from the jeweller's shop in Birchin Lane. It is very beautiful, but I do not think I could ever *wear* it.' She shivered. 'It would be grisly.'

'I don't blame you.'

'And now, thinking about it, I know that what we did was very important, but . . . I wonder if I could do any of those things again.'

Holland raised his eyebrows in obvious disbelief. 'Have another Adventure, you mean?'

'Yes.'

'Of course you could, and if Shy were here and wanted something done he would convince you in a snap.'

'But—'

'He'd tell you about some mystery or other, and offer to

show you some old pottery or the *Magna Carta*, and you would be for it.'

'*Magna Carta*!' cried Mary, 'have you seen— We meant to visit the British Museum, only our tickets of entry did not arrive in time. But that is beside the point. What I mean is, I am not very comfortable about what happened – about my part in it.'

'Well, I think you did pretty well,' said Holland, 'but it's natural to have second thoughts. An old gunner once told me that after every fight he either drank too much or got the blue devils, thinking about what had gone wrong and how he could have done things differently.'

'Really? Every time?'

'That's right. It's probably not such a bad thing to remind yourself that killing isn't all about victory and glory, but the trick is not to be too hard on yourself, especially if you have to fight again tomorrow.'

'Is that what you do?'

'Mm . . . but I have a drink too, sometimes. Not a lot, I don't,' he added, hurriedly, 'and not more than I can hold. I'm not a—'

'No, no, of course not,' said Mary, 'and no one could think it.' She continued in a consciously light tone. 'Well, I am not likely to have to "fight again tomorrow", but I am surprised to hear you encouraging me to have Adventures.'

Holland's voice was not so confident-sounding. 'I don't mean to encourage or discourage,' he murmured, 'but I think I know you, that's all.'

They walked for a while in silence, and then Mary asked, 'How did you know about the tea and how to save Susannah? It was wonderful.'

'It wasn't so much,' replied Holland. 'I had seen someone poisoned by opium before, in Madras.'

'Did that person survive? The one you saw?'

'I don't remember. Crosby-Nash put spices in the tea to disguise the smell, or else Rabelais wasn't familiar with it. I'm sure Susannah didn't know what she was drinking.'

'No, and that is what bothers me most,' Mary admitted, and she stopped walking. 'I cannot help thinking that what happened to her was actually my fault. I had kept everything from her, you see. If I had spoken about Crosby-Nash – warned her – she would have been on her guard. She did not love him – and she would have been protected!'

Holland clasped both her hands between his own. He had firmly resolved not to make any such advance, but her distress defeated him. 'No, you were right not to tell her. If she *had* known . . . do you think that she could have kept the secret from him? Not in a hundred years. And if he had thought that she knew all about him he might have done something worse.'

'What could have been worse than trying to kill her?' asked Mary, and against all reason her eyes filled with tears. She knew that she was being foolish, but she could not help herself.

'He might have made a better job of it, for a start.'

'But you think that he *did* mean for her to die?' Mary pressed.

'Probably,' said Holland, slowly, 'but we'll never know for certain. He might have hoped that she would wake up after a few hours. She had taken a weaker dose than the others.'

'I am glad I did not shoot him – not exactly because of this, but . . .'

'I'm glad you didn't too.' Presently, Holland added, 'As for Susannah, isn't it better that she doesn't know anything more about him? She's had a bad time, but now she can leave it behind, without any very terrible memories to spoil the future.'

'Yes, I see that, but it is not why I kept silent,' said Mary. 'I cannot take credit now for a . . . fortuitous result.'

'You don't have to take credit for it, but you shouldn't punish yourself for it either. We had the luck – let's leave it at that.'

Mary considered this, and then something else occurred to her. 'I might offer you the same advice, you know, not to punish yourself for consequences that you could not control.'

He stiffened as she spoke, and his fingers tightened, then loosened. Before he could let go entirely she reversed their positions, so that now his hands were clasped between hers.

'That's a completely different matter,' he said.

'No, it is exactly the same. What your parents did, or the sort of people they were, has nothing to do with you. You said before that nothing can change the past, so why not leave it alone?'

'But when I said that I meant—'

Mary could feel herself growing angry. Oh, he was a stubborn man! 'I know precisely what you meant; that what was fine for other people was not fine for you! You must sit upon your high horse, or go down with the ship, or do whatever artillerymen do when they are being obstinate.'

'But I'm not—'

'Oh yes you are. Do you remember when we thought that my uncle might have been a traitor? You told me not to mind it – that my true friends would not mind it.'

'Yes, I remember.'

She could sense that familiar wall of reserve, of . . . pig-headedness. 'And do you— Do you dare to tell me that *I* am not *your* true friend?'

A wave of colour flooded across Mary's face as she spoke, but Holland did not see it. He was looking down at her hands, so small and delicate and . . . determined, against his own.

'No.'

'Or, consider this,' said Mary, in the same urgent tone. 'Would you think any less of Susannah – *will* you think any less of her – because she was married to Colonel Crosby-Nash?'

'Of course not, but . . .' Holland paused, frowning in a way that she had never seen before, but now he raised his eyes. 'If the truth about Crosby-Nash, if that were generally known, she might suffer for it, and . . . I don't want *you* to suffer, because of me. Ever.'

'I will not suffer,' she replied, and then she smiled at him. 'It is all over, and we are both here.'

Holland smiled too, and from the back of his mind, like an insistent fly, he could hear Dick Whittington's words, spoken as they had ridden along the London road. 'After all that has happened, if you do not realise that Mary Finch is

405

no ordinary girl to whom ordinary standards apply, then I despair of you.'

From where she stood on the beach, Charlotte could just see her cousin and Mary – if she were to turn round, which of course she did not mean to do. She had been throwing sticks for Slipper, but as he was familiar with the capturing part of the game and not the returning part, the entertainment came to a swift end. Then something else caught his attention; he bounded forward and began to bark disapprovingly.

'Hush!' she urged, kneeling beside him and clamping her hand over his muzzle. 'We shall speak with them later. I do not think they want you, just now.'

Author's Note

The adventures of Mary Finch and Robert Holland in *The Counterfeit Guest* are fictitious, but they take place amid real events and involve actual people. The Naval mutinies at Spithead and the Nore are well known, but disturbances also occurred among the Guards regiments and at the Woolwich Warren in May 1797, as well as among other units. The extent to which the mutinies were simply expressions of dissatisfaction among the soldiers, gunners, and seamen, or were influenced by outsiders, is not clear. It is likely, however, that individuals hostile to the British government or opposed to the war with France would have attempted to encourage the disturbances, if they did not actually foment them. Sergeant Majors from the 3rd Regiment of Foot Guards and from the Royal Regiment of Artillery offered rewards of fifty and one hundred pounds, respectively, for the apprehension of 'evil-disposed' and 'disaffected' persons who were 'endeavouring to corrupt the loyalty of the soldiers . . . by distributing seditious writings, and by other improper means'. The document that Captain Holland reads in the barrack is a verbatim transcript of one that was actually circulated. Few details of the artillery mutiny survive, but it does seem to have been characterised by restraint and good order, and was resolved within the space of a few days. Dissatisfaction among the Guards was discovered before an actual mutiny could take place, and seems to have been cured by the rise in pay announced by the government on 24 May.

The planned attack on the Purfleet magazine is likewise fictitious, but the danger posed by the practice of allowing late-arriving barges to anchor in close proximity to the magazine was identified in the *Times* on 19 October 1864, following the disastrous explosion at a much smaller facility at Erith. The fact that other munitions were occasionally stored at Purfleet was also noted and condemned as highly dangerous.

Of the persons with whom Mary and Holland rub shoulders, Sir John Scott, Colonel William Congreve, Colonel Frederick Mulcaster and Major John MacLeod were real. Although he did prosecute a number of men for treason and sedition in the 1790s, Sir John was well known for his hesitation, rumination, and circumlocution in these and other matters. In his legal opinions to government ministers, he does refer, guardedly, to the work of government agents in uncovering possible miscreants. Whether those agents might have included someone like Cuthbert Shy cannot be known, but that a patriotic, if somewhat eccentric, gentleman of private means should have undertaken such an activity is not beyond the realm of possibility. Shy's opponent, Rabelais, is likewise wholly fictitious. There was a jeweller's shop at 3 Birchin Lane, not far from the offices of Messrs Tinker and Taylor, the noted gunpowder-makers, but the jeweller's was not called Hardy & Son's and was not, it is to be assumed, involved in espionage.

Finally, lest it be supposed that Colonel Crosby-Nash's ploy of communicating by means of his dog, Slipper, is solely the creation of the novelist, Helen Maria Williams tells of a Frenchwoman who employed a similar agent when her husband was confined in the Luxembourg prison in Paris, during the time of Robespierre. 'At length the idea suggested itself to the lady of inclosing a billet within the dog's collar; she contrived to give her husband some intimation of her scheme, which she immediately put in practice. From that period the four-legged courier, furnished with his invisible packet, marched boldly forward every day at the appointed hour through the hosts of foes, and, in defiance of revolutionary edicts, laid his dispatches and his person at his master's feet.'